CW00687699

BY HIS VOW

CALLAHAN BILLIONAIRES

TRACY LORRAINE

Development Editing by Pinpoint Editing

Content Editing by Rebecca at Fairest Reviews Editing Services

Proofreading by Lisa Staples

Photography - Michelle Lancaster

Model - Tommy Gram

The things you regret most in life are the risks you didn't take.

1

TATUM

I sit and stare at the wall ahead as the oppressive grief and sadness in the room press heavily on my shoulders.

Mom sniffles quietly next to me. But I don't look over. I can't.

It's all she's done since we got the news five days ago. She's been inconsolable.

She's had everyone doing everything for her, pandering to her grieving needs, but it's like no time has passed. She's refusing to accept the truth, and in turn, refusing to get involved with any of the arrangements.

It's fallen to me and Miles, my older brother, who's sitting on my other side, and Michael who's beside him, our father's oldest and closest friend.

Our family lawyer sits uncomfortably at my late father's desk —no doubt the reason for Mom's most recent breakdown—riffling through his briefcase to find the paperwork he needs.

To anyone else, he would appear unprepared and unprofessional. But to us, he's just Richard. A man who has been a part of our lives forever. He's reliable, trustworthy, and...a bit of a character. But he's the best. Dad refused to work with anyone else.

He continues wasting time before glancing at his watch.

What the hell is he waiting for?

He asked for us to be here for 2 p.m., and it's now almost 2:15.

I don't know about them, but I'm ready to face the inevitable and get on with my life.

Should I be more cut up about my father's unexpected death? Probably.

But I didn't have the same kind of relationship with him that Miles or our mother did.

I am neither the woman he shared his life with nor his firstborn son. I'm not even his second-born son.

I'm his daughter.

Something he'd always been bitter about.

He may never have said the words, but they weren't necessary with the way he looked at me. The way he spoke to me.

The only thing my birth brought to the table was the ability to bear children, but even then, they wouldn't carry the Warner name. And something tells me that whomever I choose to spend my life with and have my children with would never have stood up to his impossibly high standards.

He expected me to be with someone of a similar wealth and social class.

Which meant he wanted to see me marry some egotistical asshole. Basically, a clone of the man he'd trained my older brother to be. I shudder at the thought.

I don't want this life.

Sure, on the outside, everything looks great.

We've got the houses, the vacations, the cars, the designer clothes.

But it's all bullshit. A shiny veneer covering up the reality.

Like my father lying through his back teeth about his health and leaving us in the lurch with this mess.

He could have warned us. Mom could have had time to come to terms with her impending life as a widow. Miles could have stepped up at work and have been ready for his sudden promotion.

2

But no.

The all-powerful Jonathan Warner decided that the best thing for us would be the shock of finding out he had a failing heart when it was too late.

I guess we should be grateful really, that his car was parked when he suffered the heart attack that ended his life.

If he were driving, we could be in an even worse situation right now.

I glance around the room, unwilling to see most of what's around me. I have mixed feelings about my parents' house. Sure, I have some great childhood memories from this place, but they're laced with the bad ones, too. And the bad taints everything.

And nothing puts me on edge more than being in *this* room.

As children—hell, even as adults—we were never allowed to step foot in this room unless our presence had been requested.

It was our father's haven. A place he came to do...everything, I guess. Mostly things I don't have any desire to think about.

Being summoned here was bad enough. But actually stepping over the threshold and facing him, was something else entirely.

It didn't matter how bad my crime was. It could have been that I hadn't tidied my bedroom, or that one time I got caught trying to cheat on a math test. I always left wishing I were someone else. That I lived somewhere else.

It didn't matter how hard I tried, how well-behaved I usually was, or if I achieved something he should have been proud of.

It was never enough.

I always left having been reminded of my place in this house, in this family. And I always resented him that little bit more than the last time.

It's almost 2:20 when Miles's patience finally gets the better of him. "Can we get this started?" he snaps suddenly, pushing to his feet, his chair ominously rocking back on two legs behind him before he begins pacing.

I've seen my big brother in some interesting states over the years. Covered in chicken pox as a kid, tripping after his first high school party, tripping when he took a bad pill at college, and completely out of his depth but desperately trying to hide it as he took his position under our father at Warner Group LTD. But I have never seen him look as stressed or as lost as he does right now.

It's just another reason why I'm not grieving in the way that's expected of me.

I'm not sad. I'm angry. Fucking furious that our father could be this selfish to those he was meant to love. To those who depended on him.

With my anger rising and the red haze I've been drifting in and out of the past few days descending upon me, the last thing I need is to be forced to sit here waiting for nothing.

We already know what Dad's will says. Nothing Richard can read will surprise us.

It's been set in stone for years.

Mom is taken care of. Miles gets the company, And I...get the only thing he had that I deem valuable and can finally embark on the life I truly want.

I just want this rigmarole over.

"We will commence very shortly," Richard says, trying to placate Miles.

Our lawyer looks at my brother with a soft, empathetic smile on his face as he watches him pace back and forth.

I can only imagine the number of clients he's had to do this for. Each one must be hard, but after a lifetime of working together, I can't help thinking that this is even more personal than most.

But as painful as it might be for him, I doubt that's the reason he's avoiding starting this reading.

He's waiting for something.

As I wrack my brain for what the hold-up could be, the door beside me is thrown open.

Dressed in a smart suit, his hair styled to perfection, with his irritatingly square jaw and piercing green eyes, Michael's eldest son—and heir to his empire—Kingston Callahan, strides into the room as if he belongs here.

"KC?" Miles questions with a deep frown marring his brow. My hackles rise.

Sure, Kingston and Miles might have been best friends since they were in diapers, but that doesn't give him any right to be at such a private moment for our family.

Michael is one thing. But Kingston is very much another.

I jump to my feet as red-hot anger explodes within me, my blood boiling as it surges through my veins.

"I'm sorry, but this is a private family meeting," I snarl, holding my head high and bracing myself for impact.

I don't remember a time in my life when Kingston and I haven't clashed.

Growing up, our nanny tried to tell me that it was because he was the eldest of a group of brothers and that he didn't know how to handle a girl.

Personally, I've always thought it was because he's an asshole.

My words make his shoulders widen, and it's impossible not to notice the tick in his jaw before he turns his attention toward me.

The second his emerald eyes lock on mine, it takes every ounce of strength I have not to take a step back.

I've spent my life surrounded by powerful, intimidating men, but nothing ever prepared me for Kingston Callahan's full attention.

It's always been the same. From as early as I can remember, he's put me on edge. And as he grew into his gangly teenage limbs and worked his way to the top of Callahan Enterprises at record speed, it only got worse.

I'm sure it's not helped by the fact that he's hands down the most attractive male specimen I've ever had the misfortune of laying my eyes on.

Pretty he may be, but it will never, ever be enough to cover up the arrogant man who hides beneath the polished facade.

"Well," he starts, his deep, rumbling voice filling the air around me and commanding the attention of everyone in the room —even his father and Richard, who are his seniors in every sense. "I guess it's a good thing that I was invited, then."

He moves closer to me, his eyes finally dropping from mine in favor of my body.

One of his perfectly shaped brows lifts as he takes in my outfit of choice.

"At least I dressed appropriately for the occasion," he sneers before marching forward and stealing my chair.

Fire rages within me, my mouth opening and closing as numerous cutting retorts dance on the tip of my tongue, the lingering scent of his cologne wafting through my nose.

How dare he?

How fucking dare he stroll in here like his presence is required and then have the audacity to insult me?

He has no idea what the past five days have been like for me.

He has no idea that I spent all morning at the office, working with Judith, my father's personal assistant, to finalize arrangements for the funeral next week. Or that I'm on my period and all I really want to do right now is curl up in the fetal position with an IV of milk chocolate being pumped into me.

"Judgmental asshole," I mutter, unable to keep the insult to myself.

Is it the time or the place to ensure the jerk knows exactly what I think about him? No. Not at all. But I don't give a shit.

The days of me being reprimanded in this room are over. It's no longer a place where I bow down to men who think they're more important just because of the appendage hanging between their thighs.

"Okay, shall we get started?" Richard asks, clapping his hands together to ensure he steals everyone's attention.

"Is he actually meant to be here?" I ask, throwing my arm out in Kingston's direction, although I don't look at him. Asshole doesn't deserve it.

"Tate," Miles hisses. He's no stranger to our bickering. Usually, he lets us run out of steam, but apparently today is different.

"What? He isn't a part of this family."

"Nor is Michael, but you didn't complain about him being here."

"That's different," I argue, turning to the man in question. "Michael isn't--"

"Me?" Kingston pipes up with a smirk.

"Exactly," I mutter.

"Just sit down and listen to what Dad had to say," Miles demands, as Kingston makes himself comfortable in my chair, spreading his thighs wide, making the fabric of his pants stretch across his muscles.

I scoff, before ripping my eyes from the epitome of arrogance sitting there like he owns the fucking place and focusing on Richard.

It's time to get this show on the road.

Laying pages out on our father's desk, he begins reading.

As expected, the house and almost all his wealth will transfer to our mother, who continues to sob quietly throughout the whole ordeal.

Miles is to step into our father's role as CEO of the Warner Group.

He talks about changes to other roles within the organization, but unsurprisingly, there's no mention of my climb through the ranks.

I guess if I were being honest, there was a part of me that hoped he might just take me seriously for once and acknowledge that I am actually good at my job. But as his wishes about the future of the company come to an end, it's clear that there is no promotion coming my way.

My heart sinks a little. It wouldn't have made up for the years of feeling like the lesser sibling, the least important member of the family, but it might have sweetened it all a little.

Not that I have any intention of hanging around in Chicago long enough to even consider starting a new position. But the attempt to keep me here might have been nice.

I wait for my name to be mentioned, for the only thing I want from my father to be brought up. But it never is.

My heart starts to race and my palms begin to sweat.

He told me that it had my name on it. He promised me...

The room begins to spin around me as reality hits.

Was I really such an insignificant part of his life that he left me out of his will entirely?

"And that leads me to the final part," Richard says, pulling me from my thoughts.

"Go on," Michael says.

There's something in his voice that makes me look over at him. I do a double take when I find a faint smirk playing on his lips.

He knows what's coming.

I wish I could have been granted the same kind of warning, because I'm pretty sure the world being literally ripped from beneath me, would shock me less than the next words that fall from Richard's lips.

"Tatum, as per your father's wishes, you are to marry Kingston Callahan and finally merge the Warner and Callahan empires. Kingston and Miles are to work together to—"

2

TATUM

"No," I hiss, cutting off whatever else Richard had to say. He barely even glanced at me as he dropped that bomb. Did he think none of us were listening and that we'd allow him just to breeze past it? "There is no way on this Earth I'm doing that," I state, marching straight up to Dad's desk and attempting to snatch the paperback directly from Richard's hands.

When he pulls it out of my reach, I see red.

"I don't believe you," I shout. "Show me. Show me the evidence."

"Tatum," Michael says softly from behind me.

"No," I say, holding my hand up to stop him from approaching me—if he were even trying to. "This is bullshit. There is no way that Dad would have wanted me to—"

Richard spins the paperwork toward me and points toward the lines in question.

"Why?" I whisper, my eyes filling with tears as I read the exact words he just said to us. "Why would he do this to me?"

"He had his reasons," Richard muses.

"None of them will be good enough. There's no way I'm marrying that...that—" I spin around and pin Kingston with a look, but the second I register the smug expression on his face, my world tilts on its axis again.

He knew.

He fucking knew.

They'd planned this.

Our fathers.

Him.

My blood runs cold at the thought of them mapping out my entire life without my knowledge.

How dare they?

What makes any of them think they have the right to control me like that?

I'm not a puppet. I'm a human.

A fucking adult who can make her own choices, her own decisions.

Ripping my eyes from his twinkling green ones, I turn to my brother.

"Did you know about this?" I snap.

I swear to God, if he knew and was hiding this from me then—

"No," he confesses. "I had no idea."

My big brother might be like our father in many, many ways, but there is one major difference between them.

I can read Miles.

And right now, I know he's telling the truth.

"There's no way I'd have let him do this to you, Tate," he says fiercely, surging toward me and wrapping me in his arms.

I fight, I really fucking do, but the tears are too persistent, and finally, I have no choice but to let one slip free.

I hate myself for it. For appearing weak. But my world is crumbling around me and I've no idea how else to deal with this right now.

"It's going to be okay. You don't have to do anything you don't—"

"It comes with conditions," Richard interrupts.

I sigh, pressing my forehead against Miles's chest as I pray for strength.

"Of course it does," I mutter, more to myself than anyone else.

Once I've steeled myself for what's to come, I stand tall and focus on Richard, keeping Kingston and Michael behind me.

They don't deserve even a second of my time or energy right now. Ever, actually.

"What are the conditions?" I ask, already dreading the response.

"After a year of marriage, the cottage will become yours," Richard states.

All the air rushes from my lungs.

That's all I want. That little cottage in the middle of a quaint little village in the Cotswolds in England.

I'd requested to buy it several times. But he always refused. He knew it was something he could hold over me, to force me to do his bidding. Because he knew how much I loved it.

"That's not fair," I argue.

"Wills often aren't, my dear," Richard says softly. "Unfortunately, the wishes of those who've moved on often don't make that much sense to those who have been left behind."

"What else did he say?"

His eyes hold mine. Sympathy oozes from them, and my skin erupts in goosebumps.

"If you don't do this, you lose everything."

My mouth opens and closes, but no words come out.

"Your apartment, your car, your job, your trust fund. Everything."

"He can't do that," Miles roars.

"All of it belongs to your father. He can do whatever he wants."

"No, there must be a loophole. You've got to find a way around this," Miles begs.

All the while, Michael and Kingston sit behind us silently, probably enjoying the spectacle.

They already know the answer to Miles's question. Hell, even I know the answer to Miles's question. But until I hear it from the lips of the man who knows everything then—

"There is no loophole. I'm sorry, Tatum, but you have two options. Get everything you ever wanted, or walk away with nothing."

"Why?" I repeat. "Why would he do this?"

No one responds. Although I don't for a second think that it's because no one knows the answer.

The two men sitting behind me know everything.

There's movement, and all the hairs on the back of my neck lift.

I know who's going to speak long before his deep voice fills the room, but it still startles me.

"Would you all mind leaving my fiancée and me to discuss this private matter with Richard alone?"

"F-fiancée?" I stutter, my voice full of venom and disbelief. "I am not your fucking fiancée."

His expression hardens, the tendons in his neck tightening with frustration.

I stare up at him, ignoring the height difference between us, and narrow my eyes.

"I am not, and will never be, your anything."

The air crackles between us as my body burns red hot with a potent mixture of anger and disbelief.

"There has to be another way," Miles muses again, but when no response comes, he sighs and concedes.

"Come on, Helena," Michael says, pandering to Mom. "Let's leave the kids to sort this out while we have a coffee."

"Seriously?" Miles gasps. "You think we can just *sort this out*? Dad wants...Dad is demanding they—" He swallows the rest of his sentence as Michael and Mom begin shuffling around.

I catch their movement in my peripheral vision behind Kingston, but I don't look over. My entire focus is on conveying just how much I hate him with my eyes alone.

Mom hasn't said a word. Not a single word throughout this whole thing.

I know she's suffering, drowning in grief, but her only daughter has just had her life turned upside down.

Surely this is the time to pull her ass from the pits of despair. Or at least to say *something,* for fuck's sake.

Kingston's eyes continue to hold mine. His stare is cold and hard and totally unwavering. While I might be trying to silently tell him how much I despise everything about him, he's happily reminding me that I have no power here.

He has it all, and he's fucking reveling in it.

Asshole.

It's not until Mom and Michael reach the door that someone speaks.

"Tatum, I know this is a shock," Michael says. There's concern in his voice, but something tells me it's as fake as his current wife's tits. "But you need to trust your father. He knew what he was doing when he changed his wishes."

Finally, I rip my eyes from Kingston and look toward them. Michael has his arm around Mom's waist, holding her up.

She looks frail, a lot older than she actually is.

For long seconds, she stands there unresponsive, but just before Michael encourages her out of the door, she finally looks up.

Her eyes lock with mine and something passes between us.

Mom is a good person. She's always done her best for us. Unfortunately, she's also very easily led, so her best was always controlled, her intentions always steered in a certain way. And despite Dad now being gone, I have a feeling nothing is going to change. He's always going to be in her head and whispering in her ear, and if not him, then it'll be Michael.

Her lips part, and I pray that she's going to say something to help me. Some kind of advice. She's lived a life surrounded by these controlling men. Surely, she has some kind of insight that would help me right now.

But before a word can leave her mouth, her lips close again, she dips her head and shuffles out of the room with Michael hot on her tail.

With them gone, the tension immediately ramps up. The air turns thick with anticipation to the point it's hard to draw in a breath. And it only gets worse when Miles steps up to Kingston.

They might have been best friends their whole lives, but it doesn't stop them from doing what needs to be done—and it seems this is one of those moments because before Miles comes to a stop, he pulls his arm back and throws his fist into Kingston's beautiful face.

His head snaps back as a surprised grunt spills from his lips.

"No," I shriek, lunging for Miles's arm before he throws another punch.

But I'm not quick or strong enough.

Miles's bicep tenses under my tiny hands as he prepares for his second hit, and I panic.

"Stop," I beg. "Please. You're only making this worse."

It takes a couple of seconds, but my pleading cuts through his anger.

"Miles," I warn, as he shakes me off and steps toe to toe with Kingston.

Everything about them is so similar, their height, their size, and if they seriously got into it, I don't know who would come out on top. I'd rather not know. And I certainly don't want to witness it.

Miles's chest swells with anger before he seethes, "I don't know what the fuck is going on here or what kind of game you're playing, but if you so much as hurt a hair on her fucking head, I will end you."

Kingston glares back.

The air crackles loudly as we all wait for his response.

My heart is a runaway train in my chest, but the second Kingston speaks, I'm pretty sure it runs straight off the tracks.

"I can't promise you that, bro. But I can promise one thing..." I don't breathe, I don't do anything as I wait. "She'll love every fucking second of it."

I don't move fast enough. Miles is on him like a rocket and the two of them crash into the desk, making Richard screech and jump to his feet.

"Stop it," I scream. "Just fucking stop it."

I try dragging Miles away, but I don't achieve anything.

He's lost to his anger. I get it. I really fucking get it.

If I believed I could cause Kingston any physical pain right now, I'd be doing the exact same thing.

Unfortunately, I don't think there's any way on this Earth that I could hurt Kingston. He's untouchable.

Just like our fathers and grandfathers.

So why? Why did Dad think this was a good idea?

Kingston doesn't want me. He wants the blonde bimbos he usually spends time with. They stroke his ego—along with other things—and satisfy his needs. I shudder as I consider just what those needs consist of. Why would he ever agree to this? Why would he ruin his perfect bachelor life to be tied to me?

I shake my head, feeling stupid.

For power and wealth.

Is it ever anything else?

3

KINGSTON

Pain sears through my face and down my neck.

I expected it.

Although I've got to be honest, I expected Miles to keep a lid on it until we didn't have an audience.

The fact he's willingly doing this in front of both Richard and his sister shows just how un-fucking-happy he is with this turn of events.

Of course he's unhappy. What big brother wants his sister with a man like me?

Miles knows me better than anyone else on the planet. And that isn't a good thing in a situation like his.

With one more hit that makes the back of my head collide with his late father's ornately carved walnut desk, he finally takes a step back, allowing me to draw in a breath and swallow down the pain.

My eyes flicker open, and the second his shadow moves aside, all I see is her.

Tatum Warner.

Her dark hair is wild and sitting in some kind of weird bird's nest thing on the top of her head. She's wearing a massive hoodie

—one that I suspect is a man's—and leggings. Not that I can see much of her legs.

Her face is pale, bare of makeup, and her eyes are surrounded by dark circles, evidence of the toll this week has taken on her.

I grit my teeth as I try to match the image before me with what I always thought my future wife might look like.

Despite my desire to never settle down and be forced to endure the bullshit that comes with being one half of a couple, I knew that I'd eventually have to.

As the eldest son of Michael Callahan, there are certain expectations of me. Expectations that often feel like unforgiving lead weights pressing down on my shoulders.

From the day I was born, I was destined to become one of the most important, wealthy, and powerful men in Chicago.

An image of my future was painted for me from day one. The houses, the cars, the designer suits, and...the beautiful wife.

A woman from a family of good standing. Someone who would look good on my arm and portray the image my surname demands.

Sure, on paper, Tatum is the perfect candidate.

She's beautiful—even when she's doing her best to look like a tramp. She's got a surname that holds almost as much weight as mine. She's grown up in the same world as me. She understands what my life is like and the pressure I'm under.

There's just one problem...

She drives me fucking crazy.

Defiance may as well be her middle name. Everything she's ever been told to do, she takes great pride in doing the opposite—something her father didn't take very kindly to.

While I'm strategic in my ways, she's like a chaotic puppy with a squeaky toy in its mouth.

Sure, she's settled a little now she's an adult. And I can't deny that she's good at her job. A job that was never a part of Jonathan's plans for her.

She was meant to go into finance instead of marketing. He

may never have put her as high up the ranks as he immediately did Miles, due to her being a woman and Jonathan still living in the dark ages where gender is concerned, but that's not the point.

He'd carved a path out for her, and she figuratively stuck her middle finger up at him and went in her own direction.

She still works for Warner Group. She's still an asset. Just... not the asset Jonathan wanted her to be.

I'm pretty sure if I were to ask her, she'd openly tell me that Jonathan made her feel like nothing but a disappointment since the day she was born.

"What?" the woman in question snaps as I continue to stare at her and push to my feet.

Lifting my hand to my mouth, I wipe away the trickle of blood that was making its way down to my chin.

"It was hot watching you try to protect me. Maybe you will make a good wife, after all."

Some weird growl noise rumbles deep in Miles's throat while Tatum's face twists in anger.

"No, that's enough," she snaps, her arm shooting out to stop him from lunging toward me again. "You need to leave."

It takes a few seconds for her words to register, but when they do, he rears back.

"I'm not leaving you," he states firmly.

Tatum looks between us, and every time her eyes come to me, she seems to catalogue another bruise or cut caused by her hot-headed brother.

I love him like one of my own, but fuck, he's worse than Kian, my younger brother, when it comes to his temper.

"Miles." She sighs. "This," she says, gesturing between me and her, "isn't something you can fix. Apparently, Dad wanted—"

"The fuck was he even thinking?" he mutters, scrubbing his hand down his face. His knuckles are busted open, giving me a hint of what my face must look like right now.

He looks up at me, his lips twitching into a smirk as he takes in the state of my face.

Fucker knows what he's done.

I'm going to have to walk into the office looking like this.

"Listen to your sister, Miles. This is between us. Husband and wife shit."

I might be focused on Miles, but I don't miss the way Tate's lips purse in anger at my words.

"I'm not your wife," she sneers.

"Not yet. But you will be." *For once in your life, you're going to do as you're told...*

Her expression hardens, although she's pretty difficult to take seriously right now with a hoodie down to her knees and bits of hair everywhere.

"Miles, please," she begs. "We need to discuss this. Go check on Mom. I'll be out soon."

With another concerned look in her direction, Miles finally walks toward the door.

He pauses when he gets there and looks me dead in the eyes.

"I'm fucking watching you, Kingston." Hearing him use my full name makes me smile, a reaction he probably doesn't want to see.

"Miles," Tatum snaps, and finally he walks out of the room and closes the door behind us.

She stares at the dark wood as if she's praying for some kind of miracle, but sadly for her, it's unlikely to happen.

Her future has been laid out now. There's only one way her life is going.

My way.

"Tatum, Kingston, please, take a seat," Richard says, speaking for the first time in a while and reminding me that he's still sitting there.

With a nod, I move forward and drop back into the seat I stole from her with a smirk playing on my lips.

"Baby?" I ask, dragging the chair next to me closer and gesturing for her to sit.

"Don't call me that," she sneers. "Don't ever call me that."

My smirk grows.

Fuck. I shouldn't love riling her up as much as I do.

19

As a kid, it was always one of the reasons why I loved being here and hanging out with Miles. Sure, she was annoying as fuck, running around with her Barbies and other girly shit. But watching anger blaze in her eyes whenever she so much as bumped into me made it all so worth it.

"We'll see," I mutter. "At least sit down."

"I'd rather stand."

"Brat," I say under my breath.

Richard looks between the two of us as if he's watching a tennis match.

"So, what's the deal here? We get married, try not to kill each other for a year, and then I'm free?"

Richard pauses for a moment before answering, and I can't lie, his hesitation piques my interest.

I may have been aware of this part of Jonathan's will—hell, I fucking agreed to it. But I don't know the details, or even the reasons.

I just saw it for what it is. A business deal. And quite frankly, it seemed like a pretty fucking good one to me.

So, here we are.

"Yes and no," Richard finally confesses. "Your father has stipulated how he would like your relationship to progress from here on out."

"You mean he's still trying to dictate my life from the grave?" Tatum snaps.

But Richard doesn't bite.

"He has requested that you use this time of mourning to ignite your relationship. Kingston has been such a pillar of support to you during this time that you decide to finally explore what else could be between you."

"He actually said that?"

"He would like for the two of you to be seen out together, for your photographs to appear online, for your names to be entwined before an engagement announcement is made."

"This is bullshit. He wants us to have an actual relationship?" she gasps.

"It needs to look real."

"Real? Real?" she repeats as she starts pacing. "The only real thing here is how much he's fucked me over."

"I can assure you, your life could be a lot worse than being married to me," I point out.

"The state's biggest fucking player?" she screeches. "Are you for fucking real? There are a lot of things I'd rather do than this."

"Like lose it all?"

Instantly, she stills, her arms hanging at her sides and her expression softening as she thinks about the alternative.

"Your apartment, your home, will be gone. Your roommate tossed out on her ass. Your car, your clothes, every single cent of your money."

"I don't give a crap about the money, Kingston," she argues.

"You want that cottage though, don't you?"

She opens her mouth to argue, but she can't. Even I know how much she covets that place.

Every dream she's ever had ends with that cottage and a new life outside of America.

But does she want it enough?

"So, a fake relationship. A fake marriage. I assume I'm going to have to live with you?" she asks, her blue eyes holding mine.

"You'd assume correctly."

"In the guest room."

"Are you bartering here or trying to tell me?"

Her jaw ticks with irritation and her eyes narrow.

"I'm not sleeping in your bed," she states.

I smile—I can't help it.

"What's so funny about that?" she snaps.

"I give it a week before you're begging to be in my bed."

"Over my dead body. I don't even want to be in your house, let alone the same room as you."

"And yet, you've already practically agreed," I point out.

Her nostrils flare as she draws in a deep breath before turning back to Richard.

"You said a year. A year from now? A year from engagement? Or a year from saying," she shudders, "I do?"

"A year from your vows," Richard confirms.

"So, you're saying that if we don't get on with it, it could be longer?"

He nods once.

"And after that year has passed, I'm free to leave and we can divorce?"

"Yes. The cottage becomes yours along with everything else you already have. You are free to start your life over."

My fists curl on my lap as I think about her packing up her things, walking out of my penthouse, and moving to the other side of the Atlantic to start over.

She hasn't even stepped foot inside my home yet, and I already can't bear the thought of her leaving.

What the fuck is wrong with me?

This is a business deal. One that hasn't even been signed yet.

The side of my face burns as she turns to look at me.

"And you're okay with this?"

Ensuring I have a relaxed expression on my face, I turn to look up at her.

"Sure, why not?"

She crosses her arms across her chest, making me wish she wasn't covering her body with such baggy clothes so I could see the way her tits push up.

She's got great fucking tits.

Hell, her whole body is banging.

Curvy yet toned. Everything is a perfect handful, and the way her waist dips...fuck, my fingers curl again as I imagine holding her right there and—

"You won't be fucking your way around the state if we're married," she says, interrupting my little fantasy.

I quirk a brow.

"Correct me if I'm wrong, Richard, but something tells me that this is a monogamous agreement."

"You're correct, Tatum. If you agree to this, then neither of you will have any other partner during your time together."

"And if we do?" she asks curiously.

"If you do, you sacrifice everything. Just as you would by walking away right now."

"And if Kingston cheats?" she asks. The way her brow is pinched tells me that she already knows the answer to that question.

4

TATUM

A bitter laugh spills from my lips.

I don't know why I'm surprised.

Men get to do whatever they want, whenever they want, without any consequence.

I've known that for a fact for as long as I can remember.

Dad used to come and go from the house with zero consideration for the people inside.

He'd whisk Mom away on lavish holidays, leaving us behind with Lucie, our nanny, without a second thought.

He enrolled us in boarding school when he decided he wanted the house to himself.

He told us that we'd give our lives working for Warner Group. There was never an option for us to do anything else.

And that's only a few examples that I can think of right now. Thankfully, I didn't have all that much to do with him at work, but I know he was just as bad—if not worse—there.

The world we live in is controlled by men. What they say goes, and their stupid actions are brushed under the carpet.

I'm actually amazed that Dad hasn't put into this ludicrous will of his that Kingston is allowed to be unfaithful.

We all know his father hasn't been in recent years.

And mine...acid washes in my stomach as I consider how he could have treated Mom over the years.

All the business trips...honestly, I wouldn't put it past him to have had a woman in every state and every country he's been to.

They're probably all going to turn up at the funeral with handkerchiefs in hand, all trying to outdo each other on the grieving widow front.

The image plays out in my mind so clearly. It takes everything I have not to bark out a laugh.

This is it. My father has finally pushed me to my limit.

I've lost my fucking mind.

"Tatum, are you okay?" Richard asks in concern. "Do you need to step out for some air?"

"If I leave this room before we discuss all of this, there's a chance you'll never see me again," I confess, finally lowering my ass to the seat. Although not the one beside Kingston. He can fuck off if he thinks I'm ever going to follow his orders.

"Is there anything else to discuss?" Kingston asks. "We're now officially dating. In a few weeks, I'll ask you to marry me, and so on."

My stomach knots painfully. He makes it sound so easy. There isn't any kind of hesitation or concern in his voice that he's about to throw his life into chaos.

Why doesn't he care?

I know I do.

"That's basically it. There are a few other little things but—"

"Like what?"

"The prenup. Location for the wedding, honeymoon. What you're allowed access to while living as Kingston's wife."

"Whatever," I mutter. I don't care about what I'm "allowed". I don't want anything from Kingston. I have my own money. Whatever I spend these days, I've earned. I can't remember when I last touched a cent of my father's money.

"All I need from the two of you is a signature agreeing to the terms, and then I'll let you go away and process all of this."

"I have to decide now?" I blurt. "Can't I...you know, think about it?"

"What is there to think about?" Kingston asks.

Everything.

"There's only one option here, and you know it."

I close my eyes for a beat as I think about my life. My job, my apartment, my hopes and dreams for the future.

I hate that he's right.

Hate it.

Scooting forward on the chair, I hold my hand out for Richard to pass me a pen.

The metal is cool in my fingers, the weight of it almost unbearable as I drag the tip of his fancy fountain pen across the paper.

My signature is almost unrecognizable with how violently my hand is trembling.

A huge breath rushes from my lungs as I sit back and stare at the ink.

Fuck.

"Kingston," Richard says, holding the pen out for him.

"Of course."

Smoothing down his tie, he sits forward and scratches his signature beneath mine.

Unlike me, his hand is steady, his writing strong and sure.

Nothing ever unnerves this man. Even signing a year of his life away to me is just another day to him.

Right then and there, I make myself a promise.

Even if I achieve nothing else in the next year of my life, I want to find out what makes him tick, and I want to experience him lose control.

Just once.

I want to experience Kingston Callahan as a real person, not a corporate robot.

The second he sits back, I pull the door open and all but flee from my father's office.

I was wrong when I walked in there earlier. I thought hearing

26

Richard read the will would close the door on a part of my life I'm mostly happy to leave in the past.

But I have a feeling a whole new level of hell is about to start.

Pressing my hand over my racing heart, I stumble down the hallway, my only focus getting out of this house and away from everyone.

I'm almost at the front door and able to grab my bags and escape when Miles's deep voice booms down the hallway.

"Tate, wait."

I stop where I am with my hand resting against the wall.

My legs are weak and my head is spinning. The last thing I should be doing is heading toward my car.

"I can't stay here, Miles. I need...I don't know what I need."

Alcohol. You need lots of alcohol.

Fuck. I'm not even sure if that's going to be enough.

"Are you okay?" he asks quieter.

He's right behind me. The heat from his body warms mine.

I desperately want to turn around and fall into his chest. But if I do, I'm afraid I might drown in my own tears.

"Of course," I lie, holding my head up high. "It's just a year, right? It's no big deal."

"Tate, it's a massive fucking deal." Anger laces every word that falls from his lips.

"Has Mom said anything?" I ask, finally reaching for my UGG boots and roughly pulling them on as if this whole thing is their fault.

"Not really. She's gone to bed."

"Good for her," I snap. "Maybe I could do the same and sleep for the next year."

"I knew you weren't okay."

"Miles." I sigh, hanging my head as any fight I had drains out of me. "I need to go and get drunk."

I barely get the final words out before he scoops up my bags, throws them over his shoulder, and all but drags me from the house.

"Me too, Tate. Me too."

"**D**eliver those back to Tate's, yeah?" Miles asks of our father's—his—driver, Leo.

"You've got it," he agrees before closing the door behind us and getting back in the driver's seat.

"I'm not dressed for this place," I complain as I look up at my favorite cocktail bar.

"I rang ahead. We've got a back room, so no one will know."

I smile, more grateful for my big brother in this moment than he could ever know.

With his arm around my shoulders, he ushers me inside, and in only minutes, the music playing in the bar gets quieter and the door to the private room closes behind us.

Low, soft lighting fills the room and I make a beeline for one of the three velour teal couches that surround an industrial-style coffee table in the middle.

Needing a distraction, I pluck the menu from the middle of the table. I don't need it. I know the menu here by heart. But it's either read this or continue obsessing over my current situation. I know which I prefer.

"What's it going to be?" Miles asks, having already pressed the button to call a server.

"I would like," I announce firmly, "five screaming orgasms."

"T-Tate," he splutters.

"What? I've just been told that I'm going to have to be celibate for a year. I think I deserve them."

"You have to..." Miles shakes his head as he lets those words sink in. "They can't ask that of you."

"Why? Because I'm a whore?" I'm not sure if I'm joking, and neither is he, from the way he studies me after the words spill from my lips.

"Tate, that's not—"

"I'm kidding. I think. But seriously, how fucked up is this?"

He makes to answer, but a soft knock on the door, and then our server entering, stops him.

"Good evening. What can I get for you guys?" she asks, her eyes locked on Miles the entire time.

I roll mine as I sink back into the couch. Miles is hot, even I can admit that. But watching woman after shameless woman hit on him gets old fast.

"Five screaming orgasms, a scotch, and one of every sharing plate on your menu," he orders, eye-fucking her just as much as she is him.

Give me fucking strength.

"You can't fuck her," I demand the second she's gone.

"Why the hell not? She's hot."

"If I'm not allowed to have sex, then neither are you," I sulk. "It's not fair I have to deal with this shit and you don't."

"You think I don't have shit to deal with, Tate?" he asks, falling back and spreading his legs wide. "Dad has just left me in a big fucking heap of it." His head falls back against the couch, and he closes his eyes as he drags in a deep breath.

He's changed since he walked out of Dad's office earlier. Gone is the all-powerful suit that rivaled Kingston's in favor of a dark pair of jeans and a black sweater. His hair is a disheveled mess, and his knuckles are red and swollen.

My stomach knots as I remember him beating on his best friend because of me.

"What's happened?" I ask, although I'm not sure if I can handle much else.

It takes him a few seconds to respond, but when he does, I can't say I believe him. "It's nothing. Forget I said anything. I'm just...overwhelmed, I guess."

"Tell me about it," I mutter.

"I can't believe Dad has done this," he muses.

"Really? As much as I don't want to believe it, it's the exact sort of bullshit we should expect from him. Kingston though. Of all people. Why him?" I complain.

"He's not so bad."

"Of course you'd say that. I'm sure he's great to go out drinking with. You've never had to be married to him."

"Did he seriously say no sex?" Miles asks, sounding more intrigued than he should.

I sigh. "No. Dad stipulated that I have to be faithful to the marriage."

"So, you can have sex. Just...with Kingston," he says with a wince.

"Yeah, all the while he continues whoring it up all over town."

"You have to be faithful, and he doesn't?" Miles balks.

"Men get to have their cake and eat it too; you know this as well as I do." Each word that passes my lips is even more bitter than the one before.

Thankfully, our server chooses that moment to walk back in and deliver our drinks. She literally lines up the five cocktails for me.

"Are we celebrating?" she asks.

"Commiserating," I mutter, attempting to steal her attention from my brother and failing miserably.

"Oh, right," she stutters awkwardly as she slowly backs away. "Well, I hope the drinks help."

"You're still not fucking her," I repeat, reaching for my first drink and taking a massive mouthful.

Fuck, that's strong.

He studies me for a beat, thankfully swallowing any response I don't want to hear. We both already know he's going home with her—or someone—tonight, no matter how much I complain. It's just how Miles works.

"Are you going to call Lori to meet you?" he asks, confirming my suspicions. He's happy to babysit me for a while—not that I need babysitting—but not all night.

I shake my head. "No, she's got a date tonight. Been waiting ages to meet this guy. Thinks he's the one."

Miles rolls his eyes. He doesn't need to say anything. I'm well aware of his cynical views on love and relationships.

"Well, I for one hope he is," I state after draining my first cocktail and immediately reaching for the next. "Because I'm going to need to live vicariously through her for the next year of my life."

"I can't believe after everything that's happened today, you're fixating on your sex life. Aren't there bigger things to worry about?"

I glare at him.

"Firstly, if you were in my situation right now, you'd be complaining a lot more than I am, you manwhore. And second, I do not have the mental capacity to unpack the epic shit pile that was dumped in my lap this afternoon. Mourning the loss of my sex life is the easiest thing to do right now."

Miles blows out a breath and scrubs his hand down his face before muttering, "I can't believe I'm about to say this, but..." He lifts his glass and swallows the entire measure down. "You could screw your husband."

5

KINGSTON

Dad was waiting for me when I finally emerged from Jonathan's office after discussing a few things with Richard.

He wanted to know how we'd got on. I wasn't surprised.

He has a lot riding on this partnership.

Hell, we all do.

Tatum might not see it—not yet, at least. But this is so much more than just her getting the cottage she so desperately wants and keeping some semblance of her life.

This is the merger of two huge families. Two powerful and successful businesses.

It's been a long time coming.

For years, the two companies have been kept apart due to old rivalries and commitments to their own causes. But everything changed when Dad and Jonathan became friends.

When they both took their place as CEOs of each company, many thought the merger was imminent.

Yet it never happened.

They both stood strong and held the wishes of the men that came before them.

But the tide has changed.

With Jonathan's unexpected passing, the future of Warner Group now lies in our hands.

It's taken decades, but the inevitable has finally happened, and I get a hot little bonus to boot.

I can't honestly say that I'm complaining too much.

Previously, the thought of sharing anything other than my dick with a woman has been less than appealing. But suddenly, the prospect of welcoming her into my house, my bed...fuck, it stirs something within me that I've never felt before.

Tatum Grace Callahan.

Sure does have a nice ring to it.

After informing him that Tatum had agreed, I excused myself from Jonathan and Helena's house and returned to the place where I spend most of my time.

Callahan Enterprises HQ.

It's a modern, glass high-rise in the center of town. A building impossible to miss by locals and tourists alike as they pass.

We've been here almost five years now after relocating not long after I joined the company from college.

It was a smart move placing ourselves somewhere so central, so focal. It's helped push our business both here and worldwide to the next level.

You can be the best fucking business in the world, but if you don't have the right image, the right face, the right brand, then you might as well give up. Something that Tate knows all too well.

I pull my Aston Martin to a stop outside the building and long before I've hit the brake, Thomas, one of my chosen security guards, comes marching toward me.

There are only a couple of people I truly trust with both my life and my car, and he is one of them.

He eyes me closely, taking note of each bruise and cut on my face, but he knows better than to comment.

"Good evening, sir. Would you like me to park her for you?" he asks as he pulls my door wide, allowing me to get out.

"Thank you," I say coolly, passing him the key.

With a nod at the two men guarding the entrance, I march inside.

The second I step over the threshold, everything feels right in my world once again.

Any concern over Tatum and her reaction to today's revelation is gone.

When I'm here, I'm focused. I do my job, and I do it fucking well, without any distractions or drifting thoughts.

With a nod to the ladies sitting behind the reception desk, I take off toward the elevator, aiming for the one person I know will still be sitting behind his desk, completely unaware that the workday is over and most of the staff have long left for the day.

The doors open before me, revealing two young women lost in deep conversation.

Without looking, they both move to the exit, completely missing my presence.

However, it doesn't take long for one to glance up, and her gasp fills the small space around them.

"M-Mr. Callahan," she stutters, her eyes wide and her cheeks flushed. "I'm so sorry, I didn't see you there."

"No problem...?"

"C-Clare. I-I work in—"

"Hi," the other says much more confidently, stepping in and stealing my attention.

"I'm Erin. We're both in marketing," she says, her eyes holding mine for a beat before they drop to my lips.

Nice try.

"Have a wonderful evening, ladies."

I step aside to allow them to pass before walking into the elevator with the sound of their giggles filling the air.

I'm still smirking at their reaction to me when I hit the top floor.

"Good evening," I say, making eye contact with Melissa, my assistant, who's packing up her things for the night.

"I wasn't expecting you back. Can I get you anything?"

"No, thank you. Enjoy your night," I say, taking off down the hallway, passing the door to my office, and making a beeline for the one at the other end.

His windows are tinted, stopping me from seeing the man inside, but that isn't an unusual thing. He prefers to hide from the world.

I knock twice and invite myself in before he has a chance to call out to me.

The room is silent with only a light glowing on his desk, and the man himself sits with his shirt sleeves rolled up to his elbows as he types furiously on his keyboard.

"I'm busy," he barks without bothering to look up.

"Unfortunately for you, I don't give a fuck," I mutter, swinging his door closed with a bang behind me and marching into the room.

Finally, he rips his gaze from his screen and his eyes narrow as he watches me drop into the chair opposite him.

"What the fuck happened to your face?"

"Minor misunderstanding," I mutter. "It's nothing," I lie. In all honesty, it hurts like a bitch, but like fuck am I telling my younger brother that.

"Right. How did the reading go?" he asks, aware of where Dad and I have been this afternoon.

"Yeah," I say, leaning forward and resting my elbows on my knees. "It was good. Positive."

He frowns.

"What the fuck is positive in a will reading?" He grunts, pushing his keyboard back as he becomes fully invested in this conversation.

"Expansion is on the horizon, little brother," I tease.

"What does that mean? What was in Jonathan's will?"

Pushing from the chair, I walk over to his bar and grab two glasses. After pouring us a measure of scotch each, I lower his to his desk and throw mine back.

"You might want to drink that," I say, placing my empty glass on the desk as the alcohol burns down my throat.

He does as I say before I ask, "Do you want to be my best man?"

He rears back, his eyes so wide I half expect them to pop out and bounce over his desk.

"Your what?" he blurts.

"My best man," I confirm, walking back to his bar and bringing the bottle over to refill our glasses.

"Fuck off. You're joking. There's no way on Earth you're getting married."

I smirk, pushing his scotch closer.

"I am. Soon, in fact."

"To who?"

My smirk grows, excitement tingling through my veins as I think about what's to come.

"Tatum Warner."

Kian's mouth opens and closes like a goldfish before he finally settles on, "I guess that explains your ugly face. Didn't think she had it in her."

He grins at me as he sits back in his chair and takes a sip of his scotch.

"She doesn't. Not yet at least." I wink.

"You're fucking serious, aren't you?"

"Deadly. Jonathan's will states that the two of us are to be joined in holy matrimony."

"Why?"

"Why the fuck not?" I shoot straight back.

"Because she fucking hates you. Because she drives you to the brink of insanity. Because—"

"It finally joins the Callahans and the Warners together."

His expression hardens. "I'm not a fucking moron, KC. Why? Why would Jonathan sell his only daughter to you, let alone give us an in to Warner Group?"

I shrug one shoulder, equally as in the dark as he is to the finer details of this little arrangement.

I've no doubt I'll find out soon enough.

I can't imagine a man like Jonathan would make this decision lightly.

"I'll look into Warner," Kian states without missing a beat. "Something is wrong, and I'd put everything I own on it being financial," he muses.

"Whatever it is, Jonathan owed our father something to willingly hand over both his business and his daughter."

"You're seriously marrying her?"

I chuckle. "Wouldn't you?" I counter.

He doesn't respond. He doesn't need to—it's right there in his eyes.

Tatum is hot. Really fucking hot. I'm not sure there are many straight men on the planet who would turn down a shot with her.

"Marriage though, man. That shit is serious."

"It's only for a year," I reason. "Then she gets what she actually wants and starts over. We, meanwhile, will have fully merged Callahan and Warner and our empire will be growing nicely."

"And what if she catches feelings?"

"If?" I laugh.

"Arrogant motherfucker," Kian scoffs.

"What?" I ask innocently. "I can't help it that none of the ladies can resist me."

"Well, if your dick is as big as your head, I can understand it."

I flip him off with a wide-ass grin on my face.

"So, Miles beat the shit out of you. What did—"

"Whoa, you're assuming that he doesn't look worse right now."

Picking up his cell, he unlocks the screen and then slides it across the desk toward me.

"Taken less than twenty minutes ago at Maxies. I'd say he's looking pretty good."

"Fucking asshole." I scoff, remembering his blazing eyes as he rained hell down on my face.

I knew he would be pissed. Miles loves Tate something fierce, but I wasn't expecting a reaction quite that violent.

"What about Tate? How did she take it?"

"About as well as can be expected," I explain as I swallow what's left of my drink. "She wasn't left much choice but to agree, unless she wanted to walk away with only the clothes on her back."

"Why would Jonathan do that to her?" Kian asks in concern.

"Because he's an asshole." I point out.

He might never have been that way toward Miles, or me and my brothers. But we all saw the way he treated Tatum. It was like she was a second-class citizen just because she was born with a vagina. And, of course, her constant need to defy him only compounded the situation.

Did I think he'd sign her up for a marriage with me? Hell, with anyone? No, not really. But he always did like to surprise us all. I guess he's just taken it to the next level.

"What happens from here?" Kian asks curiously.

"We start dating. I pop the question. And then we say I do."

"Just like that?"

"Yep," I say, popping the p. "Just like that."

"And you've got to pretend that you like each other for the next year?"

"Yeah. Shouldn't be that hard. It's not like she's a bad person or anything. Just...infuriating."

He laughs.

"Have you told Mom?"

I stare at him. He knows full well that I haven't.

"Fuck, this is priceless," he says before scrolling through his phone for a few seconds.

"Who the fuck are you calling?" I demand when his dial tone rings through the air. It's not hard to imagine him smugly informing our mother about all this. She already has enough opinions about my life that I don't want to listen to, I don't need to give her more reason to disapprove of me.

"Who do you think?" he asks a beat before our youngest brother answers the call.

"Hey, asshole. What's up?"

While our lives are firmly entwined with Callahan Enterprises, Kieran managed to break the mold, much to our father's irritation. If we all think Tatum defied what was expected of her and broke all the rules, then Kieran fucking shattered them when he severed the chains holding him here and set his sights on playing pro football.

Dad humored him when he was younger, expecting it to be a fad that he'd forget about. He was wrong. Very, very wrong.

Kieran ended up being a first-round draft pick and has been playing for the Chicago Chiefs ever since. Fucking killing it too.

"Are you sitting down?" Kian asks.

"Yeah, hit me with it."

"Kingston is getting married."

6

TATUM

I wake with a groan when my alarm begins blaring.

Why didn't I turn that off?

Reaching out aimlessly, I smack the top of it as the irritating sound makes my head pound.

"Shut up. Shut up. Shut up," I complain, hitting it harder and finally finding the sleep button. "Fuuuuck," I groan as I pull my covers up over my head to hide.

I thought screaming orgasms were meant to be good for you...

I'm just drifting off to sleep when the buzzer starts going off in the hallway.

"Go away," I cry, burying my head under the pillow and hoping for relief from all the noise.

But it doesn't stop it.

Whoever is standing on the other side of the door isn't giving up.

It's only concern for Lori that finally forces me into action.

As I roll out of bed, cool air rushes over me, and I glance down to find I'm wearing a thin tank and a pair of period pants.

At least I look as bad as I feel.

Grabbing an oversized cardigan from my chair, I throw it

around my shoulders and attempt to smooth down my wild hair as I make my way to the front door.

The buzzer continues. Its incessant noise ripping through the apartment, making my ears and head hurt.

"I'm fucking coming," I bellow as I stumble down the hallway.

My mouth is like the bottom of a freaking bird's cage. I can only imagine how bad my breath smells.

Whoever is on the other side of this door is about to get the shock of their life.

Please be Lori.

Please be Lori.

Her bedroom door is open, and as I pass, I find her bed made and unslept in.

Hope blooms in my chest that her date went so well.

If I were a good friend, I would have stayed sober last night in case she needed a rescue. But as it is, I don't remember getting home, let alone where my cell is.

Finally, I reach the door and fumble with the lock.

I close my eyes and pray one last time that my best friend is going to be smiling at me from the other side.

"Oh, for the love of God," I complain the second my visitor is revealed. "Why are you here?" I ask, keeping a tight grip on the door and standing firm.

There is no reason for him to be at my front door this early in the morning. Ever.

Wrapping my arm around myself to cover up, I try and muster as much confidence as I can.

"I brought you breakfast, baby." He smirks before holding up what I can only describe as a bottle of Grinch vomit.

"That...is not breakfast. If you don't have any carbs or coffee, I'm not interested."

I swing my arm forward to slam the door in his face, but he sees it coming and his free palm presses against the wood long before it closes, forcing it wider.

He steps closer, his freshly showered, manly scent filling my nose, and damn it if it doesn't make my mouth water. My vision is filled with his dark navy suit as he closes the space between us.

"You don't need carbs this morning. You need something to help detox last night from your system."

I narrow my eyes at him, still refusing to allow him entry.

"How do you know what I did last night?" I snap as I'm forced to crane my neck back to keep eye contact with him.

A shocked gasp rips from my lips as he brushes against my braless chest a beat before his warm breath tickles down my neck and his lips brush my ear.

"Who do you think tucked you into bed last night, baby?"

I'm so stunned by his words that I stumble back, inadvertently giving him space to invade my apartment.

"You didn't," I seethe, watching in horror as he marches down the hallway like he owns the place.

He looks inside Lori's bedroom before continuing forward to the open-plan living area.

He comes to a stop in the middle of the large room and his shoulders tense.

If it were anyone else, I'd say they were appreciating the view of the city before them. But this is Kingston. He isn't like anyone I've ever met in my life.

Wrapping my cardigan around myself tighter, I race behind him and look around my space, instantly discovering what his issue is.

"This is...chaotic, Tatum," he chastises as I pluck one of my bras from the back of the couch and stuff it behind a cushion before he sees it.

"Maybe if you'd told me you were planning on a visit, I might have tidied up," I snap. It's a lie, and we both know it. I would never go to any special effort for him.

So our apartment is lived in, so what? We love it here. It's our safe place, our haven, our home.

How dare he show up unannounced and turn his nose up in disgust.

"It looks like a college girl's dorm room," he mutters, kicking one of Lori's discarded high heels.

"We don't all live in cold, sterile, show homes, you know," I snap, turning to look at him as he assesses the disaster that is the kitchen.

In reality, I've never been to his place; I wouldn't have a clue what it looks like. But something tells me it's far from homely or comforting, just like the man himself.

"And we don't all have takeout every night of the week," he accuses, eyeing the containers.

"We had Thai. Fucking sue me."

I stand there fuming as he clears a small space on the counter and places the bottle of vomit on the side before pulling something else from his pocket.

"Oh good, you brought rabbit food, too. Lucky me."

His shoulders tense before he looks up at me.

"Do you have any idea what kind of shit you're filling your body with?"

Jesus, who the fuck called the fun police on me this morning?

"Fun shit, Kingston. Not that you'd have any idea what it feels like to actually enjoy yourself."

"I have fun," he argues, the hard expression on his face telling a very different story.

"Bending some dumb blonde over and fucking her six ways from Sunday a few times a week doesn't cut it."

A smile pulls at his lips before he chuckles.

Fucking chuckles.

"What's so funny?" I snap. I'm trying to offend him here, not fucking amuse him.

His eyes continue to hold mine for a few more seconds, the air turning electric between us before he finally mutters, "Nothing. Where are your glasses?"

"In the cupboard where they belong," I hiss.

"Looking at the state of this place, I highly doubt that," he says under his breath.

"Why are you here?" I seethe, my hands going to my hips as I wait, very impatiently, for a response.

He searches through three cupboards before he pulls out mismatched glasses—something that I'm sure makes him twitch in irritation.

Fuck. I bet his entire kitchen matches perfectly.

He turns back to me, places the glasses on the side, and picks up the bottle as if he's about to pour me a serving of the disgusting-looking goop.

His lips move, about to say something, but the second he looks up, he seems to lose all train of thought.

My brows pinch but then my skin begins to burn, and the second his momentary lapse in judgment makes itself known, so do my damn nipples as they pebble against the thin fabric of my tank.

He swallows thickly, his Adam's apple bobbing as his eyes drop down to my feet before making their way back up.

There's a part of me that wants to wrap back up and hide, but my defiant streak is stronger and I cock a hip, waiting for his eyes to come back to mine.

"Have you finished?" I sass when we finally collide again.

His emerald-green eyes are dark and full of hunger. And damn him, because the knowledge that I just did that to him hits me right between the thighs.

Day one of my new life of celibacy is going very well.

Finally, he finishes the task at hand before pushing a glass in my direction.

"I'm not drinking that."

"You are. And then you're going to shower and dress, and I'm taking you to work."

"Why?"

"Because our new lives start today, baby." He smirks, and it does little to cool the fire raging down below.

When was the last time I had sex, I wonder.

If I knew this was coming my way, I certainly would have made better use of my final days and hours.

"Nowhere in that will did it say you were to drag me out of bed, feed me vomit, and start barking orders in my direction."

His nostrils flare. "Then maybe you should have read the small print. Drink."

He pushes the glass closer, but I hold firm.

Refusing to be baited, he lifts his own glass to his lips and swallows the "drink" down.

I get lost watching the way his throat ripples and my imagination begins to get away with me as I wonder just what he might look like if he were to lose the jacket, shirt, and tie.

I shake my head.

"If you think I agreed to this so that I could spend the next year of my life being your little bitch, then you seriously need to reconsider. I don't follow anyone's orders. Especially not yours."

Spinning on my heels, I take off toward my bedroom.

Fuck him and his pretty eyes and jawline that would cut glass. I don't need either in my life. And certainly not at this time of the morning while suffering the hangover from hell.

Asshole. I storm through my bedroom and into my bathroom. The door bangs loudly as I swing it closed behind me.

Shrugging off my cardigan, I let it fall to the floor in a heap before turning the shower on and reaching for my toothbrush.

My mouth is fucking disgusting.

I've barely started brushing when the door suddenly flies open, revealing a pissed-off Kingston. He's lost his jacket and his white shirt sleeves have been rolled to his elbows, exposing strong forearms that are corded with muscle and thick veins.

"What the fuck are you doing?" I shriek around my toothbrush.

His jaw ticks as he steps forward, his eyes holding mine.

"Drink. It," he demands, holding the glass out.

"Fuck. You."

Anger darkens his eyes before his nostrils flare with irritation.

"What's wrong? Not used to people saying no to you?" I ask, my brows shooting up so high they almost hit my hairline. "Let's get something straight right here and now. I might have agreed to those moronic terms of my father's will, but it is not because I want this. If I had my way, I would already be on a flight to England to start over."

"I didn't want his money or power, and I certainly don't want any of yours."

"I'll do what's required of me for the next year. When we're out in public, I'll put on a good show, make people believe it's real. But behind closed doors, you're nothing to me. Just like you've always been."

I cringe, hearing the words come out of my mouth.

They're cruel, fed by anger over not only his behavior but this whole bullshit situation.

He moves closer, his wide frame closing me in. My bathroom is pretty big, but with him in here, it might as well be the size of a closet.

The closer he gets, the more air he seems to steal.

"It's admirable that you think that's how the next year is going to play out, Tatum."

My breath catches as he growls my name. All the hairs on the back of my neck and down my arms stand on end as I beg the rest of my body to behave.

"A year is a long time to spend hating me."

"I've managed pretty well this far. How old are you, again? Almost thirty?"

His lips twitch.

"Nice try. You know exactly how old I am."

His free hand lands on the wall beside my head and he leans closer, surrounding me with his warmth and addictive scent.

His eyes bounce between mine, but at no point does he allow them to drop again.

Either he had a complete lapse in judgment out in the living area when he checked me out, or he's using every ounce of self-control he possesses right now.

"You need to leave." It's meant to be a demand, but it comes out like more of a plea.

His full lips pull into a panty-melting grin.

"I think it's probably for the best that you start getting used to having me around, don't you?"

"You seem way too happy with all of this."

"Just taking it in my stride, baby," he teases. "Now, drink this and get ready. We have work to do."

"You are aware that I'm on compassionate leave, right?"

"Your team needs you back at work. A lot of change is coming in the next few weeks and months. Your absence won't help."

"And who exactly made you my boss?" I snap, instantly realizing my mistake.

"The same man who's making me your husband."

Before I know what's happening, he's wrapped my fingers around the glass and taken a step back.

"It'll make you feel better," he promises.

Lifting it to my nose, I sniff the toxic-looking concoction and wince.

It smells exactly like it looks. "Day one of our new lives together," I muse, looking down at the glass as if I'm considering it. But right before it touches my lips, I move my arm, holding it over the sink and pouring it down the drain. "And it already seems you need a reminder that while I might be about to become Mrs. Callahan, I will never, ever be yours."

7

KINGSTON

I am about to be married to the most infuriating, defiant brat in the entire world.

The memory of her tipping the superfood juice down the drain this morning plays on repeat in my mind.

I was trying to help.

She was beyond wasted when I turned up to Maxies last night. Miles didn't even notice me; he was too distracted by a harem of women to see me slip into the VIP room at the back and steal his sister right from under his nose.

He was meant to be looking after her, protecting her, yet there she was, half comatose on the couch surrounded by cocktail glasses.

If I couldn't tell she was wasted by looking at her, then it was more than obvious when I slipped my hands under her body and lifted her.

She gazed up at me through glassy eyes and called me her hero.

The world is more likely to stop turning than her calling me that if she were sober.

Using the bar's back exit, I carried her out unnoticed and held her the entire journey back to her apartment.

I was expecting to find her roommate at some point, for her to be the one to cuss me out and tell me where to go for touching her best friend, but the apartment was blissfully peaceful—although a total fucking dump—as I stripped her hoodie and leggings from her body and tucked her into bed.

I placed a bottle of water and a packet of painkillers on her nightstand before storming out almost as fast as I entered.

I considered staying, letting her wake up and discover how she got back here in one piece. But one look around her room and I knew I couldn't do it.

The floor was covered in clothes, her countertops littered with makeup, perfume, and fuck knows whatever else. It was too much. Literally, too much fucking stuff.

But while I might not have spent the night to ensure she didn't swallow her tongue in a drunken stupor, I had every intention of showing my face this morning.

I knew how happy she would be to see me, and she certainly didn't disappoint.

If I weren't so furious with her, I might just laugh.

The way she looked me dead in the eye and just poured it down the sink...

I don't know why I'm surprised, but I fucking am.

With little else to do, while I wait for what feels like an eternity for her to get showered and dressed, I embark on attempting to sort her life out.

I'm not sure why I bother; she's not going to be living here for much longer, but I can't help myself.

I put the huge array of takeout containers in the trash and pile all the dirty dishes next to the sink. I would have put them in the dishwasher, but predictably, that was full of dirty dishes as well.

I set that running and immediately understand why they might not have done so before bed, because it's the noisiest fucking thing I've ever heard.

I take a step back, my heart beating a little faster than necessary, but before I manage to escape the cesspit that is their kitchen, something moving through the air catches my eye a beat before it lands on my shoulder, instantly sending pain shooting down my arm.

"What the—" I turn to the side to see a ginger cat glaring at me. I swear the little fucker is smirking, too. "Get the fuck off me, vermin," I demand as I embark on trying to pull its claws from my skin.

It hisses at me, its hackles rising higher than I thought possible. I swear to God, if the thing could talk it would be swearing at me.

"Oh, you little shit," I bark, finally managing to get a firm enough grip around its middle that I can drag it from my body, although, I'm pretty sure it takes a chunk of my skin with it.

Fuck, that hurts.

I hold the smirking terror before me and narrow my eyes.

"The fuck is your problem?" I sneer.

A door slams down the hallway, and I'm just about to launch the thing in Tatum's direction when another voice fills the air.

"Get your hands off Mrs. Meowington."

My eyes widen in surprise as Tatum's best friend runs toward me and lifts the ginger furball from my hands, cradling it against her chest like a little baby.

"What are you doing to our pussy?"

"I-I—" I stutter like an idiot. "I don't want anything to do with your pussy, Lorelei."

She studies me suspiciously as my shoulder burns and I swear blood trickles down my skin.

Fucking vampire cat.

Another door opens before heels tap down the hallway.

"What the hell is going on?" Tatum demands, looking between me, Lorelei, and the fucking feral animal.

"He was going to throw Mrs. Meowington across the room like she's nothing more than a football," the fucking tattle-tail screeches in horror.

"You what?" Tatum gasps.

"Jesus fucking Christ," I mutter, scrubbing my hand down my face. "I was not going to throw your fucking cat across the room.

Although, I should have. Fucking thing deserves it after what it did to me."

"She's scared of the dishwasher," Tatum explains.

"Are you surprised? That thing sounds like the Terminator short-circuited."

Silence falls over us as the dishwasher continues to wreak havoc behind us.

"Come on, Mrs. Meowington, you can snuggle in my room," Lorelei says in a baby voice before walking down the hallway.

"Why are you still here?" Tatum asks. "Wait...have you tidied up?"

"Someone had to, don't you think?" I deadpan.

"Whatever. Let's go," she says, pulling her jacket on and throwing her purse over her shoulder. "The sooner you're out of my apartment, the better."

"I could say the same about you."

She pauses and shoots a glare over her shoulder.

If looks could kill...

Or more so, if her fucking feral pussy hadn't gotten there first.

I grab my own jacket and throw it over my shoulder as I follow her to the front door, my eyes locked on her ass that's showcased by what I'm sure is the world's tightest pencil skirt.

Fuck knows what I've done to deserve this morning, but someone up there is kicking my ass for something.

"Why is he here?" Lorelei snaps, reappearing from her room.

She looks like she's had a very good night—and not in the way Tatum did. Her hair is a disheveled mess, she has smears of red lipstick up her cheeks, and her throat is littered with hickies.

My cock aches a little at the sight.

I could do with a night like that right about now.

"Good morning, Lorelei. It's wonderful to see you too." I smile at her, but there's nothing genuine about it.

Her eyes narrow before they drop down my body. Fuck knows what she's looking for.

"Interesting," she mutters.

"Not now, Lor. I've got the hangover from hell. I take it your date was everything you wanted it to be?" Tatum asks, raising a brow as her attention moves between her best friend's eyes and her throat.

"Oh my god, Tate. It was—"

"We don't have time for this. We're delighted you got a good dicking last night, Lorelei, but some of us have jobs to get to."

Pressing my hand against Tatum's lower back, I nudge her forward before opening the door and practically pushing her through it.

"Do you mind?" she hisses.

"No, not at all," I mutter impatiently.

"I'll call you," Tatum shouts back to Lorelei.

"You'd better. I need to know what the hell is going on here."

"I'm not sure you do," Tatum says under her breath.

"Kingston, did you know you're bleeding?" she calls before we turn the corner.

"Fuck my life."

"Karma, baby," Tatum deadpans.

She presses the call button for the elevator and the second the doors open, I push her forward.

With my hands on her hips, I spin her around and crowd her until she hits the back wall.

I stare down at her, unable to ignore the lightness in her eyes that wasn't there when she first opened the door to me earlier.

Her makeup is flawless, accentuating her natural beauty and making it...breathtaking.

Her hair is down and falling in thick, soft waves around her shoulders, and the blouse she's wearing...fuck. It's the perfect tease for what she's hiding beneath.

"And here I was thinking you had more experience with pussy than that."

My teeth grind in irritation, but there is no way she's getting the upper hand here.

"Oh baby," I purr, moving closer so nothing but the scent of her sweet perfume fills my nose. "You have no idea the things I can do with a—"

The elevator dings and the doors open. She slips from between me and the wall and walks out with her head held high.

Spinning around, I follow her and my brows pinch as she walks toward a random car with what looks like a woolly mammoth sitting in the driver's seat.

"Where are you going?" I call as people walk in both directions on the sidewalk between us.

She doesn't respond despite the fact I know she heard me.

"Excuse me," I mutter, shoving some unsuspecting guy out of the way so I can stop her before she climbs into the back of that car.

My fingers wrap around her upper arm a beat before she ducks inside.

"What the hell are you doing?" she screams as I pull her back onto the sidewalk, our bodies barely an inch apart.

"You're not getting in that car."

"Why the hell not? As you so kindly pointed out, I need to get to the office, and I'm not walking there in these shoes."

"You have no idea who that man is," I state.

"Uh, yeah, I do," she argues, holding her cell between us. "His name is Marcus, and he drives a black Prius. He's a fully registered Uber driver. He—"

"Will drive you to the outback of nowhere and leave you for dead," I point out.

"Are you hearing yourself right now? Millions of women get in Ubers every single day. How many have vanished off the face of the Earth?"

I move my lips to give her an answer, but I quickly find that I don't have one.

I fucking will, though. I'm going to find out the answer and point out to her just how unsafe it is to put her life in some stranger's hands.

"My car is over there. From here on out, you want to go anywhere, Lewis will escort you."

Sliding my hand down her arm, I entwine our fingers and turn toward my car.

"No, Kingston. That is not—"

"You're causing a scene, baby. I'm pretty sure we need to announce our relationship before giving the media an exclusive to our first fight."

"This is not a fight. This is you being totally unreasonable," she argues.

"Keeping my girl safe is never unreasonable."

I spin her around and we find Lewis standing beside the open back door to my car, waiting for us.

"Lewis, this is Tatum. Tatum, this is Lewis. I'll put his contact in your cell. Wherever you need to go, call him. He is at your disposal."

I nod at Lewis, confirming my words. Her needs come before mine now.

"Good morning, Miss Warner. It's good to meet you."

"Please, call me Tate," she says politely. "But also, don't be expecting my call. I already have more than I need from your boss."

I half expect her to hot foot it down the sidewalk, giving me little choice but to give chase, but to my surprise, she steps toward the door that Lewis has opened for us and slips inside.

Lewis's eyes meet mine and a silent conversation passes between us.

You've got your hands full with that one, Boss.

I shake my head, unable to keep the smirk from my lips.

"Good girl," I muse after sliding across the seat to sit beside her.

The second my thigh touches hers, she practically jumps to the end of the seat.

"Don't," she warns.

"Don't what?" I ask innocently.

"Don't use that tone."

"What tone?"

She rolls her eyes and sighs heavily.

"Just...just be quiet from here on out. This morning has been stressful enough already."

8

TATUM

"Stop here," I demand as Kingston pulls his cell from his pocket and scowls at the screen. One quick glance lets me know it's his Mom. I'm so not going there this morning.

Sitting forward in my seat, I get ready to escape the car I had little choice but to get into a little over ten minutes ago.

"Keep going," Kingston demands like the epic asshole that he is, letting me know that he's listening to everything despite being distracted.

Has he not already ruined my morning enough?

"Lewis," I purr, dropping my voice so it's low and husky. "Please, could you pull up here?"

"Do not use that tone with him," Kingston snaps.

"Oh, but it's okay for you to use it with me?" I counter.

"You're mine. Not his."

"Careful, Kingston. We're only one day in and your jealousy is showing."

His lips purse in anger.

"I am not—"

"Just here would be great. Thank you so much, Lewis," I say, diving for the car door before the fuming man beside me can stop me.

"Tatum, I swear to fucking God," he huffs behind me before muttering to Lewis, "Don't say anything."

"I didn't say a word, Boss," Lewis says as I reach the coffee shop door.

The second I step inside, the scent of rich beans hits my nose and my mouth waters.

Caffeine.

I get in line, my body aching for a hit that's going to help get me through the rest of the morning.

My head is still pounding steadily behind my temples and my stomach is now growling, desperate for some food that isn't pureed what...seaweed and rabbit food?

I sense him before I feel him. His presence, even when he's behind me, is powerful and almost too much to take. But knowing he's approaching doesn't stop my entire body from flinching when his arm wraps around my waist and drags me back into him.

"Do you defy me for fun, Tatum?" he whispers in my ear. The rush of his warm breath sends a shiver racing down my spine.

I swallow thickly as he holds me tighter against him, letting me feel just how hard he is in all the right places.

"You sure seem to enjoy it," I snark as the server calls, "Next."

"Hi, I'd like a cap—"

"Green tea and a granola yogurt," Kingston interrupts.

I shoot him a scathing look over my shoulder before turning back to the server.

"Ignore him. I'll have a cappuccino with a double shot, a pain au chocolat *and* a cinnamon bun. And it's Tatum," I add.

I pay and attempt to move so I can collect my order, but the solid wall of muscle behind me doesn't allow me to move with his giant hand locked on my hip.

"What is wrong with you? Can you for once just be normal?" I hiss.

"You need to eat better," he chastises.

"No, what I need is to be left alone to make my own decisions. I am an adult. He may have handed me over to you like a prized freaking cow, but I can assure you, I do not need looking after."

"I'm not sure I agree."

"I don't care," I snap, finally breaking free of his hold. "Go and talk it out with Lewis. I'm not interested."

I storm off, keeping my back to him. But he never leaves. His stare continues to burn into my skin while I wait for my order and then all the way back to the car, which he follows me into.

"Here," I say, thrusting the stupid green tea at him. "I hope you choke on it."

"I didn't actually want—" he starts, looking down at the takeout tray I pass to him.

"Then you shouldn't have ordered it. Lewis, can you please take me to my office? Fast. I've had about as much of your boss as I can stomach today."

Without any argument from the infuriating man beside me, Lewis takes off into the morning traffic.

Usually, I would wait until I got to my desk to eat my pastry to protect the Uber drivers' cars. But seeing as I don't feel the need to offer Kingston the same courtesy, I open the bag and take a massive, unladylike mouthful, ensuring I rain crumbs everywhere.

He doesn't say a word, but I'm more than aware of his attention and the fact that I'm seconds away from watching steam billow out of his ears.

Good. I'm so fucking glad that I can annoy him just as much as he does me. At least we're on the same page with something.

I've just finished by the time we pull up out front of my office building, and I make a show of licking my fingers before brushing off my skirt. Gathering my purse, coffee, and second pastry; I reach for the door.

"Wait," Kingston growls, making me pause long enough for Lewis to open the door for me.

"Thank you," I say as I step out.

The polite side of me wants to turn around and say goodbye to Kingston, but the inner bitch he seems to unleash with just his presence alone wins out.

Tugging my purse strap higher onto my shoulder, I hold my head high and step forward in an attempt to look ready for work.

In reality, my head is spinning from the events of the past six days. I've no idea how I'm going to accomplish anything, but I'm willing to give it a shot.

I expect to hear the door closing behind me, but when it doesn't, my curiosity gets the better of me and I turn to look back before reaching the doorman.

"What are you doing?" I blurt as Kingston stands from the car and does his suit jacket up before taking his briefcase from Lewis.

"I have a meeting," he informs me before stepping up to me and placing his hand on the small of my back once again as if it belongs there.

"Who are you—" I cut myself off. It's a stupid question. He's here to see Miles.

Richard's words from the day before ring loudly in my ears. Kingston and Miles are to work together to finally merge both companies and move forward; bigger, stronger, as one.

Motherfucker.

He's my boss now. And soon-to-be husband.

Could life actually get any worse right now?

It makes sense. For years, the two companies have worked side by side. Separately, they've been very successful.

But together...

We could completely dominate the hospitality and tourism sector if we played it right.

We...

I almost laugh at my stupid thoughts. Even if I wanted to be a part of it, I would never be given the opportunity.

Sure, my surname grants me certain privileges in this building.

But I'm not one of "them".

I'm not a man in a powerful suit up on the top floor of this building.

I came to terms with the fact that I'd never be as important as them years ago. I'm fine with it. It just stings every now and then.

"Good morning, Miss Warner," Garrett, one of the doormen, greets as we pass before turning his surprised eyes on Kingston. "Mr. Callahan."

Kingston might not be a member of the staff here, but that doesn't mean that people don't know who he is.

Hell, the entire city knows who the Callahan brothers are.

They're notorious.

Gorgeous. Wealthy. Charismatic. Sexy.

Three of the most eligible bachelors Chicago has to offer, and women want to try their hand at taming them.

I mean, sure, I like a challenge as much as the next woman, but putting an end to the Callahan brothers' manwhoring ways isn't something that'll be on my to-do list anytime soon.

The eyes of almost everyone in reception follow us as Kingston refuses to remove his hand and guides me toward the elevator as if I don't know where it is.

I've been navigating this building almost all my life. It's been a very long time since I've needed an escort.

There might be a small group of people who want to get into the elevator, but the second they see us—okay, him—approaching, they part like the Red fucking Sea, allowing us to step inside the second the doors open.

And to my utter horror, they don't follow us inside.

When the doors close, it's just the two of us.

"We have a board meeting this morning. But we should be done by lunch."

"I already have plans, thanks."

I keep my eyes locked on the floor numbers, wishing they'd move faster to my floor.

"I wasn't asking. I was—"

"Good," I snap, breathing a sigh of relief when level thirteen lights up and the doors open. "Have a good day, sir. Try not to make anyone cry."

I'm out of the enclosed space and marching toward my office before he gets a chance to respond.

With an accomplished smirk playing on my lips, I walk through the marketing department with my shoulders back and my head held high.

Everyone watches me with curious eyes.

I've been here since my father's passing was announced, but not to work.

No one other than senior management knows what kind of relationship we had, so I can only assume they all expect me to be an emotional wreck incapable of working.

Well, if that's the case, they're about to get a shock.

"Ten minutes, my office," I bark at my team. "I want an update about where we are with our latest campaign."

A round of agreements rings through the air and I take off toward my office, the heat of their confused and concerned stares burning through me.

I don't so much as slow until I've kicked my office door closed behind me. Once I'm confident that I'm alone, I blow out the breath I was holding and let my body sag.

I'm too fucking hungover for this shit.

Dumping my purse beneath my desk, I place my coffee on my mug warmer and open my laptop as I lower my ass into my chair.

As soon as I log in, my emails appear before me and I wince at the preposterous number staring back at me.

How is that even possible? It's been six days since I got the call and my life turned into chaos.

But despite knowing it's going to take me another six days I don't really have to get through them all, I reach for my coffee and take a sip.

I can't comprehend dealing with whatever is waiting for me in that inbox until I've managed to shake his irritating presence from my mind.

"Fuck it," I mutter, reaching for the bag that's holding my second pastry hostage.

By the time a knock sounds on my office door exactly nine and a half minutes later, I'm just swallowing the last bite.

"Come in. Take a seat." I gesture to my conference table before walking around my desk to join them.

They continue to watch me curiously. No one dares say anything until Josh, one of my interns, pipes up the courage.

"We're sorry for your loss, Tate. We're here for whatever you need."

I smile at him, feeling the sincerity in his words.

He started here fresh out of college and was pretty green with his knowledge of how the corporate world works. But he's a fast learner and he's beyond keen, and he works harder than anyone I've ever known. More than all that, he fits in. From his first day, he became part of our family, and I have high hopes for his future here.

Unease washes through me.

A future that's being discussed right above our heads at this very moment.

I've no idea if Dad laid out plans for how he wanted this merger to work. My only interest in his wishes yesterday was what he'd planned for me. Professionally, he could be about to fuck me up too.

Callahan Enterprises already has a very successful marketing department. Their Chief Marketing Officer is incredible and has taken the company, the brand, way beyond where I think even Michael imagined they could be.

But having said that, he's also a hard-ass. Something tells me that we'd clash. Badly.

Our CMO here is equally as good at his job, but he's a little more—or a lot more—personable.

I look around my team as they begin presenting their ideas for our marketing plan for next summer and I can't help wondering who will still be sitting beside me when we finally see our ideas come to fruition.

Is it wrong that I mourn their potential loss more than I have done for the actual loss of my father?

I love my team. We're a tight-knit family that works seamlessly together. We bounce off each other perfectly and we come up with some kick-ass ideas, even if I do say so myself.

"What do you think, Tate? We're torn," Josh says, pointing at two ideas laid out before me.

"Ummm..."

9

KINGSTON

"They're already in Mr. Warner's office," Judith says with a friendly smile when I march out of the elevator on the top floor of the building. Ignoring yet another text message from my mother, I drop my cell into my pocket and take off.

"Thank you, Judith," I say as I walk down hallway with my muscles pulled tight with irritation. I'm late. I fucking hate being late.

And it's all her fault.

I knock once and push the door open without waiting for a response. I already know they're waiting for me.

As I step inside, my breath catches at the sight of my father sitting in Jonathan Warner's seat at the head of the table.

I don't know why I'm surprised. He isn't the kind of man who will take too kindly to not being the most important person in the room at all times.

"Good of you to join us, Kingston," my father chides while Miles frowns.

He knows as well as I do that I don't make a habit of being the last to a meeting.

"I apologize for my lack of punctuality," I say, addressing all the men sitting around the table before pulling out the empty seat between my father and Kian.

"Good to see you're looking even uglier this morning," Kian mutters quietly as I settle.

I shoot him a glare.

"Is everything okay?" Miles asks, able to read me better than most.

"I was with Miss Warner. Helping her come to terms with everything."

"How very thoughtful of you," Dad says while the other board members nod appreciatively.

"She should be here," Miles suddenly pipes up.

"She isn't in a senior role," my father explains. "Nor is she on the board of directors."

"She should be. Half of this should be hers now," Miles argues while my mind drifts to places it shouldn't.

I picture her here with us, sitting around this table in her sinfully short skirt, her blouse teasing me with what she's hiding beneath, and her full, pouty lips that were made for kissing....

I shift in my chair as my cock begins to swell.

Stop thinking about Miles's fucking sister.

"So, as I was saying," my father continues, "we have a lot of decisions to make, a lot of changes to implement over the coming months and years, but I truly believe this merger will be a positive for both companies.

"While I might be sitting here now at the head of this table, I want to make it known that going forward, both Miles and Kingston are taking on the role of managing Warner Group.

"We will, of course, work closely together as we progress through the changes, but this is their future we're carving out, the future for their children. And after all, I'm sure more than a few of you here will agree that it's probably high time I consider taking a step back. My sons, and Miles, are more than capable of taking the reins on this while I consider doing more...enjoyable things with my time.

"Jonathan's passing is a lesson to us in many ways. Life is

short. We need to make fast yet well-thought-out decisions and think about utilizing the time and the opportunities we have wisely.

"We're a long time dead, gentlemen."

Agreement rings in the air.

"Now, and please feel free to interject, my first thought for how we handle this is..."

Dad might be right, Jonathan's passing was a surprise to all of us, but sitting there and listening to him lay out plans for the company for well over two hours, I can't help but wonder how much they'd discussed this happening. Dad sure seems very confident in his ideas.

The thought of our fathers planning what would happen in the event of Jonathan's demise behind our backs—behind Miles's back—doesn't sit right with me. But there isn't much I can do about it now.

"I need to head out," Dad says not long after the board members have left. "Call me if you have any questions about all of this."

"I have one question," Kian says, having remained almost silent for the past few hours.

I know exactly what he's going to say. He called me in the middle of the night with his findings, wanting to know what we should do about it.

"Go on," Dad says.

"What about the money?" Kian asks simply.

"What money?" Dad's expression remains neutral, but he knows.

He knows everything.

"The money that has vanished from the company in the past few months. Did you not want to tell the board about that?"

Dad's mouth opens and closes as he tries to figure out what to say.

"Jonathan ran into some unforeseen issues," he explains.

"Is that right," Kian mutters as I look between them and Miles shoots from his seat in shock.

"What money? What issues?" he demands.

Dad shakes his head. "It's nothing you need to worry about."

"Nothing I need to... Michael, you can't sit there and tell Kingston and me that we're at the top here and not clue us in as to where a significant sum of money has gone."

"It's more than a significant sum," Kian explains, much to Miles's horror.

"How much?" Miles demands.

"You are wrong for keeping this to yourself after handing us control. But if that's how you're going to play this, then you might as well leave," I tell Dad. "This is our business now, our decisions. If you feel there's anything else we need to know, feel free to tell us."

I dismiss him by turning my back to the man who's taught me everything I know.

I get they want to protect us.

But how are they achieving that without giving us the full facts?

"Kingston," Dad growls.

I don't respond as I retake my seat and pull my cell out to check my emails.

"Well, you know where I am if you need me," he mutters before leaving the room and closing the door a little harder than necessary behind him.

"What the fuck?" Miles fumes.

"Your father had a gambling problem," Kian states.

"Since when?" Miles asks on a sigh as he falls back into his seat, both of us leaving the head of the table empty.

"Since forever, if what I looked at is to be believed, but he was always relatively lucky, it seems. Until about two years ago, that is."

"How much has he lost?" Miles mutters.

Kian falls silent.

It's all the answer Miles needs to know that this is bad.

"Enough to hand his company and daughter over," he realizes. "Fucking hell."

He slumps lower in his chair and lets his head fall back.

"If this merger wasn't happening, would Warner be in trouble?"

"It could be rescued with a little restructuring, but it wouldn't be easy."

"So when Richard read the will and explained that Dad was leaving me this," Miles says, holding his arms from his sides, "he was basically fucking me in the ass just as hard as he is Tate." He glances at me. "No offense," he mutters.

"He was desperate," Kian muses.

"Desperate to ruin our fucking lives. The only one that's come out of this looking good is Mom. But then I guess she deserves that after putting up with him for so long."

I swallow nervously, remembering what Kian told me last night.

"What he's left her isn't as healthy as you might believe."

All the blood drains from Miles's face.

"How do you know all this? We only discovered the merger yesterday."

"I got access to the accounts the second I was told. I knew it was too big for there not to be something going on. And I was fucking right."

"This is fucked up," Miles mutters.

"You want to go day-drinking?" I offer, not knowing what else to suggest right now.

"Think I might have had too much last night. I woke up with this chick I have no fucking memory of," he confesses.

"She was the server from Maxies," I point out.

"How do you know that?"

"Because you were dry-humping her at the bar when I came to pick up my wife, seeing as you weren't looking after her."

His teeth grind. "Don't call her that."

"Oh, sorry. My fiancée."

"Kingston," he growls.

"What? Would you prefer me to refuse and leave her out on her ass?"

"I wouldn't let that happen," he argues. "Her position here is safe, and I wouldn't take a cent away from her."

"That's not what she really wants though, is it?"

Tatum's dream of moving to England to live in their late aunt's cottage isn't a secret.

She spent all her summers there as a kid while Miles and I were here, being forced to learn the family businesses.

I remember her constantly drawing and painting that little house. It was all she talked about.

It's why I know that I'm not risking much by agreeing to this marriage.

She doesn't want to be here. She doesn't want this life.

Once our year is done, we'll both be able to go our separate ways.

She'll get what she wants, and in turn, so will I.

Merging Callahan and Warner has been something Miles and I have talked about all our lives. Working side by side, being CEOs of our own empire, outdoing our fathers, and being the number one hospitality and tourism corporation in the country, has been our dream.

And I'm not fucking giving that up because of his bratty little sister.

So I figure we'll spend our year together, enjoy it where possible, and then embark on what we really want for our lives.

Easy. Simple.

Painless.

Minus the cat scratches.

"I can't believe you're marrying my little fucking sister."

Kian smirks. "I can. She's fucking hot. And," he adds before Miles can attempt to lay him out like he did me yesterday, "I'm pretty sure there isn't anyone else on the planet who would put up with this asshole."

"Lovely," I scoff. "Now, are we having a working lunch or what?"

"Fuck it. Yes. Let's go," Miles says, pushing to his feet and grabbing his jacket from the back of his chair.

"World domination always needs to come with a side of scotch," Kian mutters as we walk out of Jonathan's—Miles's—office.

I nod at Judith as Miles talks to his own assistant, Maddison, before the three of us walk into the elevator and descend through the building.

The temptation to stop at the thirteenth floor is strong. The need to know what she's doing—hell, if she's even here—is almost too strong to ignore.

But I do.

Eyes follow the three of us as we walk out of the building and toward Leo, Miles's driver.

He might not have got exactly what he bargained for when Jonathan left him everything, but he still did quite well out of it. And anyway, who wants to be gifted something that's running smoothly? That's boring.

This way, Miles and I can make this our own in a way we never would have been able to before.

These companies might have originated with our ancestors, but what we create by joining them together is going to be ours.

And I can't lie, that's fucking exciting.

The drive to our favorite bar is fast, and before we know it, we're sitting in the back room with a glass of scotch each and plans of expansion and growth ringing in the air.

The whole time, the only thing I can think is, there's someone missing.

Sure, Kieran isn't here because he chose his own path in life. But Tatum...she's a part of this. She's a vital member of the Warner team. She should be here planning this with us, even if she has no desire to see it out long-term.

It's in her blood.

She belongs here just as much as we do.

10

TATUM

"At fucking last," Lori cries down the phone. "I've called you, like, a million times today."

My heart aches. "I know, I'm sorry. It's been nonstop since I walked into the office this morning."

"Yeah, about that. Aren't you still meant to be on leave?"

"Yeah, well, I decided it was time to return," I lie.

"You've barely had any time off. You've been in that building every day, sorting out the shit your mother should be doing," she chastises.

"I know," I mutter. "Someone has to do it."

"Yeah, she should. It's time for her to step up."

"Lor, she can barely stand up," I point out.

"That isn't—" She sighs, cutting herself off.

She often forgets that just because she has pretty much nothing to do with her own mother, doesn't mean other people don't have obligations to theirs.

My mom isn't a bad person. She's always been there for me. Even if it was from a distance while I was away at school. Sure, she wasn't a hands-on mom, and our relationship could be a lot better, but still. She's a hell of a lot better than Dad ever was. At least she had some time for me.

"So anyway, what the hell was up with Kingston this morning? And why the fuck was he in our apartment?"

"You busy tonight?" I ask on a sigh.

"I was going to wash my hair, but—"

"Put it in an updo," I say, rolling my eyes at her insane hair routine. "We're going out. There are things I need to tell you."

"Did you fuck him?" she screeches loudly as I step into a full elevator.

Every single person turns to look at me, ensuring my cheeks blaze bright red.

"Lori," I whisper.

"Well, did you?" My lips part to tell her no, but she continues nonetheless. "I know I would have. He looked fucking delicious. Although, his hair needed messing up a little."

"I thought your date went well," I say in an attempt to change the subject.

The longer I can keep the details about me and Kingston out of the gossiping mouths of this office, the better.

"Oh, it did. He was incredible. Didn't fill out a suit in the way Kingston Callahan does, though."

"Lori, will you—" My words are cut off as the elevator stops on the second floor where the on-site gym is located and almost everyone piles out.

The second the doors begin to close, my skin erupts in goosebumps.

Dragging in a deep breath, I keep my eyes focused forward as heat begins to burn down my back.

"I know you hate him, but you can't tell me you didn't appreciate the sight this morning."

Warm breath rushes across my neck, making all my hairs stand on end.

"I'm going to check on Mom on the way home. Be ready to go in two hours?" I ask.

"You got it. Girls' night or—"

"Invite Cory. I've missed him," I confess, before a large hand clamps down on my hip.

"Okay. You got it. See you soon, yeah?"

"Yep," I agree, my voice coming out a little squeakier than I intended.

"Are you sure you're okay?" Lori asks, able to tell from just that one word that I'm not.

"Yeah, great. See you soon."

I hang up before she can say anything else I don't want Kingston overhearing.

"You lied to her," he growls in my ear, sending a shiver racing down my spine.

I buck against him in an attempt to get his hot paw off me, but all I manage to achieve is to rub my ass against his crotch.

"No, I didn't. Will you let go of me?" I demand, still unsuccessfully trying to extract myself from his grasp.

I shiver when he reaches out and pulls my hair from my shoulder, fully exposing my neck.

"Yes, you did," he states, the heat of his proximity burning down my neck. "Don't think I missed how you looked at me this morning."

"With potent disdain?" I counter.

He chuckles and fuck if it doesn't make my nipples pucker with interest.

"Sure, you keep telling yourself that."

I seethe silently as his grip on my hip tightens. I want to hate it.

I really fucking do.

Thankfully, before I get a chance to think about just how much I do like his possessive grip on my body, the elevator comes to a stop on the ground floor and the doors open.

Kingston might remove his hand from my hip, but I don't lose his touch. Instead, his palm finds a home on the small of my back again.

"You're not going out with another man tonight," he says casually as if we're discussing the weather.

"Oh, I'm sorry. I wasn't aware that you'd taken charge of my entire life."

"Tatum," he growls.

"Mr. Callahan," I counter with a smirk. "I'm not sure how many times I need to say this to ensure it gets through that big, egotistical head of yours, but I am not yours to order around. You want to play boss, go back to your own office and bark orders at your poor, suffering employees."

"Ah, but that's where you're mistaken, Miss Warner. I have just left my office, and I am ordering around one of my employees." When I don't immediately come up with a response, he continues, "You should come and visit my office next week. That way, I can give you the orders I really want to behind closed doors. Something tells me that you don't want your colleagues to see you sucking off the boss."

My chin drops in shock.

"Lewis, Miss Warner would like to go and visit her mother before returning home," he tells his driver while my Uber idles behind his fancy-ass car.

"I can make my own way home, thank you," I say, taking off toward my waiting car.

I think he's going to let me go before his hand grips mine and I'm pulled back toward him.

But he doesn't stop me at a sensible, normal-person distance. Instead, he continues pulling me until I'm pressed up against him.

"Kingst—" My voice falters when he reaches out and grazes his knuckles across my cheek before tucking a lock of hair behind my ear. "W-what are you doing?"

"Following orders," he whispers, staring me right in the eyes.

To anyone watching us—and I've no doubt there are plenty— I'm sure it looks hella intimate, and not at all like I'm two seconds from kneeing him in the balls for this very public display of ownership.

"One of us has to." He leans forward and my heart stops beating.

Surely he's not going to...

I breathe a sigh of relief when his lips press against my forehead.

Gritting my teeth, I refuse to allow myself to think about how warm and soft they feel against my skin. Instead, I try to remember all the reasons I've always hated him.

It's an easy thing to do. The man is infuriating as fuck.

"Get in the car, Tatum."

The need to defy him is so strong it burns through me like wildfire, but in the end, I choose the route of least resistance.

Plus, if we're doing this, I need to start toeing the line in public. Doesn't mean I have any intention of doing the same in private, though...

I smile up at him. To everyone around us, I'm sure it appears genuine. But I've no doubt that Kingston can see the defiance and need for retribution burning bright in my eyes.

"Thank you, sir." His eyes blaze and his jaw locks as I breathe that final word.

What a surprise—being reminded of just how powerful he is turns him on. Didn't see that coming.

I climb in the back of the car, half expecting him to follow me, but when I look back, he's still on the sidewalk.

"Aren't you coming to ruin more of my day?" I call, making Lewis smile as he moves to close the door behind me.

"Sadly, I have other plans. But you do make it sound very tempting," Kingston states before the door closes, cutting us off from each other.

Aware that I've been gifted privacy in the form of the blacked-out windows, I gaze out, shamelessly watching as Kingston gives Lewis some more demands.

He talks much more animatedly than I was expecting. Clearly, despite being boss and employee, Kingston and Lewis have bonded during their commutes together.

My eyes focus on his lips for a few seconds and my forehead tingles as I remember how they felt pressed against me.

I'd be lying if I said I hadn't imagined what it might be like to kiss him, and maybe a little more, over the years. He might have been the biggest irritant in my life for as long as I can remember, but he's also one of the hottest men I've ever had the pleasure of looking at.

Dark stubble covers his sharp jawline, and I can't help but wonder if he forgot about shaving this morning so he could get to me faster. That thought makes me happier than it should. His hair is a disheveled mess, evidence of how many times he's run his fingers through it during the day. Was he thinking about me as he did? His suit fits him just as perfectly as it did when he stepped into my apartment this morning. His shoulders are broad, his waist slim, and I know from the small amount of physical contact I've had with him that his muscles beneath the fabric are ripped. I can only imagine how he'd look without his armor. It's been a lot of years since I've seen him running around with Miles without a shirt on, and I can only imagine that very good things have happened.

It's not until I've done a whole pass of his body that I finally look elsewhere, and when I do, I shouldn't be surprised by the level of attention on him. But I am.

Men and women alike watch him as if he's some kind of celebrity. I guess in some ways he is.

Men worldwide want to be him, and women want to be beneath him.

He's an enigma. All the Callahan men are.

It's like they're born these mysterious creatures that everyone wants to try and unravel, whether it be in the boardroom or the bedroom.

Women whisper to their friends, a few shamelessly pointing in Kingston's direction.

Something uncomfortable bubbles in my stomach as I watch them strip him naked with their eyes.

Mine.

My eyes widen.

What the actual fuck?

No. He is not mine.

We might be connected in a way for the next year of our lives. But he is no more mine than I am his.

Irritation surges through me. Only, it's different from what I've felt previously today because it's aimed at myself, not at him.

I shake my head, forcing my brain to go down a different train of thought.

I wonder how many of these women he's already slept with.

I'm not naive. I'm more than aware that I'm not about to be married to a virgin. Kingston and Miles have been fucking their way around the city for years.

They may as well replace their front doors with revolving ones just to make life easier.

I shudder at the thought.

I'm so lost in my thoughts that I startle when Lewis finally joins me.

"Ready to hit the road, Miss Warner?" he asks, watching me in the rearview mirror with mischief twinkling in his eyes.

It becomes immediately clear that he's nothing like Leo, my father's driver.

"Please, call me Tate. And just so we know, this is a very rare show of obedience where Kingston's orders are concerned."

His eyes crinkle as he smirks.

"Noted. Thanks for the heads up. To your mother's, yes?"

"Please. I won't stay long," I explain.

"Stay as long as you wish, Miss—" I narrow my eyes. "Miss Tate," he corrects.

"Trust me, however long I stay will be too long right now."

"Please give her my commiserations," he says kindly.

"I will, thank you."

"I know it's cliche, but time really is a healer. Things will get better."

I sigh, gazing out at the city as is passes by.

"Yeah," I muse. "In about a year's time, everything will be a lot better."

11

TATUM

"Hey, Griz," I say, scooping up my ginger kitty the second I step into my apartment just over an hour later.

She purrs sweetly as I scratch behind her ears before I march straight into the kitchen to find her favorite treats. She needs all the treats after the way she clawed at Kingston this morning.

She certainly is my girl, that's for sure.

"Tatuuum," Lori calls from her bedroom.

"Yeah, hang on," I shout before grabbing a bag of Doritos and shaking a few into Griz's bowl, or, to use her full name, Mrs. Grizabella Von Meowington. Yes, I was very, very drunk when I named her. But to be fair, it totally suits her. She's such a princess. She'd have turned her nose up at anything more...common.

With an extra scratch behind her ear, I tell her what a good girl she is before going in search of my bestie.

I thought I needed this night out before I left the office, but after my last interaction with Kingston and then an hour of watching my mother drown in her own misery, I really fucking need this night out.

Last night, I allowed myself to wallow after yesterday's

discoveries. Tonight is about making the most of what I have, even if it's imminently about to change.

My days of living as a single girl with Lori are soon to be over, so I need to make the most of it while I can.

I've no doubt that someone took a photograph of Kingston kissing me outside the offices earlier. News of us getting close is probably already spreading around the toxic world of social media as we speak.

I come to a stop in Lori's doorway, unsurprised to find her hanging half upside down as she diffuses her hair.

"Hey," I shout, aware that she can't see or hear me.

She turns her hairdryer off and gently swings her hair around as she stands.

I roll my eyes at her. Even after all these years of friendship, her dedication to her curly hair astounds me. It's probably why she's still single. She doesn't have time for a man; she's too busy twisting, twirling, and scrunching among many, many other things.

Her eyes light up when they land on me before a wide smile spreads across her lips.

"What?" I ask nervously before moving into her room and flopping onto her messy bed.

It's a mistake. The second my back hits her memory foam mattress, all my body wants to do is sleep.

Thankfully, what Lori shows me two seconds later perks me back up.

"This," she says, holding her cell above me so I can clearly see the photograph I was just thinking about. "Care to explain why Kingston Callahan has his lips on you after being here first thing this morning?"

I groan, feeling nowhere near prepared to explain this whole shitshow. I can barely think about it without wanting to crawl into a dark closet and completely shut down.

"You fucked him, didn't you?"

"What?" I gasp, pushing myself up in the middle of her bed

and snatching her cell so I can look closer. "No, I have not fucked him."

"But you want to. I always fucking knew you—"

"Lori, I do not want to fuck him." *Liar.* "He is the most irritating man I have ever met in my entire life."

She raises a knowing brow.

"I don't," I repeat, aware that I'm not convincing her of anything.

I stare at the image of us. The lighting is perfect with the evening spring sun illuminating us in the middle of the sidewalk.

He looks...well, fucking model-worthy, like always, and I look... pretty damn good, actually. I'm wearing my sexiest skirt—total coincidence that it was the next thing in my closet this morning and not chosen for any specific reason. Nope. No reason at all.

He has one hand on my waist, holding my body against his, and the other is cupping my jaw as he presses his lips against my skin. But neither of those things is a surprise. I was there; I felt his burning touch as if he were a naked flame. What shocks me are his eyes.

They're closed.

It gives the kiss a whole new level of tenderness, of intimacy.

I swallow thickly, unable to rip my eyes away. No wonder we drew such a crowd. I'm enthralled, and I was there.

"Then you'd better have a good explanation for that, because from what I can see—"

"We're getting married," I blurt, unable to keep it in any longer.

Lori's jaw drops and she stumbles back as if my words physically struck her.

"Y-You're...you're getting m-married?" she asks in utter disbelief.

Putting her cell to sleep, I throw it to the end of the bed and push to my feet.

"I need alcohol for this conversation."

"You don't fucking say," she mutters, immediately following

me from her room and down to the kitchen. "Vodka is in the freezer."

Pulling the door open, I grab the bottle as she places two shot glasses on the counter.

I twist the top and slosh the ice-cold liquid into the glasses.

"Bottoms up, baby," I say, wincing the second I hear his voice in my mind as I say "baby."

Fuck. I need to drink him out of my system.

How is it possible that he's managed to get under my skin quite so quickly after that announcement yesterday?

I lift my glass and swallow it down in one go, loving the way it burns all the way down my throat.

I haven't had anywhere near enough to eat today to be doing shots, but fuck it.

There doesn't seem to be much in my life I can control right now, but this...this I can.

"Start talking," Lori demands as I refill our glasses before hopping up on the counter.

Griz saunters over and begins nuzzling me for more Doritos.

Leaning over, I reach for the half-empty bag and offer it up for her.

In a flash, she has her head in the bag and is chomping away on her cheesy obsession.

"Dad..." I hang my head, unable to believe I'm actually about to say these words out loud. "He stated in his will that if I want the cottage, I've got to spend the next year as Kingston's wife."

"Why? Why the fuck would he demand that?"

I shrug. "To control me? To stop me from catching the first flight to England and never looking back? Sorry," I add when hurt washes over her features.

"That's some bullshit, Tate."

"It is what it is," I mutter, swallowing my second shot.

"You don't have to agree, you know that, right?"

"I'll lose everything if I say no. My job, my life. This place," I say, letting her know that this affects her as well.

"So, you'd get another job. You're Tatum Warner. Anyone would be lucky to have you."

"Lor." I sigh, appreciating her positive thinking but totally unable to believe it. "He wouldn't have made it that easy. He's probably blacklisted me with every marketing company in the country."

She grimaces, unable to argue.

"We can get another apartment. We can—"

"Lor," I beg.

"Do you want the cottage that badly?" she asks, silently urging me to just let it go.

I nod. "I do. It's the only thing I've ever wanted."

She hangs her head. This isn't news to her. Since the moment we met at college, I've told her about my dream place in England, about my plans to relocate when the time is right.

She doesn't understand, and I get why. But it's important to me. That cottage is the only place I've ever truly felt at home. It's where my heart is.

"This is fucked up. What does he get out of it?"

"Aside from the obvious?" I ask, throwing my hair over my shoulder and sticking my tits out.

"Yeah, aside from stealing my best friend from me," she says sadly.

"They're merging Callahan Enterprises and Warner Group. Kingston stands to gain quite a bit. Miles, too, if they play it right."

"But what about you?" she argues.

"I don't want any of it, you know that."

"Another," she demands, holding her glass out.

She stares at it for a few seconds, deep in thought, before throwing it back.

"Something isn't right here. Your dad would never have willingly handed both you and the company over. Miles is more than capable; it doesn't need Callahan interference."

"He would have handed me over without a second thought, Lor. He probably expects us to fall in love and for me to pop out the next Callahan generation to take over the world."

She tilts her head to the side in thought.

"It's not going to happen. Kingston Callahan is the furthest possible from my type. He's an egotistical, power-hungry, g—"

"God?" she interrupts.

"Asshole is more like it." I scoff, jumping down from the counter and moving toward my room to get ready.

"So, what happens now?" she asks, following me.

I explain the plan Dad laid out in his will as I strip down to my underwear and then slip into my bathroom and turn on the shower.

"Two weeks? He's going to propose in two weeks?"

"We're going to fall hard and fast, apparently," I call back as the room begins to fill with steam.

"I guess when you know, you know."

"I'm in," I say, letting her know that it's safe to enter. We might be close, but we do have some boundaries.

"We've got to be married for a year, and then the cottage will be signed over to me. I'll get to keep my trust fund and everything else that should be mine."

"What about the company? You have a stake in that, surely?"

"Nothing was said about it."

"That's bullshit. Just because you have a vagina, it doesn't mean you're incapable of being senior management and kicking ass at the top."

"We both know that, but it doesn't matter. Even if they offered it to me, I wouldn't want it."

I don't need to look over my shoulder to know she's narrowing her eyes at me. This has been a topic of conversation between us more than once.

She's never believed that I'd turn down the job of CMO, if I were ever offered it.

"So you're just going to throw away your chance at meeting the one for the next year while you play house with your worst enemy?"

"It could be worse," I muse, although I don't sound very convincing.

"What does Miles think about all this?"

"You saw his face, right?"

"Oh shit. Miles did that?" she gasps. "Fuck. I bet that was hot."

"Lori," I shriek.

"What? I would happily watch those two fine specimens of men rolling around and throwing punches. I'd totally help clean up their wounds after, as well."

"Of course you would, whore," I laugh.

"Takes one to know one," she counters. "Oh, speaking of. I want all the details when you finally get to ride that stallion."

"Not happening," I state.

"What? Why not? You have to get something out of this bullshit. He's got the reputation of a freaking Adonis. If I were you, I'd be making very good use of that. It'll soften the blow of being married to the prick, that's for sure."

"I'm not sleeping with him."

She laughs.

"Lori, I'm being serious."

"So what? You're going to be married, making it look like you're following Daddy's orders while you're both fucking everyone else?"

I cringe. "I've got to be monogamous. Tell me about your date," I beg. "I can't talk about him anymore."

"My date was great. Everything I hoped for. And he was hung, too. Fucking epic," she says in a rush. "Kingston has to be faithful too, right?" she asks, swinging right back around.

"Towel," I demand after killing the water and holding my hand out.

"Tatum," she warns.

"I don't care what he does, Lor. He can fuck his way around Chicago and get dick rot if he wants, so long as he doesn't try sticking it in me."

You are such a fucking liar, Tatum Warner. Be honest, you want to climb that man like a tree.

Wrapping my towel around my body, I step out of the shower and come face to face with my smug best friend.

"I give you a week before you fall under his spell, and his body."

"Jesus, Lor. I do have some self-respect, you know."

She quirks a brow.

"What? I do. What time is Cory meeting us?'"

"Eight at Maxies. Changing the subject isn't going to work, though," she calls as she backs out of my room, ready to return to her hair.

No. I fear that telling myself I'm going to be celibate for a year isn't going to work either, but a girl can try.

12

TATUM

With a wide smile splitting my face and more margaritas than I can count right now warming my stomach, I lose myself in the beat of the music and the warm, strong hands that hold my hips hostage.

"Fuck. I love this song," I scream, my head falling back against Cory's shoulder as the heavy bass thumps through my body.

Honestly, I have no idea what the song is, but it doesn't matter.

"You're on a mission tonight, T," Cory shouts in my ear.

"Been a long week, Cor. I fucking need this," I say, rolling my body against his.

Last night was good, but every time I looked up and saw the anger lining Miles's face, I was reminded of what I was trying to forget.

And then when he abandoned me to hook up with the server, it was all I could think about.

But this, right now, surrounded by my two closest friends, losing myself to the beat as sweat glistens over my skin and my head spins with tequila, is everything.

"Woo," I cry out before slut dropping on Cory.

"Damn, girl." He groans once I'm in front of him again. "You're making me fucking horny."

Giggling like a schoolgirl, I grind my ass against his cock, instantly finding the truth in his words.

Heat rushes between my thighs. The promise of oblivion is just too much.

Fuck. I want it.

A night of mind-numbing, easy, no-strings-attached pleasure.

My old life...

Sadness washes through me as the weight of what I've agreed to presses down on my shoulders again.

Squeezing my eyes closed, I try to banish reality and pretend for a few hours that I'm the same girl who walked into my father's office yesterday.

Free, single, and ready to mingle.

More like eager and ready to get down and dirty.

I may be yearning for a quieter, simpler life in my aunt's Cotswold cottage, but I love my life here. I love Chicago. I love being in a bustling city and having everything within reach. Not to mention the nightlife, the hot men...the opportunities.

England might be my destiny. It's where I want to raise a family and grow old. But right now, I couldn't ask for more than this.

"You're going to need to look elsewhere tonight, buddy," I shout in Cory's ear as we continue to dance.

Lori is in front of us, pinned between two guys, laughing her head off at a joke we're not privy to.

Seeing her so happy makes me smile. She hasn't had it easy in life, so seeing her letting go and enjoying herself makes my heart swell with joy.

We met on our very first day at college. We were roommates.

I turned up with everything I needed, used to being educated away from home and ready to embark on this new part of my life. And then Lori turned up like a small, frizzy-haired, wide-eyed whirlwind.

She was so out of her depth that I'm not sure she even knew which way was up.

With only a small weekend bag with her belongings inside, she unpacked them and then looked at me with so much hope mixed in with the chaos, that I immediately fell in love with her.

She's strong yet vulnerable. Thoughtful yet hot-headed.

Calm yet total fucking chaos.

I love it. I love her.

We come from two completely different worlds, and yet she is single-handedly the best person I have ever met in my life.

I just wish those who are meant to love her saw her the same way I do. They've no idea how much awesome they're missing out on.

"I need to wee," I announce before spinning around and planting a sloppy kiss on Cory's cheek.

"Lor, bathroom break?"

"Yes," she cries before skipping from her dance partners.

'Drinks?' I mouth at Cory as I grab her hand and pull her in the direction of the bathroom.

"Ugh, look at the line," she complains.

My heart sinks as I take in the line of women waiting to do their business.

My eyes shoot in the direction of the stairs that lead to the VIP area.

We could be up there where I'm sure there are clean, empty bathrooms for us to enjoy. All I'd have to do is give my name and they'd unhook the barrier and wish us a good night.

But I don't want to be up there with the businessmen and minor celebrities sipping champagne and attempting to look demure while doing it.

I don't want to be demure. I want to be wild and sweaty. I want to feel my heart racing, stray hands gliding over my body, and my dress sticking to my skin.

Tonight, I don't want to be Tatum Warner with the weight of the world and an imminent sham of a marriage pressing down on me.

I want to be free, and crazy, and careless.

"Are you okay?" Lori asks, her eyes bouncing between mine.

"Yeah, of course. Why?" I ask, trying to calm my racing heart. I might want to feel it pounding, but while I'm dancing and enjoying life, not while I'm freaking out about having my life stolen from me.

"You look a little manic. Did someone slip something in your drink?'

"What? No, don't be silly. I'm just enjoying myself. Letting go."

She narrows her eyes at me, able to hear the lie in my voice.

"Tate, I know what—"

"Dance with me," I demand, reaching for her hands and spinning her around in the line.

"Tate," she warns.

"No, Lor. We're not going there. Not tonight. I need this to be a future-free night. No thinking about tomorrow or—"

"A certain man who rocks a suit like no other?" she adds.

"Exactly. None of that. Not so much as a fleeting thought about that asshole."

She smirks.

"Stop it," I hiss, knowing that her mind just ran straight to the gutter.

"Did you invite Matt out tonight?" I ask, shamelessly trying to distract her with her current online dating obsession.

She's had a few over the years, but Matt has trumped them by far. He's all she's been able to talk about for days. Honestly, I'm amazed she's allowed me to get a word in edgewise since her successful date last night.

I guess, as amazing as that was, I've kinda trumped it with my news.

Guilt knots my stomach. I don't want to overshadow her incredible date with a great guy.

"Yeah, he's out with his friends. We might meet up later," she says, her eyes twinkling with excitement.

"You really like this one, huh?"

She smiles, getting this faraway look in her eye.

"He's... perfect," she breathes, her smile widening.

Finally, she forgets about my shit and embarks on telling me every single detail about their night.

She's right. He does sound perfect. It immediately raises alarm bells.

No man is that perfect.

This is where my usually level-headed friend loses her mind.

She might be a strong, independent woman, but she's got a soft-as-hell, romantic heart locked up inside her chest, and she's desperate for it to be unleashed.

While I'm happy to stay single and play the field, kiss a few frogs, and laugh the whole time, she wants something more serious, something steady and reliable.

Her life has been anything but those things up until this point, and she's desperate to settle down with a man who worships the ground she walks on.

I've no doubt she'll find him. I just can't help worrying that she's trying too hard and attracting the wrong kind of guys.

She wears her heart on her sleeve when it comes to dating, and men know how to lure her in before quickly spitting her back out.

She's still lost in her memories of the night before when we finally get to the front of the line.

As if we're still two college students, the second a stall becomes free, we both slip inside.

I go first, seeing as she's still lost in her Matt-induced haze, and then we switch before descending on the sinks—or, more importantly, the mirrors.

Predictably, Lor immediately starts fussing with her hair.

"What?" she hisses, making me roll my eyes at her.

I shake my head. "Nothing," I mutter as I pull my red lipstick from my purse and reapply.

"You need to stop leading Cory on tonight," she says absently.

My eyes snap to hers in the mirror.

"I'm not—"

"Tate," she warns. "You know how he feels about you. You're just feeding it."

"He doesn't feel anything for me," I argue way more defensively than I mean to. "We're just friends," I say a little softer.

"You're not just friends though, are you?"

"So what, we've hooked up a few times?" My hands find my hips and I turn to her, glaring.

"I'm not judging, you know that, Tate. If you two want to bump uglies then that's up to you. But you're playing a very dangerous game tonight."

"Why? Because of Kingston?" I balk.

She opens her mouth to respond, but I don't give her time to say anything.

"He has nothing to do with this. I'm having a night out with my friends. A well-deserved night out," I add.

"Shit. I know. You're right. I'm sorry," Lori says, stepping forward and holding her arms out.

I accept her embrace and wrap my arms around her, holding her close.

"This is so fucked up, Tate," she whispers in my ear.

A lump crawls up my throat. I try to swallow it down, but it's too huge. "I know," I finally manage to say around it.

"I'm on your side. Always. You know that. I just think you should be careful. If Kingston were to see—"

I jolt back from her hug. "You think he's following me? Watching me?"

"No," she says quickly. "I don't have him pegged for a stalker type. But you know what this city is like. You can't take a left turn without someone noticing and telling anyone who cares. You're a Warner, Tate. And you're about to be attached to one of the most powerful men in Chicago. People will be watching."

"No one knows. Only you and—"

"Everyone who saw the photo online earlier?" she asks, raising a brow.

"Fuck," I groan, dropping my head into my hands.

"People know who you are, Tate. And they certainly know who he is. Like it or not, you're hot gossip right now. I bet it would take us less than two minutes searching online to find you here. If Kingston wanted to, he could in a heartbeat."

"He won't," I breathe, praying I'm right.

Lori smiles at me. "Just...don't underestimate him. You know all too well what they're capable of. Don't be naive because you don't want to believe what's possible."

With a sigh and a smile I genuinely don't feel, I let her tug me out of the bathroom and toward the bar, where we find Cory waiting with a row of shots before him.

Oh god. This is going to get messy...

That thought isn't enough to stop me, though. If anything, it spurs me on.

I swallow down the first one and reach for the second, but something makes me turn around.

I want to say that it's Lori's warning about what Kingston is capable of that sends a shiver racing down my spine, but something tells me it's more than that.

Fuck.

I scan the mass of dancers before me but come up empty. I'm hardly surprised. I can't honestly see him gyrating in the middle of a sweaty crowd.

He's more...

My eyes jump toward the VIP area upstairs.

The glass is black from down here, preventing the mere peasants from seeing the elite looking down on them.

My skin prickles with awareness, all the hairs on my body lifting.

He's there.

Watching me. I feel it.

Heat surges through me along with a powerful shot of adrenaline.

I wink, letting him know that I'm aware of him before throwing back my second shot and quickly following it up with a third.

"What the fuck are we doing loitering here? Let's go and dance."

A potent mixture of excitement and anticipation surges through my veins as I come to a stop in the middle of the crowd and drop down low again, sticking my ass out and grinding back up Cory's body.

Lori watches me with a warning dancing in her eyes.

"Call Matt," I shout. "It's time to forget reality for a few hours."

13

KINGSTON

I stand with Kian, our father, Grant, our CMO, and a few other board members of Callahan Enterprises. All of them are in their late fifties or sixties. They're all nice enough, but they're not exactly who I want to be spending my Friday night with—Kian aside, of course.

But Dad was insistent we both show our faces. The board is concerned about the merger, and who are we to refuse to have a drink with them in the hope of settling their minds? I'm not sure how this actually helps, but I guess Dad's the boss. For now...

"So as I was saying, the current market is showing an upward tick in..." I stare at Grant. I want to get excited about his predictions for our future marketing campaigns and where he thinks we should be focusing our energy in the coming months, but I can't find any kind of enthusiasm.

If I'm being honest, it's not just him. I haven't been able to focus on anything since the moment Tatum climbed into the back of my car earlier and drove off into the sunset.

We had unfinished business from that elevator and my body—my dick—has only been able to think about where things could have gone if I'd have followed her into the back of the car and demanded that Lewis took us home.

My cock stirs again just thinking about it.

Would she have continued to fight me, refusing to admit that she feels whatever this thing is that's suddenly crackling between us?

I've no idea what sparked it yesterday after the announcement.

Or has it always been there and I've been too distracted to notice?

She's Miles's little sister. And yes, while she's always been smoking hot, there has always been a barrier stopping me from actually considering her as an option. But with that gone...

"Excuse me," I say quietly as Grant continues with his spiel.

Turning my back on the group of men, I place my empty scotch glass on a tray as a waitress passes before happily accepting a refill.

I had every intention of taking a seat on one of the empty couches, but something pulls me toward the window.

Unable to ignore my gut, I move closer, sipping my fresh drink as I go.

My eyes scan the crowd below. The club is packed, filled with the best and worst that Chicago has to offer.

For a few seconds, I watch, mesmerized as the nameless, faceless bodies all move together.

Most have no idea they can be watched; they're too lost in their own worlds to worry about what anyone else is doing.

I lift my foot to take a step back when a dark head of hair and a purple sequined dress catch my eye.

My cock swells long before my brain catches up with what my body already knows.

Tatum...

My eyes lock on her as she moves toward the bar. Toward a man.

And not just any man. A man she's so familiar with she steps right into his body before reaching for the shots he has lined up before him.

My body locks up, my jaw clenching so hard I'm amazed I don't shatter a tooth or two.

I glare at him as she reaches for one of the glasses and tips it back. He watches her with heated eyes.

I know exactly what he's imagining.

Every man in this fucking place is thinking exactly the same.

She has her hair pinned up, exposing her slender neck, putting even more skin on show.

Her simple sequined dress is tiny, sitting high on her thighs and low on her chest. It glitters temptingly under the bright spotlights as they move around the room.

The desire to storm down there and drag her away from that prick is almost too much to ignore.

As if she can sense my attention, the second she reaches for her second shot, she pauses before spinning around.

Her eyes scan the crowd, searching. It's right then and there that I have it confirmed that she's feeling everything I am right now.

It makes me wonder if everything changed in her father's office yesterday like it did for me, or if I've been missing something all these years.

I sense someone stepping up beside me, but I don't look back to see who it is. I can't. I'm too desperate to know if she's going to look up and find me.

Surely, if she has any suspicion that I'm the one causing her to search the crowded club, then she has to know to look up.

I might have spent my fair share of nights down in the thick of it in the past, but it's been a while.

I don't need to anymore.

The thrill of the chase ended a long time ago.

While I was at college, I still flew slightly under the radar. But the second I started at Callahan Enterprises, my name was suddenly everywhere. I couldn't leave my apartment without women approaching me.

Obviously, I thought it was great, and I certainly made the most of the attention.

Hell, I still do. Although I've learned to be a little more selective about who I spend time with these days.

I've had more than enough crazy hookups to last me a lifetime.

"What's got you so enthr—" Kian chuckles right as Tatum figures it out and looks up.

The second she does, her eyes lock on mine and something electric crackles between us. It doesn't matter that there's glass between us, or that she can't see me.

We both know.

"Jesus. Think it's time you fucked your future wife, Bro," Kian mutters helpfully.

Silence falls between us as she winks, confirming what I already knew. She knows I'm here.

I guess the only question is...what's she going to do about it?

"Although..." Kian mutters as she swallows two more shots and moves away from the bar, "it seems she might have another man in her sights."

A growl of disapproval rumbles deep in my throat.

No one else would be able to hear it. Hell, I'm not even sure if Kian can hear it, but the fucker laughs as if this is the most amusing thing he's ever seen.

Tatum leads the guy by the hand into the middle of the dance floor before slut dropping on him.

"Oh shit. Your wife has balls of steel, man."

"And he's about to fucking lose his," I mutter darkly, my fists clenching as I imagine ripping them from his body for touching something that belongs to me.

"Ah, Kingston, there you are. Did you get my email today?" one of the board members asks.

My brow pinches as I try to force my brain to focus on anything but the woman downstairs with another man's hands on her body.

"Apologies, Chris. It's been a long day. Refresh my memory," I ask.

He frowns momentarily. It's unlike me not to have my finger

right on the pulse, but the past twenty-four hours have done a number on me. Or should I say that Tatum Warner has?

I tell myself that it's just because it's the beginning. That once we've announced our engagement and she's moved in with me, things will settle. My life will return to something akin to normal and I'll be able to focus on what matters once more.

I fear it might be wishful thinking. Especially if she keeps playing this game with me.

Chris begins animatedly explaining the contents of his email. The second I discover it's not work-related as such, but instead about his wife's cousin's experience at one of our resorts, I begin to zone out again.

How can he possibly expect me to focus on that bullshit when my soon-to-be wife is downstairs, being molested by a man who isn't me?

"Thank you for that, Chris. We'll certainly look into it," Kian says, slapping me on the back and bringing me back into the conversation I fear I was meant to have contributed to.

"Leave it with us," I say quickly, although I'm not sure he buys it.

"Actually, Chris, I wanted to pick your brain about something," Kian says, leading the older man away and toward the bar for more drinks.

As they step up to order, Kian looks back over his shoulder and jerks his chin in the direction of the stairs, silently encouraging me to go after her.

Without responding, I turn around and step closer to the window.

It takes me a second or two to locate her, they've shifted a little since I was forced to look away, but she's still dancing with that asshole who thinks he's got a chance.

I shake my head before lifting what's left of my scotch to my lips and swallowing it down.

With the alcohol warning my stomach and desire and irritation running through my veins, I take off toward the stairs without bothering to look back at the men I'm meant to be entertaining.

Fuck them. They don't need me.

Neither does Tatum, to be fair. But the motherfucker she's dancing with sure needs to know that she isn't going to be spending the night in his bed anytime soon.

She might pretend that she doesn't want to be in mine either, but I have every intention of proving her wrong.

The only place that Tatum Warner belongs is with me.

The image of her rolling around in my sheets has my cock threatening to go full mast by the time I get to the bottom of the stairs.

The music is loud down here—so loud I can barely hear my thoughts as I move through the almost unbearable heat and the scent of body odor.

If I needed a reminder of why I no longer go clubbing, then this is it.

Drinking scotch in the VIP lounge is far more my thing now.

"Fucking watch it," I bark when a guy misjudges the flat surface he's attempting to walk on and crashes right into me.

I shove him away, sending him toward the floor with one hard push.

"Fucking asshole," he slurs before rolling over like a demented turtle stuck on its back.

I force my way through the crowd, the air getting thicker with every step I take.

More than a few wandering hands brush over my body. Each time I feel someone's touch, I have to force myself not to reach out and snap their fucking wrists.

"Hey, handsome. Dance with me," a woman purrs behind me while another looks me up and down as if I'm the most delicious thing she's seen all month.

I mean, to be fair...

I shut that thought down and rip my eyes from the shameless woman in search of one that I've no doubt will be her complete opposite when I make my presence known.

With my fist curled and my grip on my sanity beginning to slip, I finally spot them ahead of me.

Tatum moves against the guy as if they do this every night of the week.

Something hot and uncomfortable explodes within me.

Lori has her back to Tatum, her tongue down some dude's throat.

She has no idea that her best friend's world is about to tilt on its axis again.

Twice in two days...

I smirk, loving how easy she makes it.

I stand there for two more seconds, camouflaged by the crowd around me like a lion about to pounce on his prey.

The guy dips his head and shouts something in her ear. She nods once before he presses a kiss to her bare shoulder, making my entire body tense with my need to rid his lips from his body as well as his balls before he steps back and disappears through the crowd.

She dances alone, but it only takes a few seconds for every man around her to notice that she's no longer got a partner.

Two step forward simultaneously, but I'm faster.

One hard look at them and they slink away, already knowing that they'd lose this battle if they started something.

Tatum Warner is mine, and no motherfucker in this club, or this city, is going to take her from me. No matter how much she might want them to.

14

TATUM

The second Cory disappears, I mourn the loss of his body heat against mine.

It's stupid. I'm hot and sweaty; the last thing I need is another person pressed up against me. But while he's—anyone's—touching me, reality is pushed to the edge of my peripheral. Nice and blurry, thanks to the tequila.

It's what I need.

I continue dancing, watching Lori with Matt who turned up only minutes ago. This is the first time I've met him, yet I feel like I know him after everything she's told me. Thankfully, he looks just like his profile picture, and we can only hope that his personality follows suit. My girl's heart can't take another knocking.

I'm lost in thoughts of them when a pair of hands grasp my hips and I'm pulled back into a hard, hot body.

I tense for a beat, but when the confident grip on my body doesn't falter, I relax.

"That was fast," I say as my head falls back against his shoulder, my eyes closed as I absorb the feeling.

A deep groan rumbles beside my ear and damn if the noise doesn't trigger something inside me.

A deep, desperate ache makes itself known.

I shouldn't do it. I know I shouldn't. Lori's warning from earlier rings loudly in my ears, as does the knowledge that he's here.

He was upstairs watching me. I know he was.

Maybe he still is...

Fuck it. I need this.

My hips roll, grinding my ass against his crotch.

He groans again, making heat flood my core.

I can always rely on Cory. Not only is he an incredible person, but he is always willing to do whatever it takes to make me happy, and of course, I do the same in return.

As my movements get more obvious, his hands slip from my hips and slide up the indent of my waist.

Everyone dancing around us fades into the distance as I completely hand myself over to him.

I gasp loudly when his thumbs brush the underside of my breasts. I'm wearing a padded bra beneath my dress—my breasts are too big to go untamed—but his touch is so potent, it's like no fabric exists.

"Oh my god," I whisper, the quiet words getting swallowed by the loud, pounding music surrounding us.

Hot breath rushes over my ear, sending a wave of desire so strong down my body that it's a miracle I don't drop to my knees right here and now and get things moving along.

He wants it. I can feel the thickness of his cock pressing against my ass.

"You're a bad girl, Tatum Warner," he warns darkly in my ear.

Something flickers deep in my subconscious, but the tequila is strong enough for it to be almost instantly forgotten.

Needing more, I wrap my fingers around his wrists and give him little choice but to take my breasts in his hands.

He groans, and I pant like a whore as he squeezes me with the most dizzying pressure.

"Yes," I cry. "I need you. I—"

My words are cut off as I'm turned around. The world spins, my vision blurring. But that's all forgotten when my front is pinned to the hard planes of his.

"Did you want to say that to my face, baby?"

My heart stops.

Sucking in a breath, I force my eyes to focus, and I find a dark gray, designer sweater in front of me.

Cory wasn't wearing a sweater. He...

My pulse races, my body temperature soaring to dangerous levels as reality rushes through me.

I wasn't dancing with Cory, and I just told Kingston that I need him.

But not him.

I told him that I needed someone else.

I. Am. So. Fucked.

Swallowing thickly, I refuse to look up, shame burning through me.

How is it that just with a few words and what I'm sure is a dark glare, he can make me feel like a naughty child?

"Look at me, brat," he demands, and the shock of his words ensures that I do just that.

My breath catches when my eyes lock on his dark and angry green ones.

I stare at him, my mouth running dry.

It's not fair that he's so hot. Why couldn't God gift these looks to someone a little less...asshole-ish.

His eyes crinkle. "Because God knows someone nice wouldn't make the most of them."

Oh shit. Fuck.

"I'm going to ask you again, Tatum, and you're going to give me the right answer." The way he says my name makes every muscle south of my waist clench tightly.

He leans in. My heart kicks into overdrive as his breath fans my face as if he's coming in for a kiss.

I know he's not, but that doesn't stop my tongue from sneaking out and wetting my lips in preparation.

He smirks, knowing exactly where my mind went.

"Did you want to say that to my face, baby?"

The words, his voice, hit exactly the same as they did the first time he said them. They shouldn't. I'm now aware that they're coming out of his mouth not Cory's, but fuck.

My nostrils flare with irritation as he holds my stare strong.

"Get fucked," I hiss, standing up to him.

"We're leaving," he states, his hand wrapping around my wrist before tugging me forward.

I wobble on my heels and crash into his hard body, my hand on his lower stomach. His muscles ripple beneath his sweater and I mindlessly slide my hand lower to feel something else equally as hard.

He stares down at me, I'm sure more than aware of my plans, but it's not until I hit his belt buckle that he stops me.

"You might be willing to embarrass yourself in public, Tatum. But I am not."

He takes off again, towing me along with him.

"Wait, I need to say goodbye to—"

I glance back to see Lori staring after me, her body still pressed against Matt's. She smirks before looking back at Kingston.

'Enjoy,' she mouths before spinning around and reaching up on her toes to kiss him again.

Cory is nowhere to be seen, but I'm confident that Lori will let him know I'm safe and he'll find someone else to spend the night with.

Despite what Lori said in the bathroom, Cory is more than happy to sow his wild oats. It isn't me he wants. Not really. I'm just easy...in more than one way.

A laugh tumbles from my throat as we emerge at the entrance of the club.

"Do you have a coat?" Kingston demands, bringing us to a stop.

I look up at him, at his hard expression and the irritation dancing in his dark green eyes, and my giggles only get worse.

"Aw KC," I tease, using the nickname he goes by when he's with his friends. "Did I embarrass you by rubbing my ass against your dick?"

"Tatum," he growls darkly, his jaw ticking with anger.

"You enjoyed it though, didn't you? I felt how hard you—"

"Do you have a coat or not?" he interrupts, cutting me off before the small audience we're gathering hears the end of that sentence. As if they can't already guess.

I roll my eyes at him and I'm sure I see a little billow of steam blow from his ears.

I stare up at him, trying to hold steady and appear strong, but I'm pretty sure I'm swaying. If I'm not, then it's the room.

"I do not have a coat, sir," I tag on with a smirk.

"Brat," he mutters under his breath before taking my hand and pulling me toward the exit.

The cool evening hair hits me and the world spins all over again.

I go from drunk to utterly wasted in two seconds flat.

"Oh my god, is that Kingston Callahan?" a woman cries from the line to get into the club.

A powerful shot of jealousy shoots through me, and long before I have a chance to think it through, I spin on my heels and find her in the crowd. I want to say it's easy, but it seems that every female before me is ogling my man.

My man.

Nope. Kingston Callahan is not *my* man.

He's just *a* man who is going to steal a year of my life when I could be out looking for the one...

"Yep, it is. But I'm sorry, he's tak—argh," I shriek when my feet suddenly leave the floor as the man in question throws me over his shoulder and drags me away. "What are you doing?" I cry as he begins marching down the street without a care in the world.

Cool air rushes over my ass and I reach up in a panic, wanting to cover myself up.

People posted innocent photos of him kissing my forehead this afternoon; that was nothing compared to this.

My cheeks heat as I try to imagine what we must look like, and it only gets worse when my fingers discover just how high up my dress is.

"Will you put me down?" I demand. "I'm showing the world my ass."

"Maybe you should have thought about that before mouthing off and embarrassing yourself," he snaps, but thankfully stops and lowers me to my feet.

"You're not worried about me," I spit. "The only reputation you care about is your own."

"Get in the fucking car before I throw you in myself."

I look forward and find Lewis idling in Kingston's town car.

He rips the door open and none too gently shoves me inside.

I should fall into the seat and be a good girl. But that's not who I am.

I am a bad girl. Especially when tequila is involved.

Pressing my knees to the seat that sits back-to-back with the driver, I bend over, resting my forearms on the wall that hides the privacy screen.

"Hey, Lewis," I purr, sticking my ass up in the air as Kingston climbs in behind me. "Are you having a good night?"

He glances at me in the rearview mirror, amusement lighting up his eyes.

"I'm having a wonderful evening, Miss Warner. Are you?"

"It's Tate," I slur. "And yes, it's been fantastic so far. Did you know that Kingston can dance?"

Lewis's smirk grows.

"I did not know that." His eyes lift to the man behind me. "Where would you like to go, sir?"

"Home, please."

The sound of his deep voice sends a shiver down my spine.

"Tatum, sit down," he demands.

"No can do, sir. I'm catching up with Lewis. Finding out if you've been nice to him this evening."

Lewis chuckles, but I quickly discover that Kingston isn't anywhere near as amused when a loud crack rips through the air.

Pain explodes before my ass cheek burns red hot.

"You spanked me," I gasp, spinning around so fast I almost tumble to the floor.

"Sit down."

In a huff, I drop into the seat I was just kneeling on, cross my arms under my tits, and glare pure death at him.

"If you're trying to scare me, you're going to need to do more than give me the stink eye, baby."

"I hate you," I seethe, as Lewis pulls away from the curb.

"Doesn't stop you from wanting me though, does it?" he pants, mimicking my reaction when he cupped my breasts on the dance floor.

"I thought you were someone else," I point out.

The air around us turns arctic, his eyes hardening and his fists curling at his sides.

He doesn't say a word. He doesn't need to.

I shiver, but it's very different from the last one, which was full of desire.

"What's wrong? Don't like the concept that a woman doesn't want you?"

"It doesn't matter what you do or don't want, Tatum. The only man you're going to be touching over the coming year is me."

"You wish," I scoff.

"No, Tatum. I don't wish. I know."

Our eye contact holds, the air crackling between us, but neither of us says a word. Not until Lewis curses at the front.

"Sorry, sir. It looks like the city is in gridlock. Getting home is going to take a while."

15

KINGSTON

Nothing but the sound of the car's engine and our increased breathing can be heard as Tatum and I continue to stare at each other.

But while I sit straight up in my seat, she's slumping lower and lower as her inebriation gets the better of her.

A borderline unbearable level of irritation continues to bubble just beneath my skin.

It's bad enough that she was dancing with him, that when she told me she needed me, she meant she needed him. Hell, she probably would have said it to anyone who was paying her attention, especially if she knew I was watching.

It's why she did it, a little voice pipes up in my head.

But it doesn't matter.

The reason behind it is pointless. She fucking did it.

And what would she have done if I hadn't stepped in?

Would she have gone home with him?

Day one and she'd have fucked everything up.

If that was her plan, why the hell did she waste our time yesterday by signing up to a year with me?

"Why?" I growl, unable to keep my curiosity to myself.

"Why what?" she slurs back, her eyes narrowing in annoyance.

She thinks I'm annoying? That's fucking rich.

"You were going to fuck him." It's not a question. It doesn't need to be.

She doesn't respond. Her glare just hardens.

"Don't ignore me, Tatum."

"Oh, I'm sorry. I thought that was a statement, not a question. If you'd like an answer, maybe consider rewording your *statement*."

My teeth grind and my fists curl on my lap.

This woman.

This fucking woman.

"You agreed to be faithful to me yesterday. For a year, you belong to me."

Her lips purse in anger, but I struggle to take the look seriously when her eyes are beginning to droop with the effects of the alcohol in her system.

"I am not a thing, Kingston. I do not belong to anyone. And least of all you."

With every word, she sinks lower in the seat.

"I am my own person. I make my own decisions. If I want to fuck anyone, then I will. The only person I won't be fucking is you."

My jaw begins to ache with how tense I am.

"You're a mess," I point out as she finally slumps to the side, her head resting on the window.

Her dress is hitched up, showing me her black lace panties beneath, and fuck if the sight of them doesn't hit me right in the dick.

I shouldn't be interested in this hot mess before me, but it seems my head and my dick are on two completely different pages.

Unlike her, I can do what I want with my life—and my body— over the next year.

I have free rein, while she has to remain faithful.

I shake my head as her lids lower, finally severing our connection.

"Fuck," I breathe, lifting my hand to comb my hair back from my face.

"Everything okay. sir?" Lewis asks, his amused eyes meeting mine in the rearview mirror.

"Wonderful, Lewis. Fucking wonderful."

He chuckles to himself as the red taillights of the cars ahead of us illuminate the front of the car.

"You've got your work cut out with that one," he says unhelpfully.

My eyes drop from his in favor of Tatum.

Her eyes are flickering as if she's dreaming already and her full, red lips are parted as she sleeps.

Even wasted and exhausted she's beautiful.

"Don't I fucking know it," I mutter, rubbing my jaw as I continue to study her. "What's the news on the traffic?" I ask after a few seconds.

"No change. What do you want to do?"

Spreading my thighs wider, I sink lower in the seat and rest my head back.

I don't want to spend all fucking night in the car, and we will if I insist on taking her home.

I shouldn't want her there as much as I do.

"Her place is closer," Lewis points out.

Yes. And so is her feral fucking cat. There's no way I'm dealing with that little fucker tonight.

Its owner is enough.

"Can you take us to the Broadway?" I ask, looking out of the window to see how far we've already made it.

"Sure thing."

Pulling my cell from my pocket, I find the contact I need to secure us a room for the night, and then I sit back and alternate between staring out of the window at the city and watching Tatum sleep.

I'm fucking exhausted and ready to crash by the time Lewis

finally pulls up outside one of our most luxurious hotels in the city.

"Here you go, sir."

He pushes his door open ready to help us out, but the doorman is already opening my door.

"Good evening, Mr. Callahan," he greets. "It's a pleasure to have you with us tonight. Can I be of assistance with your guest?" he asks politely, glancing very briefly at Tatum.

"That won't be necessary, but thank you," I say as I move closer to her.

Slipping my arms beneath her body, I lift her into my chest before attempting to get out of the car without sending us both crashing to the sidewalk.

"Sir, I have a blanket," Lewis says, rushing to our side the second my feet hit the ground and covering Tatum with it.

"More than she deserves," I mutter under my breath.

With a brief thank you, I march into the hotel, and, without stopping at reception, I head straight for the elevator.

Tatum barely makes a noise as I carry her inside. She's dead weight in my arms, her breath tickling over my neck as she continues to sleep.

"I hope you enjoyed your night, Brat. There isn't going to be a repeat anytime soon," I warn despite the fact she can't hear me.

No wife of mine is going to be going out and getting so wasted she has no idea who she's dancing with, or whose bed she'll end up sleeping in.

I shake my head, my grip on her tightening. I'm beyond pissed that she'd be so reckless, so careless for her own safety.

Tonight could have gone in a very different direction for her very fast.

And then what?

I let us into the best room I was able to secure at such short notice, carry her over to the bed and lay her out.

"No, Kingston," she moans, her arms wrapping around my neck and attempting to pull me with her. "Don't go."

Reaching behind me, I pull her arms away and let them drop to her sides.

"I don't think so," I say before taking a massive step back from the bed.

I stand there for longer than I should, staring at her in a way I shouldn't.

Her dress is now totally around her waist, letting me see just how tiny her panties are—and just how long her legs are.

I squeeze my eyes closed as I get assaulted by an image of them wrapped around my waist as I—

"Fuck."

Spinning on my heels, I march toward the bathroom, dragging my sweater off as I go.

Kicking the door closed behind me, I turn the shower on hot and shed the rest of my clothes.

With steam quickly filling the room, I step under the scalding water and tip my head into the powerful stream.

I focus on breathing, on inhaling one deep breath after the other and attempting to talk myself down.

Tatum is passed out in that bed, and it's all I can do not to think with my dick.

Two weeks ago, it would have been easy to dump her in here on her ass and walk out without a second thought.

But that was two weeks ago.

Before I discovered what our fathers were planning.

Before Dad sat me down and explained what they wanted from me.

Before I agreed to tie myself to her for the next year of our lives.

Before I agreed to make her my wife. To be her husband.

Now...now she's all I can fucking think about.

Mine...

She is fucking mine, and yet, she's doing everything she can to piss me off and to prove to me that what we've both agreed to was the worst fucking mistake of our lives.

Only, it's not.

For some ungodly reason, I don't regret it.

Sure, we might only be a day in. But I already know that I'm not going to.

Life was getting mundane.

Predictable.

I worked, I fucked, I worked some more.

Rinse and repeat.

Well, Tatum has certainly stopped that merry-go-round.

In only a few hours, she fucked up my status quo and dragged me out of monotony and into a whole new world, mostly full of irritation and pent-up frustration. And should we mention desire?

Reaching out, I wrap my hand around my length.

I'm hard. Painfully fucking so. And the second I tighten my grip, a groan spills from my lips.

I stroke myself faster, my entire body locked up with my need for release.

Closing my eyes, I think about her out there in her tempting little dress.

It would be so easy to tuck my fingers under the lace of her panties and slide them down her legs. I could spread her thighs wide and take in what will no doubt be the best part of my wife.

My mouth waters just thinking about tasting her. About running my tongue through her folds and lapping at her juices.

My movements become borderline violent as my balls begin to draw up.

I imagine dropping to my knees at the end of the bed, wrapping my hands around her thighs and dragging her to me.

"Fuck. Fuuuck," I groan, as my cock jerks in my hand and I come in the shower.

My heart pounds as I find an unfulfilling release delivered by my own hand.

"Shit," I hiss, reaching out and resting my palm on the cool tiles.

I need more than that. More than I'm able to give myself.

More than some random woman can give me.

Without thinking, I look back over my shoulder.

I need her.

Anger surges through me and I slam my palm down on the wall.

I don't need her.

I don't fucking need anyone.

I'm Kingston Callahan. I already have every single thing I need.

I did this to secure Warner Group.

This is about business. Nothing else.

It is not about pleasure, or being driven to the brink of insanity by the woman out there or her fucking pussy.

Reaching for the bottle of branded shower gel before me, I angrily scrub myself, desperately trying to remove her scent from my body.

Killing the shower, I reach for a towel and wrap it around my waist.

I walk up to the sink, staring at myself in the mirror.

Lifting my hand, I push my sopping hair back from my brow and have a serious word with myself. Never before have I been so torn over what I want and what I should do.

It's Friday night, I should be out finding a woman to warm my bed, not jerking off in the shower like a loser over a woman who drives me to the brink of insanity.

Tatum is just another woman.

Okay, so she might be the only one I've ever met who's point-blank turned me down. But she is still just a woman.

She is no more special than any other.

Feeling a little better and more in control, I scoop my clothes from the floor and march out of the bathroom with my head held high.

Everything is great until I turn the corner and see her.

16

TATUM

My body burns up as I watch Kingston emerge from the bathroom with only a towel wrapped around his waist and water droplets on his skin.

Fuck. This night just took a very enjoyable turn.

Dropping my eyes down his body, I shamelessly feast on him.

Tanned skin, hard muscles, a scattering of dark hair that directs me down to the towel and what is hiding beneath it.

"I thought you'd passed out," he mutters, sounding nothing but pissed off with the current situation.

"You should be so lucky," I sass back, making his expression harden.

"What's wrong, KC? All work and no play makes the King all tense and angry?"

"Shut the fuck up, Tatum. I'm not in the mood for your shit."

"Then why are you here?" I counter. "You could have left me in the club." He scoffs, letting me know exactly what he thinks of that suggestion. "You could have left me here. I'm not going to die."

Something flashes in his eyes, and I'm pretty sure it's hope that maybe I would, to get him out of this bullshit arrangement.

"So?" I ask, pushing myself so I'm sitting and resting back on my palms. "What happens now? You've got me in your fancy hotel room. You're all but naked and I'm..." I kick my heels off and lift my feet, placing them on the edge of the bed with my legs spread.

Shameless hussy, Tatum Warner.

I banish that little voice of reason in my head.

Who the fuck cares?

Kingston sure doesn't. He and Miles make a hobby out of seeing how many women they can tap in one weekend; why shouldn't it work the other way around?

Maybe I should make a play for all the Callahan brothers. That's the sort of hat trick I can get on board with...

"Keep your fucking eyes and hands away from my brothers, Tatum," Kingston warns, letting me know that that wasn't an internal thought.

Damn tequila.

"Or what?" I taunt, dropping back to my elbows.

"Or fucking nothing."

He moves closer and my heart rate kicks up a notch.

His eyes hold mine for a few seconds before he finally loses the fight with his self-control and they drop to my body, lingering for longer than polite on my lace-covered pussy.

"See something you like?" I tease, spreading my legs wider, and offering myself up to him.

"I'm not some sleaze you picked up in a club, Tatum."

"I'm more than aware of that, husband," I breathe, my voice raspy and full of need.

His jaw ticks and his Adam's apple bobs as he swallows.

I run my eyes down the length of his body again and smirk when I find that he's beginning to tent his towel.

My fingers twitch with my need to reach out and rip it from his body.

I gasp as he suddenly leans over me, and as his hands press to the mattress on either side of my head, my arms give out and I collapse back.

"Kingston," I breathe, my eyes searching his, desperately trying to figure out what he's thinking.

"You're a bad, bad girl, Tatum." He dips his head, his hot breath rushing over my skin, making my core flood with heat. Just his breath alone is intense; I can only imagine what his touch will do. "I think it's time someone finally taught you a lesson."

"Oh my god," I whisper, desire coursing through my veins.

His knuckles brush against my hips before he grasps my dress and none too gently drags it up my body.

My skin burns as his eyes feast on me. Needing more, I reach for the front clasp of my bra and flick it open.

"Make me yours, King," I moan, the room spinning around me.

"You're fucking trouble, Brat. You've no idea what I want to do to you."

"Do it. All of it. Please."

I wake with a start, my heart racing and my entire body covered in a layer of sweat.

My core aches, my clit pounding.

"Kingston," I whisper. "Please." The words spill from my lips without instruction from my brain. My body has taken on a life of its own.

I need him. I need him to continue, to give me the release my body is so desperate for after his teasing.

It was bad enough dancing together and feeling his excitement pressed against my ass. But seeing him in that towel, feeling the heat of his body looming over me, his hot breath rushing over my skin...

"King?" I call a little louder when I get no response. "KC?"

Ripping my eyes open—a fucking challenge, seeing as my mascara has turned into superglue—I search the room around me for him.

"Shit," I hiss, closing my eyes again and falling back onto the bed.

Grabbing a pillow from the other side of the bed, I pull it over my head and try to figure out what the fuck is going on.

He was here. I know he was.

There's no way I made all of that up.

I wasn't that drunk...

Was I?

I squeeze my eyes closed and try to make sense of what actually happened last night and what was a figment of my horny, overactive imagination.

I remember dancing, but that was with Cory. But I remember turning around and staring up into an angry pair of green eyes. Eyes that sent a shiver down to the tips of my toes.

I remember getting in a car and taillights. Lots and lots of taillights.

I remember him.

Inches and inches of bare skin wet from the shower. I remember the scent of his aftershave filling my nose. Hell, I can still smell it. If I didn't already know that I was in the room alone, I would be convinced he's still here.

Pulling the pillow from my head, I look at the other side of the bed, trying to figure out if he slept here with me.

He was here with me. I know he was.

It wouldn't be my first salacious dream about my brother's best friend, and something tells me that it won't be the last.

Throwing the pillow down, I groan, frustrated with myself for getting so drunk that I don't remember details from the night before.

My need for the bathroom effectively pauses my pity party for one, and I reluctantly swing my legs out of the bed.

My toes sink into the thick, soft carpet and I groan.

I don't need to look around to discover where I am.

It's the confirmation I need to know I left with him.

I left the club with Kingston Callahan, and he was so ashamed that he dumped me at one of his hotels and took off. I knew I meant nothing to him. But being beneath his hookups is a whole new low. It stings.

He takes woman after woman back to his bed. They're allowed in his inner sanctuary, even if it is for a few pleasure-filled hours. And here I am, about to marry the asshole, and I get dumped here like I'm some kind of hooker he's trying to hide from the world.

I pad through to the bathroom, and it's not until I'm sitting on the toilet that I look around.

It's not the first time I've been inside a Callahan hotel, and something tells me that it's far from being the last, but still, the mass of Callahan branding takes me by surprise. It really is impossible to forget where you're staying.

I do my business before stumbling toward the sink to get a look at the state of myself.

"Jesus Christ," I mutter when the reality of the situation appears before me.

It's no surprise he did a runner. No one wants to wake up to this mess.

It takes a few seconds for me to rip my eyes away from the disaster that is my hair and face, but when I do, my gaze drops to what I'm wearing.

A white shirt with the Callahan logo over my breast.

My bare breast...

The memory of me exposing myself to him reappears in my mind.

It was just a dream, right?

I didn't actually...

My groan bounces off the shiny white tiles around me as mortification threatens to swallow me whole.

I showed him my tits and he still ran.

I'm not sure if that says more about me or him, if I'm being honest.

After attempting to clean up, I return to the room, my need for a caffeine hit the only thing spurring me on.

But when I get out into the bedroom, I discover my worst nightmare.

There is no coffee machine.

"How is this even possible?" I mutter to myself as I embark on checking all the cupboards. "There has to be a coffee machine in a

Callahan hotel."

But after searching through every single possibility, I still come up empty-handed.

"Fucking stupid hotel." I scoff as I wake up the tablet beside the bed so I can order room service.

"Coffee, coffee, and more coffee," I say to myself as I order the largest on offer. "Oh, and bacon. I need bacon."

With nothing else to do but wait, I find my purse on the nightstand and pull my cell out.

My stomach knots when I find messages from Lori and Cory, both individually and in our group chat.

I open Lori's first, knowing that it's going to be safer.

She knows what's going on. Hell, she's all for me hooking up with Kingston.

And she only proves I'm right when I find a whole stream of messages first wishing me a fun night and then more from only an hour ago, demanding details.

Shaking my head, I come out of that conversation and hesitantly open Cory's.

> Cory: Lori said you left with Kingston Callahan. What the hell? I know he's fucking loaded and all, but seriously? I thought you hated the guy.
>
> Cory: I'm sorry, that was uncalled for. You can go with whomever you want.
>
> Cory: Are you okay? Reply so I know he's treating you right.

My heart aches reading his messages.

I hurt him last night.

I led him on to sate my own need for attention and then I dropped him just as fast.

I open up our group chat to find more of the same. Them freaking out that Kingston has fucked me into some kind of pleasure-induced death.

If fucking only.

I quickly reply, letting them know that while I might have woken up in some kind of hell, I'm pretty sure I am still alive. The hangover is evidence of that.

Dots start bouncing as one of them replies, but a knock at the door has me putting my cell down and racing over.

I glance down at myself a second before I pull the door open, questioning my state of dress, but the lure of coffee means I throw caution to the wind.

Ignoring the person holding the tray, I focus on the contents, excited to see my caffeine hit, but I don't find it.

In its place is a glass of very familiar-looking green stuff.

My blood boils as fury wraps around me.

"Where's my coffee?" I demand.

"I'm sorry, Miss. Your order was changed," the poor guy standing before me explains.

"Well, change it back. I need coffee."

"I'm sorry, I'm afraid we can't do that. Please enjoy," he says, thrusting the offensive drink toward me.

I have little choice but to take it, and the second I do, he hot-foots it down the hallway.

Pussy.

Kicking the door closed behind me, I look between the glass of gunk and my cell.

Kingston is going to pay for this.

17

TATUM

Anger doesn't even begin to explain the eruption within me when I stalk back into my hotel room with a tray in my hands.

"Fucking Grinch juice. Fucking Kingston Callahan," I mutter darkly as vivid images of all the ways I could cause him pain for this emerge in my mind.

I dump the tray on the nightstand and glare at the green gloop as it sloshes from side to side.

Nothing about it is tempting. Not a fucking thing.

With a sigh, I snatch the bottle of water from the tray and twist the top.

The coolness might be refreshing as I swallow, but it has nothing on a nice strong cup of coffee.

"Asshole," I mutter, going in search of my cell again.

I decide against replying to Lori's messages. Way too much has happened—or not, I don't know—to attempt to explain it over the phone.

I flop back in the bed, my stomach rolling horribly as I bounce before the line connects and starts ringing.

"Ah, here she is," Lori sings happily.

"Why are you so cheerful?" I groan, wincing at the lightness in her voice.

"What isn't there to be cheerful about? I had an epic night, as I'm assuming you did, and now I'm on the way to have a fucking awesome Saturday."

"Hmm," I hum in response to her assuming my night was awesome. "What are you doing today that's so incredible?"

She barks out a laugh. "You're funny, Tate."

"Am I?"

I stretch my legs out and sigh as my muscles relax.

She laughs again.

"Room 1008, right?"

I squeeze my eyes closed. "What the hell are you talking about?"

But before she can answer, there's a knock on the door.

My anger surges immediately and I jump up faster than my head can cope.

"Can I call you back?" I ask, hanging up before she gets a chance to respond.

Once I'm confident I'm not about to collapse, I grab the glass of green shit, ready to tip it over the motherfucker's head the second I open the door.

My hand trembles with a mixture of anger and anticipation as I pull it open. I'm poised and ready to attack when I'm interrupted.

"What the fuck are you doing?" a very familiar, very female voice shrieks a beat before I tip the stuff over her head.

"Lori?" I ask, confusion fogging my brain.

"Yes. What the hell?" She snatches the glass from my hand and hesitantly sniffs it. "How is it possible that it smells worse than yesterday's?" she mutters with her top lip peeled back in disgust.

"Why are you here?" I ask as she slips past me and into the hotel room.

Without saying a word, she takes the glass to the bathroom and tips it into the sink.

"That's the only place that deserves to be. Why aren't you ready?" she asks, looking me up and down as I stand in only my Callahan Enterprise shirt.

"Ready for what?"

She shakes her head, smirking at me.

"Kingston called me earlier. Invited me to come and spend the day in the spa with you."

"H-he what?" I balk.

"I know, right? I was surprised too. But he said—"

I tune her out as I snatch my cell up and call his number, immediately putting it on speaker so Lori can hear.

"Kingston Callahan," he answers like a douche. He knows it's me. My name—or some version of it—just flashed up on his screen. Why be such a pretentious dick?

"What the hell are you playing at?" I snap.

"I don't know what you're talking about. How are you feeling, baby?" he asks, faking concern.

If he's doing it for Lori's benefit, he can cut the act. She isn't going to be fooled by him, free day at his fancy spa or not.

"Wonderful, thank you. Why is my best friend standing in front of me ready for a spa day?" I demand.

"Because I've booked you both in for all the works. Thought you'd need the relaxation after last night."

I roll my eyes at him and when I look up, I swear that Lori is swooning.

I frown at her.

She's smarter than this.

"Why?"

"Why not? You're there. The spa is there. Did you have any other plans for today?"

No. "Maybe."

"Well, if you did, cancel them. I promise you'll have a better day with what I have organized."

"You wanna bet?" I mutter under my breath.

"Make the most of it. The salon is expecting you as well. You'll be ready for next Friday's gala."

"Gala?" I parrot.

"Have you not looked at the diary I shared with you this morning?"

The red haze of anger begins to descend again.

"No, Kingston. I have not looked at your diary."

"It's not mine. It's ours, baby."

My teeth grind.

We have a joint diary. Of fucking course we do.

"What if I'm busy?"

"You're not. I'm expected to attend, and in turn, so are you. It's the perfect night to confirm what everyone will already know by then."

My hand begins to tremble as I picture him making a spectacle of our relationship in the middle of some swanky gala with all of Chicago's elite watching.

My stomach knots.

I might have grown up attending these kinds of events, but I have never, ever wanted to be front and center.

Before me, Lori lifts her left hand and wiggles her ring finger.

Oh my god, no.

"I'll check my schedule."

Kingston chuckles as if he knows more than I do.

To be fair, he probably does. Nothing about this situation has been a surprise to him.

For all I know, every single minute of my life from the second I signed that document yesterday has already been mapped out.

I've probably got a wedding dress waiting for me somewhere with my name on it.

"Spend the day with your friend, Tatum. Relax. The next few weeks and months are going to be hard. Take the time while you can."

"Why are you being so nice?"

It's the last thing I'd expect if my hazy memories of the night before are correct.

"Just enjoy yourself, yeah?"

I'm about to respond, but the line cuts dead.

"Please don't tell me that you're going to refuse all this?"

"Lori," I warn, already picturing myself walking out of the room and then the hotel with my middle finger held up to the security camera so he can see it.

"What? He's playing games."

"So? We've got a spa all to ourselves. A salon. Take what you can get while it's on offer. Make him hurt for playing games later."

"To ourselves?" I ask, ignoring most of what she said.

"That's what he said to me."

"He can't shut the entire spa on a Saturday so we can have it to ourselves. That's insane."

"He's Kingston Callahan; he can do anything his heart desires. And right now, he wants to make you happy, so take it."

There's another knock on the door, but I'm too lost in all this to move, so Lori is the one who answers it.

"Thank you," she says softly before returning with a massive black box with a silk gold ribbon tied around it.

I glare at it, wishing I could see what's inside before pulling the lid off.

She sets it down on the bed and places her hands on her hips.

"Go on then. I'm dying here."

"What did he say to you this morning?" I ask, studying her closely.

"Nothing. Why?"

"You're very Team Kingston right now," I accuse.

Her chin drops. "What? That's insane. I'm Team Tatum, always. I just...I agree that you could use a day of relaxation. You've got the funeral next week. Now this gala. Him. It's just what you need."

Unable to argue with her reasoning, I reach for the box and pull the ribbon loose.

Inside, everything is covered in gold tissue paper.

I pull out the parcel and inside, I find a tiny gold swimsuit.

"Wow," Lori breathes as I hold it up against my body.

"He has seen me before, right? I have boobs. Like...real boobs."

She laughs.

"And..." I turn the bottoms around. "Where is the back of these?"

"I guess this explains why he shut the spa," Lori muses. "What else is in there?"

"What's that supposed to mean?" I demand.

"He won't want anyone seeing you in that."

"You will," I point out.

"Babe, I've seen you in way less many, many times. I don't think it's me he'd be worried about."

I shake my head and drop the offending swimsuit onto the bed before returning to the box.

"That's it," I say. "This massive box, for that." I point at the scrap of fabric.

Lori shrugs.

"Put it on then. We've got nothing but pure relaxation waiting for us downstairs."

I want to argue. To tell Kingston where to go and cut this stupid swimsuit up into tiny bits and mail it back to him. But then I see the excitement in my best friend's eyes and I swallow it down.

I'm not the only one who needs this.

I'm not the only one with issues right now. She needs to take a step away from life and just be for a few hours. Maybe it'll help her figure her shit out. It sure isn't going to fix any of mine.

Muttering my unhappiness over this whole situation, I snatch the swimsuit from the bed and stomp through to the bathroom.

To my astonishment, when I inspect it closer, I find that it's actually my size.

That bit of knowledge raises just one too many questions about how well my soon-to-be husband knows me.

Ignoring everything, I pull the fabric on, astounded to realize that for such a small thing, it holds the girls up pretty well.

But while I might be happy with that, the ass is an entirely different situation.

Twisting around in the mirror, I stare at my practically bare behind.

I'm fairly body confident. I mean, I'm no size zero. I have curves and some cellulite in all the normal places. I try and take care of myself and ensure that my curves are as toned as they can be. But standing in only this tiny swimsuit pushes me right to the edge of my comfort zone.

If I didn't know that the spa was going to be empty, I'd be questioning my life right now.

"I'm going to make you pay for this, Kingston Callahan," I promise before re-twisting my hair up into a messy bun, splashing my face with water and pulling the door open.

"Oh holy hell, Tate," Lori says, her eyes widening as she takes in my outfit—or lack thereof.

"The fuck are you doing?" I shriek when she holds her cell up like she's taking a photo. 'No. Delete that right now."

"Oh, whoops," she says with what I'm sure she's hoping is an innocent smile.

"What do you mean, 'whoops?'"

Snatching her cell from her hand, I stare down at the screen to see a photo of myself in a message chat with... Kingston.

And he's already read it.

"I hope you suffocate in the sauna," I hiss, thrusting it back at her as the dots bounce with his reply.

I don't want to know what he has to say to that.

I don't.

I don't.

I—

Lori's smile grows.

Damn it.

"What did he say?"

She looks up at me and smirks.

"Maybe you should ask him."

She makes a show of putting her cell to sleep and then sliding it into her purse.

"Grab a robe, Tate. The spa is calling," she sings before walking toward the door.

Unable to do anything but follow orders, I pull the thick

toweling of the Callahan-branded robe around myself, slip my feet into the slippers, and follow her, muttering, "There had better be coffee down there."

Problem is...I already know there won't be.

And I'm proved right when we emerge in the spa to find glasses of green juice waiting for us.

Wonderful. Just freaking wonderful.

18

KINGSTON

I sit at the conference table in my father's office while Kian points at a spreadsheet full of numbers and graphs.

I'm meant to be focusing on the impact our acquisition of Warner Group will have on our forecasting and profit margins moving forward.

But all I can think about is how Tatum looked in that gold bikini.

I knew the moment I saw it that it was made for her. But there was no way of truly appreciating just how incredible it would look on her.

My cock swells at just the thought while Kian drones on.

I should be paying attention. This is important. But fuck. I can't get my head out of the gutter.

It's bad enough that I cleared the entire spa so I could watch her on CCTV without worrying about any other man turning up and looking at her. But knowing I've got the image Lorelei sent me burning up my cell is something else entirely.

I've spent longer than I'll admit to anyone staring at it as I've jerked off in the past couple of days.

With Kain's voice a distant memory, I pull my cell from my pocket and unlock it.

The temptation to look at the photo burns through me, but instead, I open the notification I just received letting me know that her lunch has arrived.

I smirk thinking about her reaction to it.

I woke her up with a healthy and nutritious breakfast this morning, and I've got the abuse for it sitting in my messages.

"Kingston." Awareness tingles through me, but it's not enough to pull my attention from my cell as I wait for a reaction. "Kingston."

"Kingston," Dad barks, successfully dragging my eyes from the screen.

"Yeah?" I ask, trying to play off the fact that I've not paid an ounce of attention.

"If you don't want to be here right now, just fuck off," Kian snaps as my cell buzzes in my hand.

"I'm here." I grunt, attempting to ignore the burning need I have to look down. "I've just got some emails that need my attention," I lie.

Both Dad and Kian glower at me.

It's unlike me not to be fully focused in our meetings. But I can't fucking help it.

"It can wait," Dad says without enquiring about what I'm dealing with.

Dad has been slowly trying to pull back from the business, but despite his desire to embark on retirement, he's still managing to be his overly-involved self with everything.

We've been running this place successfully for a while now, but Dad's always been there watching our moves, double-checking our figures, and questioning our decisions.

It's not necessary. We both know what we're doing. We were fucking born for it, after all.

It's time.

Even more so now that we have Warner Group and Miles with us.

The three of us have got this. We have the skills, the

dedication, and the hunger to take both companies to places they've never been before.

"Just..." I look down at my screen and my smirk returns.

> Tatum Warner: As much as I appreciate you sending something edible for a change, I have lunch plans so it was unnecessary. I'm sure my team will enjoy it. I'll get them to send their thanks.

"Something funny?" Kian asks, when my smothered grunt turns all attention on me again.

"Everything is good. Please continue," I say, placing my cell face down on the table before me.

"Not what I asked, but whatever," Kian mutters as I repeat Tatum's message in my head.

She's lying. I had IT hook me up with her diary. I know she has back-to-back meetings today—none of which are lunch meetings.

It's why I sent sushi. She can eat bites between them. It's easy. Healthy. Filling.

I want to prove her right. Let her know that I know everything about her schedule.

I warned her on Saturday morning when I dropped the gala dinner on her. I already knew she didn't have plans. I also knew that she'd try to convince me she was busy.

She's underestimating me. I want to say that she really should learn, but I'm already addicted to proving her wrong and being one step ahead.

Knowing that she's in her office eating some decent food, I finally turn most of my attention to my little brother as he geeks out over his spreadsheets.

Knock. Knock. Knock.

I stand on the other side of Tatum's office door and

wait. It's not often I do so, but my need to be at least semi-professional stops me from just barging in.

The attention of everyone in her office burns into my back as I wait for her to respond. Everyone bar her immediate team, that is. I already know they're inside with her.

"Come in," she calls out a handful of seconds later than polite.

Excitement bubbles inside me as I twist the handle and push the door open.

Silence greets me as I step inside, but somehow it gets even quieter when my identity is recognized by everyone around the conference table in her room.

It's nowhere near as big as the one I've spent most of the day being bored around while thinking about her, but it's decent enough to give her some kind of power trip, I'm sure. She might not be where she deserves to be in this company based on her surname alone, but she's still doing alright for herself, and without the kind of step-up that Miles received when he finished college.

Tatum's expression hardens as she glares at me. The air crackles between us, and I've no doubt that her team can sense it.

"Mr. Callahan, what can we do for you?" she asks tersely.

"Good evening, Tatum," I say, forgetting about the formalities. The only time I'm going to use a surname to address her in public —hell, even in private from here on out—is going to be as Mrs. Callahan.

My dick stirs in my pants just thinking about it.

Beg for it, Mrs. Callahan...

"Sir?" she repeats when I don't respond.

"I've come to take you home before we go out for dinner," I say with a smile on my face.

Tomorrow is her father's funeral. Everyone sitting around the table will be aware of that, and if we're going to ensure those closest to her believe this relationship is real, then they need to see me being the support she needs during this time.

"Thought it might help take your mind off things," I add.

"Aw, that's sweet," one of the older ladies around the table gushes.

My eyes find hers and I nod, silently thanking her for her support.

"I-I already have dinner plans tonight. But t-thank you for the invitation." She stutters over her words, letting me know just how fake the gratitude is.

"You're going home to spend the night alone." Her eyes widen in surprise as I relay her plans for the evening. "We can do better than that, Tate." I wink and the woman who was already swooning practically melts into her chair.

"I'm sure you can, Mr. Callahan, but I'm busy right now and I actually do have plans later."

Dropping my briefcase beside her desk, I shrug my jacket off and throw it over the back of her chair, moving around her table and pulling out a spare seat. I straighten my tie and then set about rolling up my sleeves, more than aware of Tatum's heated stare.

"I can wait. Please," I say gesturing to the paperwork spread across the table. "Continue. I'd love to hear what you're planning. I have a vested interest now, of course." I wink at the woman before scanning the rest of the faces around the table. Most look tense and confused, but there is one, a young kid—probably fresh out of college—who looks like he's planning my murder as he glares at me.

Alright, kid. Stand down. Your boss is mine.

Figuratively and literally.

Tatum glares at me from across the table. She's debating doing as I say or defying me and calling an end to the meeting.

There are ten minutes left of their workday. She should continue. It would be bad practice for her to let her team out early while senior management sits around her table, but unlike Tatum, I've long stopped underestimating her.

Her eyes narrow at me before she responds. "As I was saying, I think we're moving in the right direction here." She points at a piece of paper in front of the kid. "I think this is the one we should be focusing on. Well done, Josh. You've knocked it out of the park."

He preens like the cat who got the cream, lapping up Tatum's praise like it's the best day of his life.

Kiss ass.

I chuckle quietly.

"Did you want to add something, sir?" Tatum asks, turning all eyes on me.

"N-no," I say, fake clearing my throat in an attempt to cover my reaction to his bullshit "You're right. This is great."

Tate glowers at me, holding my eyes dead as she dismisses her team, telling them to make their changes ready to get together again on Wednesday.

"Was that necessary?" she barks the second Josh closes the door behind him.

I sit back in my seat and cross my arms over my chest.

"I've no idea what you're talking about," I say quietly as she begins gathering up the paperwork.

"You bulldozed my meeting for absolutely no reason at all."

"No, I came to invite you to dinner," I argue.

"And I declined the offer. You should have left."

"Maybe I wanted to see if my new acquisition is working to my advantage."

"You know exactly how well Warner Group is doing. You don't need to sit in one of my meetings to confirm that," she grumbles.

"Well, maybe I have more interest in this department, this manager," I emphasize, "than anywhere else in the company."

She sighs as if she's already exhausted by this conversation. By me.

Scanning her office, I notice how much tidier and more organized it is than her apartment. My gaze is almost back to her when I spot the empty tray her sushi would have been delivered on earlier.

"I see you enjoyed your lunch," I muse, unable to hide my smirk.

"My team did," she says, raising her chin in defiance.

"Sure," I concede. She's lying. We both know it. But I'll let it slide—for now.

"What did you really want, Kingston?" she snaps once she's standing behind her desk as if she's ready to run out of the door and never look back.

"Like I said, I came to take you for dinner."

"And I said I'm not interested. I'm busy."

"You're lying," I accuse, pushing to my feet and stalking around the table toward her.

Her expression hardens and her lips press into a thin line as irritation floods through her veins.

"We have an image to portray now, Tate." Her eyes remain locked on mine as I close the space between us. The second I come within touching distance, I reach out and tuck a stray lock of dark hair behind her ear.

She's tied it up. When she first walked into her office this morning, it was loose and around her shoulders.

It's pretty down, but when she has it pulled back, it accentuates her features, makes her eyes look bigger and even more mesmerizing. Her lips...

My eyes drop and her breath catches as my fingertips brush the shell of her ear.

Her tongue sneaks out, wetting her bottom lip and telling me everything she refuses to with words.

"Let's show the world how good we could be together, baby. It's part of the deal, after all."

Her eyes search mine, anger and hunger dueling within them.

She wants to say no. To forget everything she agreed to and live her life how she sees fit. But she can't. She has too much riding on this working out.

My hand brushes down her bare arm, causing goosebumps to erupt, and the second my fingers meet hers, I grasp them and tug her closer, dropping my mouth to her ear.

"Be a good girl, Tatum. Come to dinner with me. I'll make it worth your while."

19

TATUM

I lie in bed and stare up at the ceiling as images from our meal last night play out in my mind.

I held firm on not going until we walked out of the building to find Lewis waiting for us. By the time Kingston pressed his hand against my lower back, directing me toward the open door, I knew it was over.

We had eyes on us. All I could do was smile and greet Lewis as I climbed in the back.

I can tell myself all I want that I thought my argument about being busy might eventually fly, but I knew the truth then, and I still know it now. It was never going to work.

From the moment Kingston stepped into my office, nothing I said would have mattered.

He's Kingston Callahan. He always gets his way.

What I wasn't expecting was for him to be the perfect gentleman and for the night to turn out to be the best date I've ever had.

He was thoughtful and attentive, and when he asked me a question, he actually listened to the answer like he genuinely wanted to hear it. It was mind-blowing, and nothing like I've ever experienced from him before.

He's always been my older brother's best friend, who never had time for Miles's annoying little sister. But last night, I wasn't a little sister. I wasn't an employee. I was just Tatum, the woman on a date with one of the city's most eligible bachelors.

Even now, with the bright light of a new day streaming through the curtains I failed to close properly last night, I'm as confused as ever.

Something unexpected and totally unwanted flutters in my stomach as I think about the end of the night when he delivered me home. He didn't come up. He didn't even attempt it. Instead, he walked me to the main doors of my building before twisting his fingers with mine and pulling me close.

The heat of his body practically burned mine through our clothes, and I'd be lying if I said that desire wasn't thrumming through my veins.

It has been all night.

The eye contact, the way he watched me from across the table, the innocent little touches he gifted me. All of it was beginning to drive me crazy.

More than crazy.

I shouldn't have wanted to drag him up to my apartment as much as I did, but I couldn't help myself.

Thankfully, one of us wasn't fueled by desire and had managed to keep his head. Either that or the chemistry I was feeling was totally one-sided and he hadn't even considered the possibility.

I shake my head. Surely not.

It can't be possible. The air was practically crackling between us.

He had to have felt it...

My heart sinks a little and embarrassment threatens that he didn't.

His actions outside sure led me to believe he didn't want me like I did him.

He didn't even follow through on his promise of making it

worthwhile...assuming a happy ending was where he was going with that comment.

Rolling over, I press my face into my pillow and scream quietly, needing somehow to get rid of the frustration and lingering desire I've been unable to shift.

All he did was brush some of my hair behind my ear and then kiss my cheek as he wished me goodnight.

Kissed my freaking cheek.

This is Kingston Callahan we're talking about. I don't think he's ever only kissed a woman's cheek before.

Along with my brother, he's the ultimate manwhore.

They always have been.

So why am I different?

Because he's been told to spend time with you...

I slam down those stupid thoughts.

I refuse to allow myself to even consider that I'm not worthy of a man like him.

I am. Hell, if we're being honest, I'm worthy of a lot better.

He's arrogant, egotistical, powerful, dangerous...and not just with the way he makes me feel.

I've never cared to dig into anything I've seen in the past that appeared to be untoward, but I know that not all of our fathers' business deals were above board. Some of our clients...well...the less I even think about it, the better.

I don't want to know. I have never wanted to be involved any deeper in the family business than I am right now.

I have my team, a role I love. That's all I ask for.

I have every intention of doing my job until I deem the time is right to start over in the place that truly owns my heart.

"What do you mean it isn't on the system?" Lori shrieks from the other side of my ajar bedroom door. "I booked it. Hell, I put it in myself. I know it was there."

"Fucking hell," I mutter as I throw the covers off and pad toward the bathroom while she continues to rant on the other side of the door.

I freshen up before going to find out what's going on.

I didn't get much sleep last night. Between reliving every element of our "date" and the impending dread of what today is going to hold, I mostly just tossed and turned and watched the clock tick around. I'm feeling it now, too. My eyes are sore, my body is sluggish, and my head already pounds gently, a sure-fire sign that I'm stressed.

"Fucking assholes," Lori mutters to herself as she paces back and forth in our living area.

She's got her cell clutched tightly in her hand and Griz watches her with a confused expression on her face.

"What's going on?" I ask, gently scooping Griz up and snuggling her against my chest.

When I fell asleep last night, she was cuddled up with me, but she must have gotten fed up with my restlessness and retreated to her own, much more peaceful bed. The only place I know she won't have gone is in with Lori. That girl snores like a freight train to the point that even Griz can't put up with it.

Griz purrs as I tickle her ears, and it instantly makes me feel better. A snuggle with my girl always helps me put things into perspective.

"My leave for today has magically disappeared. I'm meant to be in the office right now," she explains angrily.

"Oh," I say, my heart sinking at the thought of not having her with me today.

"I'm not going in. Obviously," she states fiercely, rolling her eyes. "There is nowhere else I'm going to be today than by your side. Fuck them."

"Lori, it's your job. I know it fucking sucks, but still. You need it."

"I don't care. Today is too important for them to ruin."

"It's really not," I mutter. I'd happily go to work today instead of the show I'm going to be forced to endure. Spending the day as Jonathan Warner's grieving daughter is the very last thing I want to do right now.

"It is, Tate. I'm not letting you do it alone. No fucking way. They can fire me if they want. Screw them."

"Lori," I warn.

"I'll get a waitressing job. Sweep the streets. I'm done with them. This is the last straw, I swear—"

"You need to calm down. It's not that big a deal."

"Tate." She sighs, stepping closer and tickling Griz's head. "You have been there for me every single day since we met. You've picked me up and put me back together time and time again. But you...you're so fucking strong, level-headed, and...stable. I've never been able to repay you so—"

"I love you, Lor. But you really don't need to—"

"I do. Fuck work. Fuck my stupid boss. I'm spending today with you, and tonight we're getting off-our-heads drunk. And I might just ring in sick tomorrow as well," she announces.

She won't; her work ethic is too strong. But I appreciate the sentiment all the same.

"Come here," I say, holding my arm out for her to join our snuggle. She's getting all angry and emotional, and I fear I'm already going to have to deal with enough of that today without her joining the party.

"Okay," she says after a few seconds. "I think I'm good now. You want coffee?"

"Yes. God yes."

She laughs as she walks into the kitchen and grabs my favorite mug.

"So, I saw some pretty cute pictures of a certain date last night. Care to spill the deets?" she says.

I sigh, hating that I'm going to have to be honest.

What I want to say is that he was the irritating asshole we all know and love and it was nothing but a turn-off.

But that's far from the truth.

"It was amazing," I confess in a rush as I settle on a stool at our breakfast bar.

"Oh?" she asks, looking over her shoulder with intrigue glittering in her eyes.

"He was just—"

The buzzer goes off and my spine straightens.

"No," I breathe, immediately picturing Kingston standing at our front door with a bottle of that green shit in his hand.

Every freaking day he's attempted to get me to drink it. And every day, no matter how he delivers it, I dump it down the drain.

"Oh my god, Tate. That is totally him," Lori says excitedly.

"You do know this is an arranged-marriage situation, right? He doesn't actually want me. Or the other way around."

Her brows lift in suspicion. "Is that right?" she taunts irritatingly.

"Yes," I snap as the buzzer goes off again.

"Well," she says, gesturing in the direction of the front door.

"I'm not going."

"I thought you were meant to be supporting me today."

She winks and blows me a kiss as I slip from the stool and stalk toward the front door, still with Griz in my arms.

I don't bother looking through the peephole. What's the point? I already know what awaits me.

A hot-as-hell man wearing a pristine black suit and carrying a health drink made by the devil himself.

I'm just not lucky enough to find anything else.

I pull the door open, and the second I do, I'm assaulted by his scent.

My mouth waters instantly and I'm taken right back to last night when he pulled me up against his hard body.

Damn it.

No. Damn him.

He shouldn't look or smell this good.

It's not fair.

"Good morning," he says, his deep voice washing over me like thick, delicious silk.

My skin erupts in goosebumps but thankfully, it isn't my reaction to him that captures his attention.

His eyes drop to Griz as she snarls at him.

He stares at her with a deep frown between his brows.

"It's so weird. Pussy usually loves me."

I allow myself to drop my eyes down his body and appreciate just how freaking good he looks.

It should be illegal.

But then I come up short at what he's holding.

Surprise, surprise.

"Was there something you wanted other than to insult my pussy?" I ask, my brows lifting.

"I would never," he says quietly. "I'm sure she's beautiful once I get to know her."

The chemistry I remember all too well from last night crackles between us.

"I brought you breakfast, and then I'm going to escort you to your parents'."

"I'm more than capable of getting there myself," I mutter, taking a step back to let him in.

I can stand here wearing only a tank top and booty shorts, blocking his entry for the rest of the floor to see, or I can concede to what we both know is going to happen anyway.

"I'm aware of that. But given the significance of the day, you shouldn't have to."

"Right," I mutter, letting my nose lead the way toward the freshly brewed coffee.

His stare burns into my skin, and when I risk a look back, I find his gaze locked on my ass.

Hmm...proof it wasn't totally one-sided last night, maybe?

"Kingston," Lori muses. "What a surprise."

"Lorelei," he greets.

"Would you like a coffee?" she asks a little reluctantly.

It's funny seeing her reserved attitude toward him when she's been so pro him in private.

I guess she's just as confused as I am about all of this.

"Not necessary," he says, placing the tray and bag in his hands on the counter. "I have everything covered."

"I'm not drinking that shi—" My words are cut off when I find that there's more in the takeout tray than just a green juice.

There's also coffee.

Two large coffees, in fact.

"Skinny cappuccino with a double shot and extra foam?" he asks, holding a cup toward my best friend.

Her chin hits the floor right alongside mine.

"How? How did you know that?" I whisper.

He turns to me, my coffee in his hand with a devastating smile spread across his face.

Fuck. I was right earlier.

This man is beyond dangerous.

20

KINGSTON

Tatum is stoic as we stand beside the grave, waiting for her father to be lowered into the ground.

Since the moment we arrived at her parents' house, she's barely said a word.

It's the first time I've appreciated the change in her.

In her apartment, she was more than happy to give me shit—although the coffee delivery certainly softened the worst of that.

Any other day, I'd have stuck with the juice and a bottle of water, but she deserved the pick-me-up this morning.

And looking at her now, I'm so glad I did.

The second Lewis turned into her family's estate, her mood completely changed.

She shut down.

Most would probably assume it's because of what the day represents, but something tells me that it runs much deeper than that. I'd hazard a guess to say it has a lot to do with the reason she's a marketing manager for Warner Group and nowhere near the CMO, which is where she should be—and not just because of her name.

Before storming into her office yesterday and disrupting her meeting, I spent most of the afternoon digging into everything Tatum has ever done for Warner Group.

Now, I may not be a marketing expert, but I know good campaigns when I see them. The increase in sales that quickly followed are more proof I don't need that Tatum has been seriously undervalued in Warner Group.

Because of her father and his old-fashioned ways? Quite possibly.

That realization doesn't sit right with me.

How does Miles get to graduate college and walk straight onto the senior management team but she doesn't?

She is equally as talented and as good at her job as Miles. Hell, possibly more so.

He's never had to prove himself. She does every single fucking day.

Helena continues to cry as we stand listening to the minister as he says his final words. Miles and my father stand on either side of her, helping to hold her up, while Tatum stands beside me with Lorelei on her other side.

She hasn't shed one tear. Hasn't even looked close.

Her expression is hard. Completely closed off.

To an outsider, she might look like she doesn't care that they're burying her father. But they'd be wrong. She cares. Possibly too much. And a hell of a lot more than she's letting on. It's just in a very different way from everyone else here.

Only Tatum can understand the relationship she had with Jonathan. Sure, she could attempt to explain it, but we'd never understand. We couldn't. And she doesn't need us to. She just needs us to be here.

She draws in a deep breath as the coffin is slowly lowered into the ground.

Helena wails, turning everyone's attention to her. Just in case anyone missed her grieving widow status.

She's hurting, I get it. But she has two children.

They may be adults, but they have lost their father. Doesn't she want to think about that, and support them, instead of expecting them to hold her up?

Not that Tatum is making much of an effort.

I can't help but wonder if her opinion of her mother right now is similar to mine.

I reach out, my fingers brushing against her warm, soft skin.

I expect her to pull away, to refuse the contact. But to my surprise, she doesn't. Instead, she lets my fingers entwine with hers, even squeezing a little as if to silently thank me.

A weird warmth spreads through my chest at the thought of being important enough to support her right now.

It's taken every ounce of my self-restraint not to spend the day obsessing about last night.

It was...everything.

Once she dropped her guard and stopped fighting me, our evening was...easy.

I've never felt so relaxed while spending time with a woman before.

She was interesting, funny, and smart. So fucking smart. Honestly, she blew me away.

Everything about our night, her, was perfect.

I shake my head, trying to banish the confusion the last few days with this woman has instilled in me.

I signed a business deal. A way to grow Callahan Enterprises.

I didn't agree to anything else but loaning her my second name for twelve months and ensuring we both get what we want out of her father's death.

So why is it that as Helena throws a single rose on her late husband's grave, all I can think about is backing her daughter up against a tree and starting this marriage the right way?

My vision has long blurred as I focus on my imagination instead of reality, so when Tatum turns and presses her face into my chest, putting her back to the scene before us, I couldn't be more surprised.

I move on autopilot, my arms lifting to wrap around her.

She doesn't make a sound or do anything. She's like an immoveable rock against me.

As much as I might like that she's using me for support, I also hate how high she's built her walls.

They feel impenetrable right now.

Movement to my left catches my eye, and when I look over, I find Lorelei studying us closely.

'What?' I mouth.

She's made it more than clear that she doesn't like me. I couldn't care less about that. But it will certainly make my life easier over the next few months if I can get her on my side. Her and the fucking cat.

Every time they both look at me, I just know they've got their claws out, ready for a fight.

I'm still healing from my last rendezvous with the damn cat.

Lorelei shakes her head before shuffling closer, gripping Tatum's shoulder, needing to be there for her as well.

We all stand there while the committal is brought to a close. People begin to shuffle away, but Tatum doesn't move.

Neither does her mother, but I'm hardly surprised. I bet she'd sleep out here with him if she had a chance. At this point, I'm not sure if that's romantic or just pathetic.

"Baby, we should go," I say softly.

Lorelei's eyes widen, but I don't give her a second of my attention. She can think what she likes.

A second later, Miles turns around and his eyes immediately find mine before dropping to his sister in my arms, and then back up again.

Any hit of the grief he was just feeling is instantly banished, replaced by unfiltered anger.

The bruises might have started to fade since he showed me with his fists last week how thrilled he was with this plan, but it's clear he's far from over it.

"We should go," I say softly, my eyes holding Miles's but my voice soft for Tatum.

She shakes her head. It's so slight that I don't think I'd know if she weren't pressed against me.

"You go. We'll meet you back at the house," I say, looking between Miles and Lorelei.

Miles wants to argue, but thankfully, he decides that now is not the time, and after giving me a long hard glare—a warning—he takes off with a concerned-looking Lorelei by his side.

Dad and Helena are the last to leave. Helena clings to him like she'll die without him.

I guess it's a good thing that Dad's latest wife decided funerals were too depressing and turned down the invitation to join him. Her words, apparently, not his.

"Tatum?" I whisper when it's just the two of us left. "What do you need, baby?"

She doesn't react for long seconds, but eventually, she pulls away from me, and with her head bowed, she walks toward the freshly dug hole in the ground where her father has been laid to rest.

I let her go, giving her space to do whatever she needs.

My heart thunders in my chest as I watch her. Her pain is palpable, but once again, I can't help wondering if it's more than just loss.

She stands there unmoving, staring into the Earth.

The sun continues to shine down on us, and the birds overhead continue to sing.

As funerals go, it's pretty perfect with the beautiful spring weather and the promise of new life popping up around us.

Cathartic, in a way.

As one door closes, more open up all around us.

I guess all that matters is which ones we choose to walk through.

I give her as long as I can, but eventually, my need to support her gets too much and I step up behind her.

Wrapping my arm around her waist, I pin her back against me and tuck my face into her neck.

"I should be sadder than I am," she confesses after long, agonizing seconds.

"There is no right or wrong way to feel, Tatum."

"Everyone expects me to be devastated. I should be devastated."

"No one expects anything. They didn't know what it was like to live with your father. Only you know the relationship you've had."

"He's given me everything," she whispers.

"Has he?" I don't mean the simple question to come out as bitterly as it does.

Her breath catches as she hears it, but I doubt she understands what I really mean. As far as she's concerned, I'm just as bad as they are.

"You're shivering. We should get back."

I've no idea how she can possibly be cold with the warm sun beating down on us, but she's trembling.

"I'm not cold. I'm...I don't know." She sighs.

I hold her tighter. "Let me take care of you."

It takes her a long while to reply and when she does, it knocks me sideways.

"I don't know how to let you do that," she confesses quietly—so quietly, I have to wonder if she was hoping the words might get swept away by the light breeze before they hit my ears.

"We can bail on the wake, if you like," I offer. "We could go and do something else instead."

"I can't," she says sadly, lowering her head. "Everyone expects—"

"Fuck everyone, Tatum. This isn't about them. It's about you."

"No," she says, a bite of anger entering her tone. "It isn't about me. It's about him. It's always about him."

My lips part to respond, but for once, I don't have any words.

She's right.

So painfully right it cuts down to my soul.

"Okay, we'll go. But the second you're done, tell me and we're out of there."

She nods once before twisting out of my hold and marching toward the parking lot.

I watch her go for a beat, in total awe of her strength.

Tatum Warner is a force to be reckoned with, and something tells me I've already fallen under her spell.

21

TATUM

The warmth of Kingston's hand resting on the small of my back continues to radiate through me.

It's been the same since the moment he first held my hand at the committal. He hasn't left my side once. His support has been unwavering. And I'm not sure how to feel about that.

I thought it was going to be Lori who held me up today. Never in a million years did I think I'd be craving Kingston's strength instead.

"Here you go," the girl in question says, passing me another glass of champagne.

"Thank you," I say in a rush, immediately lifting it to my lips. The bubbles pop against my lips before coating my tongue and then rushing down my throat.

It's my fourth glass...possibly my fifth.

As much as I don't have any intention of getting blind drunk to deal with all this bullshit small talk with people who may or may not be lying about actually liking my father, there is no way I can do it sober.

Kingston continues to talk to the couple before us as if he's known them all his life. What do I know? Maybe he has. I don't recognize them, although they seem to know exactly who I am.

Miles is currently with Michael, schmoozing with Warner Group's senior management. And Mom...well, she got so drunk that she had to be taken to bed for a lie down about thirty minutes ago.

A few people have started to leave. Hell knows that I'm more than ready, but despite not wanting to be here, it seems wrong for me to be one of the first to disappear, especially with our host out of commission.

"Not gonna lie, Tate, this is a fucking snoozefest," Lori teases as she looks around the room.

"Pretty sure that's standard after a funeral, Lor."

"Yeah, I know. I just thought...I dunno, all these millionaires might be a little more...charismatic."

I can't help but laugh. Lori might have been a big part of my life for quite a few years now, but she hasn't actually dived into this side of it. She's attended a handful of events with me, but there is usually some kind of entertainment as a distraction. This right now is...well, dull.

"Money doesn't buy everything," I deadpan, avoiding pointing out that almost everyone around us smashed through the millionaire threshold a while ago.

The wealth in the room doesn't even bear thinking about. It's hard for me to comprehend, let alone Lori, who grew up in a small town in California with barely a dollar to her name.

"Nope, personalities are free." Lori laughs, draining her glass.

"Well, I wish you all the best with everything," the man talking to Kingston says, dragging my attention back to them.

"Thank you. I'm sure it's going to be beneficial for everyone involved."

He turns into me, our bodies close. He's doing a fantastic job of ensuring that everyone who cares to look knows there is something going on between us.

Add that to the images that have already surfaced of us outside Warner Group together, leaving the club, and then at dinner last night, and I'd say we're doing a pretty good job of making this fake relationship look like it's blossoming nicely.

Bitterness twists at my insides. Sure, having him beside me today has been nice...more than nice. But knowing that we're deceiving everyone—that we're playing a twisted game to ensure we both get what we want—makes me feel a little sick. No, a lot sick.

All of this for a house. For a company acquisition.

It's insane. Totally insane.

But then he leans closer and his warm breath tickles down my neck, making my brain short circuit and forget all rational thoughts in favor of filthy ones that shouldn't have a place in my head.

"Did you want to get out of here?" he whispers in my ear.

Goosebumps erupt and a shudder rips down my spine.

I might not be able to see him, but I feel his cheek move against mine. He felt it, and the smug jerk is smiling.

"I'm not sure if I can—"

His hand lands on my hip and he tugs me closer.

"You can do whatever it is you want to do, Tatum."

Excitement flutters in my belly as he amps up the charm and ups the ante. "Is that right?"

"Yep," he agrees. "Right here, right now, you can do anything."

"Hmm...the possibilities are endless."

"They'll be even more so when we get out of here and are alone."

My body temperature soars. Gaining his sole attention shouldn't have this effect on me. He's my brother's manwhore of a best friend. I should be immune to his charms.

I pull back so I'm able to look into his eyes. They're dark. Hungry. The sight of his desire makes my own quadruple.

"Can you take us home, please?" I say, trying to keep my head.

The champagne is working its magic, and everything feels just a little too possible right now.

"I'll take Lori home," he states. "I have other plans for you."

Placing my hand on my waist, I pop my hip, giving him all my sass and defiance.

"On second thought, we'll just call an Uber."

His eyes narrow and even more butterflies take flight in my stomach.

Oh, I love this game.

Maybe the next twelve months won't be so bad after all...

A s we pull up on our street, Kingston is still touching me. My threat of calling an Uber went down about as well as I expected it to, and not ten minutes later did we say goodbye to Miles, who looked thoroughly pissed off about our sudden departure, as Kingston was practically dragging me away from the house.

I felt bad. Miles doesn't deserve to deal with all of this alone.

"Who organized the funeral?" Kingston had whispered in my ear as Lori climbed into the back of his car.

He knew. He always seems to know.

He was right. Judith and I organized almost every second of today. Miles was too busy picking up other pieces that had shattered around our feet when we got the call to say that Dad had gone.

But that doesn't give me the right to abandon him today.

I sigh as Lewis brings the car to a stop. Every inch of my body aches. All I want to do is pull on my pajamas and curl up on the couch with Mrs. Griz and some very strong alcohol. Maybe a tub of ice cream to go with it.

Kingston's hand grips my thigh harder as Lori grabs her purse and twists around to leave.

"I'll meet you upstairs," Lori says, looking between us. I've no idea what she can see on my face, but Kingston's expression is hard.

She's gone before I get a chance to say anything or even attempt to follow her.

"You're not going up there," he states the second the door has closed.

"It's my home. All I want to do is--"

"No, it's not your home anymore."

"King." I sigh. I have nowhere near enough energy to deal with his bullshit right now.

"Very soon the press is going to be printing our engagement photos," he explains, making my stomach tighten with anxiety.

I've never been one to dream about my big day and my perfect man. Sure, I want to find the one, but anything beyond that...I've always been happy for it to be a surprise. But learning that my wedding is going to be taken out of my hands in every single way—including the man I'm to marry—isn't exactly something I'm anticipating.

"It's time, Tatum."

I shake my head.

Why today? Why can't we do this tomorrow?

Because you'll be strong enough to put up a fight.

He knows that I'm at rock bottom, and he's going to use it to his advantage.

His eyes search mine. If he's trying to see just how broken I am, then I fear he isn't going to have to look very hard.

"Let's go home, baby."

A lump crawls up my throat. It's so huge that I don't stand a chance at swallowing it down.

My nose itches as tears burn the back of my eyes.

His grip tightens again in silent support, and I finally manage to rip my eyes away to look out the window and to my building.

"I'll need to get some things," I whisper. Mostly, I need to get Griz. I know Lori will look after her, but there's no way I'll settle long-term without her.

"I'll take care of everything. Come on," he says, wrapping his arm around my waist and tugging me into his body. "Let me look after you, baby."

I take in a shaky breath as I accept my fate and snuggle into him.

His heat warms me from the inside out and damn if it doesn't make everything just that little bit better.

"We're going home, Lewis," he tells the driver, forcing a lone tear to spill from the corner of my eye.

This is it. This is the beginning of a whole new life.

One that I'm not sure I'm ready for.

"Tatum. Baby." King's deep, raspy voice flows through my ears, bringing me back to reality.

I take a second to try to remember where I am.

His arm is still wrapped around me, and I have the steady beat of his heart in my ear.

Sucking in a deep breath, I'm hit with a shot of his manly scent.

"Let me look after you, baby." His words from earlier come back to me and the lump of emotion returns to my throat.

"We're home," he says, lifting his hand from my waist to gently stroke my head.

"I-I'm awake," I rasp.

He doesn't say another word as he helps me from the car and then leads me into his building.

The doorman nods at us before we step into the private elevator.

I might not have been to his place before, but I've spent enough time at Miles's penthouse to have an idea about what I'm walking into.

The air around us crackles with the electricity that I'm becoming used to when we're alone as we ascend through the building.

"I've made a few changes since our agreement," he says, shattering the silence.

"Changes?" I ask, still a little too sleepy to understand.

"New furniture," he clarifies.

"You don't need to do anything special for me. No amount of new furniture is going to make me want to live here with you."

I glance to my right just in time to see his reaction to my comment.

"You can't honestly think just because I agreed to this charade that I'm actually happy about it?"

His shoulders square as the lights on the panel in front of him let me know that we're almost there.

My new home...

"Trust me, Tatum. You've fully expressed your displeasure over all of this."

The second the doors part, I march out as my irritation with this man gives me a second wind.

I've no idea where I'm going, but I figure there will only be so many options. A private elevator to the penthouse doesn't usually lead to a series of over-the-top apartments.

A huge set of walnut double doors with shiny chrome fittings await me.

"Go on," Kingston encourages. "I've already given you permission to access everything."

"Lucky me," I mutter as I grip the handle and watch a little light turn green before the locks disengage and allow me to push the door wide open.

22

KINGSTON

I stand back and just watch as she throws the door open and looks inside my apartment.

Our apartment.

Our home.

My heart thunders in my chest as the enormity of this makes my hands tremble at my sides.

I've never had a woman here for more than one night.

Sure, some have wanted a longer visit, but it's never been in the cards for me. And plus, no one has ever held my interest long enough for me to even consider an extended stay. We have our fun, but once we've both got what we needed, I'm over it.

But watching Tatum walk into the entryway feels entirely different from anyone else who's ever stepped foot in my space.

She moves deeper into the apartment and I'm powerless but to follow her.

Her eyes are everywhere as she slowly moves toward the living room.

She lingers on an abstract painting I bought at an auction in New York a few years ago, but while I sensc her questions, she doesn't speak a word.

She walks into the living room, but despite the changes that have taken place here today, I can't take my eyes off her to look.

She gasps in surprise before walking toward the floor-to-ceiling windows.

I get it. I've hands down got the best view in the city, but honestly, what's outside has nothing on what I'm looking at.

Her black jacket fits her like a second skin. It nips her in at the waist before flaring out to accentuate her hips and ass that's wrapped in a form-fitting pencil skirt. It hits just above her knees, showing off her shapely calves and then her hot-as-hell black shoes.

I make my way back up and focus on the curtain of thick, dark hair that falls around her shoulders.

I love it. The thought of wrapping the length of it around my fist and—

I scrub my chin, wishing I could see her face, her reaction.

"Tatum?" I finally say, unable to stand the silence any longer.

Her shoulders rise as she sucks in a deep breath before spinning around and giving me what I need.

She looks exhausted. Today has taken a toll on her. It's why I needed to get her out of there when I did.

One more glass of champagne and she'd have lost the tight control she had on herself.

I could feel it slipping, and all I could think about doing was getting her somewhere safe, somewhere she could embrace whatever she's feeling.

Grief. Relief. Fear.

I know I'm feeling a little bit of each; I can only imagine the wide range of emotions that are warring inside her right now.

She licks her lips before doing another sweep of the room. I follow her lead and do a double take.

It's my apartment, only it's not how I left it.

I spoke to Melissa, my assistant, last night, asking her to find someone to help me out. My apartment was exactly what it needed to be. A bachelor pad. It suited me. All clean lines and empty surfaces.

I don't spend all that much time here, and when I do, I want it uncluttered and stress-free. But with Tatum moving in imminently, I needed to make some changes.

She's going to be forced to live here with me for a year. The least I can do is try to make it comfortable for her.

I've seen her apartment. Hell, the place gives me nightmares. But it's also told me a lot about how she likes to live her life.

My dark gray couch now has a blanket artfully draped over the back. A pink blanket. There are also a handful of cushions scattered over it.

I shake my head and rub the back of my neck.

Who knew agreeing to an arranged marriage included the addition of fucking cushions to my life?

There's a vase of matching pink roses on the coffee table and when I look up, I find another huge bouquet in the middle of the dining table and more in the kitchen.

"This is—"

"Yeah," I agree, still rubbing the back of my neck. "Welcome home."

"You did this. For me?" she asks, turning to face me.

I shrug one shoulder, somewhere between embarrassed and confused by the changes.

Reaching out, I take her hand before gently pulling her toward the stairs. There are two guest bedrooms on this floor, but I have zero intention of letting her stay in one.

If she's here in my apartment, then she's in my bedroom as well.

"So, this is where all the magic happens," she deadpans as I take in the colossal new bed in the middle of the room. Just like downstairs, it's much softer than its black metal-framed predecessor. The heavy oak is warm and homely, and the new bright white sheets really set it off.

"Tatum," I warn.

"There's really no need to try and cover up the kind of life you live, Kingston. I'm more than aware of how many women have rolled around in that." She jerks her chin toward the bed.

"Is that right?" I mutter, walking around her and pulling my tie free.

"You're a player," she states. "If you're not figuring out how to take over the world at work, then you're fucking your way through fifty percent of the population."

My brows rise.

"Says the virgin."

Amusingly, she has the decency to blush a little. It's cute.

"Never said I was an angel. But I also haven't stood you in front of my bed like I expect you to sleep in it after..." She trails off, deciding against whatever she was going to say next.

I shrug off my jacket before unbuttoning my shirt and dropping it into the laundry.

She's still standing motionless, staring at the bed as I walk up behind her.

She gasps the second I press my body up against her back, and then she shudders as I dip my lips to her ear. Just like she did at her parents' house before we left.

My cock swells, remembering just how needy she was. Her body was screaming at me to take her, to give her the escape from life she so desperately craved while stuck in that situation.

I release a breath, letting it rush over her skin, loving the way she shudders again.

"No one has slept in that bed, baby. Not a single person," I confess, my voice deep with my need to test it out.

"W-what?"

"It's new, Tatum. It's ours."

A laugh of disbelief erupts from her throat.

"You seriously think that—"

I spin her around, cutting off her question.

But while I stare down at her, desperate to see into her eyes, to understand what she's thinking, she keeps her gaze locked on my bare chest.

"Eyes, Tatum," I demand.

She swallows thickly but doesn't do as she's told.

I don't know why I'm surprised.

This is Tatum Warner, after all.

Reaching out, I tuck my fingers under her jaw and force her head up so she has no choice but to look into my eyes.

"Do you always have to be such a brat?" I ask darkly.

One corner of her lip twitches in a smirk.

"I'm not sleeping in your bed, Kingston. I'll wear your ring, take your name, and keep up this farce, but that's where this arrangement ends."

My own smirk grows at her blatant lie.

"I think we both know that's not how this is going to go," I tell her, dipping my head until our noses are almost touching.

Her breath rushes over my face and her blue eyes darken even further.

My grip on her hip tightens and I pin us as close as possible, letting her feel every inch of what she's doing to me.

"You don't need me. You can have any of your harem keep you satisfied over the coming year," she sneers, jealousy dripping from every word.

"But what about you?" I ask, neither confirming nor denying that I'll be doing what she suggests.

"What about me? I've got a perfectly good vibrator that'll do the job when the need hits."

"Wow." I laugh. "You must have been with some really shitty guys if you truly think a vibrator will satisfy you well enough."

Her eyes narrow and her lips press into a thin line.

"I think you've been missing out, baby," I say, dipping lower as if I'm about to prove my point with my actions as well as my words.

Her mouth pops open in preparation, but at the last minute, I release her and step back.

"Come and check out the closet. I have some things in there for you."

I take off, pulling the doors to my closet and giving it a double take.

One side has always been empty. But that is no longer the case.

I haven't bought her much, just a few things I thought she might like or need.

I sense her step up behind me before I see or hear her.

"You're fucking crazy," she says, ducking around me to see the rails and shelves of clothes, shoes, and purses.

"There's lingerie in those drawers, too."

Okay, I lied. I may have gone a little over the top with my personal shopper.

"Kingston." She gasps after pulling the top drawer open to reveal lingerie sets in every color of the rainbow. "I don't need or want any of this stuff."

"And yet it's yours," I state simply as I undo my pants and shamelessly push them over my hips then tug them and my socks off.

"I have every intention of seeing you wrapped in every inch of lace in those drawers in the coming months," I confess as I walk toward my own side and grab a pair of gray sweats. That's the magic ingredient when it comes to women, after all, right?

Her gaze makes my skin burn and I turn back toward her, shamelessly letting her see the goods. I might still be wearing my boxers, but quite honestly, they're doing a pretty shitty job of hiding anything right now.

She takes her time working her way down my chest, and the second her eyes drop to my dick, I swear the electric current that races through me should be powerful enough to take me out.

How did she do that?

There are feet between us. Yet with just her presence and her eyes, she has the ability to affect me more than any other woman I've had the pleasure of spending time with.

"Well, you can keep dreaming about that," she mutters, her eyes still blatantly on my hard cock.

I smirk. The words that are coming out of her mouth are such bullshit. Her body...now that tells the truth. And it's screaming at me that it wants the same thing I do.

Finally, I bend over and pull my sweats up my legs. Putting on clothes isn't in line with the fantasy in my head, but it's the right thing to do.

I want her. I'll make no secret of that.

I'm pretty sure I could have her, too.

But not today. Not while she's suffering and feeling vulnerable.

Well...not unless she begs.

I swear she stops breathing as I step closer to her.

"Get comfortable. You'll find toiletries in the bathroom. Meet me in the kitchen when you're ready."

"What if I'm never ready?" she whispers, staring up at me like I might hold all the answers.

"Then I'll come and find you. You don't need to worry about that."

Leaning forward, I finally give her the kiss I teased her with earlier, although it's nothing like the filthy, desperate type that was filling my mind. Instead, it's a chaste one to the corner of her mouth.

Even still, her lashes flutter closed and she lets out this little whimper that makes my chest tighten and my heart thump harder.

"Relax, Tatum. This is your home now. With me."

I take off without another word, leaving her, no doubt, with her head spinning and her heart pounding.

Fuck. I know mine are.

There is only one thing I know for certain right now.

These next twelve months are either going to be the very best or the very worst of my life. Only time will tell which way it's going to go.

23

TATUM

The sound of Kingston's footsteps fades as he hits the bottom of the stairs, and I finally kick my heels off.

Inhaling a deep breath, I count to five before I release it again in the hope it helps ground me.

Today, I've gone from watching my father get lowered into the ground, to getting tipsy while pretending to grieve, to standing in the closet of my new home with my soon-to-be husband showing off his new lingerie purchases.

I'm not going to lie; it hasn't been anything like I thought it would be.

Saying my final goodbyes to Dad was a headfuck all in itself. Watching Mom crumble and Miles mourn, hurt. It hurt more than the loss did. But even still, I couldn't do anything. It was like I was there in body but not in spirit. Like I was watching everything play out from a distance, not experiencing it firsthand.

It was weird.

Even now having been through it, I still can't get my head around how detached I felt from the entire thing.

It wasn't until Kingston reached for my hand and pulled me closer that I started to really feel anything.

Sure, there was some grief in there. But mostly, it was disappointment and contempt.

All my life, Dad ensured Miles had everything. I might have had the same access to money, the same education, but that was where it ended. Standing there at that grave, that became all too real. Miles now has everything, no questions asked, but in order for me to get any kind of inheritance, I have to jump through a million hoops.

I have to marry someone. Be a wife to a man I never would have chosen for myself just to get the one thing I truly want.

It's not about the money. I couldn't give a crap about that.

I earn my own money, pay my own way, and I'm more than happy to continue that way.

But that cottage...I just can't let my dream go.

I squeeze my eyes closed and immediately see two children and a dog running around the backyard that's filled with beautiful blooms.

My heart aches for it. For the lifestyle, for the peace.

I love Chicago, but it's full-on, and I don't ever see that changing.

Especially not with the new merger.

With a sigh, I take a step back so I can really appreciate the beauty of this closet.

The left-hand side is his. There are rows and rows of tailored suits of every shade. The shelves of shoes are endless, and when I move closer, I find that his collection of designer watches is showcased with a glass top.

I'm no stranger to wealth. I grew up with access to everything my heart desired. But even still, seeing it laid out so blatantly before me makes me do a double take.

I haven't lived like this since I started college. And even before then, I spent most of my time at a boarding school.

Shaking my head, I walk back to my side and begin pulling draws open and checking out what else he's bought me.

I find everything. Literally everything I could possibly need to live here. I wouldn't need to move a thing in.

Maybe that's his plan.

He might be forced to live with me, but maybe my baggage is a step too far for his fancy penthouse...

But then I think of the scatter cushions, blanket, and flowers downstairs. His confession about the bed behind me being new.

Those aren't the actions of a man who isn't fully in this.

With a million and one opposing thoughts spinning around my head, I try to decide what to wear.

My need to shed my depressing black dress and jacket is too much to ignore.

Especially when I pull a drawer open and find tanks and sweats staring back at me.

He literally has thought of everything.

In seconds, my outfit, and thankfully, my bra, has been discarded on the floor and I'm pulling the softest sweats I've ever felt up my legs as I slip the tank over my head.

I feel better immediately.

Leaving the closet behind, I go in search of the bathroom. It's not hard. There is only one other door in this room.

"Wow," I breathe as I step inside. It's impressive.

Everything is white marble with black and chrome accents. The bathtub is big enough for at least six people. I shudder as I think about Kingston hosting a party in it and rip my eyes away.

The shower would easily fit the same number of people with its multiple heads and jets covering the ceiling and walls.

There are impressive double sinks with absolutely nothing on display.

It's exactly how downstairs would have looked before the cushions appeared.

Like a show home.

I get it. This is just a place Kingston comes to get away from work. But just like my father, and now Miles, that isn't all that often.

They don't spend days slobbing around on the couch eating nothing but popcorn and ice cream and binging on movies. That's just not the kind of life they live.

It's why none of them understand my obsession with that little Cotswold cottage.

"Fuck," I breathe when I open one of the hidden cupboards and find all my usual products. "How?" I muse. How could he possibly know what I use? He's been in my bathroom once. There is no way he'd have memorized all my favorite brands and products. It's impossible.

I tie my hair up in a messy bun before reaching for my cleanser. I take my time wiping my makeup from my face, washing today down the drain before putting everything away and heading out.

The moment I open the door, the scent of something hits my nose and my stomach growls.

Led by my hunger, I move toward the stairs, assuming that he's ordered in.

It's not until I'm halfway down that I discover that isn't the case at all.

Over the soft music that is filling the apartment, I hear a familiar sizzle of a pan, and then Kingston's voice as he sings along.

With my curiosity spiked, I creep down the rest of the stairs as silently as I can. I need to catch this rare species unawares.

My hand lifts to cover my mouth when I find him wiggling his ass at the stove as he stirs something in a pan and continues singing.

This is not a version of Kingston I have ever experienced before.

With one hand gripping the rail, I stand there watching him perform and attempt to keep my giggles to myself.

I can totally get on board with this side of the infamous Kingston Callahan.

I don't know what I do, I'm pretty sure I don't make a noise or move, but after a few more seconds, Kingston goes still, his spine straightening and his hips slowing.

Before he can turn around and discover me watching him in his natural environment, I take a step forward.

"Well, well, well, who knew the great Kingston Callahan could cook?" I tease as I move toward the kitchen island and the closest stool to me.

His gaze holds mine for a beat before it drops. I try not to react, I really do. But my body acts on instinct and my shoulders roll back, ensuring my tits stick out a little more.

His eyes widen as they trail down my body, and when he hits my toes, he works his way back up again.

My blood begins to heat and my heart races.

You hussy. All he's done is look at you.

He drags his bottom lip between his teeth before his signature smirk appears.

"There's a lot about me that you don't know, baby." He winks before turning back around and pouring some kind of sauce into his pan.

"It smells amazing," I say, unable to ignore it as I hop up onto the closest stool.

Abandoning the food, he stalks to the other side of the kitchen.

He's still shirtless—risky decision while cooking—and his muscles pull and twist as he moves. Even more so when he reaches into a cupboard for something. What that something is passes me by as I shamelessly indulge in his god-like body.

I startle when he slams a glass down in front of me and fills it with a very healthy measure of scotch.

I look up, my eyes instantly locking on his amused ones.

"See something you like, Tatum?"

"Not really. Can't say I like scotch all that much."

His eyes narrow, but the heat in them doesn't lessen.

"Good thing I wasn't talking about the scotch then, wasn't it? Drink," he says, sliding it closer without giving me a chance to respond.

"But I don't—"

"I said drink," he repeats.

The need to fight burns through me, but then I look into his eyes and it melts away.

I reach for the glass and my breath catches as our fingers collide. Electricity shoots up my arm and our eye contact holds.

The air between us turns thick with sexual tension and I struggle to catch my breath.

The second he pulls his hand away, my entire body runs cold. It's the most bizarre thing.

Without thinking, I lift the glass to my lips and swallow down the contents in one go.

The second it hits my throat, I realize my mistake.

I cough and splutter as the strong alcohol leaves a fiery trail all the way to my stomach.

Kingston watches me suffer with an amused expression on his face.

"Don't give me that look. I told you I don't like it," I snap.

He chuckles before turning back to dinner.

"Trust me, it'll help you relax."

His insinuation irritates me. "I don't need to re—"

He turns around and glares at me.

"What?" I hiss.

"Do you argue with everything I say for fun? Is it some kind of game to you?" he asks, looking genuinely interested in my answer.

"I don't like being told what to do."

"I've noticed," he mutters, setting two plates on the counter before placing a pile of fresh noodles in the center.

"As if you're any better." I scoff.

"I'm the boss. No one tells me what to do," he says, puffing his chest out.

"Right," I mutter as he loads colorful veggies onto the noodles before sliding the stir-fry toward me.

"You're a bit of a health freak," I point out.

He takes the seat beside me before picking up his fork and twisting some noodles around it.

"I'm conscious of what I put into my body. I need it at peak performance at all times." I scoff at that. "That doesn't make me a freak."

He pushes his food into his mouth, his eyes holding mine as he chews.

How is it possible that he even looks hot eating?

Wrong. So freaking wrong.

"Shame you aren't so selective about what bodies you put yourself into," I mutter under my breath as my eyes briefly drop to his crotch.

Jesus, is he still semi-hard down there?

I look away as quickly as I looked, my cheeks heating like I'm a teenager with my first crush.

"You sound a little jealous there, baby."

I scoff. "Hardly. I couldn't care less who you stick your needle dick inside. I'm more concerned about how many unsuspecting women you're infecting."

"Needle dick? Infecting? I'll have you know that—"

"Spare me," I say, spearing a baby corn with my fork and holding it up with a smirk. "I have no interest in discussing details."

Sticking my tongue out, I lick the drop of sauce at the end of the piece of corn.

"Mmm, delicious," I say before sucking it into my mouth.

Out of the corner of my eye, I see his chin drop in shock before I bite it off.

He shakes his head as he chews.

"Maybe I was wrong. The scotch was a bad idea."

"Whoa, wait up. Did you just admit you were wrong?" I ask in astonishment.

"Maybe. I said maybe," he argues.

"Close enough," I mutter as I refill my fork. For all his annoyingness, he actually is a damn good cook. A hell of a lot better than Lori and me, that's for sure.

24

KINGSTON

I shouldn't like having Tatum in my home as much as I seem to.

After dinner, I poured us both a glass of wine and she curled up on the couch while I tidied up. She offered to do it seeing as I did the cooking, but I wouldn't hear of it. She's had a day of it. She deserved to put her feet up.

By the time I joined her, her glass was half empty and she was smiling at something on the TV.

She looks good. Too fucking good.

Her simple white tank shows off her tits to perfection. It's all I can do to keep my eyes away from her cleavage.

The sight of her in sweatpants does something to me as well. It shouldn't. They're not meant to be sexy, but damn...

She hits pause on the series she chose to watch and climbs to her feet.

"Bathroom," she says before stepping between me and the coffee table. Only, she doesn't lift quite high enough so her toes hit the top of my foot and she stumbles.

"Whoa," I say catching her a beat before she crashes into me.

"Sorry, sorry," she mumbles, a bit of a slur to the words.

Glancing at her wine glass, I find that it's empty again. As is the bottle next to it.

Her eyes find mine, and instead of immediately jumping up and running away, she stays where she is. Her eyes search mine, looking for...fuck knows what.

"Tatum?" I whisper, my fingers twitching around her waist.

It would be so easy to lift her and place her on my lap. But I can't.

Not tonight. And not when she's under the influence.

I might be a man who always gets what he wants. But not like that.

I earn everything I get. I don't just take. Ever.

"Bathroom," I say, reminding her of the reason she got up in the first place.

"Mmm," she hums, still staring at me. "You've got really pretty eyes. Did you know that?"

I smile as I wait for the insult that's no doubt about to follow. But it never does.

Instead, she says, "I could look into them for hours."

"Oh yeah?"

"It's funny," she muses, making me raise a brow at her to encourage her to continue. "I always thought they'd lead directly to a black soul."

Ouch.

"Well, I'm sorry to disappoint."

She doesn't say anything for the longest time, and I start to wonder if she's ever going to.

But just as I'm about to set her back on her feet on the other side of mine, she blurts, "You're not what I was expecting."

"No?"

"I mean, you are. You're still an egotistical asshole but...there's more, too."

"Should I take that as a compliment?"

She shrugs. "Take it however you want," she says before wiggling out of my hold and stumbling toward the bathroom.

My eyes don't leave her until she turns the corner and disappears from my sight.

"And yet you're everything I was expecting, and then some," I muse into the silence.

While she's gone, I get up and get us both glasses of water.

She might want to embark on a second bottle of wine, and I'm sure if she were home right now, Lorelei would let her. But I'm not Lorelei.

When she returns, she takes one look at the fresh drinks and rolls her eyes, although she doesn't comment.

She drops back down onto the couch, but she's noticeably closer to me than she was previously.

"You okay?" I ask as she grabs the new blanket from behind us and pulls it over her legs.

"Cold," she says simply before pressing play on her program again.

I've kinda figured out what's going on, but I'm having a hard time focusing on it. Everything is hard—pun intended—with her here in my apartment with me.

It's weirdly comfortable, and I'm not sure how I feel about it.

"Are you going to look at this?" she asks when my cell lights up on the coffee table.

I glance over and smother a moan when I see Mom's name.

She does too and I cringe. She's aware of my strained relationship with my mother but it's not something we've delved into yet, and I'm more than happy with that.

"Nope," I say before silently reaching out and dragging her even closer.

"King." She gasps as I tuck her into my side and wrap my arm around her. But nothing else follows. Instead, she just gets comfortable and continues to watch.

Hours pass as we move silently from one episode to the next. We both get up to use the bathroom, but when we return, we're still close, still touching in some way.

"God, that feels good," Tatum moans as I pick up one of her feet that's resting in my lap and press my thumbs into her arch.

My dick instantly hardens as her moans of pleasure fill the air, and when I glance over at her, I find that I'm not the only one affected by my innocent massage. Her chest is heaving and her nipples are pressing against the fabric of her tank.

"King," she groans, sinking farther into the couch, her eyes still glued to the TV.

Her other foot shifts and grazes my dick, and I swear it nearly fucking goes off from that simple touch alone.

I'm in fucking trouble here.

"Don't stop," she begs, making me realize that I've been too focused on watching her than anything else.

When I still don't move immediately, she turns to look at me. "King, wha—" She swallows whatever she was about to say the second her eyes find mine.

Something electric sparks between us and everything else fades into the background.

Her foot moves again, but this time, I don't think it's a happy accident.

I grit my teeth as I try to talk myself down from pouncing on her like a feral, horny animal.

"Tatum, are you being a brat again?" I warn.

Her lips part, her breath rushing past as she considers my words.

"You wouldn't want me any other way."

She grazes me again, and this time I have to shut my eyes, instantly giving away just how close to the edge I am already.

So much for my fucking reputation.

Dropping one hand, I grip her ankle, stopping her from moving by holding her against my aching length.

"You're asking for something I can't give you, Tatum," I explain quietly.

"From what I'm feeling, I think you can."

I swallow thickly.

"I'm not very good at doing the right thing," I explain.

She laughs. "Don't I fucking know it. I'm only here because you agreed to a very wrong thing."

"Matter of opinion. There might be a lot of things I regret in my life, but something tells me that a year of this, of you, isn't going to be one of them."

Her eyes narrow in confusion, as if what I just said makes no sense.

None of this right now should make any sense, but instead, it all just feels right.

Music fills the room, signaling the end of the episode, and without looking, I reach for the remote and kill the TV.

"Are you taking me to bed, Kingston Callahan?" she purrs like the seductress she is.

There's a reason she has a reputation of her own. One that Miles has been eagerly trying to avoid hearing about for the past few years.

"Y-yeah," I stutter, hating that she can hear the hesitation. "You've had a long day, and a lot of alcohol. You need to sleep it off," I explain, pushing her feet toward the floor in the hope of encouraging her to move.

It's either that or I drag her sweats down, spread her legs and—

"Fuck. Come on. It's time for bed."

Ripping the blanket that's hanging over her waist, I throw it to the other end of the couch and grab her hand, pulling her to her feet.

"Ohh, someone is feeling impatient."

My teeth grind as I climb the stairs, tugging her along behind me.

A smart man would deliver her to one of the guest rooms and close the door behind her. Out of sight, out of mind.

But I'm not feeling very smart right now.

I don't stop until we're in the bathroom and I place her in front of her sink before passing her a toothbrush and toothpaste.

Side by side, we clean up and get ready for bed. The entire time, my dick is more than obviously trying to punch its way out of my clothes.

"I need to shower," I state once I'm done. "Go and get into bed."

She turns to watch me as I turn on the shower and then drop my sweats.

"Do you...do you have a side?" she asks, her eyes jumping between mine and my cock.

"A side?" I ask with a frown.

"Yeah, you know. A side of the bed you prefer to sleep on."

I shake my head, perplexed that she needs to ask.

"What?" she asks, seeing my confusion.

"You sleep on the side closest to the bathroom."

Her brows pinch. "Why?" The fact she's even asking tells me all I need to know about the men of her past.

"Because men always sleep closest to the door."

A smirk kicks up the corner of her lips. "Is that right?"

"Yeah," I confirm, leaving little room for argument. "Now go and get in bed. I won't be long."

Turning my back on her, I shed my boxers before stepping into the water.

She doesn't leave, preferring to watch me wash.

Reaching for my shower gel, I squirt some onto my palm before rubbing it over my body.

My cock bobs before me, desperate for attention. But as hot as it would be to jerk off right here and now with her watching, I refrain.

The second I reach out to turn the water off, she turns and bolts from the room.

I've still got a smirk playing on my lips as I wrap a towel around my waist and march out of the bathroom.

I find her standing at the windows, staring at the sleeping city before us. And she's still there after I've found a clean pair of boxers.

I'd usually sleep naked, but something tells me that might be pushing it too far tonight.

One day...

"Come on, baby. It's time to put an end to this day." I don't mean for it to sound as depressing as it does, and I regret the words instantly.

I pull the sheets back and climb into my side and wait.

She spins around and studies me.

"Tatum?" I ask when she doesn't make a move to join me.

My heart rate picks up at the thought of her refusing to sleep here.

She glances back at the stairs and then at me again.

I've no idea what kind of decision she makes in that moment, but I soon discover that whatever the reason, she makes the right one.

The second she tucks her thumbs into her sweats, I stop breathing, waiting for her to reveal more skin to me.

Sure, I've seen almost all of it before. But changing her when she's passed out drunk and watching her get undressed are two very different things.

Her sweats hit the floor, revealing the tiniest pair of black lace panties I've ever seen.

Fuck. She is not playing fair with those.

She takes a step forward and every muscle in my body pulls tight.

"Turn around," I demand.

"W-what?"

"Slowly, spin around. I want...I want to see."

Her eyes narrow but after a second, she surprises me by doing as she's told for once.

I guess she doesn't need to fight it when she knows that what she's going to reveal would knock me on my ass, if I weren't already on it.

"Fuck," I breathe when I get sight of her ass and that teasing strip of lace that disappears between her cheeks.

My fingers twitch with the need to pull it free and drag the sinful thing down her thighs.

All too soon, she's facing me again and climbing into bed.

She turns her back to me and doesn't say a word about the little show she just put on that has me as hard as nails.

Unwilling to let her fall asleep without her knowing how she affects me, I roll over and spoon her, ensuring my dick is nestled right against her ass.

"King," she moans as I wrap my arm around her waist, giving her little chance of escape.

"I've got you, baby."

She wiggles her ass, tempting me, teasing me, and I press my lips to her shoulder.

"Trouble," I muse.

"I'm not doing anything," she whispers. "It's your dick that's poking me in the ass."

I laugh, unable to deny the facts as I pepper kisses toward her neck.

"So, you're totally unaffected by this?"

"Yep. My body has no interest in yours, Kingston."

"Liar."

Silence fills the room; the only thing that can be heard is our increased breathing.

"Prove it."

25

TATUM

My dare hangs heavy in the air as I wait for how he's going to respond.

My heart thumps in my chest, but it's got nothing on the pounding in my clit.

I want to stay it started at the same time he decided to give me a foot massage, but I'd be lying.

It started way, way before that.

It's wrong. My body shouldn't be as in tune with his as it is.

I should be turned off by him.

I am turned off by him...but also...

As gently as I can, I grind my ass back again.

A filthy groan rumbles deep in his throat and his fingers twitch against my stomach, threatening, teasing.

I know what he's capable of. There isn't a female out there who hasn't happily shared her pleasurable experiences with this man as wide as she can in the hope of fame and fortune.

Unlucky for them, they never got a callback.

And lucky for me...I'm here, hoping to reap the benefits of all his practice.

I should be disgusted by his manwhore ways. I always

chastised Miles for the way he treated women, and Kingston hasn't been any better.

But right now, I don't care about the past, about who we've been with before or how many of them there were.

It's about us.

Just me and him and this burning chemistry between us.

It's been building since we signed that paperwork, and it doesn't seem to be diminishing.

Maybe we need to do this.

Maybe if we give in, it'll put the flames out and we can then focus on what's important. Surviving the next year together.

My brain misfires, forgetting everything I was just thinking about when Kingston exhales, sending a rush of warm breath over my neck and chest before his hand slides downward.

Oh my god.

Heat rushes to my core, the pulsating between my thighs becoming almost unbearable.

I stop breathing. All I can think about is his hand moving lower.

Then it does. Slowly. So fucking slowly.

I don't know if it's because he's testing me, giving me a chance to stop him, or if he's just teasing me.

I'm never going to find out, because I'm not asking him. Now isn't the time for words.

I need actions.

I need them so fucking badly I could cry.

Today has been...a lot.

The alcohol has worked to a point, but I need more. I need a bigger distraction—one that will turn my body to goo and send me off into a blissful sleep.

And then he's there, his fingertips dancing along the edge of my panties.

How I don't moan or beg for him to continue I don't know.

My body burns up and I shift, brushing my ass against his length again.

He's big. I knew that from the gossip. But seeing the way he tented his boxers earlier, feeling his thickness beneath my foot... it's more than I imagined.

He pushes beneath my panties and I bite down on the inside of my lips to stop me from crying out in delight.

"Fuck," he groans, his lips pressed against my shoulder again when he discovers how wet I am. "You need me, don't you, baby?"

I don't respond. I couldn't even if I wanted to.

The way he circles my clit with the perfect pressure, at the perfect speed, I forget words even exist.

Shamelessly, I part my legs, giving him the access he needs to do the job properly.

"Dirty girl," he muses darkly, although he immediately takes advantage of the situation and pushes two fingers inside me.

Finally, a moan spills from my lips.

It's too good. His thumb is on my clit and his fingers are inside me.

My body is strung so tight that all I can do is ride the waves and wait to be washed up on shore, exhausted and satisfied.

"Oh god," I moan, rolling my hips in time with his thrusts.

"That's it. Be a good girl for me and let me feel you coming on my fingers."

Oh shit.

He has a dirty mouth.

Of fucking course he does.

"King," I moan, unable to stop myself. Thankfully, I'm too far gone to care.

Pleasure builds. I feel myself climbing higher and higher. My toes curl against the sheets and lights begin to flash behind my eyes.

I'm vaguely aware of the fact that it shouldn't be this good just from someone's fingers, but it's too late.

One more graze of that magic spot inside me and I go flying off the edge.

I cry out his name again as he curses behind me.

His dick is painfully hard against my ass as he moves with me, but at no point does he get it out.

He finger-fucks me through every second of my release, and it's not until I'm relaxed, my breathing heavy and erratic, that he finally pulls his fingers free.

I watch with wide eyes as he lifts his hand. For a second, I think he's going to demand I clean them, but then he diverts them from my line of sight, over my shoulder.

It doesn't matter that I can't see. I know what he's doing. And it's only confirmed when he moans wantonly.

"So fucking sweet for such a brat," he muses before wrapping his arm around me again and pressing his palm flat against my stomach.

"King, what—"

"Sleep, baby. You need to rest."

He relaxes against me, his head falling to the pillow.

I want to argue. I want to demand he roll over and repay him.

But also...I'm exhausted.

Only seconds after thinking of all the things I could do to him in return, I drift off into a deep, peaceful sleep.

"You have got to be kidding me," I say the next morning when I join Kingston in the kitchen.

He's already dressed and ready for work. I, however, have just rolled out of bed. My hair is a bird's nest on top of my head, my eyes are puffy, and I'm pretty sure I've still got a pillow crease in my cheek.

What I need is one very strong coffee.

And yet, there doesn't seem to be any in sight.

"You actually make this shit?" I snarl as I start rooting through the cupboard for the coffee machine.

Surely, he has one. This is America. A coffee machine is as guaranteed as bacon in the refrigerator.

Oh my god, tell me he has bacon.

I pull the heavy refrigerator door open and study the shelves.

"What are you doing?" he asks, amusement filling his voice.

"Seeing how much of a freak you really are."

He laughs. "It's too late now, anyway."

"Why's that?" I ask, my head still stuck inside.

"You already agreed to marry me."

"Ow," I cry, banging my head on a shelf.

"What exactly are you doing?" he asks, abandoning his blender in favor of getting a closer look at my fridge inspection.

"Looking for bacon."

"Bacon?" he asks, confused.

"Yeah. I need to know if you have any—"

His hand moves over my shoulder and he grabs something from a pile.

"Happy?" he asks, showing me the packet.

I breathe a sigh of relief.

"Now your coffee machine?" I ask hopefully.

"You don't need coffee, Tatum," he states, going back to put the lid on his health drink concoction.

"And this is where we disagree."

"You need vitamins, minerals, potassium, magnesium, antioxi—"

I cut him off. "No, I need caffeine."

"Give me two weeks," he says before turning the blender on and transforming his mixture of random shit into the green goop I know and hate.

"No," I state, placing my hand on my hips and glaring as hard as I can for this early in the morning with no coffee in my system.

"Two weeks, and I promise you'll feel better than you ever have."

I can't lie. Feeling better within myself does sound appealing. But then he removes the jug from the blender, and I change my mind.

He pours the juice into two glasses before passing one over.

Immediately, he lifts his to his lips and takes a big gulp.

I cringe.

How is he not gagging?

Cautiously, I lift it to my nose and sniff.

Yep, same as all the previous days.

"Have you even tried any of the ones I've delivered to you?" he asks, lifting a brow in question.

"Uh..."

"You've got to give it a chance, Tatum." I stare at him, wondering if he's talking about the juice or this whole situation. "Just try it. I promise you, it's not that bad."

I refuse for another few seconds before I reluctantly lift the glass to my lips and take a tentative sip.

I'm fully expecting it to taste like I'm drinking dirty toilet water. But the second it hits my tongue, I discover I'm wrong, and sadly, he's right.

Not that I'm going to tell him that. His ego is already inflated enough.

I pull the glass away and curl my lips in disgust. "It's vile," I lie.

"Well, it's that or water. Your choice."

"Or...I order takeout like a normal person."

He shakes his head before finishing his drink.

"I've got an early meeting," he says, placing the empty glass in the dishwasher. "But Lewis will come back and take you to work."

"That's not necess—" His glare ensures I cut myself off. There are some arguments I might stand a chance of winning. Like hopefully the addition of a coffee machine in his fancy kitchen. But getting myself to work isn't going to be one of them. "Okay, thank you. I start at—"

"Eight-thirty and finish at five. I know, Tatum. I've got meetings all afternoon, but I'm hoping I'll be able to pick you up. Thought we could go out to dinner, celebrate you moving in."

My eyes widen.

"Have I moved in, though? None of my stuff seems to be here."

"You don't need to worry about that. I have it all under control." His cell buzzes on the counter and he snatches it up and pockets it. "I've got to go," he says in a rush, stepping closer and dropping a kiss on my cheek. "Have a good day, baby. Try not to miss me too much."

He's gone before I get a chance to register the kiss or his words, but as the door slams behind him, I find that I'm clutching my cheek like a sap.

"Yeah," I muse. "I'm sure I'll cope."

Despite his words, the first thing I do once I'm alone is have a thorough search for a coffee machine.

It's pointless, though. He really doesn't have one.

What kind of man have I agreed to marry exactly?

26

TATUM

"Oh my god." Lori gasps, a wide smile on her face as I explain all the details of my first night at Kingston's apartment.

We're in our favorite Italian restaurant after a long day at work, catching each other up on everything that happened since she left me behind in the back of the car.

Admittedly, my night was much more exciting than hers, seeing as she watched a movie, refused to open her emails knowing that she was going to have to deal with her boss for taking the day off, and curled up with Griz long before midnight.

"And he didn't demand you return the favor?" she asks, a little too loudly.

The older couple at the next table both turn to look at us.

"Will you keep it down? It's bad enough that the whole world knows we're seeing each other thanks to all the photos circling online."

"You could try to stop looking so cute and into him when you're out in public," she suggests.

"Fuck off," I hiss. "I am not into him."

She raises a brow.

"Oh, that's right, he was more...*into you* last night."

187

I groan. "I knew I shouldn't have told you that."

"Oh no, you so should. It was hot."

Heat unfurls in my lower belly as I think back to how it felt last night to have his fingers on me...in me.

Yeah. It was so fucking hot.

So hot that it's been the only thing I've been able to think about all day.

By the time five o'clock rolled around, I can't lie, I was actually feeling a little bit giddy about seeing him. So when his message came through that he was stuck in a meeting, my heart sank a little.

After giving myself a good hard talking to, for allowing him to get under my skin quite so quickly—pun intended—I called Lori for a distraction.

Thankfully, she'd had a shitty day and was more than happy to indulge in pasta and prosecco.

"It was a one-time thing," I mutter, twirling my fork around in my tagliatelle.

She chuckles, not believing a word of it. "Sure it was."

I drop my fork without eating any and let out a sigh.

"It has to be, Lor. I can't afford to be reckless here. This is a business transaction. Nothing more, nothing less."

"Maybe so, but you can totally have fun while you're at it."

"He's Miles's best friend," I argue.

"So? Miles is a big boy—so I've heard." She winks, and I groan in disgust.

"Never say that again, please," I beg. "And don't even think about—"

"I'm not going there, don't worry. He's too...rich for me."

I shake my head, loving my best friend more than ever.

There have been so many people who have entered my life with one goal in mind, and every single one revolved around our wealth.

But Lori is the exception to the rule. She loves me despite my family's money, and I love her even more because of it.

She isn't friends with me for an easy ride, and she never got close to me so she could be introduced to Miles or any of his friends.

I shudder at the thought of her going after Kingston.

Mine...

I draw in a sharp breath, utterly horrified about where my mind just went.

Kingston Callahan isn't mine, and he never will be. We're just...borrowing each other for a year to get what we want.

Business deal.

Business deal.

Business deal.

If I repeat those two little words enough, surely it'll help remind me?

"He's also now technically my boss, and there is no fucking way I'm going there. As far as I'm concerned, I dodged a bullet by not being allowed to spend my time on the top floor of the building. I don't need to be screwing one."

"But you'll be married to one, so you may as well reap the benefits. Especially when you know they're good."

I'm about to respond, but someone walks up to our table and pulls the spare chair out.

"Sorry I'm late," Kingston says, his voice all deep and sexy.

I stare at him in disbelief as he slips his jacket off and places it on the back of the chair before lowering himself into it.

Not a word is said around our table as he reaches up and releases his tie a little, undoing his top button as if he plans on getting comfortable.

He might still look irritatingly hot, but he's not quite as put together as he was this morning. I get lost for a few seconds, watching as he rolls his sleeves up to his elbows, exposing his strong, corded forearms before my eyes lift to his face.

He didn't shave this morning, so now he's sporting more than just a hint of a five o'clock shadow. His hair is messy, as if he's spent half the day dragging his fingers through it. And his lips—

"What the fuck are you doing?" I finally blurt, forcing myself to stop checking him out.

Our server comes over and places a glass of scotch before him.

"Thank you," he says, immediately reaching for it and bringing the glass to his lips. "Can I please have a glass of red wine with my steak?" he asks, not even bothering to say what red he wants.

The server nods and scurries away to do his bidding.

"I'm sorry," I say, shaking my head. "Who exactly invited you?"

He's about to answer when another thought hits me.

"How did you even know we were here?"

A smirk spreads across his lips.

"You're soon to be my wife, baby. I know everything."

"I'm not sure if that's sweet or borderline stalker," Lori mutters into her glass before swallowing a huge mouthful of prosecco.

Kingston follows her lead and swallows his scotch in one.

"Here you go, sir," the server says, appearing with his wine and pouring a little into his glass so he can approve it.

He swirls it like an asshole before sniffing it.

My eyes collide with Lori's.

'Give me strength,' I mouth, much to her amusement.

"Fantastic as always, thank you," Kingston says, cutting through our silent conversation.

"Your steak will be just a few moments," she assures him before disappearing again.

"Good choice, ladies," he says before taking another sip of his wine. "So what are we talking about?" He looks between the two of us as if he's seriously expecting us to continue like he didn't just interrupt us.

When neither of us responds, instead just staring at him in shock, he figures out his answer.

"Ah, I see," he muses. "Lorelei, did Tatum tell you just how much she enjoyed her first night in our apartment?"

My cheeks burn at the insinuation.

"I hear you have pink scatter cushions and a blanket," Lori

deadpans. "Didn't see you as a blanket kind of man, I've got to say."

"Never judge a book by its cover, Lorelei," he says as his dinner arrives. "Please..." He gestures to our half-eaten meals. "Don't stop on my account."

He picks up his knife and fork and dives in while we continue to stare at each other.

'Sorry,' I mouth to my best friend.

She shakes her head, an amused smile playing on her lips before she focuses back on her food.

We eat in silence for a few minutes before Kingston groans and pulls his cell from his pocket.

"Sorry," he says. "I need to take this."

I want to chastise him, but honestly, what's the point? He's going to do whatever he wants, no matter what I say.

I might like to fight with him, but I'm not sure now is the time or the place. Instead, I choose to glare at him, silently letting him know how irritating I find him.

"Okay, that's fantastic. Yeah. Yeah. No." He smirks, and it spikes my curiosity. "No, she won't be requiring the contents of the top drawer of her nightstand."

My chin drops as realization hits.

"Oh, her passport is in there. Yeah, she'll need that. The Rampant Rabbit can stay, though."

"Kingston," I hiss, fury bubbling up inside me.

"Sorry, hang on a minute," he says before lowering his cell a little and focusing on me. "Are you going to need lube, baby?"

Lori loses the fight with her amusement and barks out a laugh while I pray the floor will open up and swallow me whole.

"You're a fucking asshole. I can't believe I'm stuck with you of all freaking people."

Reaching out, I snatch his cell from his hand, moving faster than he anticipates.

"No, don't pack the lube. Kingston much prefers it when I fuck him dry. Make sure the extra-large strap-on is in the box, though. He loves that bad boy."

Lori loses control over her laughter and all but falls off her chair as I throw Kingston's cell onto the table and jump to my feet.

Without looking back, I march straight into the ladies' bathroom with my chest heaving and fury coursing through my veins.

"Asshole. Fucking asshole," I mutter to myself as I pace back and forth, attempting to calm the fuck down.

All of this...the agreement, moving, becoming a wife...it's all just too much to take.

Shaking my arms out at my sides, I try to talk myself down.

It's fine.

Everything is fine.

You're just marrying him.

A year.

It's nothing.

Twelve little months.

Three hundred and sixty-five days.

It'll fly by.

Before I know it, it'll be this time next year and I'll nearly be free.

I could be planning my new life in England.

I could—

The door crashes back against the wall behind me and I lurch forward in shock.

I should have seen it coming, but I thought Lori would be the one to come and check on me when I didn't return after a couple of minutes.

Who am I kidding; she's probably still laughing.

"You think you're funny?" Kingston growls, stalking toward me like a lion going after its prey.

I shrug. It's a move that I know all too well will piss him off, but I can't stop myself.

He closes the space between us with only a handful of wide strides. I back up, but there is only so far to go before I bump into the wall.

I suck in a sharp breath, but he's so close that the only thing I smell is his aftershave.

And hell, it's mouthwatering.

"You're trying to control my life," I state, my voice high-pitched and irritating. I'm mad, damn it. I can't help it.

"You agreed to this," he counters, his voice calm and unaffected by my outburst, although the pulsating muscle just beneath his jaw tells a very different story.

"I agreed to put up with you for a year. I didn't realize that included you stalking me, inviting yourself to dinner with my friend, and stopping me from having fucking coffee."

I gasp as his hand darts out and he collars me around my throat.

I stare up at him with wide eyes as my pulse pounds against his fingers.

"Just getting to know Lorelei better, baby," he says softly, totally at odds with the dangerously possessive way he holds me. His thumb moves, grazing over my pulse point.

A shiver races down my spine and I can't help but arch against the wall, my body desperate to feel his up against me.

"She's important to you, so she's important to me."

I narrow my eyes.

"Cut the shit, King. This isn't a fucking game. It's my life."

"A life you're trying to make very hard," he warns.

"What the fuck is up with you tonight?" I snap.

"I've had a stressful day. I'm hungry," he adds. "And yet my steak is sitting out there while I'm in here taking care of you."

"I don't need taking care of, Kingston. I can look after myself."

He dips his head, letting his nose brush along the line of my jaw until his lips are at my ear.

"It sure seems like you have enough toys to do so," he muses.

"Fuck you. What I do with my body is absolutely none of your business."

He leans forward, pressing his length against me, pinning me against the unforgiving wall.

"That's where you're wrong," he rasps in my ear a beat before his fingers brush my thigh.

"King." I gasp as they move higher. "No, you can't."

I try pushing his arm away, but he's having none of it.

"Fight all you like, Tatum. It only makes it sweeter."

He pulls back and his blazing green eyes lock on mine.

My breath catches at the uncontrolled inferno I find staring back at me.

"All day," he says, his fingers tucking under my panties, "all I've been able to think about is how tight your pussy is. How sweet it tastes."

"Oh god," I moan as he circles my clit. "King."

"Fuck," he groans, his eyes shuttering as his name echoes around us. "So fucking wet for me."

I shake my head, attempting to argue with his words. It's pointless; he can literally feel the evidence.

As he plunges two fingers inside me, the sound of me sucking him in is unignorable.

My entire body burns red hot as he really starts to work me.

My head falls back against the wall and my eyes close.

"Oh no," he says, slowing his pace and letting my approaching release ebb away. "You watch me as I do this. I want you to know exactly who owns your pleasure right now."

My chest heaves as I fight to hold his eyes.

I could refuse. But where would that get me?

Probably back at the table with a cold dinner and a desperate pussy. Doesn't sound like much fun, if I'm being honest.

"Who owns you, Tatum?" he demands.

Fury shoots through me at his blatant claim of ownership.

I clench my jaw to bite back a seething comment but then he bends his fingers just so and everything melts away.

I'm right there, teetering on the edge of the cliff. I'm ready to dive, to fall headfirst into mind-numbing pleasure.

But he doesn't let me. He holds me right there, torturing the words out of me.

And then the anger comes back full force.

How dare he?

How dare he try to own me and control me like I'm his fucking toy.

"I hate you," I seethe, glaring pure death at him while trying to ignore the fact that tears of fury burn the back of my eyes.

Now is not the time to lose control to this man.

But all he does is smirk, his eyes darkening with desire as he holds my orgasm hostage.

"Tatum," he growls. "Who do you fucking belong to?" He rolls his hips and I moan, feeling his solid length against my hip.

Fuck him.

Fuck him and his cocky smirk and big dick.

His thumb grazes my clit, sending pleasure shooting through me, and I cave.

"You, King. I belong to youuuuu," I cry as he lets me fall.

"Christ." He grunts as I suck his fingers deeper, embracing wave after wave of pleasure.

"Now," he says, his fingers still inside me. "Tell me that any of those toys in your top drawer can give you that."

A cocky smirk appears on his face. He knows how good that was. He knows I can't.

Arrogant jerk.

I was wrong last night. He isn't sweet and thoughtful. It was an act. He is the power-hungry, egotistical asshole I had him pegged as.

This time when I shove his hand away, he lets me.

Pulling his fingers from my body, he instantly lifts them to his lips and licks them clean.

My lower stomach tightens with desire, but I force it down as I march into a cubicle before slamming and locking the door as the sound of his laughter ripples through the air.

27

KINGSTON

I walk out of the ladies' bathroom with a shit-eating grin on my face and my dick trying to rip a hole through my pants and collide with the woman who's been serving our table.

She looks at me, glances at the door I just emerged from, and then back to me again.

"I wasn't paying attention," I say seriously.

Her eyes widen as if her brain has just suddenly jumped into action.

"Uh...yeah, sure," she agrees before practically running for the door that has a staff-only sign on it.

I make use of the facilities, reluctantly washing Tatum's scent off my fingers before returning to the table.

I want to say that my face is all business, but the second Lorelei glances at me, I know I'm not fooling anyone.

"What's that look for?" I ask flatly when she grins up at me with a naughty glint in her eyes.

She knows.

"Oh, nothing."

Her eyes drop to my crotch. I'm sitting at the table; she can't see anything, but it doesn't matter.

She knows how much I'm suffering.

"You really are much more giving than I expected you to be."

"Like I said, never judge a book by its cover."

"Hmm." She studies me as she sips her drink.

My first clue that Tatum is returning is when Lorelei's eyes shift over my shoulder. The second is the shiver of awareness that rips down my spine.

Silence surrounds us as she retakes her seat, reaches for her glass and drains the contents.

"I was going to suggest dessert, but it seems you've already had yours," Lorelei deadpans, making Tatum snort prosecco through her nose.

E xactly as I'd planned, there was a small huddle of press when we finally emerged from the Italian restaurant. Tatum might have thought it was a coincidence, but in my world, there is no such thing. Everything is planned, calculated, and executed exactly the way I want it.

Jonathan Warner wanted our blossoming relationship to be documented as part of this partnership, and that is exactly what's going to happen.

All week, there have been photos floating around of us. Some are totally innocent, others much more intimate, showing us getting closer.

They're perfect for the rush announcement we're going to be making very soon.

The gossip-hungry city is already speculating about where our relationship is going to go. It only seems right to give them what they're demanding.

After taking Lorelei home, Tatum and I make our way to my penthouse. Silence fills the car, and despite her allowing my hand on her thigh, there is no other contact between us. She's barely said a word to me since returning from the bathroom, and I'm struggling to get a read on her.

It's putting me on edge, not knowing what she's thinking, how she's feeling.

I hoped that getting her off might make her relax a little. I could tell she was tense from the first moment I saw her sitting at the table. I knew my presence was going to make it worse, but it was the perfect opportunity.

She's still silent as Lewis pulls the car into the underground garage and opens the door for us.

The second we step into the elevator, the air is charged with chemistry, and it only gets worse the higher we get.

She stands tense beside me; any relief she may have found in that bathroom seems to have been forgotten.

She didn't want to come back here last night, I understood that. But I'd hoped that today might have been a little different. Especially now that all her stuff is here.

She gets to the front door before me and marches inside.

"I wasn't sure where you'd want everything, so I asked the movers to put your boxes in the guest room at the end of the hallway," I explain.

She comes to a stop in the middle of the living room and looks around with a deep frown between her brows.

"Where's Griz?" she asks before turning to me and staring as if I have a fucking clue what she's talking about.

"Griz?" I ask. What the fuck is a Griz?

She sighs, disappointment coming off her in waves.

"Mrs. Grizabella Von Meowington," she says seriously.

I blink, desperately trying not to laugh.

Who the fuck calls any animal a name like that? It's got to be some kind of animal cruelty, I'm sure.

"What?" she snaps. "I'm not living here without my cat."

"I'm not having a cat in my apartment," I state, cringing at the thought of all the cat hair. The litter box...

And of course, there's the small fact that the little fucker hates me.

"But you want me in your apartment," she states, placing her hands on her hips.

"Yeah, you. I didn't sign up to spend the next year of my life getting mauled by Satan."

Her lips thin. "Griz is the sweetest. If you didn't start the dishwasher, she'd have been lovely."

One of my brows lifts.

"She can stay with Lorelei. In a home she knows. She doesn't want to be here." Fucking hell, I'm making excuses for a fucking cat.

Tatum fumes, glaring at me with nothing but hate in her eyes. "But she's my cat."

"And you're going to be my wife," I fire straight back.

Her lips purse and her face heats.

"You're unbelievable," she says, throwing her arms out to her side.

Before I can figure out what to say next, she spins on her heels and storms down the hallway toward the guest rooms.

I wince as the first door she gets to goes flying back into the wall, but when she discovers that it isn't full of boxes, she continues to the next door, and then the next, no doubt leaving a trail of destruction in her wake.

Fucking hell. This is why I've never wanted a relationship, I muse, combing my fingers through my hair as I watch her finally find the right room.

If I thought she'd abused the previous doors then I was very, very wrong, because I swear the force she slams this one with as she closes herself inside has the power to rock the entire building.

"Fucking hell," I mutter to myself as I pull my tie from around my neck and shrug my jacket off, throwing it over one of the kitchen stools before marching toward my drink cabinet.

I pull out a tumbler before filling it with a generous measure of my favorite scotch and taking a sip, hoping that it'll wash away the frustration—and lingering desire—bubbling up inside me.

There are some bangs and crashes from down the hallway. I try to ignore it, but it's harder than I expect.

With a sigh, I grab a wine glass and fill it from a bottle in the fridge before taking it down to her as some kind of peace offering.

She'd better like it, because she can bet her ass I'm not conceding on the cat thing.

Everything goes quiet inside the room the second I knock on the door, but she doesn't respond.

Reaching for the door handle, I press down and push. I was half expecting her to have barricaded herself in, so I'm pleasantly surprised when it opens.

"What the—" I stand in the doorway and just stare.

There is stuff fucking everywhere.

If I didn't know any better, I'd have thought the boxes had exploded.

With her ass in the air, Tatum doesn't so much as pause.

"I brought you a glass of wine," I say hesitantly, lingering on the threshold.

But still, she doesn't react. Instead, more and more clothes are moved from the box she's bent over, flying across the room and landing wherever they fucking want.

"Tatum," I snap.

Nothing.

Fuck. This woman.

She's even more infuriating than I expected her to be.

"Fine. If you're going to be a child about this, I'll drink the alcohol."

She doesn't respond or react.

The second I close the door behind me, I lift the glass to my lips and drain it.

But it's not enough.

How the hell am I meant to survive a year of this?

———

"That's fantastic. Could you put it on the counter right over there, please?" Tatum says, her voice as sweet as sugar.

My brows pinch as I descend the final few steps of the stairs.

200

"You got it, love," a deep voice responds, making my hackles rise.

"What's going on?" I demand, racing into the room and setting my sights on the delivery man that Tatum is smiling at like he's personally delivered her heaven.

I might not look at her, but I know she turns her eyes on me. The electricity in it zaps right down to my cock.

"Thank you so much," Tatum gushes, turning up the charm to piss me off.

The guy is young, and I guess, pretty hot, if you're into that kind of thing.

He has dark tattoos up both his exposed arms and gauges in his ears. Not Tatum's type at all—not that it seems to bother her.

"Let me see you out," she purrs before walking around in front of me to direct the guy to the front door, which I seriously hope hits him on the ass on the way out.

"Tatum," I growl when I finally turn my eyes on her and discover what she's wearing...or not.

Her black booty shorts barely cover her ass, and her tank is—

She shrieks when I reach out and tug her back into my body, locking my arm around her to stop her from following him.

The guy turns, his eyes immediately snagging on Tatum's tits.

"Leave," I growl darkly.

The guy swallows nervously before darting out of the room. Only a second later, the sound of the front door slamming fills the apartment and Tatum begins to fight.

"Get off me, you Neanderthal," she cries, twisting and turning to make me loosen my grip.

Never going to work, baby.

I stalk forward, giving her little choice but to move with me until I pin her hip against the counter in front of her new delivery.

"What is this?" I demand quietly, my lips brushing the shell of her ear.

She didn't emerge from the guest room once last night. I lost count of the number of times I talked myself out of going down there.

I knew it would only end in a fight. Didn't stop me from imagining all the ways I could fuck the anger out of her, though.

My cock swells now just thinking about it. Having her round ass pressed against it sure doesn't help either.

"I've no idea what you're talking about," she breathes, her voice low and raspy.

Fuck, it's hot.

I squeeze my eyes closed, trying not to think about how it might sound while she's on her knees staring up at me, telling me how much she wants to suck my—

"Tatum, what is this?" I ask again, desperately trying to stay on track.

She tries to buck against me, but it's pointless. With a granite counter in front of her and me behind, she's stuck until she gives me what I need.

"A coffee machine," she finally concedes.

"Why is there a coffee machine in my apartment?"

"Our apartment," she counters, being the smartass I know her to be.

"We're not married yet," I warn.

"Then why am I here?"

Because it's where you belong…

"You know why," I hiss, refusing to even consider my previous thought.

"You don't get to control my life or my body, Kingston."

I move my hands from her waist and cup her tits, squeezing in a way that makes her moan in pleasure.

"Is that right, baby?" I whisper in her ear.

"I hate you," she seethes.

I smirk, hating that she can't see my reaction to her barbed words.

"No, you don't. You just hate that I'm not punishing you in the way you want."

"W-what are you—"

I grind my dick against her ass before releasing her and stepping away.

202

"Asshole," she hisses.

I hold my hands out at my sides and smirk.

"What you see is what you get, baby. I hope you enjoy your caffeine hit, but don't enjoy anything else." My eyes drop down her body, lingering on the juncture between her thighs.

"You don't get to tell me what I can and can't do."

"Fine. Defy me. See if you think it's worth it."

Her eyes narrow and her lips purse. All it does is make my smile widen.

Without another word, I grab my briefcase and march toward the front door with her eyes drilling into my departing back.

28

TATUM

My email dings and I reopen the window to see what it is.

It's pretty much how my day has gone. I try to focus on a task but quickly get distracted and flit to something else.

I'm not usually so eager to open my emails, but that ding holds the promise of another distraction.

"What the—"

From: Warner Group HR
Subject: Annual leave request approval.

I click to open the email and scan through the details before picking up my phone.

It rings once before connecting.

"Good afternoon, Warner Group HR department. Gabby speaking. How may I help you?"

"Gabs, it's Tate," I say quickly. Gabby and I are pretty friendly. We've had more than a few nights out. Not so much recently as life has taken us in different directions, but I guess that's how it goes when a single girl finds her man. "I just received an email telling me that my annual leave for tomorrow has been approved."

There's a beat of silence that's suspicious as fuck.

"Y-yeah. It's late notice, but the rest of your team are in tomorrow so I don't see why there would be an issue."

"I didn't book it."

"Oh...umm..."

As she hesitates, my cell buzzes with an incoming message.

> Unknown: Good morning, Tatum Callahan. This is a reminder about your personal stylist appointment tomorrow at 10:00 AM. Your stylist will meet you at the address provided on your booking.

Anger begins to bubble up within me.

"Tate, are you still there?" Gabby asks.

"Uh, yeah," I mutter.

"I'm sorry. I was just doing my job, you know?"

"Yeah," I muse. I might not have heard her confession, but I know exactly who is behind this. I didn't need the surname in the booking confirmation to verify it. "I get it. Could you do me a favor?" I ask, aware that I might be about to ask too much.

"Sure. What is it?"

"If he ever does anything like that again, call me before you do anything about it."

Again, she hesitates. I get it. Kingston Callahan isn't the kind of man you defy lightly. "Y-yeah, sure."

"Thank you, I really appreciate it. I should let you go," I say, preparing to hang up.

As I pull the handset from my ear, Gabby calls my name.

"Yeah?"

"Is everything okay? Kingston was..." Trust her to see beneath the surface. I guess that's one of the reasons she's so good at her job.

"Yeah, Gabs, everything is fine. I've got it under control."

"Okay, good. If you need anything, you know where I am."

"Thank you. Enjoy the rest of your day."

"You too," she says before the line cuts.

I'm about to find Kingston's contact and rip him a new one down the line for trying to control my life yet again when another appointment confirmation comes through. This time for hair and makeup.

"Oh, for the love of God," I mutter, finally locating him and pressing call.

It rings and rings, but he doesn't answer.

"Fuck," I bark, pushing from my chair and storming out of my office.

I've no idea where I'm going or what I'm doing, but I need to move. I can't sit in there fuming at that infuriating man.

I knew I started a war by ordering that coffee machine yesterday, but fuck it. I'm more than ready to fight.

Kingston: Can't talk. In a meeting with K and M.

I stare at his message and then look up at the ceiling.

Could he be...

Without thinking it through, I storm toward the elevators and step inside the second one stops.

Pressing my pass to the security panel, I press the button for the top floor. It's about the only thing my surname grants me in this place. An all-access pass...not exactly the thing dreams are made of.

"Good afternoon, Tate. Is there anything I can help you with?" Judith asks the second I storm toward her.

"Are they here?" I demand.

She stares at me but doesn't dispute my suspicion. I take that as the confirmation I need and march down toward my brother's office.

Our father's office is closer, but something tells me he won't have relocated there yet. He's going to want the home comforts of the office he's made his over the past few years.

"Tate," Judith calls.

"Don't worry, I'll keep you out of this," I call back over my shoulder before coming to a stop outside Miles's corner office.

The door is closed and the glass has been darkened, stopping me from seeing inside.

They're in there, though. I can sense it.

I knock once, just as a courtesy, before swinging the door open and surging inside.

"Tate?" Miles says, jumping from his seat with concern on his face.

I never come up here, so I'm not surprised he assumes something is wrong.

But it's not my brother I focus on. It's the man sitting beside him.

"You," I seethe, pointing right at him. "What the hell are you doing?"

"Right now, I'm in a finance meeting with the CEO and CFO of your company, Tatum. What are *you* doing?"

"Me?" I gasp, turning my finger on myself.

"Yes, you. You're the one who stormed in here looking like you're about to blow."

"Maybe we should take a break," Liam, our CFO suggests, looking totally out of place as I glare at Kingston.

"Not necessary," the asshole says, finally pushing his chair back and standing. He stalks toward me with a blank expression playing on his face. "Tatum is overreacting," he explains.

"Overreacting?" I shriek.

"Oh Jesus," Kian mutters, looking between the two of us with a wince.

"Tatum, can you bottle this and deal with it later?" Miles suggests. "This is kind of important."

"More important than your best friend trying to control my life?"

"I booked you a few appointments. Most women would love a spur-of-the-moment treat. I guess I should have known you wouldn't be one of them."

"What the hell is that meant to mean?" I seethe.

"You're not fucking normal, Tate," Kingston announces to the room.

"Me?" I ask, shocked to my core. "I'm the weird one? Says the man who doesn't even own a coffee machine?"

"She's got a point there, Bro," Kian laughs, earning himself a seething look from his big brother.

"I'm with them. Coffee is life," Miles agrees.

"Can we talk about this later?" Kingston asks, scrubbing his hand down his face. "Maybe after you've calmed down a little?"

"Calmed down?"

"Fucking hell, man. How have you managed to get so much action when you can't even talk to a woman?" Kian teases.

"I'm going to hurt you," Kingston warns.

"Oh, I'd like to see you try."

"Go back to work, Tate," Miles says, attempting to usher me out of his office.

Anger vibrates through me as I keep my eyes locked on Kingston's.

"What? I was doing something nice for you. It's not like you even deserve it."

"The only person who is in the wrong here is you," I spit.

"I'll see you at home later, baby. I'll see what I can do about expelling some of that pent-up anger you're harboring."

"You'll be so lucky," I shout as Miles finally gets me out of the room.

"Seriously, Tate," he hisses. "What the fuck are you doing?"

"I'm not doing anything," I fume. "If you want to accuse anyone of anything then you need to be looking at your best friend. He's an asshole, Miles."

"I'm fully aware of Kingston's qualities."

"Qualities." I scoff.

"Listen," he starts, holding my shoulders as if I'm a little kid again, "I don't fucking like this either. The thought of the two of you..." He shudders. "But the alternative would mean I have to see you lose everything." His eyes search mine, and I see pain and regret swirling around within his depths.

"You decide not to do this, I'll back you all the way, but there is only so much I can do. All this bullshit is tied up with Dad's will."

"I know," I mutter, my anger starting to ebb away.

"We've just got to make the best of it for now. It's not forever."

"Feels like it," I muse.

"Just think of the outcome. That'll be worth it, right?"

As he continues to study me, I can't help but wonder if he's silently begging me to say no and turn my back on all of it.

I can't, though. Even if Aunt Lena's cottage wasn't at the end of this, I'm not the kind of woman who will back down from a challenge.

If I were, I certainly wouldn't be standing here right now.

"Yeah." I sigh, the rest of the anger seeping from my body, allowing exhaustion to take its place.

I didn't get much sleep last night. I was too angry, too confused. Too...I don't even know. Overwhelmed, maybe. And I missed my Griz.

"You should go home, Tate. You look like you could use a few hours to yourself."

"I've got all of tomorrow, thanks to that jerk."

"Well, maybe he was on to something. The last ten days have been stressful for all of us. There's nothing wrong with admitting that and taking some time."

I swallow, trying to force down the lump of emotion that's crawled up my throat.

"Go home, Tate. Relax. We've got a big night tomorrow, and plus, you deserve it. Something tells me that the crazy has only just started."

Nerves begin to flutter in my belly as I think about what tomorrow night might hold.

Callahan Enterprises are sure to steal all the awards on offer; it's how these kinds of galas usually go for them. But I can't help but think that Kingston has an even bigger show planned.

A plan involving me. A very public one to abide by my father's wishes.

I sigh, unable to fight anymore.

"Yeah, okay," I concede.

"Work will still be here next week," he says with a sad smile.

"Everything is going to be okay here, right?" I ask. I don't know the details about the reasons behind our father's demands and sudden decision to merge with Callahan Enterprises, and to be quite honest, I don't want to know. I just...I want Miles to have a future. One that he deserves. One that he's worked his ass off for.

"Yeah, there's nothing to worry about. KC and I have got this," he says with a cocky wink.

"Hmm...that's partly what I'm worried about."

He shakes his head.

"You know, there's a spare office up here now," he says, shooting a look over my shoulder in the direction of Dad's lair.

"Oh yeah, because that would go down so well."

Miles shrugs. "It's where you belong."

"It absolutely is not, but I appreciate the sentiment all the same. You should get back in there."

He nods once. "Call me later, yeah? I'm worried about you."

"No need, big brother. I'm more than capable of handling shit myself."

"I know. That's why I worry."

He kisses me on the cheek before turning back toward his office.

"Everything will work out, Tate," he promises before slipping back into his room.

I sigh and my shoulders sag in defeat as I make my way back toward Judith.

"Oh my goodness," she gushes the second she sees me.

She's out from behind her desk before I can stop her and pulls me in for one of her signature hugs.

The second she squeezes me tight, I finally let go.

"It's okay, sweetie. I've got you," she soothes. "Everything is going to be okay."

29

KINGSTON

By the time I got home last night, Tatum was already asleep.

After seeing the state she'd left my kitchen in—on purpose, of course—I almost woke her, dragged her out there and demanded she cleaned up her shit.

But then I remembered what Miles said to me after she stormed out of our meeting earlier.

"I know it's not in your nature, but be nice to her. She might be putting on a brave face, but she's struggling."

It was those words, and those words only, that made me walk into the guest room and gently sit on the edge of the bed beside her.

It took more restraint than I'm willing to even think about to only reach out and tuck a lock of hair behind her ear.

What I really wanted to do was brush my fingertips over her cheek to find out if her skin was as soft as it looked and then drag the sheets from her body to see what she was wearing beneath.

I know what Miles said was true. I know she needs me to be gentle with her despite how she acts. It's a front, a facade to make it look like she's coping.

She is not coping.

Since the moment Miles said those words to me yesterday, I regretted how I spoke to her in front of Kian and Liam. But I saw red when she accused me of controlling her life. I was trying to do something nice...

I pause before reaching for the door handle.

She's inside and hopefully ready for the night ahead.

Despite my suspicions that she'd turn everyone away, I've had confirmation from each of her appointments that they went smoothly.

That means she should be ready.

I'm late. I hoped I wouldn't be, but my last meeting of the day ran over, so now I'm left with only twenty minutes before we need to leave for the gala.

Rolling my shoulders, I attempt to brace myself for what I'm about to be faced with.

As well as missing her last night, she also didn't emerge from the guest room before I left this morning.

She's giving me the cold shoulder, and I don't fucking like it.

The second I step into my apartment, her sweet scent assaults me. It makes my mouth water.

"Honey, I'm home," I shout, shaking my head as I say those unbelievable words. I never wanted a serious relationship like this. I knew that, ultimately, I'd have to settle down eventually. Callahan Enterprises will need a next generation at some point. But I was nowhere near ready for that shit.

But right now, I can't deny that something feels very, very right about coming home to Tatum, even if there's a very high chance that something unbelievably hard and painful might just come flying toward my head.

I've no idea why the thought of her being so violent brings a smile to my face, but as I walk down the hallway in search of her, I can't fight it.

That is, until I see her standing at the windows, looking out over the city wrapped in a stunning, fitted gold dress.

"Oh shit." I gasp, my eyes tracing the lines of her body, my cock swelling in an instant.

She stills but otherwise doesn't react to my presence.

"You've got fifteen minutes," she says coldly, refusing to face me.

"That's ten more than I need. Turn around," I demand.

She doesn't move.

"Look," I say softly, knowing that I need to be the bigger man here, "I'm sorry, okay? I thought I was doing something nice by arranging today. I knew you didn't want to come, so I thought the least I could do was—"

"Thank you," she says, interrupting my apology. When I look up, my eyes collide with the reflection of hers in the window and my breath catches.

I've no idea what this...this thing is between us, but it's potent, powerful, and it doesn't seem to be diminishing.

"I appreciate what you've done. I just wish you didn't spring it on me like you did. If you'd have just told me instead of blindsiding me with it—"

"You wouldn't have agreed," I point out confidently.

She chuckles. "Probably not, no," she concedes.

"Can you turn around? Please," I ask again.

"Go and get ready, Kingston. You don't want to be late for your big night."

Relenting, I spin on my heel and march toward the stairs.

I know the second she turns to look at me—my skin burns beneath my suit—but I don't turn around.

She wants me to wait, and I will respect that. It'll only be for five minutes, after all.

I strip off my clothes and throw myself into the shower, and in only minutes, I'm out again and pulling my dinner suit on.

Something flutters in my stomach as I march toward the doorway five minutes before Lewis expects us for the journey to the hotel where tonight's event is taking place.

As I descend the stairs, I find her in exactly the same position she was standing in when I left; only this time, when she hears my footsteps, she spins around.

My eyes widen and my chin drops as I take in the true beauty of the woman before me.

Her hair is pinned up in an intricate updo and her makeup is light but flawless, accentuating her large eyes, high cheekbones and full lips. It almost makes her slender neck look longer than I'm sure it is as my eyes drop to the plunging neckline of her dress.

It's...fuck. Sinful.

"Kingston," she teases. "You're drooling."

Without thinking, I lift my hand to my mouth.

She smirks before her laughter fills the room.

"You look amazing, baby," I say, as I drop down the final step and approach her.

As I study her, I almost blurt out my plans for the weekend. She's just chastised me over not telling her what I'm scheming up, but despite knowing that this is the most perfect opportunity, the words refuse to leave my mouth.

"Are you ready?"

Her eyes narrow and she studies me for a beat. If I didn't know better, I'd say she's nervous.

"Y-yeah," she stutters, confirming my suspicion.

She reaches for her purse and tucks it under her arm before turning toward the front door.

"Tonight is just a formality, you know that right? Nothing will be expected of you," I say when I catch up to her.

"I know. I'm just not feeling very...peopley."

"Just a few hours then the only person you have to deal with is me."

"Is that meant to make me feel better?"

I laugh. What else can I do?

With my hand pressed against the small of her back, I guide her into the elevator.

But instead of standing side by side like we have on every other journey up here so far, I turn into her body and back her up against the wall.

"King." She gasps, her hands wrapping around the railing to steady herself.

"Did I already tell you how beautiful you look tonight?" I whisper, letting my lips brush her cheek as I move toward her ear.

"N-no."

"Well, you do. You're easily going to be the most stunning woman in the room tonight."

"You're lying."

Pulling back, I look her dead in the eyes.

"I'm not," I state. "Every single man in that place is going to wish they were me."

"Not as much as the women are going to wish they were me," she counters.

"Is that your way of telling me that you think I look good too?"

She scoffs. "You know you do."

"Maybe I just want to hear you say it," I muse, my eyes dropping to her glossy lips, trying to imagine how they'd feel pressed against mine.

I don't make a move to find out, but I do step closer and press my hips to hers.

Her breath catches at our contact and her pupils dilate.

"King," she warns, her eyes dropping to my lips as if she's having the same thought.

"Yes, baby." I smirk.

"You—" The elevator dings and the doors open behind me. But I don't move. Not until she finishes whatever it is she wants to say. I raise a brow for her to continue. "You've looked worse."

Her lips twitch, threatening a smile, as the air between us crackles loudly.

"I'll see what I can do to improve further," I say before taking a step back, but not before I snag her and tug her with me.

She shrieks as she fights not to stumble in her shoes while keeping up with me.

Lewis is already waiting for us next to a limousine when we emerge in the underground garage. His eyes barely glance in my direction; instead, he focuses on Tatum. I understand why, but that doesn't stop something ugly from unfurling inside me.

"Wow, Tate, you look—"

"Focus on your job, Lewis," I bark, making him blush.

"Yes, sir," he says before pulling the back door open for Tatum to slide inside.

My eyes hold his for a beat, but when he smiles at me, I can't help but return it.

Lewis isn't a threat. Not only is he too old for Tatum—I hope —but he's as trustworthy as they come.

The journey to the event is short and charged with sexual tension. We sit side by side and my hand rests high on her thigh the whole way.

The temptation to put the divider up and turn my full attention on her is almost too much to deny. But there's something that stops me. I tell myself it's that she doesn't want to be ruffled when we emerge in front of a mass of photographers, but deep down, I think it might be the fear of being rejected.

The feeling is alien. I'm pretty sure it's not something I've ever really felt before, and I don't fucking like it.

I have never second-guessed my actions before. If I want something, I fuck the consequences and take it.

But there is something different with Tatum tonight.

Maybe it's just the pressure of our first official public appearance as a couple. Or maybe it has something to do with her silent treatment and the pressure I'm putting on myself.

Or more likely, it has something to do with the impending question I need to ask her.

There is no reason to be apprehensive about it; I already know her answer, but for some weird reason, I want to get it right.

Sure, this whole thing is one big fabrication, but still, she deserves for it to be memorable. We're both going to have a lot of life to live after this bizarre year, and there's a part of me that wants her to remember our time together fondly. I also want her future husband to have a lot to live up to, because I'm nothing if not competitive.

We're only a few minutes out when she turns to me. She doesn't say anything for a few seconds. Instead, she silently studies me with a small frown between her brows.

"Are you okay?" she asks, her eyes bouncing between mine.

"Yeah, why?"

"You seem...nervous?"

I laugh it off. "Nope. Just ready for this night to be over so we can be alone, now that you're talking to me."

"We've got a few hours yet. There's every chance you could fuck it up again," she muses.

"You don't think very highly of me, do you?"

She smiles. "There are plenty of things I know you're good at, Kingston. A serious relationship isn't one of them."

"Says the expert," I mutter. "How many have you been in exactly?" If I didn't already know the answer, then her tight expression would tell me. "Admit it, neither of us knows what we're doing right now."

The car comes to a stop, but we don't look away from each other.

"Never has a truer word been spoken. Are you ready for your big night, hotshot?"

"Always. Ready to show the world that you're my girl?"

"Not even close," she answers honestly.

The door opens beside me and the noise from outside breaks through the tension.

I squeeze her thigh in support before sliding from the seat and stepping out.

Cameras flash around me, but it only gets worse when I lean into the car and help her out.

Our names are called as we move toward the entrance with my arm locked around her waist. We turn this way and that, giving the media—and her late father—exactly what they want.

30

TATUM

It doesn't matter how long I sit here or how many people I talk to, how many condolences on the loss of my father or congratulations on my new relationship with Kingston I receive, my unease over what tonight holds never leaves me.

Every time Kingston moves suddenly, my stomach turns over, thinking that this is the moment he's going to successfully turn all eyes on us—on me.

The welcome drinks go down a little too easy, and long before the meal arrives, I'm feeling a buzz thanks to the minimal food I've eaten all day. I couldn't; I was both still too mad at Kingston and nervous about what the evening was going to hold.

There was a reason he wanted me to look my best, and it's more than just wanting me to make him look good by being on his arm, I'm sure of it.

Miles keeps one eye on me all night, as if he's expecting me to bolt any minute or possibly lose my shit like I did yesterday.

Both Kian and Liam are here, and every time their eyes turn on me, my cheeks heat with embarrassment. I shouldn't have done that yesterday. It was unprofessional of me. But the red haze descended, and I couldn't stop myself.

I want to say that it was a one-time reaction, but Kingston drives me so crazy that I'd probably be lying.

Dessert plates are cleared away, and still, nothing happens as we wait for the award ceremony segment of the night to begin.

Callahan Enterprises will win; they always do. It was one of the things that used to drive Dad crazy being the best friend of the man who owned and ran the most successful hospitality company in America. But the truth is, Callahan Enterprises has always, and will always be bigger than Warner Group. Well, maybe that's no longer true, now they're one and the same.

Warner Group's ethos was always to keep things smaller and more personalized for our clients. Callahan Enterprises has bigger ambitions. It's why they now have resorts on every continent and are growing that number on a weekly basis.

They're bigger than I think they ever expected. But it works for them. And other than nights like these, Dad was always proud of his friend's achievements.

The master of ceremonies starts with the smaller awards. While most of the room falls quiet, our table seems to continue their conversations, as if what is happening on stage right now is below them.

It annoys me that Michael ensures our attention is on him as he tells some bullshit, chauvinistic story. All the while, the woman —Martha—sitting beside him smiles up at him like he's just hung the moon. Clearly, she only cares about the size of his wallet—or something else, gross—or she's just plain stupid, because if Kingston or Miles were telling a story even close to the one he is right now, then I'd have long ago stabbed them with the knife the server forget to collect on his last pass.

I respect Michael as a businessman, every now and then as a father, but right now, as a human being, and a man, he's fallen very short of the mark.

Turning my attention to the stage, I listen as someone gives a thank-you speech. It's not exactly exciting and the man isn't going to win any awards for public speaking any time soon, but he's obviously proud of his achievement and his joy brings a smile to my lips.

"Do you know him?" Kingston whispers in my ear, sending a shiver down my spine.

"Nope. Would rather listen to him than your father right now, though," I whisper back.

"My father and alcohol don't mix very well."

"So I see." It's not the first time I've experienced Michael under the influence, but usually, I have the pleasure of being at a distance.

"As soon as we can get out of here, we will," Kingston promises, making me sit up a little straighter.

"I can't wait," I murmur.

"Here you go," Kian says, appearing beside me with Miles next him, their hands full of drinks.

"Thank you," I say when Kian hands me a new glass of champagne before handing one to his date. She's...exactly the kind of woman that the Callahan brothers usually entertain. She looks good on his arm and is done up to the nines, trying way too hard with nothing of any interest to talk about. Safe to say, the two of us won't be building a friendship anytime soon—not that I suspect I'd get the chance, even if she wanted to. She'll be out of favor come morning, I've no doubt. It's how they roll. New day, new woman.

"Having fun?" Miles asks with a knowing wink.

"Best night of my life," I deadpan.

"Who'd have thought a life with KC would be so thrilling, huh?"

"Hey, I know how to give out thrills," Kingston argues.

"And the less said about that when it involves my sister the better."

"Aw," Kingston muses, nuzzling my neck right in front of my brother. "She loves my thrills, isn't that right, baby?"

Miles's jaw pops with irritation as he watches his best friend manhandle me.

"There isn't enough scotch here tonight for this."

"What?" Kingston laughs. "You started it."

"And on to our last award for the evening," the master of ceremonies says.

Proving that they all are half listening, a hush falls around our table.

"The prestigious Hospitality Industry Leader is..." He goes on to explain just how competitive the award is and how so many of the businesses in attendance tonight deserve it, but the moment he begins noting the successes of the winning business, it's more than obvious who it's going to. Again.

"Once again, I am proud to award this prestigious achievement to..." He pauses for dramatic effect. "Callahan Enterprises."

The room erupts into applause as a spotlight illuminates our table, ensuring every single set of eyes turns our way.

Michael preens in his achievement, but he doesn't get up to accept his award like I'm expecting him to. Instead, it's Kingston who moves.

But he doesn't stand, oh no. He shifts his chair back a little and reaches for me. My heart jumps into my throat.

Oh god, no. Please do not do this now.

My body temperature soars, and I swear a trickle of sweat runs down my spine.

But when he moves again, thankfully, he doesn't drop to one knee or pull out a ring. Instead, he leans in.

My heart skips a beat.

So many times over the past few days I've thought he was going to kiss me. Despite my better judgment, I've been desperate for it.

This was not how I thought it was going to go.

One second he's got his hand wrapped around my neck and is staring into my eyes as if I'm something special, and the next, his lips are on mine.

My entire body locks up in surprise. I stop breathing despite the fact my heart is beating at a million miles a second.

No sooner has it started is it over.

It's a chaste kiss. But that doesn't mean I don't feel it all the way down to my toes.

When I open my eyes, I have to blink twice, because the person I was expecting to see before me isn't there.

The attention of everyone around our table burns into me, but I ignore them in favor of searching for the man who just tilted my entire world on its axis.

I find him striding toward the stage like a man on a mission.

Desire pools below my waist just watching how he confidently moves across the stage and shakes hands with the master of ceremonies.

He hands Kingston the microphone and goosebumps race across my skin in anticipation of hearing his voice filling the entire room.

A weird sense of pride washes through me as he steps up to the podium and prepares to speak.

Before he says a word, he finds me in the crowd.

Our eyes lock and a strong wave of desire floods my system.

Right now, he's in full arrogant businessman mode. He's everything I hate about the world we were born into. But that's the last thing on my mind.

All I can think about is the way his lips felt against mine. How every single one of his touches, innocent or not, makes me burn up inside.

The second his deep voice hits my ears, every single hair on my body lifts and tingles erupt. The reaction is so strong, so visceral, I don't even get a chance to question it.

"Thank you. As always, this award means the world to us. We give our lives to—"

"You're good for him, you know."

Shocked by the words spoken quietly in my ear, I rip my eyes away from Kingston as he continues with what is quite clearly a well-practiced acceptance speech.

I want to watch him, soak up everything that is the confident CEO, but his brother apparently has something important to say.

222

I look into a set of green eyes that are just a shade darker than Kingston's and wait for him to continue.

"I know you might not believe me, but since this..." he says gesturing to me, "started, he's... different."

"More pissed off, you mean?"

Kian laughs. "Well, aside from that. He's lighter. There's a twinkle in his eye that I didn't realize was missing until recently."

"Pretty sure that's just his level of irritation hitting max."

He laughs again. "You could have a point there. But I think it's more than that."

The crowd around us erupts in another round of applause and I look up just in time to see Kingston lift the award and stalk across the stage.

No sooner has he turned to walk down the stairs than he finds me again.

My breath catches, and without thinking, I lift my fingers to my lips, remembering how he felt pressed against them.

Regret sits heavy in my chest that I missed his speech.

Our eye contact holds as he makes his way back to our table, but someone steps in front of him, congratulating him on his win, and severs it.

"See," Kian muses. "I don't think I've ever seen him look at a woman like that."

"Stop," I breathe, unable to believe that this is anything but business.

It's not.

He's said it time and time again.

This is a business deal.

That is all this is to him. A way to ensure that he gets to receive that award, and many, many others, in the coming year.

It's just a business deal...

I'm still repeating those words over and over in my head when Kingston finally rejoins our table and slams the award down, and everyone around me erupts in excitement.

I want to say it's infectious, but I struggle to find my enthusiasm.

"I'm sorry. Excuse me," I say before pushing my chair back, grabbing my clutch and trying to escape.

"Tatum?" Kingston asks, catching my fingers in his before I manage to run.

"I just need to use the bathroom," I lie.

I make the stupid mistake of looking up before I bolt. The sight of the confused frown on his face makes the emotion bubbling up within me so much worse.

"I'm sorry," I say again before rushing away, my gown billowing around my legs as I go like some kind of golden Cinderella.

If only I had a carriage outside, ready to take me away from all of this...

31

KINGSTON

I watch her go with my brows pinched in confusion.

What just happened?

I thought she was happy. I thought we were celebrating. But she looked about two seconds from vomiting right here.

Fuck. I can't keep up with her emotions. They're like a pendulum swinging from side to side but without any rhythm.

A hand lands on my shoulder, startling me.

"What the fuck are you doing? Go after her," Kian says in my ear.

"I-I—"

My eyes snag on Miles. Thankfully, he's too distracted by the woman at his side to notice his sister's sudden departure.

Briefly, I glance at his date.

She's exactly the kind of woman I would usually bring to these kinds of events. She comes from money, is used to being around these kinds of people and events, and is happy to go along with anything provided it helps her climb the social ladder.

Kian's date is the same. Beautiful, sure. But something tells me it's only skin deep.

It's only tonight that I've discovered how fake and unfulfilling that kind of date is.

Sure, it's going to lead to a pleasurable night for both of them. But is that really enough?

That thought gives me whiplash.

Of course it's enough.

That's all I want.

Surface-level pleasure.

Fuck anything deeper. That's not—

My eyes turn toward the now-closed doors that Tatum ran through.

Or is it?

"But what if she doesn't want me to," I argue like a fucking pussy.

"And what if she does?"

His words linger in my mind for a few seconds before I take off in pursuit of my girl.

My girl...

More than a few people try to stop me to catch up and congratulate Callahan Enterprises on our success tonight, but I manage to dodge all of them.

Pushing through the double doors, I look left and then right, trying to decide which way she went.

The bathrooms are left, but the exit is right.

It takes me another second to decide, and I follow my gut.

She was lying to me.

I take off, my wide stride eating up the space between the event and the exit, and the second I storm through the doors and into the night, I discover that I was right.

"Tatum," I shout when her gold gown catches in the hotel lights as she rushes toward where a taxi loiters by the curb.

She doesn't look back or stop, but her steps do falter.

I take off running, refusing to give her a chance to escape. Or get farther, anyway.

She's about to reach for the back door of the car when I get to her. Wrapping my fingers around her upper arm, I manage to drag her back before she makes contact with the handle.

"Tatum," I growl.

"Let go," she says, refusing to look up at me.

"No. I'm not letting you run from me," I argue, pulling her into my body and wrapping my arms around her. "What's going on, baby?" I ask, my voice softening as my heart rate begins to slow.

I want to say it's racing because I chased her, but I fear it might be for another reason.

She keeps her eyes locked on my chest, refusing to connect with me.

Reaching out, I tuck two fingers under her chin and give her little choice but to look up at me.

My breath catches at the emotion glistening in her eyes.

"Tatum?" I whisper, hating the sight of tears barely holding onto her lashes. "What's wrong? What happened?"

She shakes her head, biting down on her bottom lip in an attempt to stop it from trembling.

"I need to leave," she finally says.

"Okay," I agree, trying to force a smile onto my lips. "All you had to do was say so."

She stares up at me, her eyes saying all the things she's refusing to do with words.

She wanted to leave *without* me.

Yeah, not happening.

"Come on. Let's get out of here."

"I can take the—"

"Absolutely not," I growl as I entwine our fingers to stop her from escaping again.

Pulling some notes from my pocket, I push them through the window at the waiting driver before apologizing and taking off toward the valet.

I pull a ticket from my pocket and pass it over, much to Tatum's confusion.

"I had Lewis bring my car."

"Why?"

Turning her into my body, I press my hand to her lower back and pin our hips together.

Desire races to my dick, making it swell against her.

"I thought we could do our own thing tonight."

She nods once before leaning forward and resting her head against my shoulder and wrapping her arms around me.

My heart thumps against my chest as I think about how intimate we look right now.

But instead of checking to see if anyone is taking a photograph, I lower my head and press my lips to her hair.

She shivers against me, goosebumps rising on her skin. Wrapping my arms around her, I attempt to keep her warm while we wait.

It shouldn't be long.

Silent seconds pass as we stand there waiting.

There are so many things going unsaid between us, but I can't find the energy to say any of them because I don't want to ruin this. Whatever this is.

Eventually, a familiar rumble hits my ears and when I look up, I see my Aston Martin moving closer.

"Time to go, baby," I say, reluctantly peeling her from my body and leading her toward the car.

She barely glances at my car, which is a damn shame because she's beautiful. Almost as beautiful as the woman who's about to get into the passenger seat.

It's not until I join her and grip the wheel that she speaks.

"Are you sure you should be driving?"

"I would never put you at any risk, Tatum. You have my word."

No sooner than I deliver that promise do I press my foot on the gas, and she shrieks in shock as we dart forward.

"Put your belt on, baby. I'm about to rock your world."

"In a car this small?" she deadpans, looking back to find there aren't any seats. "I highly doubt it."

I make a mental note to take her out in my Range Rover one day soon before I take a right that will lead us to the freeway and really let her see what my girl can do.

"Oh my god," she gasps. "Are you sure you're not drunk?"

I chuckle. "I'm sure. Now relax. We're going to be driving for a while."

"Why? Where are we going?"

"Will you shout at me if I say that it's a surprise?" I edge.

She shoots me a glare and I grin back at her.

"This is a good one." I hope.

"I'll reserve judgment for now."

"I wouldn't expect anything else," I say as I change lanes to head out of Chicago.

"Get comfortable." I turn the music up.

"Comfortable?" she balks. "Have you seen the size of the underwear I'm wearing right now? There is nothing comfortable about wearing a skin-tight body sock to keep all your wobbly bits in."

"You don't have any wobbly bits."

"You just haven't had a chance to see them yet."

Yet.

"Are you sure about that?" I counter, glancing over and letting my eyes trail down her body.

"Stalker," she mutters lightly.

"I think you secretly like it."

"And I think you're delusional."

Silence falls between us as I drive, but it's not uncomfortable. If anything, it's the complete opposite.

Eventually, though, the question nagging at the back of my mind becomes too much to ignore.

"Why did you run earlier?"

"King." She sighs, sinking lower in the seat and wrapping her arms around herself. "I don't want to talk about it."

"You freaked out," I muse, hoping that if I get close enough to the truth she might just confess.

She grunts, confirming that I'm on the right track.

"Because I kissed you."

She shakes her head.

"You can't tell me that you didn't want it. I can read you, Tatum. I know you did."

"King, that's not—"

"So, what was it?"

"Nothing?"

I chuckle. "Sure. Where were you going to go?" I ask, changing tactics.

"I don't know. I'm not even sure I'd have gone. I just...I needed a moment. Everything got too much. Kian said something and—"

"Motherfucker. Do I need to break his nose?"

She laughs sadly. "No. He didn't mean anything by it."

"What was it?" I edge, doubting that she'll confess.

"He said that I'm good for you. That you're different now that we're...whatever we are."

"Getting married?" I ask.

"Hmm."

I take a turn, letting her hum linger between us while I think about what she's trying to tell me.

We've probably covered another five miles in silence before it hits me.

"You thought I was going to propose," I blurt, mentally patting myself on the back for figuring this woman's mind out.

"N-no, that's—"

"Yes, you did. That's why you looked so horrified when I moved and refused to look at me."

"King," she warns, letting me know that I'm right.

"Did you want me to?"

"NO," she shrieks, sitting up straighter.

"Okay, so why are you upset that I didn't?"

"I don't know, okay? Everything is so fucking confusing right now. I don't know if I'm coming or going or which way is up."

"I get it. Trust me, I do," I assure her.

"Do you? Because from where I'm standing, everything is just rosy in your world. You're growing your empire, winning awards, and not batting an eye about suddenly having to share your life and your home with me. This massive thing has happened and you're just acting like it's another day. Like you're not about to promise yourself to your best friend's sister and pretend to the world that you're madly in love."

"Things could be worse," I confess, amused that she thinks I'm handling this that easily.

"Things seem pretty fucking bleak to me right now."

"Then you're not looking at it the right way," I muse, casting a glance her way. "Right now, you're sitting in the front of my car, looking hot as fuck."

She shifts in the seat, making me wish it were lighter so I could see the blush that blooms on her cheeks.

"You know, you still didn't tell me that I looked good tonight," I tease, remembering our conversation from earlier.

Her attention makes my face heat as I focus on the road ahead.

"I'm pretty sure your ego is already inflated enough. You don't need me making it any bigger."

"But you think I look hot?"

She sighs. "Yes, Kingston. You look hot in a dinner suit."

"Now was that so hard to confess?"

She thinks for a moment, refusing to answer.

"How long are we driving for?"

"Get comfortable," is the only answer I give.

32

TATUM

I awake with a start. My heart is racing, my skin is clammy, and between my legs throbs.

"Oh my god," I whisper as I press my face into the pillow.

There is only one man's face in my mind, and from the way my body is singing, I know exactly what I was dreaming.

Stupid, traitorous body.

We hate him, remember? I silently fume at myself.

I draw in a deep, hopefully calming breath, but the scent that fills my nose isn't familiar.

I sit up quickly and look around. It's dark. So dark I can barely see anything. But it's enough to confirm that I don't know where I am.

Reaching out, I find the other side of the bed empty.

What the fuck is going on?

The last thing I remember was being in Kingston's fancy-ass car.

I vaguely remember my eyes getting heavy as the gentle purr of his engine lulled me to slumber.

Surely, I didn't fall asleep so hard that I have no memory of getting in here?

Oh my god. I lift my hand to discover what I'm wearing.

A t-shirt and...

Fucking hell.

My heart continues to race but for an entirely different reason from when I first woke.

Not willing to sit here in the dark, silently freaking out, I slide my hand toward what I hope is a nightstand and possibly a lamp.

I feel around until I find it, and to my relief, soft light fills the room.

"Oh my god," I breathe. The bedroom is stunning. It's all cream and gold and soft fabrics.

I don't need to catch sight of the branding on the bottle of water next to me to know who this place belongs to.

I shake my head as the soft sound of water fills the room.

A shower.

Swinging my legs off the side of the bed, I go in search of the man who brought me here.

My search takes me to an enormous walk-in before I find a half-open door.

As I close in on him, the sound of the shower gets louder.

It should be enough to stop me, but seeing as he must have carried me out of the car and then stripped me—again—I'm not feeling too worried about overstepping where privacy is concerned.

Pressing my hand to the door, I slowly push it open.

The bathroom is just as stunning as the bedroom with huge white marble tiles and gold accents, but it's not the decoration that captures my attention. That is the god-like man standing under the rainfall shower.

He has his head tipped back, his eyes tightly closed. Every single muscle in his chest and stomach are tense, allowing the torrent of water to rush over the deep lines and ridges. One of his fists is curled tight by his side, exposing the thick veins that run down the length of his forearms but it's where his other hand is that mesmerizes me.

All the air rushes from my lungs as I watch him stroke himself.

Holy shit, he's...impressive.

His hand is pretty big. Every time he's held mine, it's totally engulfed my smaller one. But compared to his dick...

Holy freaking baby Jesus.

No wonder this man is the cockiest motherfucker I've ever met.

Heat surges through my body, the lingering desire from my dirty dream about this very fine man returning in full force.

Reaching out, I grasp the doorframe as my knees threaten to buckle beneath me.

He has no idea I'm here.

I should back away and leave him to his...self-care.

I'm about to do the right thing when he lets out the most erotic moan I've ever heard in my life.

Liquid lust pools between my thighs and my knees become weak all over again.

I'm not a huge porn watcher; I've indulged on occasion, but I mostly find it unfulfilling. But this...this is the most erotic, sexiest thing I've ever had the pleasure of laying my eyes on.

My grip on the doorframe tightens as his pace increases with every second that passes.

He strokes himself almost violently, his muscles pulling even tighter.

Another groan slips free as his release approaches.

My heart pounds and my body temperature is at melting point as I find myself along for the ride with him.

I'm pretty sure it would only take one light touch to my aching clit and I'd go off like a rocket.

Suddenly, his movements falter and I know he's there, finding the ultimate pleasure while he thinks he's alone.

I need to run.

In only seconds he's going to open his eyes and find me standing here like a creep.

But my legs refuse to follow orders. My feet are glued to the floor.

"Tatum," he groans, and fuck, am I glad I stayed put.

My hand lifts and claps over my mouth to keep the loud gasp that wants to break free.

He's thinking about me...

His chest heaves as he rides out every second of his release.

He lets himself go, leaving his still semi-hard dick standing proud of his body.

My mouth waters as I fight to rip my eyes away from it.

"I know you're there," he suddenly says, scaring the everloving shit out of me.

Fuck. Fuck. FUUUUUCK.

I take a hesitant step back, desperately wanting to believe that I imagined him saying those words and that I wasn't just caught shamelessly watching him jerk off in the shower like a creep.

Newsflash, Tatum. You are a massive creep.

Shit.

I take another step back before I risk looking up.

He's looking at me, I know he is. My skin is burning with its attention, but I can't face him.

Embarrassment and desire heat my cheeks as I shift on my feet, conflicted about what to do next.

"Look at me." His demand cracks through the air like a whip, and I'm powerless but to follow orders.

My eyes jump to his and I audibly gasp. I swear I must suck all the air from the room, because it's impossible to breathe again while I'm ensnared in his trap.

"King," I whisper, not knowing if I want to run in the shower and demand he show me what else he's capable of with that body, or spin on my heels and sprint as far and as fast as I can away from him.

His eyes crinkle with amusement; it's the only way I know he's smirking, because I can't look away from his dark green orbs.

"Go back to bed, Tatum."

"W-what?" I breathe.

"Go back to bed. It's the middle of the night and you need to rest."

Rest?

Rest is the very last thing I need right now.

"Do as you're told, baby."

"Why?" I sass. "Will you punish me if I don't?"

His eyes darken dangerously and my stomach knots.

"Don't push me right now, Tatum."

"What if I want to?" I taunt, jutting my chin out in defiance.

His jaw ticks in irritation.

I shriek as he suddenly surges forward.

In a heartbeat, he's standing right in front of me, still gloriously naked, and from the way something brushes my hip, I'd say he's fully hard again.

His fingers grip my jaw. It's not painful, but the threat of it being so is right there.

He lowers his head until his nose almost brushes mine.

"It's late, baby," he says, his voice softer than his actions. "Let's go to bed."

His eyes bounce between mine for a few seconds before he lets me go as quickly as he grabbed me, snatches up my hand and marches toward the bedroom, towing me behind him.

The sheets are still pulled back from when I got up and he pulls me onto the mattress, gets in behind me—still freaking naked—and flips the covers over us.

"Kingston, I—"

His arm snakes around my waist, dragging me back against his hard, and still wet, body.

"Sleep, Tatum."

I fall silent for a moment, too shocked by the turn of events to find any words.

"Where are we?"

"Surprise, remember? You can find out in the morning."

"Why are we here?"

"So you can watch me jerk off in the shower every chance you get," he jokes, letting me see a side of him that not many others do.

"You loved it." I giggle.

His grip on me tightens, the thickness of his cock impossible to ignore as it presses against my ass.

I'm not wearing any panties; it would be so easy for him to...

"Get those thoughts out of your head, Tatum," he orders like the demanding asshole that he is.

"I'm thinking of all the ways I can kill you in your sleep," I lie.

"No, you're not. You're trying to scheme up the best way to ride my dick."

I hmpf, which totally gives away that he's right. But I'm so horny I can barely think straight.

"Sleep, Tatum. It'll be worth it."

Rejection sits heavy in my gut.

"Don't you think I'm hot?" I blurt like a moron.

He chuckles. Fucking chuckles.

The warmth of his breath tickles over my neck and makes my already pebbled nipples press harder against the fabric of the shirt I'm wearing.

"Baby, you already know the answer to that."

"So why aren't you interested in—" I cut myself off as I hear my own words.

What the fuck am I doing?

I'm practically begging the manwhore that is Kingston Callahan to fuck me.

Jesus. Have some fucking self-respect, woman.

"Do you know what? Fuck it. Do whatever you want. I'll just have my own shower tomorrow."

A beat of silence passes.

"Do I get to watch?"

"You're infuriating," I hiss.

"So are you. Maybe we are a match made in heaven after all."

"No, we're a match made in hell," I spit bitterly.

I've no idea what my father was thinking.

Punishment.

And from the way Kingston is punishing me right now, I'd hazard a guess that the two of them were in it together.

What did I ever do for him to hate me so much?

Just because I was born with a vagina, not a dick swinging between my legs, it doesn't make me a lesser person.

I am capable of all the same things that Miles and Kingston are. But no.

My importance has been reduced to nothing but a business transaction.

My only use is to become a fake wife.

I guess I should be thanking my lucky stars that there was no stipulation of popping out little heirs.

Acid burns up my throat at the thought of being forced to reproduce under these conditions.

The emotions I was battling with earlier in the evening come bubbling back up and a single tear slips from my eye, instantly soaking into the pillow.

Maybe Kingston is right. What I really need is to sleep, not to ride his dick.

But the latter would be so much fun...His dick is so pretty, and big, and...

His snore fills the room and I blow out a slow breath as I try to calm the raging emotions swirling within me.

He shifts and his hand slides up, cupping my breast.

There's a part of me that loves it. Being in his arms, protected by him. It's...overwhelming. But there's also a huge part of me that hates it.

It's only been a few days, but I'm getting too used to having him in my life, and I fear that as time goes on, it's only going to get worse.

It's why I never should have signed that contract in my father's office.

I should have thought of myself more. The cottage is just a house, at the end of the day. There will be others.

But I only have one heart...

33

TATUM

The next time I wake, the room is still pretty dark, but it's more than obvious that it's daylight. The bed beside me is cold and empty.

I stare at the crumpled sheets, the only reminder that last night was real and not a part of my filthy imagination.

Desire stirs beneath my waist as I think about him in the shower.

Everything about it was perfect. Like it had been plucked from my dirty mind and played out right in front of me.

I banish thoughts of what happened after. If I dwell on it, I'll only end up pissed off before I've even seen his face for the third day in a row.

I'm tired of fighting. Of being angry at him for...just being himself.

I've always known him to be a self-centered, arrogant jerk, so I should expect the bullshit he's pulled. But it's winding me up more than it ever has.

I need to let it go and just roll with the punches. It would be so much easier. And a lot less stress-inducing.

But it's not going to happen. I spent years following the orders of a powerful man because I didn't have any other choice.

The second I heard that Dad had passed, I vowed to never be under the control of a man again.

It's almost laughable, what happened in the days following that promise.

No. I made the choice.

I could have said no.

I could have walked away from it all...

He's still pulling the strings, a little voice says in my head.

He may no longer be here, but he still has control. He is still getting his way.

With bitterness sitting heavy in my stomach, I throw the covers back and march toward the bathroom. My steps falter the second my eyes land on the shower, and I immediately see Kingston standing there naked, his head tipped back and his cock in his hand.

"Fuck," I breathe, and I attempt to force it from my mind and focus on what I need to do.

I need to forget about how hot that was, about the way I offered myself up to him, only to be rejected.

I refuse to feel less of a woman, of a person, because he apparently isn't interested in what I have to offer.

But he is...there was no mistaking how hard he was before he fell asleep. His body wanted me. His head just clearly wasn't on the same page.

Will I ever be more than Miles's annoying little sister?

I step up to the sink and look at myself in the mirror.

I didn't get a chance to take off my makeup last night, and I look like a trainwreck.

My eyeliner and mascara are smudged around my eyes, making me look even more exhausted than I feel. My hair is a disaster. It's still up with a million bobby pins in it, but it's all lopsided, a bit like I've had the best night of my life...

If fucking only.

I find my toiletries lined up on the counter, and after brushing my teeth, I set about removing the evidence of the night before.

I don't bother changing, so when I step out of the bedroom a while later, I'm still wearing what I assume is one of Kingston's t-shirts.

The second I pull the bedroom door open, sunlight sears my eyes, and my gaze locks on the view from the other side of the building.

Wow.

Through the floor-to-ceiling windows is a lake. The water is still, the sun glittering on the surface. And beyond that, there's nothing but forest.

It's stunning.

Silently, I move closer, utterly enthralled by the peacefulness of the scene.

It's not until I'm halfway there that my skin begins to prickle with awareness.

Ignoring him and the effect he has on my body, I keep moving, desperate to get lost in the serenity of where he's brought me.

"Where are we?" I ask again.

He refused to answer every time I asked yesterday. Maybe things have changed now the sun has risen.

"Kohler."

"Wisconsin?" I ask.

"Do you know of another?"

"Do you need to be such a smartass? You're ruining it," I hiss.

I can practically hear the cutting remark he wants to respond with, but for some reason, he holds it back.

"It's beautiful," I breathe instead, trying to change the subject.

"Yeah," he muses. "The view is pretty fantastic from here, too."

My heart skips a beat, and before I know what I'm doing, I've spun around.

He's sitting in a chair wearing only a pair of gray sweats and a smirk.

It shouldn't be as hot as it is.

His eyes are dark and intense and locked firmly on me.

My stomach flip-flops, and it only gets worse when his gaze drops and he leisurely takes in every inch of my body.

I might be wearing his t-shirt, but the way he's looking at me, I may as well be standing here naked.

"You stripped me last night," I blurt, the words escaping without permission.

"Hmm," he hums, his thumb dragging across his bottom lip as his eyes make their way up to mine.

My breath catches when our gazes collide.

"You were right," he says, confusing me.

"I was?" I ask, my voice annoyingly raspy from just one heated locked stare with him.

Shut that shit down, Tatum. You do not want him.

"Yep. Your panties were fucking massive."

Credit where credit's due, he tries to keep a straight face, he really does. But only a second later, one side of his mouth twitches.

"Yeah, all right. Laugh it up. I wouldn't have been able to wear that dress without them, so—"

"Bullshit. You've got a banging body, Tatum."

His compliment is such a shock, I lose all train of thought for a hot minute.

"One that I didn't give you permission to look at, let alone undress."

"If you're expecting an apology, you're going to be waiting a long fucking time," he confesses before pushing to his feet and moving closer.

The air around us turns thick as my heart rate increases.

"What are we doing here?" I ask, trying to keep a level head as his scent floods my nose.

He gets so close that I have no choice but to tip my head back to keep my eyes on his. It's either that, or I look ahead...right at his bare chest.

I swallow thickly and try to keep the image of him in the shower from my head. Obsessing over that isn't helping anyone.

He reaches out and I gasp as his knuckles brush along my cheek before he tucks a lock of my hair behind my ear.

"I thought you could use a weekend away."

"Why?" I breathe.

He shakes his head, his eyes searching mine.

"You're still thinking about it, aren't you?" he correctly guesses.

"I've no idea what you're talking about."

He smirks. "Of course not. That's why your pupils are dilated, your chest is heaving, and your nipples are hard beneath my shirt."

"Kingston," I whisper, although I'm not convinced it isn't more of a whimper.

"And something tells me that if I—"

"Oh my god," I gasp when his fingers brush against my thigh.

"If I were to explore a little more, I'd find you wet and ready for me."

"Never," I hiss.

"Such a pretty little liar, Tatum," he muses as he traces my lips with his pointer finger.

"I-I'm not," I argue, but I quickly discover he's not going to find out the truth for himself because he suddenly backs away and stalks over to the small but luxurious kitchen.

"I'll get you back for work on Monday morning. But we're spending the weekend here. You're going to kick back, chill out, and rest," he instructs before pulling open the refrigerator and emerging with—

For the love of fucking God.

"I want a coffee," I argue, barely restraining myself from stomping my foot on the floor like a toddler.

He smirks as he pours the homemade juice from the bottle and into a glass—as if that makes it more appealing.

"You can have one. After you have this."

I want to argue, I really fucking do, but I'm scared that if I utter even a word, he'll take the coffee option off the table and leave me without any caffeine hit.

Admitting defeat, I stalk over, wrap my hand around the glass, and bring it to my lips.

Without thinking, I tip it back and swallow it down without coming up for air.

Honestly, it isn't even that bad, but there's no way I'd admit that after the fuss I've made.

The second I've drained the glass, I slam it on the counter before staring him dead in the eye and licking my lips.

"Coffee, please," I say in the sweetest voice I'm capable of while forcing a smile onto my lips.

"Of course, baby," he teases before turning around to the coffee machine, popping a pod in and hitting the start button.

The scent of rich coffee fills the air and my mouth waters.

Now that's how you start the day.

"Hungry?" Kingston asks after delivering my mug of liquid gold.

"Uh...yeah, I guess."

He quirks a brow.

"You need to start taking better care of yourself, Tatum."

"I go to the gym." I scoff. I also eat a lot of chocolate, cake, and drink way too much coffee and alcohol, but he doesn't need to know that.

"Looking after yourself is more than just working out. It's about what you put inside your body."

"If only," I mutter, earning a heated glare from Kingston.

"Are you really bitching at me for doing the right thing?" he asks incredulously.

"We're not discussing this," I snap.

"You started it."

"How very mature of you."

Both of his brows lift this time.

"What are you feeding me? Rabbit food?" I guess.

He shakes his head and turns away from me as I sip my coffee.

To my surprise, he pulls a jug of batter from the fridge and sets it beside a frying pan.

Next comes bacon, then eggs, and mushrooms.

Okay, maybe I can work with this.

The scent of frying bacon fills the air and my mouth waters while my stomach grumbles.

The meal we had at the gala last night was incredible, but the portion sizes were on the small side.

I watch him work in silence, and before long, he slides a plate full of freshly made pancakes, bacon, eggs, and mushrooms toward me.

"Eat up; you're going to need the energy for what I've got planned."

I don't say anything despite the many responses that dance on the tip of my tongue.

He waits for it, but when no words pass my lips, he takes a seat beside me at the island and starts on his breakfast.

The silence isn't uncomfortable, per se. But it's not entirely comfortable either.

We're both on edge, and there's a very heavy sexual tension hanging around us.

But neither of us acknowledge it or make a move to shatter it.

"That was good, thank you," I finally say once my plate is empty.

"You're welcome," he says before taking my hand and pulling me from the stool.

"What are you doing?"

"We're getting ready to go out."

"Go out? I thought we were relaxing."

"We are."

"Going out isn't relaxing in my book."

"Then maybe you should take a page out of mine," he counters before releasing my hand in favor of placing a suitcase on the edge of the bed and unzipping it.

The second he flips the lid open, I discover that it's packed full of my things.

He rummages through before pulling out a pair of cut-off shorts, a long-sleeved Chicago Chiefs t-shirt and a red set of lingerie. A set he chose. And then to top it off...a thick pair of socks.

"Interesting choice," I muse, staring at the items laid out on the bed for me.

"Get dressed," he instructs before turning his back on me and reaching for another case.

He grabs what he needs before shamelessly shoving his sweats from his hips, leaving him standing there gloriously naked. I'm powerless to do anything but gawp.

"The sun will only be up for so many hours, Tatum," he mutters without looking back to confirm that I'm doing nothing but staring.

"You've got a nice ass for a jerk."

"Pretty sure you like more than just my ass," he counters as he pulls a pair of shorts over his boxers and then reaches for a t-shirt.

When he turns around fully dressed, I'm still standing in the shirt I slept in.

Folding his thick arms across his chest, he raises a brow.

"What? You're not watching me dress," I sass.

"You just watched me," he points out.

"I didn't have much choice. You just stripped off."

"You could have looked away," he argues. "Just like you could have walked away last night."

My lips purse.

Why didn't I just walk away? It would have saved a lot of frustration.

Part of me expects him to stay put and force me to change in front of him, but after a few seconds, he concedes and walks toward the door.

"You've got ten minutes."

"But I need to shower," I argue.

"Shower later. We have places to be."

34

KINGSTON

It's fourteen minutes later when the door to the bedroom finally opens and Tatum steps out with a smirk playing on her lips.

Little brat was in there waiting, just to piss me off.

My eyes hold hers for a beat, silently letting her know that I'm aware of her devious plan, before they drop to her bare legs.

Fuck. Those shorts are sinful. The thick fluffy socks should probably be off-putting, but if anything, on her, they only add to the whole look.

"What the hell are those?" she balks, her eyes widening on the pair of shoes in my hand.

"Hiking boots. What do they look like?"

Her eyes narrow in irritation.

"I'm not going hiking, Kingston. You can forget it."

"Why's that? Are you too much of a princess to get a little sweaty in nature?"

Her nostrils flare as she glares at me.

"I thought we were meant to be relaxing. Hiking is not relaxing," she states fiercely.

"Getting out into the wilderness is very relaxing. Cutting off the rest of the world. Breathing in fresh air—"

"My god, you're a tree-hugger hiding in a fancy suit, aren't you?" She laughs.

"There is nothing wrong with enjoying the outdoors. There's more to life than what I can see from my office and penthouse."

"Said like the spoiled billionaire you are." She taunts.

"There is more to me than that," I argue, irritated by her assessment of me. Sure, my life mostly revolves around work. But there are other things in my life I enjoy. Prior to finding myself in this situation with her, I was quite fond of spending as much time as possible entertaining women. That seems to have gone out the window; I may as well find pleasure elsewhere.

Fucking hell, what is this woman doing to me?

I actively chose to go hiking instead of throwing her over my shoulder and taking her back to bed.

It's what she wants. Her body is screaming for it.

So is mine, and it's getting harder and harder—pun intended—to do the right thing.

She's been forced into this. I'm more than aware of that. I'm pretty sure that in a few years, hell, even in a few months, that she's going to regret it, and I don't fucking want that.

I don't want her to look back at our time together and feel regret and loathing. I want it to be different.

I want us, this arrangement, to be different.

Is holding off taking what I want going to help? In the grand scheme of things, probably not.

She might have agreed in Jonathan's office last week. She might have signed on the dotted line and handed herself over to me. But I'd be fooling myself to think she'd had even a second to consider what she was doing.

She was pressured into it. Blackmailed because of her love for that little cottage.

There was a part of me that didn't think she cared enough to go through with it. It's just a house. Bricks and mortar. It's replaceable. Replicable.

I truly thought she'd tell us to shove it and walk out of that office with her head held high. We all know the money wouldn't be enough to sway her. She's better than that. Unlike most of the women I spend time with, she doesn't care about wealth or her place on the social ladder. She doesn't want all the money in the world or the lifestyle that goes with it. She wants to work at a job she deserves because of her determination and talent, not because of her surname. I do not doubt that if she were allowed, she'd be working for any other company than Warner Group right now. But there are some arguments that are just too big to win, and working for a competitor would have been that.

Time has passed now. She's had time to think, to consider her options.

She could still say no. I couldn't blame her if she does.

But until I hear her answer from her own lips, nothing more is going to be happening between us.

I want to know she's fully in this with me before I give any more of myself to her.

Although I fear she's already taken more than I was willing to give.

"If you say so," she mutters.

"What about you, baby? Want to show me that you're not a prissy princess who's scared of getting a little dirty?"

"You're an asshole, you do know that, right?" she snaps as she marches toward me and snatches the boots from my hand.

"I might have been told a time or two." She scowls at me as she drops her ass to the couch and pulls the boots on.

"Let me," I say when she begins battling with the laces.

I drop to one knee in front of her and reach for them.

The air between us turns thick, but I refuse to look up until I have her securely into her boots.

"There," I say after tightening a double knot like a good Boy Scout before I finally lift my eyes to hers.

The second our gazes connect, she gasps.

My heart pounds against my ribs.

Since the first moment Jonathon brought this situation to my attention along with the stipulations he required, thinking about asking her to be mine hasn't been very far from my mind.

It might be fake, but it should still be special.

We're both going to have to remember it for the rest of our lives, so it needs to be something worthy of the memory.

Jonathan wants our union to be public. That's why Tatum expected me to do it last night. I understand her reasoning, I really do. But despite having to follow the rules laid out for us, for once, I don't want to make a spectacle of the whole thing.

People are watching, watching closely, and I want it to look as authentic as possible.

Sure, we've known each other our whole lives, but it's fast. Really fast.

In two weeks, we've gone from never really being seen together to forcing our relationship into the limelight.

The skeptics are going to be all over it. And we can't have that.

Any whiff that this is fake, and it'll be all over.

"Ready?" I ask, barely able to force the word out before I push to my feet.

"I can't wait," Tatum deadpans as I turn my back on her.

"Cell phones stay here. It's just you, me, and the great outdoors today."

"You really do know all the things to say to a girl, huh?"

"Many would think this is romantic," I mutter, more annoyed than I should be that she's not seeing it that way.

"I'm sure many would say anything is romantic just to get the chance to touch your dick."

I watch her walk toward the door and pull it open.

"Obviously, I've got a very nice dick," I say with a cocky grin playing on my lips.

She scoffs. "Your ego can only get you so far, King."

"I know. You'll find out soon."

She shrieks as I slap her ass the second I've caught up to her.

"Jerk," she mutters as I catch her hand and drag her down the path toward the lake.

The beauty of the place is impossible to ignore, and we both fall silent as we take it in.

The soft lapping of the water fills the air along with birdsong and the trees rustling in the wind.

It's so peaceful.

Perfect for this weekend.

"Come on, I've got so much more to show you."

We walk along the path that wraps around the lake. It takes a few minutes, but the roof of another cabin eventually comes into view.

"How many are there?" Tatum asks.

"Ten. All hidden in the trees for total seclusion."

"It's incredible. I didn't know you had a place here," she muses.

"Been keeping tabs on my business deals, baby?" I ask, my chest tightening at the thought of her paying any kind of attention to the things I do.

"Uh...no, not really. Miles often talks about them, though." And then the warmth is gone.

"Right," I mutter as I tug her to the left when the path forks. "Well, this is something of a passion project. I've had my eye on it for a long time, but it doesn't fit into Dad's ideals for acquisitions," I explain like she cares about any of this.

"Why not?" she asks, surprising me.

"There's a five-star retreat close, along with another resort of ours. He thinks the market is too saturated."

"But you disagree," she guesses correctly.

"That, and I don't like people telling me no."

"Oh, really? I'm shocked."

"Funny. So anyway, I need to come up with something epic to prove him wrong."

The side of my face tingles with her attention, and when I look over, I find her studying me with narrowed eyes.

"You want to prove to him that you're capable of taking over, and this is your way to do it."

"He already knows I'm capable, Tatum. He's trained me himself."

"Okay, he might know, but you want him to truly see it, believe it."

I shrug one shoulder.

Praise from our father has never been batted around all that freely over the years. So I guess, yeah, I do want to hear him say that I was right and that I've done a good job here.

It's not going to be for a while, though. While the cabin we're in might be finished to a level that's almost worthy of a Callahan resort, the rest of the place leaves a lot to be desired.

The estate itself is huge. The potential here is even bigger.

I can see it. It's just going to take a fucking massive investment and some serious vision. Thankfully, I have both of those, so I'm confident that I can make it work.

Fuck the haters.

We continue walking in silence after I don't respond to her last statement. I don't think she needs one. She knows.

Minutes tick on as we head toward the main building. The second the roof appears in a break in the trees, excitement stirs within me. And then the building reveals itself.

"Oh wow, that's...huge."

"That's what she said," I deadpan.

"I see what you mean, though. It needs a lot of work."

My grip on her hand tightens as we move closer.

Pulling a key from my pocket, I open one of the side doors, and after placing a hard hat on her head, I tug her deeper into the building.

She listens as I point out different elements of my vision for the luxury health and wellbeing retreat I'm envisioning here.

She listens and even offers up some of her own suggestions here and there. Hearing her talk about my baby lights something up inside me. She gets it in a way most others don't. Even Miles wasn't as excited as she is right now when he visited with me a couple of months ago. Sure, it was much more of a shell than it is now, but as I watch Tatum spin around in a circle, taking in the room that will one day be a restaurant, goosebumps erupt across my skin. She can see what I can. I know it.

We don't leave a room undiscovered, and by the time we walk out, Tatum's eyes are alight with ideas, her excitement palpable.

"What now?" she asks with a smile playing on her lips.

Reaching my arm out, I point to a peak in the distance.

"We're going to see what the view of this place is like from up there."

"Fuck off. That's like...a mountain."

"Sure. It's totally the Mount Everest of Wisconsin," I tease. "Do you think you're man enough to get up there?"

"Man enough? Kingston, I'm a fucking woman. I can do anything a man can do and then some."

Slipping her hand from mine, she takes off down the path with determination coming off her in waves.

I totally agree with her. This beautiful, deviant, hot-headed woman is capable of anything but... "You're going the wrong way," I call with a laugh. "You're heading to the parking lot."

"I knew that," she announces confidently. "I was just checking to see if you did.'

I'm laughing hard as she stomps in front of me and heads in the opposite direction.

"Are you coming, or am I climbing this mountain alone?"

35

TATUM

I'm dying.

I. Am. Fucking. Dying.

My chest is heaving, and my heart is pounding harder than I'm sure it ever has in my life.

I go to the gym. I thought I was pretty fit.

Well...turns out I am not.

Jesus.

Resting my palms on my knees, I look ahead to see how much farther the summit is.

Summit. What a joke.

I might keep calling it a mountain, but honestly, it's barely even a hill.

What the hell is wrong with me?

"We're nearly there," Kingston says with a smirk playing on his lips.

I'm pretty sure it's been a permanent feature on his face since the moment I took off in the wrong direction.

"Go on ahead," I say, waving both him and his stupid cocky smirk away.

"Aw, baby. I wouldn't dare complete this once-in-a-lifetime experience without you."

"I hate you," I seethe, finally standing up straight.

My head spins and I take a step back to steady myself.

"Shit." He gasps, rushing forward to catch me.

Totally unnecessary, but I appreciate the gesture all the same.

When it's just the two of us like this, it's almost possible to forget who he is and what a massive asshole he can be.

Since the moment we left the cabin, he's been sweet, and honest, and maybe even a little vulnerable as he talked about his vision for the vast resort behind us.

I could see it. The way he laid it all out for me in such detail. I could see every one of his clients sitting there sipping on his special green juice as they took some time out from reality to relax and rejuvenate.

Fucking green juice.

I bet I wouldn't be having this issue right now if I were able to have my standard three coffees before leaving the house this morning.

"It's the air," I explain. "There is like, no oxygen up here."

He tries to hide his amusement, he really does. But the second I look at him through my lashes, he bursts out laughing.

"Baby, your old apartment has a higher altitude than this hill."

I shrug, unwilling to comment on what is so obviously a fact.

"Come on," he says turning his back on me.

"What?" I ask, not believing what I'm seeing.

"Jump on. We'll do it together."

"King, you can't carry me. I weight a to—"

"It's either on my back or I throw you over my shoulder," he warns, shooting me a wicked look.

I consider my options for a moment. Piggyback and look at the stunning view, or over his shoulder and stare at his ass. I mean, I've had worse decisions to make in my life, that's for sure.

But he soon makes it for me and lowers down.

"Hop on, baby."

I move on instinct and grab his shoulders before jumping.

"Oh my god." I squeal as he takes off running with me clinging to him for dear life.

I'm pretty sure I was ten the last time someone gave me a piggyback. And that someone was Miles, and he tripped and sent us both flying.

I banged my head so hard, I saw stars for days. Or at least, that's what I told him to make him feel bad.

"You're fucking crazy." I squeal when he doesn't so much as slow down.

"Takes one to know one," he counters as he climbs the final slope toward the edge of the 'mountain.'

"Wow," we both breathe simultaneously as the valley below appears.

Lake Michigan sparkles away in the sun. It looks beyond inviting.

"Do you think it's cold?"

"You're shitting me," he pants, finally putting me back on my feet. "It's spring. It'll be fucking freezing."

"I guess. It looks so calm and—"

"Cold?" he finishes for me.

I laugh. "Yeah, I guess," I muse before shuffling closer.

"What are you doing?" Kingston asks in a panic as his hand wraps around my forearm, stopping me from getting closer to the edge.

"Well, I was considering throwing myself off and seeing how I fare," I deadpan before shaking him off and lowering myself to my ass, my legs dangling over the edge.

"Crazy fucking woman," he mutters before dropping down beside me.

The wind blows around us. It's not cold, but that doesn't stop me from shivering.

Without missing a beat, Kingston wraps his arm around me and tugs me closer.

I nestle into his side as the scent of fresh air, nature and him mingle in my nose.

I like it a lot more than I should.

Neither of us says anything as we stare out at his passion project in the distance. The sun is glinting in the windows on the left-hand side of the building, but the rest is hiding in the shadows. A little like a phoenix rising from the ashes.

"I don't think you need to worry about your father being right. This place is incredible. It's going to be an asset to your portfolio," I say confidently.

His grip on me tightens, but he doesn't say anything for the longest time.

"We'll see what the future holds."

"How very modest of you," I tease.

"Can't always be full of confidence," he muses.

"You mean arrogance," I correct.

"Same thing."

I laugh. "If you say so."

A loud squawk fills the air before a massive bird of some sort flies overhead before diving down into the valley on the hunt for some food.

"This is nice," Kingston muses.

"Yeah," I agree. "It's nice to learn that you're not always an asshole."

A chuckle rumbles in his chest. "Don't tell anyone."

"I wouldn't dare. Imagine the chaos that would ensue if everyone realizes their boss is a sap who loves nature and gave their best friend's little sister a piggyback."

I continue staring out at the view, but I'm achingly aware that Kingston has turned his eyes on me, and not just because the warmth of his breath hits the top of my head. I feel his attention all the way down to the tips of my toes.

Has it always been like this between us?

No. It was always hatred and irritation.

This...this attraction is new.

New and powerful. And fucking terrifying.

"You're not just Miles's little sister, Tate."

My heart skips a beat, hearing him shorten my name. It's stupid really, but I'm only ever Tatum, brat or baby to him. Sure, the latter gives me full-body shudders whenever the word leaves his lips. But hearing him call me Tate, like my friends do? It's a whole new weird level of intimacy between us.

"No?" I whisper, desperate to know what I am if not that. "So what am I?"

He makes a weird noise in the back of his throat like he's catching a word he doesn't want to spill free.

"It changes daily. I couldn't possibly choose one."

Time seems to speed up as we sit here. A few wispy clouds dance across the sky as the air blows gently around us and birds fly overhead.

Our shadows shift and morph as the sun moves closer to the west as the day progresses.

It's calm, relaxing, and comfortable.

It's...everything I didn't know I needed.

The space between here and Chicago is in contrast to the closeness between us right now.

I'm not entirely sure what it means at this moment in time, but we're going to return stronger, ready to face whatever is going to be thrown at us next. It's a weirdly comforting thought.

I've no idea what time it is or how long we've been sitting here when Kingston finally speaks.

"We should probably head back," he says quietly, as if he doesn't actually want to but knows we must before it begins getting dark.

"Yeah," I muse, reluctantly pulling away from his warmth. "Although I don't think I can get up."

He laughs at me as he jumps to his feet and holds his hand out.

I slip mine into it, loving the way tingles shoot down my arm. It's the same every time he touches me, and I'm quietly becoming addicted to it.

He tugs me to my feet but doesn't let go fast enough, and I stumble forward into him.

His arms wrap around me, and he holds me close.

He stares down at me as the air crackles around us.

"King," I whisper.

His eyes bounce between mine and my lips.

Kiss me.

My heart races, my temperature spikes, and my mouth runs dry as I think about how easy it would be to take our innocent kiss from last night to the next level.

The pull to him is too strong and I stretch up, lifting onto my toes, but right before I get to do anything, he releases me.

"The sun is going to start setting soon," he says before capturing my hand and turning to walk back down the hill.

Disappointment sits heavy on my chest as I trail behind him.

Being rejected for a second time in twenty-four hours stings badly, I won't lie. But I know it's for the best.

If we act on the attraction building between us, then I've no idea where it's going to leave us.

Business deal.

Business deal.

Business deal.

The sun is setting by the time we get back to our cabin, casting the air around us in a beautiful pink-orange hue. The second I see it in the distance, I begin hobbling faster, tears of relief burning the backs of my eyes.

The temperature has dropped significantly, and my skin is covered in goosebumps.

"Wait there," Kingston demands after pulling his boots off and marching into the bedroom.

"Sure thing, boss," I mutter, saluting him behind his back, swallowing my threatening emotions finally being back causes.

"Don't think I can't hear your sass," he shouts back.

"I'd be disappointed if you couldn't," I counter before limping to the kitchen to find some alcohol and something to eat.

I want a shot of vodka, a packet of chips, a chocolate bar...some kind of naughty snack after all the miles we've done, but I come up short-handed.

I don't want a fucking carrot stick. Jesus. This man is certifiable.

Settling for a bottle of water and an apple, I defy orders and go in search of him.

No sooner have I stepped into the bedroom does the scent of something floral hit my nose. The sound of running water fills my ears, but it's not the same as the shower last night.

I come to a stop in the doorway and stare at him as he stands in front of the massive bathtub, watching it fill with fluffy white bubbles.

"I've always seen you as more of a shower man, if I'm honest," I tease.

His shoulders tense, the fabric pulling tighter across them. "Do you ever do as you're told?" he asks without turning around to look at me.

"Nope. Where's the fun in that?"

He shakes his head before wrapping his hand around the back of his neck and rubbing his muscles.

I take a step forward, the pull I feel toward him too powerful to stop me.

Suddenly, he spins around and his gaze locks on mine.

"It's for you. Relax," he says before slipping around me and moving toward the door.

"W-what about you?" I stutter, hating how disappointed I am that he's not going to get in with me.

"Don't worry about me," he says as he grabs the door handle to close it behind him.

"But what if I do?" I ask.

But I'm too late.

He's already gone.

36

KINGSTON

nock. Knock. Knock.

"Yeah?" Her voice floats through the air and fuck if my dick doesn't react.

I've been rocking a semi all fucking day. There aren't enough unsexy thoughts in the world capable of sinking it.

It doesn't matter how many times I tell myself that I need to wait, that I need to hear her answer; my body craves her in a way I was not expecting.

She's always been hot, sure. But this attraction, this chemistry between us is off the charts. I'm at the point of needing her more than my next breath. It's all I can think about.

"Can I come in?"

"If you're asking if I'm naked, then yes, I very much am," she counters, making me smirk.

"Good. That's what I was hoping for," I say as I push the door open and march in.

Sadly, she's totally covered in bubbles, but that doesn't mean she doesn't look hot as fuck. Her cheeks are pink from the heat of the water and her hair is up in a messy bun, but she's got sweaty strands sticking to the side of her face and neck. Just like she would after an hour or two rolling around in my bed...

"You're staring," she points out, barely able to contain her smile.

I shrug one shoulder. "Want to return the favor?" I ask before reaching behind me and pulling my t-shirt from my body.

"Wh-wh—" She swallows her words as I turn around and tuck my thumbs into my shorts and boxers.

My skin prickles with her attention as I step into the shower and turn it on. I get blasted with ice-cold water, but it does very little to deal with my boner.

There's only one thing that's going to get rid of that...

Reaching for my shower gel, I make quick work of washing up, ensuring I keep my back to her at all times.

I might be up for giving her a thrill again, but I've got to keep some things secret. Like how much I want her...

As soon as I'm done, I reach for a towel and wrap it around my waist. One look down and I know that I'm not going to hide anything when I do turn around.

I mean, I could walk out of the room like a crab to try and hide it, or I could just—

The second I face her, her eyes drop to my wet chest and then lower.

Her chin drops and her tongue sneaks out, licking across her bottom lip.

Fuck. That does not help.

"I've ordered dinner. It'll be an hour," I inform her, ignoring the elephant in the room. "I'm going to leave something on the bed for you to wear." I pause. "Please, wear it. And do your hair and makeup."

"But we're staying in." She frowns.

I smile at her. "Staying in is the new going out, baby," I explain.

She raises a brow, but the soft smile playing on her lips lets me know that I've got her.

"Be a good girl, Tate," I say, remembering how her entire expression softened when I used her nickname earlier. "And I might make it worth your while."

I move toward the door before she gets a chance to respond.

"You've said that before, and I don't remember it being anywhere near worth it."

"Well, maybe tonight will be your lucky night." And mine.

I close the door softly behind me before getting dressed and leaving my outfit of choice for her laid out on the bed as promised.

Honestly, I'm not expecting to see her wearing it when she walks out of the bedroom in the near future. It's why I place two other options in the closet and then take her suitcase with me into the living area to ensure the only way she can truly defy me is to come out naked—and I can say for sure that I would not be complaining about that.

I might have been the one to plan this night, but even still, I'm surprised by it when I emerge from the bedroom and look around.

I shake my head in disbelief. How did my life go from a new woman every night of the week to having only one in my head, only one that my body is interested in?

Okay, yeah, part of tonight is about getting her into bed, but I don't need to be going to these levels. She's offered herself up to me more than once now. I'm the one that's holding back.

I've no idea when hell froze over, but apparently, it has, because I'm standing here surrounded by more romance than I knew existed just because I want to make her smile. Because I want her to look at me and see more than her brother's annoying friend, the man she has to marry.

I want her to see me for me. Not KC, the player. Not Mr, Callahan, the businessman. I want her to see Kingston, the man who can't stop thinking about her, the man who wants to make this year we have together as enjoyable and as easy as possible.

Hell, who am I kidding? I want her to see that and so much more. Just like I do when I look at her.

"Are you happy, sir?" the young woman who has assisted me with this asks.

"Yeah, it looks incredible," I say.

"The food is in the oven. It'll be ready in about forty minutes."

"Thank you."

"I hope you have a wonderful night."

She fusses with a few final things before she bids me farewell and disappears.

Nerves flutter in my stomach as I look around the room and then focus on the bedroom door.

Tatum is...bewildering. Sometimes I can predict exactly how she'll react to things; other times, I get it very, very wrong. Last night was a case in point.

I never in a million years would have thought she'd run because I didn't propose and she didn't know how to feel about it.

I also didn't expect her to fall into my arms and shatter while allowing me to hold her together.

After a few minutes, there is noise on the other side of the cabin, letting me know that Tatum is out of the bath.

It only makes the flutters in my stomach worse.

I've never doubted myself and my decisions before, but there is something about Tatum that makes me feel like a teenage boy who has no idea how to talk to a girl again.

I waste the next forty minutes pacing back and forth through the cabin as our dinner bakes in the oven. It smells incredible, and my stomach growls loudly every few minutes.

I stare at the clock on the wall, watching every minute pass slowly and painfully.

She's going to torture me by making me wait again, I've no doubt.

Fuck. This was a stupid idea.

Lifting my hand, I comb my fingers through my hair, dragging it back until it hurts in the hope that a little bit of pain will sort my head out.

Standing at the floor-to-ceiling windows that showcase Lake Michigan, I focus on the stars that are reflecting in the inky, dark water.

My breath catches when a door behind me opens. I glance at the clock to see that she's early.

Little minx is teasing me.

"Oh my god, Kingston." She gasps, taking in what I've done.

Drawing in a slow, calming breath, I close my eyes for a beat before turning around.

Oh my god, indeed.

"Tatum," I whisper, my eyes darting around her, not knowing what to focus on first.

The black, figure-hugging dress with thin straps and a square neckline I left out for her is as perfect as I imagined.

No, that's bullshit. It's better.

How that is possible, I have no idea. But it is.

She takes a step toward me, her hips swaying, her small fists clenching beside them as if she's just as nervous as I am.

"You look incredible. That dress—"

"It's beautiful. Thank you. This place...how did you—"

"I had a little help. The bath was a distraction," I confess, feeling my cheeks heat as I glance around at the vases of roses, the flickering candles and the fairy lights that are strung up everywhere.

"It's incredible. You did this for me?" she asks in disbelief, her eyes getting a little glassy.

"Nah," I say, making her rear back. "This is just how I like to spend my Saturday nights."

She raises a brow.

"It's usually me in the bubble bath, though."

She shakes her head, smiling at me like I'm the biggest idiot she's ever met.

"You take bubble baths?" she asks, placing her hand on her waist and popping her hip.

"No. I haven't been in a bathtub since I was about eight."

"We're going to have to fix that," she muses, moving closer again. "So," says, glancing between me and the decorations around us. "What's this all about?"

"A date."

"A date?"

"Dinner is nearly ready. Staying in is the new going out, remember?"

Reaching out, I twist my fingers through hers and tug her forward, closing the final few inches between us.

Her soft curves press against the hard planes of my body. My fingers grip her hip, pulling her in tight enough to me that she can't possibly miss the thickness of my dick against her stomach.

"I remember," she whispers, gazing up at me.

Her red lips call to me.

"If I didn't know any better, I'd say you were trying to seduce me, Mr. Callahan."

I chuckle. It's breathy and full of desperation.

"I'm not sure any trying is necessary," I confess.

She gasps at the insinuation.

"I'll have you know that I'm—"

I lean in, letting my lips graze her cheek before getting to her ear.

"Soaking fucking wet for me," I whisper, loving the way she shudders against me.

"For you? Never."

"Such a pretty little liar," I muse before dropping my lips to the sweet spot beneath her ear.

"Oh my god," she moans as I gently suck on the sweet patch of skin. She sags against me, letting me know that my previous words are more than true.

I lick her skin, tasting her before forcing myself to step back.

"Would you like a drink?"

It takes her a moment to respond, and I can't stop the cocky smirk that spreads across her lips as she watches me stalk toward the kitchen for two glasses of champagne.

She's going to say yes.

She has to say yes. We can't go another night without doing something about this tension between us. It's at its boiling point, and I can't wait to discover just how explosive it is when we finally let it bubble over.

She lets out a little shriek when I pop the cork on the bottle of fizz. I pour us both a glass before walking back over to her and handing her one.

"Are we celebrating?" she asks, studying the bubbles before glancing back up at me.

"Us."

"King, there is no—"

"To our future. Our union."

"Do you celebrate all your business deals like this?" she asks, her eyes bouncing between mine, silently begging for me to tell her no.

"I've never had a business deal quite this important before. I'm flying by the seat of my pants right now."

"Well, I can assure you, you're doing a fantastic job."

My chest puffs out at her praise. Never before have I cared about a woman's opinion of me outside of my skills in the bedroom. But suddenly, I want Tatum to think that everything I touch turns to gold, that I'm so much more than I truly am.

37

TATUM

Kingston is nervous.

I was suspicious of him the second I stepped out of the bedroom and saw the set of his shoulders as he stared out of the window, the way his entire body flinched when I first spoke. But the second he turned around and I saw the slight frown on his brow and the unease in his eyes, I knew.

It made my stomach bottom out.

If a man as powerful and sure of himself as Kingston Callahan is nervous, what the hell does that mean for me?

I take a sip of my drink, the bubbles exploding against my tongue before the cool champagne slides down my throat.

It's good. Really good.

Not that I'm surprised. This is Kingston I'm standing in front of. He wouldn't have anything but the best.

"Come on," he says, sliding his hand into mine and pulling me toward the door that leads to our deck.

Fairy lights are strung up everywhere, illuminating our little slice of heaven along with flickering candles.

It's incredible. Way more than I would have thought he was capable of in the romance department.

He leads me over to the table. It's set for two, and after placing the bottle of champagne in the ice bucket, he pulls out my chair for me.

"Who knew you could be such a gentleman," I tease as I take a seat.

"I have plenty of talents that you've yet to discover, Tatum," he says in a deep, rumbling voice that makes tingles shoot around my body.

I'm strung as tightly as a fucking bow.

Lying in that bath, the temptation to deal with the situation myself was strong, especially when he decided to gate-crash and give me a little show.

Fuck. That was hot.

Not as hot as last night, though. That was next level.

"I hope you're hungry," he says before abandoning his glass and heading back inside.

As soon as he appears in my vision through the window, my eyes lock on him and I watch as he pulls something from the oven.

He's dressed in dark gray dress pants that hug his ass and thick thighs in the most delicious way, and a simple white button-down that's undone one too many buttons to be professional with his sleeves rolled up to his elbows.

His hair is messy, like he ran his fingers through it after his shower and hasn't bothered touching it again since, and he's got the perfect amount of stubble on his chin.

I bet it would feel incredible between my thighs...

I shake my head, trying to force it out of the gutter.

It's getting harder and harder to do the more time I spend with him.

He turns around to place the baking tray on the side, and he looks up before I have a chance to avert my gaze.

My breath catches as chemistry crackles between us.

His lips twitch as he discovers I'm watching him before they pull into the most incredible smile.

This is the real Kingston Callahan. The one not many other people get to see.

He makes quick work of dishing up our dinner before striding back toward me.

"Wow, that looks amazing," I say when he lowers a chicken dish before me. "And it smells—"

"Not as good as you," he says, cutting me off as he takes his seat opposite me. "See, being stuck with me isn't so bad, is it?"

"The night is still young, Kingston," I tease as I lift my knife and fork, cutting into my chicken to find a creamy sauce inside.

He barely moves an inch as I lift the fork to my lips.

His eyes drop to my mouth and he watches, enthralled as I take the piece of chicken and chew.

Oh my god.

I'm pretty sure my eyes roll back, it's so good.

"Fuck," he breathes, shifting a little in his seat.

I lick my lips, making the most of having his heated stare on me.

"Eat," I say. "It's so good."

His eyes jump between mine and my lips before he mimics my move, sweeping his tongue across his bottom lip before murmuring, "What's on my plate isn't what I'm craving."

How I don't drop my knife and fork on the table, lie back, and offer myself up for his dinner, I don't know.

"Do those lines actually work for you?" I ask innocently.

"They sure do. And they're working like a charm right now."

"Pfft. So full of yourself."

"I'd rather fill you."

"King," I warn, trying to discreetly rub my thighs together under the table.

His eyes drop and my cheeks blaze.

He knows.

Finally, he picks up his cutlery and begins eating.

I do the same but it's hard to focus on the delicious food with the air so thick with tension around us.

"Dessert?" he asks once I've placed my knife and fork together on my plate.

My eyes drop from his in favor of his body.

I can't really see any of it with the table between us, but I've seen enough now to be able to use my imagination.

"Not yet," I say before picking up my champagne and draining the glass.

It's my second, and I can already feel the buzz in my veins.

"We've got all the time in the world," he says.

After abandoning the dirty plates inside, he returns and leaves the door to the cabin open, letting soft music spill out into the night.

I expect him to retake his seat, to continue to drive me crazy with his dirty talk and dark, hungry eyes.

I'm torn between thinking he's winding me up for his own amusement, or building me high so that when we finally collide, it's mind-blowing.

The devil on my shoulder is hoping for the latter, while the angel who tries to keep me on the right track is trying to convince me that it's the former.

It's the simplest way to handle this...transaction.

It may be the simplest, but if I'm being honest with myself, it isn't what I want.

But he doesn't make it to his side of the table. Instead, he stops in front of me and holds his hand out.

"If you think I'm going hiking now, you really need to reconsid—"

"Dance with me."

"W-what?" I stutter, blindsided by his question.

"Dance with me," he repeats, holding strong.

"Uh...okay," I whisper, placing my hand in his much larger one, allowing him to pull me to my feet.

With my heels on, there is less of a height difference between us, but he's still a head taller than me.

With my chin tipped back, I keep my eyes on his as he pulls me into his body and slides his hands down my back, stopping just before the swell of my ass.

My body aches for him, and when he presses me against him, I discover that I'm not the only one.

He's hard and ready. All he needs to do is break through whatever keeps holding him back and we can finally shatter this tension between us.

If we stand any chance of getting out of this shitshow with our sanity intact, then we need to do this. It needs to happen.

My heart threatens to pound out of my chest as we begin to move together. It's slow and sensual, and way, way too much, considering who I am dancing with.

My head screams for me to take a step back and put a stop to where this is heading, but my body...my body is desperate for more, for this powerful connection that is only getting stronger and stronger as the seconds go on.

The music continues and the light breeze blows around us, but I'm nowhere close to being cold while I'm in his embrace.

Resting my cheek against his chest, I close my eyes as I focus on the steady beat of his heart.

It's racing as fast as mine.

As if we're no longer two people but one.

"Tatum," he whispers before his lips press against the top of my head.

Desire unfurls in my stomach.

I want to feel those lips in so many other places, but I refuse to ask. I've already shown my hand one too many times regarding what I want from him.

If tonight is the night we take things to the next level, then he's going to need to be the one to make the first move.

And if that happens, all I have to do is hope that he can see it through to the end. I can't do another night where he pulls back at the last minute.

My palms slide up his back, loving the way his muscles ripple with my touch, before I drag my nails back down.

He groans the most erotic noise I've ever heard before his hand slips lower.

I gasp when he squeezes my ass just hard enough to hurt in the best kind of way.

Pulling my cheek from his chest, I look up at him.

His eyes are dark, his expression tight.

"King?" I whisper, my heart suddenly racing for a whole other reason.

He looks like he's freaking out.

Fuck. He's going to—

"No," I cry when he releases me and takes a step back. "No, don't do this."

I don't mean for the pleading words to break free. But they do, and they hang heavy in the air between us.

His chest heaves as he stares at me as if he's just seen a ghost.

"What's wrong?" I whisper, unsure if I should be hanging around to watch this or running for cover.

A man like Kingston doesn't show vulnerability lightly, and when he realizes the kind of top-level freakout he seems to be having right now, I'm not sure I want to be the one in the firing line as he tries to assert his dominance again...or maybe I do.

Fuck. This man is so fucking confusing.

I take a step back, unaware that I've decided that the best course of action here is to retreat.

He's frozen in place, his eyes locked on me.

"I'm just gonna—"

"Wait," he commands, the power in his voice at odds with his behavior.

"Uh...okay. I-I'm not sure—oh my god." I gasp as he suddenly sinks to the floor and... to one knee.

Time doesn't just stop.

It totally fucking freezes.

I stop breathing and all of my senses refuse to cooperate as he slowly reaches for the railing, revealing a small black box.

My hands tremble as he brings it to a stop between us.

I can't look at it. I can't rip my eyes away from his as he gazes up at me.

Awe.

I'm pretty sure that's what I can see in his expression.

But why?

This isn't real.

He isn't seriously asking me to marry him.

Well, he is...kinda.

But...it's not real.

He doesn't love me. He doesn't want to spend his life with me.

I'm not the one.

I'm just the one who'll help him hit the next high with Callahan Enterprises.

He only wants me for the next twelve months so he can get what he wants.

So I can get what I want...

Suddenly, none of that seems quite so important as it did only a few minutes ago.

With him down there and holding a ring, it suddenly all seems very real.

Marriage.

A year.

I'm going to be a wife to a man I'm not sure I even like.

My breathing begins to get erratic as a million and one thoughts race through my head.

What the hell am I doing?

What the hell have I agreed to?

"Tatum," he says, his voice surer than it was a few moments ago.

He's found some composure now that he's done what he needed to do.

I kick myself for not figuring it out the second I stepped out of the bedroom. I expected it to happen last night in front of everyone. I thought it had to be public. I never even considered—

"Will you marry me?"

38

TATUM

I stare down at him in disbelief.

I knew it was coming. Maybe not tonight or like this.

Alone

But seeing him down there isn't anything like I expected.

I thought it would feel like a joke. An act.

I don't know what it is, but this feels real.

His nerves are palpable. The way my heart races and my hands tremble are very real.

Too real.

He stares up at me, his dark green eyes boring into mine.

The air between us is charged, but it's more than just the chemistry I'm becoming accustomed to when we're together.

"Tatum?" he whispers, pointing out that I haven't said anything in a really long time.

A small frown creases his brow as his eyes bounce between mine.

Waiting.

Lifting my hand, I pinch the pendant of my necklace between my fingers, fidgeting it as I try to find some kind of equilibrium.

His frown deepens and concern darkens his eyes.

Is he honestly worried that I'm going to say no?

Can I even say no?

I signed the paperwork. I agreed to this. I thought that the proposal was going to be some elaborate public show.

This...this is intimate. Romantic.

This isn't telling the world and trying to convince them that our fake union is real.

It's...

"Tate, you really need to say something right about now," he mutters, still down on one knee before me, his hand trembling as he holds out the ring.

"I-I know, I'm sorry. I just—"

He jumps to his feet the second I apologize, and disappointment flashes across his face. He tries to cover it, and he probably thinks he does, but his poker face isn't good enough.

"Wait," I say, reaching out and wrapping my hand around the side of his neck.

His pulse flutters rapidly against my palm, giving away everything he's trying to play off.

I hold his eyes firmly and continue. "I'm sorry. I just got a little lost in the shock of it all. Can you please get back down?" I ask, my voice quiet, nervous.

"B-back down?" he parrots.

I nod, biting on my bottom lip as the weight of what I'm asking him begins to press down on me.

Slowly, so fucking slowly, he sinks back to one knee before me and holds the ring out.

"Go on," I whisper.

He sighs, a smirk threatening as he understands what I'm asking.

"Tatum," he starts, "will you do me the honor of making the next year of my life probably the most insufferable, and annoying, and impossible one I've experienced yet?"

I can't help but laugh.

I make a show of considering it, but I'm going to need more than that.

"Everything I have, you're welcome to borrow, and I promise

to give you more thrills than anyone else is capable of, leaving you wondering how you're going to continue life without me."

"Idiot," I mutter, my smile wide and honest.

"So, will you?" he nudges.

"Will I?"

He shakes his head, losing patience with me.

Start as we mean to go on, right? What did he say about me being insufferable?

"Tatum," he warns, causing tingles to erupt between my thighs. "Will you be my wife?"

I suck in a breath, allowing myself one more second to consider just how fucking insane this is before I give my answer.

His eyes widen in impatience and his jaw ticks, but I don't make him suffer any longer.

"Yes, Kingston. I'll marry you."

I tell myself the words spill from my mouth as I think about that little cottage and its cute garden. But the truth is, anything outside of this moment, this man, is far from my mind.

In a rush, he flips open the ring box. I hadn't even realized that he didn't show me what was hiding inside before.

"Oh my god," I gasp as the stunning yet simple round solitaire ring sparkles under the soft glow of the fairy lights strung up around us.

It's huge. At least five carats.

It's...too much.

Plucking it from its velvet cushion, he holds it out for me.

"Kingston, that's...massive."

He smirks, and I roll my eyes, knowing exactly what's coming next.

"That's what they all say. But it's yours now, baby. Enjoy it." He winks, and a laugh tumbles from my mouth.

"Such an idiot."

He shrugs as he slides the stunning ring onto my finger. It's cool and heavy, and...so beautiful.

My chest tightens as I stare down at it. The meaning behind it, even if it is fake, still feels too real.

A lump crawls up my throat and tears burn the backs of my eyes.

I'm engaged.

One of the moments every girl dreams of, just happened to me.

I knew it was coming. It's fake.

But still, it feels magical. It feels—

My thoughts vanish in a heartbeat as Kingston surges to his feet. His huge hands cup my jaw as he steps up to me, the heat of our bodies melding together before he drops his lips to mine.

Everything stops.

His fingers twitch. It's the first sign that he's not going to pull away this time.

The second is the delicious sweep of his tongue across the seam of my lips, silently begging for entry.

My knees give out and I stumble backward. But he's right there, pulling me back into his body with one strong arm locked across my back.

"Don't fight me, baby," he whispers against my lips. "I can't hold back any longer. I need you."

All the air rushes from my lungs and he makes the most of my parted lips.

His tongue plunges into my mouth, searching out mine.

The second they collide, all bets are off.

My fingers sink into his hair, his hands drop to my ass, and we lose ourselves in each other.

It's been a long time coming. We've been dancing around this for days now, and it's just as electric as I thought it would be.

I gasp when he lifts me, sweeping my feet right off the ground as if I weigh nothing more than a feather.

He moves, but I don't pull away from his kiss to look where we're going. With any luck, it's the bedroom.

My ass presses against something and he releases his grip on me, his hands skimming up my waist, making my back arch for more of his touch.

His lips move from mine, kissing a wet trail along my jaw and then down my neck.

My eyes flicker open, and I absently notice that I'm on the railing. But despite knowing I could fall back and probably break my back any second, I don't release Kingston and hold on.

Instead, I make the possibly stupid decision to trust him. After all, it doesn't feel like he's going to let go anytime soon.

"Fuck, Tatum," he groans, his hands pressing against the small of my back, ensuring we're pinned together tight enough that I can feel him hard and ready against me.

Wrapping my legs tighter, I press my heels into his ass, silently letting him know that I feel it.

"Please," I whimper, my head falling back when he sucks on the sensitive patch of skin beneath my ear. "Kingston."

"Fuck, I'm already addicted to hearing my name roll off your lips," he confesses as I tug at the fabric of his shirt, pulling it from his pants and lifting it up his body.

He flinches the second my fingers touch his warm, smooth skin.

"More," I beg. "I need more."

"No stopping," he murmurs, dragging his lips across my cheek and back to mine. "Never again."

His lips claim my mine his grip on my body stopping me from pulling his shirt from his body.

Abandoning the fabric, I go for the buttons instead.

My hands tremble and I fumble with each one as our kiss gets wilder and more frantic.

My body burns red hot, my heart racing, my skin on fire.

I've never felt like this before. Sure, there have been plenty of guys I've wanted. But never as fiercely as this. It's never been this...this powerful. This all-consuming.

The second I have the final button open, I run my hands up the expanse of his chest, indulging in his hard muscles, warm skin, and the tickle of the smattering of dark hair.

His entire chest vibrates with a moan when my hands sink

over his stomach. His abs bounce beneath my touch as his grip on my hips turns painful.

It's not enough.

My fingers find his belt and I quickly unbuckle it and pull it free from the loops.

"Take me inside," I beg into our kiss.

He stills, our lips still pressed together, our heaving breaths mingling.

"Tatum," he whispers, moving his head so his brow touches mine a beat before his eyes open.

My breath catches at the unfiltered desire staring back at me.

I undo his pants and slip my fingers beneath them and his boxers, but a second before I make contact with him, I'm moving.

"Kingston," I cry as he suddenly throws me over his shoulder and spanks my ass.

"Dirty, dirty girl," he muses as he marches into the cabin and kicks the door closed behind him.

Reaching out, I grab his ass and squeeze as hard as I can.

He rewards me by spanking me again, but long before the sting of his hit has faded, I'm placed back on my feet in front of him.

He shrugs off his shirt, letting it flutter to the floor before he toes off his shoes and pushes his pants from his hips, leaving him standing in only his black boxer briefs that do very little to hide what's going on beneath.

My mouth waters as I stare down at the head of his dick poking above the waistband.

"Keep looking at me like that and you'll spend the night on your knees, Tatum."

My breath catches and my eyes roll up his incredible body. It's not news to me that he puts as much effort into his body as he does at work. But knowing it and seeing it—feeling it—are two different things.

I sweep my tongue across my bottom lip, looking up at him through my lashes.

He smirks, shaking his head slowly.

"One day, baby. I'm going to take you up on that offer," he rasps. "But tonight isn't about me."

Placing his hands on my shoulders, he spins me around.

I shudder when his fingers softly brush against my neck as he pushes my hair over one shoulder.

His lips connect with my skin next, peppering kisses down my spine until he meets his fingers that have the zipper firmly in his grasp.

"Kingston," I breathe as he pulls it down slowly until the fabric pools around my feet, leaving me standing in only my lace panties.

His knuckles bounce down my spine and my entire body pricks with goosebumps. My breasts are heavy and my core aches.

As much as I love this tender side of him, what I need right now is for him to throw me on the bed and take me hard and fast.

Gentle can come later. Everything can come later.

But right now, I need—

"Turn around," he demands.

Without question, I do as I'm told, and I find him gloriously naked with his thick, hard dick jutting out from between his thighs.

My mouth runs dry as I stare at him.

He's a god. And something tells me that every single rumor I've ever heard about his skills is true.

For long, agonizing seconds, he does nothing but stare at me with his chest heaving and his cock bobbing with excitement.

And then, just as I think he's going to go back on his words from outside, he leans forward, grips the back of my thighs, and flips me onto the middle of the bed.

I land with a gentle bounce and look down to see him pressing his knees to the end of the bed, the look in his eyes predatory.

It's everything.

And then some.

39

KINGSTON

I crawl closer, staring down at her with what I'm sure is nothing but awe in my eyes as I drag her panties down her legs.

She's fucking magnificent.

The flush on her cheeks that spreads down to her chest, the fullness of her tits, and her pink peaked nipples that are begging for my mouth. The dip of her waist, the flare of her hips and the—

Gripping her knees, I force her legs wide, exposing her to me.

My eyes hold hers for a second longer, letting her see everything I'm feeling right now before they drop and sweet fucking shit...

If that isn't the holy grail of pussy, then I don't know what fucking is.

Her skin is smooth, pink, glistening, and ready. No, desperate.

I know the fucking feeling.

Fuck. I can already see how fucking perfect it's going to look, stretched wide around my cock. I can feel her squeezing down on me. I can feel her rippling as she comes all over me.

My cock weeps for her, desperate to feel everything I've been vividly imagining.

"Kingston," she moans, rolling her hips in the hope of enticing me closer.

So un-fucking-necessary.

Leaning over her, I plant my hand beside her head and duck down to claim her lips again.

Kissing has always just been a prelude to the real thing in the past, but one sweep of her tongue against mine, and I suddenly understand what all the fuss is about.

It's so much more than just a warm-up.

She trembles as I slide my other hand up and down her body, touching every inch I can and learning the lines of her curves.

I groan as she drags her nails down my back, trying to speed me up.

Fuck. I don't need any fucking encouragement, but I'm trying to do this right.

She deserves more than a quick fuck to find our releases.

This is...this is more than that.

"I swear to God, if you don't stop teasing me, I'm going to—"

"What, baby?" I ask, my lips tracing across her jaw. "What are you going to do?"

Sliding my hand down her stomach, I push myself up so I can look into her eyes as I give her what she needs.

I push my hand between her thighs, my fingertips dancing over her sensitive skin.

Her eyes widen and her pupils dilate.

"Please," she whimpers, her hips jumping from the bed to try and force my hand.

"Greedy little thing, aren't you, Tatum?" I muse.

"I need you to touch me, King."

My chest swells, hearing her call me that.

Fuck yeah.

"OH MY GOD," she screams when I push my hand lower and plunge two fingers inside her.

"Eyes, Tatum. I need you to know who's doing this to you."

"I know," she pants. "Trust me, I know."

As I pump my fingers in and out of her, watching her fight to keep her eyes on me as her fingers twist in the sheets, I can't help but remember who this is beneath me.

My best friend's little sister.

I never had to promise him that I'd never go after her. It was more than obvious that neither of us could stand each other from a very young age.

My smirk grows. Just look at how that turned out.

"Good. And don't fucking forget it."

I kiss her again, fucking her mouth just like I am her pussy until she's trembling and chasing her release.

"King, please," she gasps the second I release her lips.

"Not yet, baby."

"Oh god, yes," she cries when I crawl down her body and drop onto my stomach between her thighs.

"Been looking forward to my dessert," I confess before leaning forward and licking up her pussy, letting her taste flood my mouth. "Fucking delicious," I mutter before diving back for more.

With my mouth on her clit and my fingers deep in her cunt, I work her until her back arches off the bed and she screams out my name.

Makes me feel like the motherfucking king that I am.

I kiss and lick my way up her body. Her fingers twist in my hair in an attempt to make me move faster.

The second I'm within reaching distance, she lifts from the bed and swipes her tongue across my lips, tasting herself.

"Filthy," I muse before deepening the kiss once more as I wrap her legs around my waist.

My dick brushes against her pussy, the heat of her practically burning me.

Her nails scratch my scalp before she begins clawing at my shoulders. She's rough enough to draw blood, and I fucking love it.

"Animal," I mutter as I reach for myself and press the thick head of my cock against her entrance.

Her muscles ripple, desperately trying to suck me deeper.

Squeezing my eyes closed, I attempt to dig up some self-control so I don't blow the second I push inside her.

I've been with more women than I care to even try to count, but none of them matter. Right now, this moment. It feels like the first time all over again.

"King, I need you," Tatum begs, her wide, dark eyes staring up at me.

"Fuck. Hearing you say that does things to me."

She circles her hips and I grit my teeth.

"Please," she whispers. The plea is so quiet, so soft, I'm not even sure it's real, but it's enough to shatter the thin grip I have on my control.

My hips punch forward, and I fill her pussy in one swift move.

She cries out as her body fights to adjust to my size.

I, however, just grit my teeth and fight to hold still.

"Move, please," she begs, her hands sliding down my back to grab my ass and pull me even deeper.

"Fuck," I groan as her pussy ripples.

I was wrong earlier.

This is better than anything my imagination could come up with.

"Tatum, you feel fucking incredible," I groan through gritted teeth.

"Fuck me, King," she whispers. "Let me feel you."

Dropping my head to hers, I hold her eye contact, our increased breaths mingling as I do as she suggests.

All the air punches from my lungs as I pull out and then push back inside.

Fuck.

We've barely started, and I already know this is going to be the hottest sex of my life.

Wrapping my hand around the back of her neck, I angle her head exactly as I want her and crush my lips to hers. She groans, her legs tightening around me as I increase the pace.

"Yes, yes, yes," she cries into our kiss.

It's wet, frantic and desperate.

Our hands are everywhere, scratching and groping as our movements become more and more erratic.

"Oh god. Oh god. Oh god," Tatum begins chanting, her pussy clamping down on my dick as she approaches the end.

Sitting back on my ankles, I grip her hip in one hand while pressing my thumb from the other against her clit.

"Not God, baby," I taunt, our eyes locked as she begins to lose control. I press harder before circling the little bud of nerves. "Your king."

"Oh fuuuuuck. Kingston," she cries, her body convulsing as she falls over the edge.

She squeezes me impossibly tight, leaving me with no other choice but to crash with her.

My dick jerks violently inside her, filling her with everything I've got.

I don't realize that I've collapsed on top of her until she shoves at my shoulder, trying to remove my weight.

"Oh shit," I grunt, rolling to the side.

She tries to slide away, but I'm not ready for that. Nowhere fucking near, in fact.

"No," I grunt, wrapping my arm around her waist and pulling her closer.

"King," she shrieks as I roll onto my back and take her with me.

Her legs land on either side of my hips, her chest pressed tightly against mine.

My heart still races, and something tells me that hers is too.

My dick rests happily beneath her pussy, the thought of my cum leaking out of her right this second making it stir again.

Resting her head against my chest, she lets out a sated sigh as I run my hand down her back.

"That was—"

"Incredible," I finish for her.

"Unexpected and reckless," she corrects, an edge of anger in her tone.

I know what I just did, but I'm not sorry about it. There was no way there was going to be anything between us.

"Why? Did you think I was going to be a fumbling idiot?" I laugh, choosing to focus on her first comment.

She chuckles her frustration ebbing away. "I think we both know that you've had enough practice to ensure that wouldn't be the case."

"So, what's so unexpected?"

She doesn't say anything for a few seconds, and a little unease begins to trickle through my veins.

"I thought..." she starts but quickly cuts herself off when she moves her hand, her new ring catching her eye.

She holds it up, admiring it.

I'm not normally a jewelry kinda man, but even I can admit that it's a beautiful ring. It called to me the day I went shopping. I've no idea how, but the second I saw it, I knew it was meant for her.

"I thought that once we'd done that, it would be out of my system and I'd be able to put it behind me and move on," she says absently, as if she's talking to herself.

"But now?" I ask, my deep voice startling her.

"I..." She sighs before finally looking up at me.

My breath catches at the honesty in her eyes.

"I want to do it again already," she confesses.

I swallow thickly. My cock is already prepared for round two.

I thrust up, letting her feel just how much I agree with her before I lay my arms out on the bed at my sides.

"Use me, baby. Take everything you need from me."

"King," she whispers, dropping her gaze to my chest.

Reaching out, I tuck two fingers under her chin to force her eyes back to mine.

"What, baby?"

"We shouldn't be doing this. It complicates things."

"Does it, though? Because to me, right now," I say, grinding myself against her again, "it feels like the simplest, most obvious thing in the world."

I flip us again, finding my home between her thighs and sliding back inside her.

Both of us sigh with pleasure. A million and one things are dancing on the tip of her tongue, but I silence all of them with another earth-shattering kiss.

This time isn't as frantic or as desperate as the first time.

We needed that to take the edge off.

This time is gentler, slower, but it's no less full of passion and desire.

It's like nothing I've ever experienced before, and for now, I refuse to think too much about that, because the truth of what's building between us is nothing but terrifying.

It's a business deal, and this right here is one of the benefits.

And just like that, I manage to spend the rest of the night lying to myself as we reap the benefits of this arrangement over and over until we both pass out, exhausted and sated, knowing that we've got a whole year to worry about what's really happening here.

Not that it really matters. Right now, we're in a bubble. A bubble where the outside world doesn't factor. But come Monday when we return to Chicago, everything is going to change all over again.

We won't just be two people letting the world see our relationship developing. We're going to be an engaged couple with a fast-approaching wedding.

She just doesn't know that part yet.

40

TATUM

I wake burning hot and pinned to the mattress—and not just by the massive diamond that's weighing down my hand.

It takes a second for everything that happened last night to fully come back to me, and the moment it does, my temperature rises that little bit more.

Fuck.

Kingston was like a man possessed.

Talk about going from zero to sixty. Jeez.

It was worth the wait, though.

My core clenches as I think back, and the ache that comes from the move is enough to let me know I'm going to be feeling the side effects for a while.

I don't think I've ever had a night like it.

No. I *know* I've never had a night like it.

It wasn't just the insanely good sex, either. Yeah, that was mind-blowing in all the right ways, but it was so much more. The reverent way he touched me, the emotion in his eyes as he stared down at me. It was...all-consuming.

But as much as I want to revel in the way he holds me close in his sleep, my need for the bathroom means I have no choice but to slip from under the dead weight of his arm.

He moans and shifts as I climb from the bed, but he doesn't wake.

I watch him for a few seconds, unable to keep the soft smile from my lips.

He looks so much...nicer in his sleep.

The hard expression, the impenetrable eyes are long gone. Although, if I'm being honest, I haven't seen either of them since I woke up here.

He's...he's been an entirely different person. A person, I hate to admit, that I quite like. He's sweet and thoughtful, funny and vulnerable. All the things he isn't in Chicago. All the things I didn't think he could be.

Moving before he catches me being a creeper, I scan the room. It's the first time I've seen him surrounded by chaos. And by chaos, I mean our discarded clothes.

Reaching down, I swipe his shirt from the floor and shamelessly lift it to my nose. Breathing in, I revel in his manly scent as it floods my senses. All the hairs on my body lift as goosebumps race over my skin.

His scent alone shouldn't have such a visceral effect on me, but I can't help it. One sniff and everything from last night begins playing out in my mind like a high-definition movie.

And fuck, it was hot.

Pulling his shirt over my head, I let the soft fabric float around me as his scent fills the air.

With my heart beating wildly in my chest and every muscle in my body aching, I rip my eyes from the sleeping man before me and pad through to the bathroom.

I do my thing before stepping up to the sink and reaching for my toothbrush.

Looking up, I find that my eyes are alight with happiness—or it might just be the post-orgasm glow I haven't experienced in a while, I'm not sure. My hair is a wild mess. Honestly, I look like I've been dragged through a hedge backward. My lips are still swollen from all the kisses, and my neck and chest look a little like I've been mauled by a dog.

My heart continues to race as I lose myself in memories, the giant diamond on my finger glittering under the bright spotlights above me.

I'm so lost in my own head that I don't notice someone else walk into the room, so when a large pair of hands land on my hips and lips brush the side of my neck, I shriek around my toothbrush.

My eyes find his in the mirror, and even without seeing his mouth, I know he's smiling.

"Good morning, baby," he muses, his voice raspy with sleep.

"Hey," I mumble around my toothbrush before it's pulled from my mouth. "Hey," I repeat, only for an entirely different reason this time. "Oh my god," I gasp in horror. "You did *not* just do that?"

My stomach turns over as I spin around and reach for *my* toothbrush that is now inside *his* mouth.

He moves before I can make contact with his hand, and I find my arm pulled behind my back before he pins me against the counter with his hips. His naked hips.

Oh god.

My stomach rolls again, but this time it's not in disgust but desire.

"Baby," he mumbles, "this is nothing after what we shared last night."

His eyes search mine so intently, I can't help but wonder if he's trying to work out if I'm thinking about it or not.

"That's not the point," I argue. "That is gross. Last night was..." I trail off, unable to find the right word. A word that won't increase the already massive ego he has.

"Was?" he asks after throwing my toothbrush into the sink.

"Not gross?" I reply intelligently.

His eyebrows lift in amusement. "Not gross. I guess it could be worse."

Wrapping his hands around my waist, he lifts me until I have no choice but to sit on the cold granite counter.

He steps between my thighs, wrapping my legs around his waist.

His hard dick brushes against my pussy and I shudder, desire rolling through me.

Twisting his fingers in my hair, he drags my head back, positioning me exactly where he wants me.

His warm, minty breath rushes over my face as he studies me.

"King?" I whisper.

"Fuck. I love it when you moan my name."

"I didn't—" My words are cut off as his lips brush over mine.

At first, it's innocent, but then he pulls my hair, sending a shot of pain down my neck. I gasp in shock, and he makes the most of my parted lips by plunging his tongue past them.

He kisses me as if I'm the most important person in the world.

The only girl in the world...

My hands slide up his arms and over his shoulders before my fingers thread into the short hair at the nape of his neck.

He groans into our kiss, his hips rolling against my pussy.

Despite the soreness, I ache to feel him inside me again.

Reaching between us, I grab his dick and put it into position.

"Aren't you sore?" he whispers, kissing along my jaw.

"I don't care." It's true.

His eyes open, holding mine captive.

I lean forward, mourning the loss of his lips, and he smiles.

"I care, Tatum. There might be many, many things I want to do to you, but I can assure you, hurting you isn't one of them."

My breath catches at the sincerity in his words.

"You good there for a minute?" he asks.

I want to cling to him, to stop him from leaving me, but I refrain. The less I look like a crazy, sex-starved fool, the better.

And that's all it is. The lingering high of all the orgasms. It has nothing to do with how I feel for him. I don't feel anything for him, so it's a moot point.

I shake my head as he approaches the bathtub, wondering if I'm going to be able to lie to myself for an entire year, all the while calling myself Mrs. Callahan.

My ring catches my eye, but I don't allow myself any time to focus on it—not while I have a naked man pouring bubbles into a tub.

Fuck. His ass is something else.

Hard. Round. Perfect.

I squint at the little red marks on his skin.

Did I—

He turns around, and my beautiful view of his ass turns into something else entirely.

"Well, good morning, Mr. Callahan," I muse, resting back on my palms while shamelessly staring at his hard dick.

I spent more than enough time worshipping it last night. He knows how I feel; there's no point hiding it.

"See something you like?" he asks, his voice deep with desire as he reaches for himself, wrapping his fingers around his shaft.

Fuck.

My eyes jump to his.

"You shouldn't look so good naked. It's not fair."

"What's not fair right now is that you're still wearing my shirt," he counters.

He stalks over, gently stroking himself as he does before reaching out and dragging his shirt from my body.

I squirm on the countertop, desperate for him to touch me.

But he never does.

Instead, he just wraps his hands around my waist and lifts me.

"Take me back to bed," I whisper in his ear, making him chuckle.

"Does your brother know you're a sex maniac?"

"I sure hope not. And if you feel like telling him, that's at your own risk. We already know he can overpower you in a fight."

"Not true," he states.

"Umm..." I trace the lingering darkness around his eye with my pointer finger. "If last week taught me anything, it's that—"

"I let him make those hits. I deserved them for what I was doing. Don't think that just because I didn't fight back, I can't."

I chuckle. "Sure."

I groan when he lowers me into the bathtub, the hot water soothing my aching muscles.

"You're a brat," he points out as he releases me.

"You love it," I taunt, watching the way his eyes widen and his chin drops.

"You drive me crazy."

He stands tall, making no attempt to hide just how much he loves my sass.

"Oh yeah, you look *so* turned off right now."

I reach for him, wrapping my fingers around his velvet shaft and stroking him. Once. Twice...

He groans loudly, his dick jerking happily in my hold before he grabs my wrist, stopping me.

"Brat," he muses, making me pout when he removes my hand from my new favorite toy and takes a step back.

"You're not getting in?" I ask, disappointed.

"Relax," he says, continuing to back up toward the door.

"If you're disappearing out there to jerk off, at least send me a video," I shout once he's slipped around the corner.

The only response I get is his loud laugh that echoes off the walls.

"Asshole," I mutter, sinking into the hot bubbly water, sighing in contentment.

Noises come from the other side of the door, making me believe he hasn't gone to jerk off, but he's gone for long minutes. "Oh Mr. Callahan, a girl could get used to this." I sigh, sinking lower.

"Is that so?"

I startle, sloshing water everywhere as I bolt upright.

He saunters in, still as naked as the day he was born, with a smirk playing on his lips and two mugs in his hands.

Two?

"What's that?" I ask, already knowing from the scent that fills the air that at least one is coffee.

"Don't get used to this," he says before placing both mugs on the side.

The sight of thick, perfectly white foam greets me before I glance at his.

"Tea?" I blurt.

Okay, so I might not have been expecting him to have a double espresso or anything, but...I should have guessed.

"Green tea," he explains before gesturing for me to slide forward so he can get in behind me.

His strong, thick thighs wrap around my body. His still-hard dick brushes against my back before his arm wraps around my waist, pulling me against him.

We slide lower, sinking into the bubbles together.

His lips drop to my ear, and I shudder as his warm breath races down my neck.

"I like this," he whispers, his hands beginning to roam. "I like having you all wet for me."

"Kingston," I moan when he cups both my breasts, squeezing just so before flicking my nipples with his thumb.

"You moan my name so beautifully."

"L-last night was..." I start, barely able to form words as he continues teasing me.

"Amazing? Incredible? Mind-blowing? Best night of your life?" he offers up as one of his hands descends my body.

Oh god.

"A one-off," I whisper. But I already know I'm lying through my teeth. With the lack of conviction in those words, he knows I am too. I mentally kick myself for not being stronger.

He cups my pussy. His hold is possessive and weirdly erotic, considering he's not really touching me. Not the good bits, anyway.

He chuckles darkly.

"This pussy is mine now, Tatum. You said yes. You gave yourself to me. There is nothing that is going to be a one-off with us. If we're doing this, we're doing it properly. And I have every intention of treating my wife the way she deserves."

41

TATUM

The rest of our weekend is a dream.

After our bath, Kingston made another incredible breakfast and we spent almost the whole day lounging on the couch, watching Netflix and laughing.

It was incredible. It was also mind-blowing.

I've never spent time with him before that wasn't hard work and full of snide insults and bickering. So just...enjoying each other's company was bizarre.

Nice, but bizarre all the same.

He spent the whole day touching me somehow—a hand on my thigh, his fingers toying with my hair. It was comforting in a way I never would have imagined.

And when we went to bed last night? Phew.

I thought I'd experienced good sex before, but man, Kingston Callahan blows everything I've known before out of the water.

He is a god. Although, I have no intention of telling him that.

His ego already barely fits through a standard door.

And I'm pretty sure that me screaming his name last night over and over could have given him a clue.

We both fell asleep sated and exhausted. It was blissful.

Something I could easily get used to, despite knowing that

getting attached to this man and his magical cock is the worst possible thing I could do.

He shifts behind me, his hand brushing down my side.

It's the dead of night, but still my body comes alive at his innocent touch.

His hand continues down to my leg, and the second his lips brush against my shoulder, I realize that maybe it's not quite as innocent as I thought.

"King," I moan as his fingers tighten around my thigh and he spreads me open.

"So wet for me," he groans when his fingers collide with my center.

"Oh god."

The way he touches me...it's too good to be true.

In only seconds, he's fully dragged me from sleep and has me riding the edge of pleasure.

"More, King. I need more." I gasp, my pussy contracting, desperate to feel something inside.

"Dirty girl," he muses before shuffling forward.

I gasp as the thick head of his cock brushes against my entrance.

"Yes," I cry, more than willing to be anything he wants me to be as long as I get what I need. "Oh god," I moan as he pushes inside. I'm sore, but in a really good way.

"Fuck, baby. I can't get enough of this," he whispers as he pushes deeper inside me.

His grip on my hip tightens until his fingertips are digging in so hard that I know I'll have bruises in a few hours.

Not that I care. The only thing I care about right now is getting more of him and everything he can give me. Nothing else matters.

Just us.

We move together in perfect sync. It's slower than last night, but no less intense. If anything, it's more.

With nothing but darkness surrounding us and our increased

breaths and groans of pleasure, it feels more intimate than being able to see each other.

"I'd happily wake up like this every morning." He groans in my ear as his hand slides to my clit, giving me the extra push I need to find my release.

"King. King. Oh god," I moan as pleasure shoots from my core, saturating every single one of my nerve endings.

"Tatum," he breathes, his hot breath rushing over my neck and sending another bolt of pleasure through my body as he spills inside me.

As our highs melt away, neither of us moves. He doesn't pull out of me, and I don't make any attempt to force him to do so.

I'm too content, too relaxed. Too...happy.

My body might be singing, but my head tells me to sleep.

It's the middle of the night. We've got to be up early for him to deliver on his promise of getting me to the office at the start of the day.

I'm just drifting off when a thought hits me.

A thought I should have considered before now.

"You haven't used a condom all weekend," I whisper into the darkness.

He sighs. It's as if he's been waiting for me to question it. Which I should have done before I let him inside me the first time, but...

I squeeze my eyes closed as I chastise myself for being so reckless—I fear with both my heart and my body.

"You're on the pill, baby."

I grit my teeth as irritation surges through me.

"That is not the point, Kingston," I snap.

My attempt to get away from him is ruined when his grip on my waist tightens, pinning me to his ridiculously hot body.

"I'm clean, baby. I know you are too," he says softly as he looms over me.

"How? How do you know that?"

"Tatum," he growls.

"No, don't give me that deep sexy voice in the hope I'll forget how annoying and over-powering you are. You looked into my medical records."

He doesn't say anything. Not that I needed the confirmation. He's already guilty as charged.

"Did you want something between us?" he asks.

No. "We need to be sensible."

He drops lower, letting his lips brush over the shell of my ear. "Where is the fun in being sensible, baby?"

I shake my head, losing the fight with my self-control when he's so close, when he's hardening again inside me.

Rolling me onto my back, he lifts my foot to his lip and trails kisses down my sole. It tickles, but it also burns in the best kind of way.

"See," he says, thrusting forward and ensuring he hits that magic spot deep inside me. "Sensible never feels this good."

"Kingston." It's meant to come out like a warning, but I fail miserably.

Dropping my foot, he falls over me, his hands landing on either side of my head, pinning me in place.

"Give me another one, baby. Let me feel how much you love my dick before we have to return to reality."

My heart sinks into my stomach and my eyes dart toward the clock on the nightstand.

Fuck.

He didn't wake me just for a middle-of-the-night fuck. We need to leave.

Disappointment trickles through my veins.

I'm not ready.

Returning to the city means leaving all this behind.

An unexpected lump crawls up my throat.

Sensing my imminent breakdown, Kingston's eyes search mine. It terrifies me what he might see staring back up at him, but I'm powerless to conceal it.

I already know that he'll demand I open my eyes if I try and hide it.

"Tatum," he whispers, dropping lower, his nose brushing mine.

"Don't," I croak, embarrassed that I'm on the verge of tears while he's deep inside me.

I tell myself it's exhaustion and the effects of one too many orgasms, but I know I'm lying to myself.

It's more than that.

He's more than that.

"You're incredible," he murmurs before stealing my lips in a filthy, all-consuming kiss.

The bright lights of the city shine in the distance and the knot in my stomach tightens.

I'm not usually an anxious person, but returning after our weekend away...everything feels...I don't know. Wrong, I guess.

Or maybe right.

Fuck knows. I'm so confused by everything.

I shouldn't have enjoyed the weekend with him as much as I did.

I shouldn't have delighted in discovering a different side to him.

I shouldn't want it to continue as much as I do.

But I can't help it.

I fear that Kingston has lured me into his trap, and it's going to be harder than I ever appreciated to escape.

Do I even want to?

Just as it has for the entire weekend, my cell sits turned off in my purse.

I should feel guilty for shutting off from the rest of the world, but Kingston assured me that Miles knew where we were if we were needed.

Selfishly, I needed this weekend.

We needed this weekend.

I feel like we're returning stronger. That our fake union might just be a little more believable now.

Fake...is that still what this is?

I let out a pained sigh as I stare at the lights ahead of us.

"Enjoy your job that much, huh?" Kingston asks teasingly.

"I love my job," I counter. "I'm just not sure I'm ready for reality yet."

I startle when his warm hand lands on my thigh and squeezes lightly. "We can go back."

I glance over at him, hating being so vulnerable with him but equally unable to stop.

"I'd like that."

"We can go anywhere you want. We've got resorts or property in almost every corner of the globe. The world is your oyster, baby."

I smile, appreciating the sentiment despite not wanting to use him for free vacations over the coming months.

I might be about to marry into the Callahan family because of a property, but it isn't one of theirs I want. I don't want a penny of the Callahan money. I just want what I was promised. What should be mine.

Another sigh slips free.

"You don't want to travel?" Kingston enquires.

"Of course I do. Who doesn't want to experience all the world has to offer? There is so much more than Chicago. Than America."

His grip tightens, reminding me just how much I like his touch. "Stick with me, baby. I'll show you the world."

"That sounds a little too romantic for this situation, Kingston."

"There are no rules here, Tatum. If I want to give you something, I will. Just like this weekend."

"Well, you certainly gave me something," I say, my thighs clenching. I'm pretty sure I can still feel what he gave me dripping from inside me.

"I wasn't talking about my dick, but it's good to know where your dirty mind goes, baby."

"Pfft. Of course you weren't." I roll my eyes and shake my head.

"I'm more than happy to, though. My dick had a fucking fantastic weekend getting to know your pussy. He's very much interested in repeating it as often as possible."

"Please don't talk about your dick as if it's its own person. It's weird."

He chuckles as the buildings around us grow the deeper we get into the city.

The Warner Group building is looming closer and closer. As is reality.

It's only been a weekend; not that much could have changed.

My eyes drop to my hand as I consider this, focusing on my new piece of jewelry.

Or everything could have changed.

Nerves swirl in my stomach as I consider what's next for us.

A big announcement, I guess. Public wedding planning. A ceremony that's going to have press coverage in order to fulfill my father's bullshit demands.

I hate being center of attention.

He knew that as well.

Probably why he did it.

Take away the one thing I truly wanted and force me into the spotlight to get it back.

Sounds just like the vindictive shit he was capable of.

I'm about to ask what happens next when Kingston pulls the car to a stop outside the building I've spent most of my life in.

"So, I guess the weekend is over then," I mutter sadly.

I wasn't lying before. I do love my job.

It's just...everything seems a little harder right now.

Life is harder.

It's why this weekend was so incredible. The stress of everything seemed to just vanish.

"I'm not sure what time I'll finish later, but I'll try to come and pick you up," Kingston offers.

"You don't need to do that," I say as I turn to look at him. "I know you're busy and—" His fingers press against my lips, stopping me from saying anything else.

"If I can be here to pick you up, I will be here. I want to be here." His eyes search mine, letting me see the truth within them.

My heart begins to race and my hands tremble.

For a man who's been forever single and only used women to get his kicks, he sure is good at this romance thing.

He damn well knows it too.

"Okay?" he asks, still holding my lips hostage.

I nod my head once. I've discovered this weekend that fighting isn't the only way to have fun with him. Sometimes, agreeing and being a good girl has its benefits too.

Pacified by my response, he lets his hand drop, but before I can turn away to get out, his fingers grip my jaw and he leans forward, brushing a sweet kiss on my lips.

It's teasing in all the right kind of ways. And when he wishes me a good day and unclicks my seat belt for me, I'm nothing but a puddle on his passenger seat.

Maybe him coming back to pick me up after work won't be so bad. Hell knows I'm going to spend all day thinking about how that kiss could end.

"Have a good day, baby."

"You too. Try not to take over the entire world."

"I'll do my best. Just think though, soon you'll get half of everything I take over."

With those ominous words floating around my head, I climb out of the car, nod in greeting to our security guards, and make my way up to my floor.

42

TATUM

The anxiety I was feeling in the car as we drove into the city only gets worse with every set of eyes that follow me toward my desk.

"Good morning, Tatum. Can I get you a coffee?" Josh asks as he rushes over.

"Y-yeah, that would be great," I mutter, my skin prickling as almost every person on the floor stares at me with a varying array of emotions on their faces.

Most are happier than usual, and others look confused.

"W-what's going on?" I whisper, feeling like I've missed out on something huge.

His smile widens as he stares at me. "Congratulations, Tatum," he says quickly before spinning around and marching toward our break room to make my coffee.

I quickly scan the office full of intrigued faces before I turn toward my office and rush inside.

Digging around inside my purse, I search for my cell.

The second it's in my grasp, I turn it on, only to find the red dead battery sign flashing at me.

"Fantastic," I mutter as I dump my purse on the floor, drop into my chair and reach for my charger.

The seconds seem to turn into minutes as I wait for it to power up, and the second it does, it lights up like a Christmas tree with notifications.

The majority are from Lori, but there are loads of others as well.

I'm staring at them all filling my screen when it begins ringing in my hand.

"Hey, Lor. What's—"

"That ring is fucking gorgeous," she shrieks down the line.

"W-what?"

"And it was so romantic. Like, every girl's dream proposal."

My hand trembles and my heart begins to pound. "W-what are you talking about?"

I don't know why I'm asking; I already know the answer.

"Tate, the photos are everywhere. It's the most romantic thing I've ever seen."

"Where?" I ask, turning my computer on.

She laughs. "Literally everywhere. Wait...you didn't know?"

My breathing becomes erratic as my web browser finally opens and I click onto a popular gossip site.

"Oh my god," I whisper as a very clear photograph of Kingston and me on the deck of that cabin appears before me.

Private.

I thought it was private.

I thought it was just me and him. Something that we'd shared between us. A moment where everything changed, where the chemistry that was crackling finally bubbled over and we gave in.

I scroll down, ignoring whatever the journalist has written, and focus on the images.

Images that I didn't consent to.

Images that—

A bitter laugh full of disbelief spills from my lips as I stare at a photo of me sitting on the railing, the two of us making out like teenagers.

Maybe it was stupid to think that we'd shared something over the past two days. Maybe I was a naive little girl, thinking that our fake arrangement was turning into something.

As I stare at the image, a single tear runs down my cheek.

I was wrong.

Everything about this is nothing but a business deal.

Fuck. I'm so fucking stupid.

I gave him the benefit of the doubt. I let him sweep me away in all of this.

I let him play me.

"Fuck," I groan, slumping back in my chair as if all the wind has been knocked out of me.

"Tatum, talk to me. Didn't you know about this?"

"Does it look like I knew about this? I'm molesting him, Lor."

"Not exactly. You're both fully clothed. It's sweet."

"It's fake. All of it is fak—" A knock on my office door cuts my words off before Josh pokes his head in with my coffee in his hand.

Lifting my hand, I wipe the tear trail from my cheek and try to pull myself together.

"I don't think that's—"

"Thank you, Josh. Could you let the others know that we'll meet in thirty? I had a few ideas over the weekend that I'd like to discuss in regard to the campaign."

"O-of course," he stutters, his eyes bouncing between mine, my computer screen and the wall behind me. "See you soon," he says before backing out of the room.

"So he's still hot for you then," Lori deadpans once she's confident the door has closed behind him.

"Focus, Lor. Josh isn't an issue here."

"Is there even an issue here? Didn't you sign up for this?"

"I thought he was going to do it Friday night at the gala. He didn't and instead, he swept me away for a romantic weekend in the woods.

"It was so perfect, Lor. Everything about that place, about him—"

"Uh oh," she says, hearing what I'm not saying. "You're falling for him, aren't you?"

"What?" I shriek, trying to sound offended by the mere suggestion. "No. Of course I'm not. I can't stand him."

"But you just said—"

"I didn't know that it was photographed, Lor. I didn't know that photos of me were going to end up all over the internet without my permission. That's not right."

"Maybe not, but it's not something you can really stop when you're publicly dating a man like King—"

"If we were in Chicago, yeah, I'd let you have that. But we were in the middle of fucking nowhere, Lor. No photographers followed us there. If they did, there would be photos of what we did during the day. He did this."

Betrayal drips through my veins. It's bitter, poisonous.

I thought we were...connecting, growing.

But in reality, all he was doing was focusing on the end goal. Ensuring he hit all the requirements of my father's will to get what he wants.

Warner Group.

He wants to acquire my family company to further his own career, his own wealth.

He isn't interested in me. In a relationship with me. In a future with me.

He was just making all the right noises to ensure I go along with him.

Fuck.

"Maybe not, Tate."

"Why are you defending him all of a sudden?" I snap. "I thought you hated him."

"I thought you hated him," she counters.

"I do. I need to go."

"Me too. Lunch?" she offers as olive branch.

"Tacos?"

"Whatever you want."

"Okay. Normal place?"

"You got it. See you in a few."

She cuts the call before I do, and I slump back in my chair.

He did this. I know he did.

I keep my cell on silent all day. The thing doesn't stop. People I know message to congratulate me, and random unknown numbers call incessantly. I can only assume that they're reporters wanting to get firsthand information on the engagement that's sent the entire city into meltdown today.

I knew Kingston had a public image, that he was often photographed and talked about in the local media. But I had no idea it was to this extent.

Ten minutes before I was due to leave the building to meet Lori, she called me to say that she was bringing the tacos to me.

She explained about the crowd of journalists outside her building wanting to ask my best friend questions, and then she tried to play off what it was like downstairs. But the second she left, I walked toward the window and looked down.

The crowd made my heart drop into my feet.

Dad wanted this.

He knew what a public engagement and soon-to-be wedding would do, and he demanded it.

Why?

Why would he do this to me?

My team has been incredible. All the questions dancing on the tips of their tongues have thankfully remained inside their mouths. The only thing they said is congratulations, and a couple of the female members of my team asked to look at my ring, which of course they gushed over.

Why wouldn't they? It's gorgeous.

But it's now also tainted.

With a sigh, I begin to pack up my things in preparation for leaving.

The crowd is still there. It seems like no one has forgotten the news or had anything else to distract them with.

My stomach knots just thinking about getting through it all.

I haven't heard from Kingston all day. His silence is confirmation I don't need that he did all this. That his romantic weekend was a setup and nothing else.

Did he even mean any of it?

I'm blinking back tears once again when a knock sounds on my door.

Attempting to swallow down the emotion bubbling up faster than I can control, I call, "Come in," and wait to see who wants me.

It's not him. I already know that. He wouldn't have knocked. He wouldn't have given me that courtesy.

"Hey," a familiar voice says the second the door opens.

"Cory?" I gasp.

He hesitates a little before I urge him to come in.

"So..." he starts, his eyes running up and down the length of me. I've no idea what he's looking for, or if he finds it, but his gaze finally locks on mine.

"So..." I echo, my stomach twisting up. I haven't really spoken to him since our night out. Things have been too crazy. But now, staring into his eyes, I regret not making the effort.

He's been a good friend to me. A very good friend.

"You're marrying Kingston Callahan," he blurts.

"Fuck, Cory," I breathe, dragging my hair back from my face.

"I thought all those images circling last week were fake," he admits. "I couldn't believe that you, of all people, would fall for him."

"Cory, that's not—"

"You're wearing his ring, Tatum."

Hurt flickers in his eyes, making me feel like the worst friend in the world.

"I know. Things have just been crazy since Dad died and—"

He smiles softly before cutting me off.

"It's okay, Tate. You don't need to explain."

"But—" He crosses the room and wraps me in his arms.

I almost shatter right then and there. Tears burn the backs of my eyes and make my nose itch, but I fight it.

I can't lose my shit here, I just can't. There are too many eyes on me.

I need to get home, lock myself away, and then I can deal with everything.

Home...

Do I even have one of those right now?

I suck in a ragged breath, but before I can release Cory, my office door flies open and heavy footsteps storm inside.

"What the fuck are you doing?" a deep, angry voice barks. "Get your hands off my wife."

43

KINGSTON

Anger surges through me at the sight of another man touching Tatum.

No. He's not just touching her. He's fucking holding her.

Comforting her.

Before I can think about my actions, or calm myself down, I've crossed the room, fueled only by my need to protect her, to make her mine.

My hand wraps around his upper arm, and I drag him away from her.

Thankfully, he releases her. If he didn't and dragged her with him, so help me fucking God.

"Kingston, what the hell?" Tatum shrieks as I throw the guy across the room, sending him crashing to the couch that sits beneath her window.

Ignoring her, I turn to the guy, looming over him as he fights to right himself.

The second he looks up, I recognize him.

He's the guy Tatum was dancing with last weekend.

The guy she would have gone home with if it weren't for me stepping in and taking what's mine.

His eyes lift to mine, but unlike I was expecting, there is no fear, no hesitation as he stares back at me.

"She is not your wife," he states coldly.

"Semantics. She will be. Soon. Very soon."

A shadow appears beside me, but I don't turn to look at Tatum. My attention is laser-focused on her friend instead.

My mouth opens to speak, but she beats me to it.

"You need to leave."

A smirk curls at my lips, but when the guy moves, it isn't in the direction of the door, and he's no longer glaring at me but looking at Tatum.

Ripping my eyes from his, I focus on my fiancée.

"Me?" I ask in disbelief. "You want *me* to leave?"

"Yes," she states fiercely, her hands resting on her hips.

I don't need to look at her little friend to know he's got a smug grin playing on his lips.

"But I was going to take you to dinner. Then we've got a meeting with—"

"No, Kingston," she spits, making me rear back. "I'm not going anywhere with you."

"Tatum, that's not—"

"You heard her," the guy says, puffing his chest out and stepping between us. "She doesn't want to go with you. I suggest you fuck off back where you came from. She is not interested."

"The ring on her finger would suggest otherwise," I happily point out.

His nostrils flare, and if I were to look down, I suspect I'd see his fists curled, ready to throw a punch or two in my face.

"Just go, please," Tatum says, her voice quiet and broken.

Looking over the guy's shoulder, I find her standing behind him with her arms wrapped around her waist and tears filling her eyes.

"Baby," I breathe.

"No," she spits, her voice much stronger than she looks.

The air crackles between us as our silent battle of wills continues.

"W-what's going on?" I ask, confused.

She shakes her head, a bitter smile pulling at her lips.

"The photographs, Kingston." She laughs again, but there is no amusement in it, only pain. "I-I thought—" She cuts herself off. "It doesn't matter. We're done here."

"No, Tatum. We're not done here. This isn't—"

"Leave, please." The fight has gone from her voice. I hate it.

"Okay," I concede, willing to give her some space. "But this isn't over, Tatum. This is so not fucking over."

I hold her eyes for a few seconds before looking back at her "friend."

"You hurt a single fucking hair on her head, and I'll make sure you regret it for the rest of your life."

His mouth opens to respond, but I've no interest in his answer.

Instead, I spin around and storm out of Tatum's office, leaving her behind.

Every single set of eyes still on this floor turns to me and watches every second of my lonely retreat to the elevator.

It isn't very often I don't get what I want, and I don't fucking like it.

When the elevator doors open, they reveal a handful of Warner employees. A couple I vaguely recognize, but the rest are strangers.

One, a member of senior management, I believe, looks as if he's about to say something, but one hard glare in his direction and he shrinks back as if he's attempting to vanish into thin air.

Holding my head high and keeping my shoulders square, I draw in deep, calming breaths as the elevator descends through the building and releases me on the ground floor.

Again, the attention of almost everyone down here turns my way, but I don't return any of their stares. My focus is on my car loitering at the curb.

Lewis steps out the second he notices me, but I'm faster and reach for the door handle before he can.

"Wait, you've got—"

My eyes land on the woman sitting in the back seat, and I'm granted a moment of relief from the irritation of the past thirty minutes.

"Well, if it isn't Mr. Callahan," my visitor taunts. "Good day at the office, sweetie?"

"Fuck's sake," I mutter lightly, although I can't fight the smile that pulls at my lips.

"Get the fuck in, asshole. I think it's time we caught up, don't you?"

I glance at Lewis, who is also smirking, before climbing into the car.

"Long time no see," I mutter as I get comfortable.

"Time makes the heart grow stronger, don't you think, KC?" She winks, and I finally crack.

"Fuck. It's good to see you," I groan as I sink lower in the seat and tug at my tie, the facade of the hard-ass businessman shattering with every second that passes.

"So..." she starts. "You're engaged, huh? I wasn't expecting to see that when I woke up this morning."

"Yeah, yeah," I mutter, rubbing my hands up and down my thighs in the hope of ridding the unease that's running rampant through me from seeing Tatum with another man.

I feel her eyes on me. My skin prickles with awareness, but I refuse to look at her, too terrified of what she'll see in my eyes.

It's been a very long time since we knew each other intimately, but still, she still has the ability to see more than anyone else.

"Just spit it out, Aubrey," I hiss as Lewis pulls away from the curb. I haven't told him where to go; I can only assume that he's following orders from the woman sitting beside me.

There aren't many out there who would try to take control when it comes to me. But Aubrey Kendrick is one of them.

"You're on edge. I don't think I've ever seen you anything but completely sure of yourself."

"Gloat away. It doesn't happen very often," I mutter, hating that she's witness to this right now.

But equally, aside from my brothers, or now Tatum, Aubrey is the only one I trust enough to see me when I'm not at my strongest.

"Me? Gloat?" She gasps, pressing her hand to her chest. "I would never."

"Pfft. Where are we going?"

"Good question," she says, tapping her bottom lip in thought. Suddenly, she scoots forward and speaks to Lewis.

If I cared, I could listen and learn our destination. But I don't. My head is still back in Tatum's office.

"Okay, sorted," she says, sitting back beside me. "So, Tatum Warner. Your best friend's little sister. How and when did all this come about?"

I glare at her.

"Why don't you tell me? It seems that you already know all the details."

For a lot of years, I had no idea how Aubrey seemed to know everything. She'd find me in places I'd never expect. She'd walk up to me like she was expecting to see me while I stared at her in shock. It was fucking weird.

But then one day she decided to trust me with the truth, and everything started to make sense. Why she was hanging around with the corrupt businessmen my father associated with. Why she seemed to be dating men at least double her age when I knew for a fact that she didn't have any interest in them.

"What?" she asks innocently. "I would be a really shitty friend if I weren't keeping tabs on what's going down in your life."

"Some might consider it being a normal friend, Aubs," I counter.

She scoffs and waves me off. "I'm not going to lie, there was a moment when I thought hell had frozen over. I mean, the great Kingston Callahan getting married. But then, I did some more digging."

"Aubs," I warn. "I thought I told you not to do that shit."

"What? Sometimes I just can't get over my curiosity. Especially when it involves my favorite billionaire," she mocks.

"I need alcohol for this," I mutter under my breath, knowing full well that she won't miss it. Aubrey misses nothing.

"Well, lucky for you, we're heading to the perfect place."

A few minutes later, a familiar restaurant appears beside me and things feel a little more possible.

The best whiskey and steak in the state. That is exactly what I need right now. Maybe hold the steak.

"Brilliant," I say, climbing out of the back of the car the second it comes to a stop, but before I march toward the entrance, I lean back inside and demand Lewis return to the office and do whatever it takes to ensure Tatum gets home safely.

"Good evening, sir. Do you have a reservation?" the young guy says, stopping me from inviting myself to select a table.

"No."

"Oh," he says awkwardly, shrinking under my gaze. "Well, I'm sorry, but—"

"Mr. Callahan, how wonderful to have you back. Are you looking for a table?" Rob, the owner, says, interrupting his young sidekick.

"That would be wonderful," I say as Aubrey steps up beside me.

"Right this way then. Harry, please can you get a bottle of Macallan for Mr. Callahan and his guest," he says over his shoulder as we move toward the back of the restaurant to the private area Rob has set up for some of his best-paying diners.

"Oh, to know people in high places," Aubrey teases as I glance back to see the red-faced server running toward the bar like his ass is on fire.

"Here you go," Rob says, gesturing to a booth with high-backed bench seating and some fancy indoor plants to ensure total privacy from the diners on either side of us.

"Your drinks will be right over. I'll be right back with some water and to take your orders," he says after handing over the menus.

I place mine straight on the table, not needing to read it to know what I want.

In seconds, two glasses and a bottle of their finest Macallan appears before us. The poor kid's hand shakes as he pours us both a measure. It's not helped by the way Aubrey stares up at him, batting her lashes and turning the charm up to one thousand.

I kick her under the table, silently chastising her, but I also can't help laughing.

She has this innate ability to lure in men of every age, culture, and religion. It's a gift. One I'm not sure she's happy to have, but she uses it to the best of her ability nonetheless.

"Thank you so much," she purrs the second he successfully puts the bottle down without spilling any. Honestly, it's a miracle.

She smiles at him as he backs away, only just catching himself from tripping over his own feet and crashing to the floor.

"You can't help yourself, can you?" I mutter before taking a sip of my drink.

Fuck. That's good.

She shrugs. "It's fun." She throws back her drink without so much of a wince before slamming the glass on the table and staring me dead in the eyes. "So, tell me everything."

44

TATUM

"He's hot when he's angry."

"Cory," I gasp, although honestly, it's the kind of distraction I need.

"What? I'm just saying."

"Fuck. This is all such a mess."

"You're telling me," he mutters as he drops into the chair beside him and studies me closely. But before long, his eyes inevitably drop to the rock on my finger. "You're seriously engaged to that asshole?"

I'm not sure if the look in his eyes is pure disbelief, disappointment, or something else entirely.

A bitter laugh spills from my lips.

"Yeah," I confess. "I'm actually engaged to that asshole."

"Why?" he blurts, unable to believe what he's hearing.

I roll my eyes. "Because I'm madly in love with him and his overbearing, asshole ways."

"Did you want to try that again and at least try to make it sound believable?"

"I'm too exhausted."

"You know what you need? Margaritas."

"No. What I need is carbs and sleep." It's been hours since those tacos, and I'm starving.

"Okay, carbs and margaritas, and then I'll take you home to sleep. Wanna invite Lori to join us?"

I shake my head as I pack my things up. "She's got a date with Matt."

"Again?" he asks, surprised.

I get it. There aren't many men who get this far with Lori. She's usually self-sabotaged the possibility of a relationship by now.

"Yep. Matt is special."

"Good for her. Shall we?" he asks, pushing to his feet and holding his arm out for me.

"Don't let me get drunk."

He laughs. "You do know who you're talking to, right?"

"I'm going to regret this," I mutter as I continue finishing up for the night.

My email pings with something that needs my immediate attention, and I sit down to deal with it while Cory scrolls through his phone.

Focusing on work might be the last thing I need right now, but I have to admit, it does help distract me.

It's almost thirty minutes later when I finally close down my computer and stand.

"Okay, we're good to go."

"Thank God. Those margs won't drink themselves."

"It would probably be better for my body tomorrow if they did," I deadpan as I throw my purse over my shoulder and head for the door.

Cory hops up from his seat, pockets his cell, and eagerly follows me out.

"So, what's going on with you?" I ask once we're securely in the elevator.

He chuckles. "Nothing anywhere as close as entertaining as what's going on with you."

"Humor me."

"Okay." He smirks, thinking for a moment. "You know that couple I spent time with a month or so ago?"

I roll my eyes. "The couple who gave you the best night of your life? How could I forget?"

"Man, it was good," he says dreamily.

"Not good enough to share all the juicy details, though," I point out as we descend through the building.

"Nah, they're all for my dirty mind only," he teases.

"Boo, you're no fun."

"I think they would argue that fact."

"Whore." I laugh.

"Takes one to know one," he counters, more than happy to give as good as he gets.

It's one of the many things I love about Cory. He's just so easy—and I don't mean sexually, although he is pretty easy there too—but our friendship is just so easy. We can be ourselves one hundred percent and it's totally okay. It's safe. We can say anything we want and know we won't be judged.

We continue with our friendly bickering as we move toward the exit. With my attention focused on my friend, I miss the crowd outside. But one incredibly bright flash catches my eye, and I turn their way.

"Oh, holy fuck," I gasp.

"You're hot news, babe."

"I don't want to be hot fucking news," I complain as two men in black suits none too discreetly talking through earpieces head our way.

"Miss Warner, if you'll follow us, we'll escort you to the car," one of them instructs.

"Did Kingston instruct you to be here?" I ask, my eyes locked on his.

He doesn't answer. But he doesn't need to.

Kingston has orchestrated all of this. Maybe I should see it as sweet and thoughtful that he's ensured I have a way to get through the hoard of journalists all wanting the first interview about our bullshit union. But right now, I'm finding it more overbearing and controlling than I am sweet.

"This is fucking bullshit," I mutter so that only Cory can hear.

"I've got an Uber waiting. You don't need to do as you're told." His words are like music to my ears.

"What's the car?"

He pulls his cell from his pocket and shows me the picture of the black Prius that's waiting for us.

"Ready to run?" I ask, a shot of adrenaline saturating me.

"Oh hell, yeah."

Cory grabs my hand, and together we dart around the security guards and rush toward the front doors and the awaiting press.

Chaos erupts, but neither of us stops running as the space around us gets smaller and smaller.

"Tatum, how does it feel to be engaged to Kingston Callahan?"

"Tatum, can we see a close-up of the ring?"

"Tatum, were you expecting him to pop the question so soon?"

"Tatum, how does it feel to snag Chicago's most eligible bachelor?"

The security details are behind us; I can feel their presence as we set our sights on the car.

Lewis stands beside Kingston's car, his hand poised ready to pull the door open to let us escape.

But just before he does so, we dart to the right, to the car idling behind him.

"Tatum, what are you—"

We dive into the back of the car and fall about in fits of giggles.

Fuck. I needed that. Today has been too much.

"Step on it," Cory demands, and thankfully, the driver follows orders and pulls away from the curb as the crowd moves closer.

"Oh god," I cry as we're thrown back into the seats when he floors the gas and speeds away from the Warner Group building.

"Now, that's what I'm talking about," Cory shouts excitedly. "That was fun. You're like...a celebrity."

My stomach knots. "I'm really not," I mutter.

"Didn't you hear them all calling your name? Girl, you're the hottest thing in Chicago right now."

"Please stop," I beg. "I want to be an invisible thing."

"Should have thought about that before you attached yourself to the hottest man in the city then," he counters.

"If only it were that simple."

"Well, I guess the heart wants what the heart wants," he swoons.

His brows pinch when I groan.

"What? What am I missing?"

"Not here," I whisper, shooting a look at the driver, who I'm sure is more than interested in the drama of my life. "Where are we going?" I ask instead, changing the subject.

"Trust me, T. You're going to love it."

Cory wasn't wrong. The small family-run Mexican restaurant is perfect.

We're hiding down a backstreet with no chance of anyone finding us.

He made sure our Uber driver took an extra-long way here to ensure we lost anyone who might have been following us.

I found it hard to believe that the journalists would go to that length. I'm just me. I'm nothing special. Camping outside Warner Group is easy, but chasing me around the city is something else entirely.

"Oh my god, these are so good," I slur as the remainder of my most recent cocktail disappears down my throat.

We've eaten our body weight in nachos, and my blood is buzzing from the tequila shots and margaritas we've consumed.

It's been perfect.

So fucking perfect.

"I love you, Cor," I say, wrapping my arm around his shoulders and holding him tight. "You're such a good friend."

"Love you too, T," he says, kissing my temple.

It's innocent and comforting. Just a friend being there for another friend.

It's exactly what I need.

Admittedly, I should go home.

My cell has long died, thanks to all the calls and messages. Mostly from Kingston, after I forced him to leave my office.

I've no idea where he went or what he did. I like the idea that he went home alone to sulk. But this is Kingston we're talking about. I'm not sure sulking is in his vocabulary. If he doesn't get what he wants, he smashes down every single obstacle in his way until he does.

Another two margaritas that I don't remember ordering arrive as the server clears our empty plates.

Resting my head back, I lose myself in stupid thoughts about our weekend.

How was it only hours ago that we drove back into the city blissfully happy?

It feels like a lifetime ago now.

Waking up with his hands on my body, feeling him pushing inside me.

"Oh shit," Cory gasps, his eyes widening as he stares at his cell.

"What?"

"Nothing. Nothing. It doesn't matter."

"Oh no, you're not pulling that shit with me." Reaching my hand out, I snatch his cell from him and scroll up.

I've no idea what I was expecting, but honestly, it wasn't to see a photo of Kingston's hand pressed against a woman's back as he helps her into his car.

Lewis is standing there watching like it's nothing.

"Maybe it's an old picture," Cory adds.

"It was posted forty-five minutes ago," I point out. "Who is she?"

"No idea. The article doesn't name her, and there is no way of telling in that photograph."

I shouldn't care. And it certainly shouldn't hurt. But fuck. It does.

Betrayal drips through my veins like poison.

Ripping my tear-filled eyes from the screen, I look up at my friend.

A weird mix of anger, frustration, and regret war inside me.

I can sit here and be disappointed at Kingston for going out with someone else all I like. But I'm doing the exact same thing. And with the man he watched me dancing with, no less.

But still, I'm pissed at him. The stunt he pulled with photos of our private moment at the cabin is unacceptable.

He didn't even give me a hint that it was going to be front-page news this morning. How fucking fair is that?

I'm about to demand that Cory call us another Uber when a shadow falls over our table.

Glancing up, I find two familiar suited men staring back at me.

How did they find us?

"Can you come with us please, Miss Warner?" one asks, his voice leaving very little room to argue.

I want to, though. Of course I do. It's how I roll, defying the orders of every controlling man that I can. But something tells me that arguing right now would be a bad move.

"What about Cory?" I ask.

"I think Mr. Denham needs to go home, don't you?" he states, lifting a brow as I gasp as the realization that they know who he is.

Fuck.

My heart rate increases as I think about the possible fallout from this.

Kingston is going to be pissed. That's a sure fucking bet.

But could that be a good thing?

Desire sits heavy between my thighs.

No. No. It's a really bad thing.

Keep your head in the game, Tatum. Do not give in to the tequila and a hot man.

"Fine. Cory, I'll call you, okay?"

Leaning over, I kiss his cheek, but before I get a chance to say anything else, I'm none-too-gently dragged away from him.

"I don't think that's a good idea, do you, Miss Warner?" the other man growls.

"I can do what I want. No one owns me. And my name is Tate," I spit before marching toward the restaurant's entrance.

I want to say that it's smooth, that my legs work as they should and that I look like a put-together, sophisticated, intelligent woman.

But then I go over on my ankle and bump into the table beside me, knocking over a water jug. Thankfully, the table is empty and waiting to be cleared, but there are enough diners in here to witness my drunken antics. And not only that, but when I glance up at the windows, I find cameras pointed in my direction.

Fuck my fucking life.

"We're going this way," a deep voice demands before I'm turned around and directed toward the back of the restaurant.

There's a car idling outside the back door and Lewis sits behind the wheel, ready to whisk me away.

I let out a sigh as one of the men opens the door for me and then joins me in the back once I'm safe, while the other sits up in front with Lewis.

"Good evening, Tatum," Lewis says, his eyes finding me in the mirror.

"Don't give me that look, Lewis," I mutter.

"Home?" he asks, although I don't know why he bothers. We all know that I'm going to be going wherever Kingston wants me to go.

That's my life now. I'm the little lady who has to do as she's told.

A bitter laugh spills from my lips.

Did he really think that I'd fall into line that easily?

He knows me better than that, surely. Or did he think that a

325

handful of orgasms delivered by his skillful body would soften me? Make me more pliable to his wishes?

"Do I actually get a choice?" I ask irritably.

Lewis wants to say something. I see his jaw move as if he's going to, but then he changes his mind.

Probably for the best.

I don't want to go to Kingston's penthouse. I want to go home. I want to put on my pajamas and curl up with Griz.

The thought of my fluffy terror makes a smile tug at the corners of my lips.

I sit forward, swaying slightly as I do.

"Lewis," I ask sweetly.

"Tatum," he counters, studying me as closely as he can in the rearview mirror as he navigates the backroads of Chicago.

"Can we make a detour, please? It will only be a short one. I just need to pick something up."

45

KINGSTON

I didn't go home after dropping Aubrey off at her hotel. Instead, I made the possibly stupid decision to swing by Kian's place.

I was already a few too many whiskeys in, and the second he saw the look on my face when he opened the door to me, he immediately passed me another.

He wanted details, but to my surprise, he never asked. Instead, I turned the conversation to work, and that was how it stayed as we worked our way through half a bottle of his finest.

It was good.

Nice.

But it wasn't where I wanted to be. Not that I thought anything good could come out of thinking about being at home with Tatum after our interaction earlier.

I had more chance of her cutting my throat after what I did, than I did her wanting to jump my bones and give me a nice little repeat of our filthy weekend.

She's furious with me. I saw that in her eyes the second I walked into her office.

But what did she expect? She knew the terms we're bound to.

Surely, she didn't honestly expect the weekend to stay between us. Did she?

"Shit," I mutter, resting my head back as Lewis drives me home.

"She's home safe," he assures me, his eyes meeting mine in the mirror.

I think of her getting drunk with him tonight.

The second she swerved Lewis when she finished work earlier, I was alerted to her defiance.

The need to leave Aubrey behind and go and find her myself was strong, but as much as I hated the thought of her being out with another man—a man who clearly wants her—I knew nothing good could come of it.

I was angry, and so was she.

My fists curl on my lap as I remember the way they danced together last weekend. So familiar. Too familiar.

Anger licks at my insides and I sit forward, already impatient to be home. To see with my own eyes that she's there and untouched.

Fuck. I swear to God. If he touched her...

I fidget all the way back to my apartment. Lewis keeps one eye on me, but he doesn't say anything.

He's been with me long enough to know that no words will help.

I need action. And they can only happen with her.

The car has barely stopped moving when I push the door open and jump out.

"Is that—"

"You can go home, Lewis. Thank you," I state as I march toward the elevator that will take me to her.

My foot taps against the floor and my fingers drum on my thighs as the car moves slower than I'm sure it ever has before.

The second the doors part, I burst out, my impatience getting to be too much.

The door unlocks the second I press my hand to it, and I rush inside.

Her scent lingers in the air and my mouth waters.

The sweetness of it melts some of the anger that has me in its tight hold as I march through the living room.

The lights are off aside from a lamp in the corner, but I don't need light to illuminate my way around my own home.

My foot collides with something on the floor that goes scooting across the wood flooring and disappears under the couch.

Before Tatum, I'd have had to find what it was and put it where it should be. But all I can think about right now is her. Fuck whatever I just kicked under the couch. If it were important, it wouldn't be on the floor.

The huge clock on the wall catches my eye as I move to the base of the stairs.

It's late. Too fucking late for a Monday night. But it's a bit too late to do anything about it now.

I pause and weigh my options.

The hurt in her eyes earlier tells me that she'd have retreated to the guest room again.

But there was more than hurt. There was anger and frustration too. And those two usually lead to Tatum's defiance.

Making a decision, I lift my foot and begin climbing the stairs, praying that I know my fiancée as well as I think I do.

Silence greets me when I get to the door, but I quickly find that the blinds have been closed, and upon closer inspection, there's a Tatum-shaped lump in my bed.

I might still be frustrated by her actions earlier, but knowing she's in my bed, waiting for me does things to my body.

In record time, I've shed my suit and thrown my boxers in the laundry.

She can be as mad as she wants, but I refuse to put a barrier between us.

I take a piss and brush my teeth. I want to say that my movements are fluid and easy, but honestly, the whiskey is hitting harder than ever.

I stare at myself in the mirror as I stand at the sink and smirk. My eyes are wild.

Fuck. I really hope my girl is about to be as wild in my bed.

My cock stirs as I remember how filthy she was this weekend.

Fucking perfect is what she was.

Annoying little Tatum Warner...who'd have thought it?

She grew up to be a fucking seductress extraordinaire.

Abandoning my toothbrush, I flick the light off and blindly make my way to the bed, my cock rising higher with every step I take.

Waking her up and pushing myself inside her feels like a year ago now.

I need it again.

I need to feel her tightness, her warmth wrapped around me, sucking me deeper.

Approaching the bed, I reach out for the covers and gently pull them back.

My knee hits the mattress, and I'm about to lower myself down when a weird hissing fills the room.

Too confused to register it, I continue.

My ass is just about to touch the sheet when it turns into a loud growl and then something sharp and really fucking painful swipes across my stomach.

"What the fuck?" I bark, jumping out of bed and reaching for the light. "Shit," I hiss as the room illuminates, making my eyes water and my head spin.

I've had too much fucking whiskey for this bullshit.

"What are you doing?" Tatum slurs, letting me know that I'm not the only tipsy one after the events of the day.

My vision clears and so does the ginger ball of fluff that's sitting in the middle of my fucking bed, baring its fangs at me.

"Me? What am I doing? What the fuck is that doing?" I retort, pointing at the feral animal making itself at home where it doesn't belong.

"*That* is my pussy."

"No, Tatum. Your pussy has way less hair and is much friendlier than that thing."

"Please use her name, she isn't a thing."

"Her name," I echo as blood trickles down to my much-less-interested dick.

Funny how one type of pussy can make it deflate just as fast as a different kind can make it grow.

"Yes, asshole," she seethes as she climbs to her knees and pulls the cat into her arms. "Her name."

"I don't fucking remember that."

She glares at me, silently demanding I at least try.

I throw my hands up in frustration.

"Princess Sparkles Glitterpants?"

Her lips twitch at my stupid suggestion, but she doesn't allow the smile to fully form.

"Don't be ridiculous. I'd never call a cat that."

"Oh, so her real name is so much better?"

"Her name is perfect for her. Isn't it, my pwetty kitty?" she says, tickling the cat behind its ear.

"Right. Great. Can we go back to the part where she made me bleed?" I say, finally looking down at the very obvious scratches across my stomach.

Blood trickles from each one, racing down toward my pubic hair.

"Aw, she was protecting me."

"You don't need protecting from me," I mutter, disgruntled. "You're going to be my wife, remember? You're going to be mine."

Tatum grits her teeth, her jaw popping with irritation.

She doesn't immediately snap back, and I'm not sure what to make of that.

"Whatever," she mutters, placing the cat back down in the middle of the bed and climbing to her feet.

She stumbles, letting me know she's drunker than I first thought before she stalks toward the bathroom.

My eyes follow her every move while the cat continues to snarl at me.

I might have signed up to marry Tatum, but I never signed up to house a feral feline. As if Tatum's catty side isn't enough...

"What?" she snaps, shooting a look over her shoulder and finding me watching her.

"You look hot," I state, letting my eyes drop down her body.

She's wearing a white tank and a gray pair of panties. Simple but so fucking hot.

"And you look like an overbearing asshole, but do you see me staring?" Defying her words, her eyes drop to my dick. Or maybe it's to the wound on my stomach, I'm not entirely sure. But my dick jerks happily regardless.

Before I find any words to come back at her with, she disappears into the bathroom.

Spinning around, I stare at the creature in my bed.

"Don't you have anywhere else to sleep?" I snarl, glaring at it as hard as it is me.

Who knew cats were capable of dirty looks?

Or maybe it's not cats and just this devil incarnate disguised as a cat.

Its hackles rise and I get another shot of its vicious teeth.

Brilliant. Just fucking brilliant.

The toilet flushing drags me from my staring competition with the fluffy pussy, and I march toward the bathroom.

"You owe me," I state.

"How do you figure that?" she asks, watching me in the mirror as she washes her hands.

Her eyes are wild and unfocused. Her hair is a mess and her cheeks are flushed.

She looks incredible.

"I'm bleeding because of you."

"Debatable," she mutters under her breath.

"My first-aid kit is down there," I say, pointing to the drawer beneath the sink. "I need cleaning up."

"I'm sure you're more than capable," she counters.

"As I said, you owe me."

46

TATUM

The air turns thick as we stare at each other.

Do I feel bad about the fact that Griz attacked him? Honestly?

No, not really. If I'm being truthful, I expected her to do so.

She's nothing if not protective, and there was a twisted part of me that wanted him to know that someone can do a proper job of looking after me. Not that I want him to, of course.

But...

Fuck.

My head is too fucked up with all the tequila, and I'm royally screwed.

"I don't owe you anything after what you've done," I state, taking a step toward the door.

I turn my back on him, and I've almost escaped when he speaks.

"They were just some pictures, Tatum."

I still, anger coursing through my veins.

I don't want to react. I shouldn't react. But the tequila is stronger than my self-control and I spin back around, my eyes narrowing on his before I spit, "Just some photographs. Is that what you really think?"

He shrugs. He really does think that.

Nothing more than images.

Emotion creeps up my throat and tears burn my eyes.

It really meant nothing to him.

"Yeah, sure. They're just photos," I say sadly before turning back around so I can escape him.

I've already given him too much. He doesn't need to know that I'm not just angry about how he announced our engagement, but I'm also hurt.

It's bad enough that he has the power to hurt me at all.

I don't want him to know that he's done it as well.

"Tate, wait," he calls before I manage to leave the room.

My head drops, but I don't stop.

I can't.

I can't allow him to see the tears and pain in my eyes.

But he's faster than me, and his warm hand wraps around my upper arm, stopping me from going anywhere.

Before I know what's happening, he's spinning me around, cupping my jaw, and tilting my head up so I have no choice but to look into his eyes.

"Baby?" he whispers, searching my eyes.

"Just leave it, King."

His brows pinch as he continues staring at me, but he doesn't say a word. He's so out of his depth right now.

I try to jerk away from him, but he holds me tighter, stopping me.

"Please, just—"

"I'm sorry," he finally says.

My lips part to say something, but I quickly find that I have no words.

Instead, more tears flood my eyes until one finally falls free.

"Fuck, baby. I didn't mean to—"

"It's okay," I whimper.

"It's really fucking not. You're crying."

"I'm drunk and emotional. I just need to go back to bed," I ramble, embarrassed that I've reacted so strongly to all of this.

It shouldn't matter.

It's just a business deal.

"You think that because I shared the photos, I don't care. That that moment out on the deck, or what followed, didn't matter," he guesses.

"They don't matter. I'm just stupid. I'm going back to bed."

He lets me turn away, giving me the impression that he's going to allow me to escape, but it's all an illusion.

I shriek when my back is suddenly pressed against the cool wall and the warmth of his big body burns the front of mine.

"Just let me go," I beg, refusing to meet his eyes.

"No fucking chance, baby," he says before ducking down and brushing his lips over mine.

"King," I mumble against his lips.

"Let me make it up to you, baby."

"Sex isn't going to fix this," I argue as he presses his hard length against my stomach. Tempting me.

"Didn't say it would. It'll make it sweeter though."

"I knew we shouldn't have slept together," I state, turning my head away, but it doesn't deter him.

"You're wrong," he groans as his lips graze down my throat, making my skin erupt with goosebumps. "It was the best thing we ever did."

"You need to stop," I say, twisting my fingers in his hair to pull him back, but as I do, he sucks that sweet spot beneath my ear and I find him doing the exact opposite.

"They might have the photos, baby. But they'll never know what it felt like."

Oh god.

"I'll never forget what it felt like when you said yes."

"I didn't have a choice," I argue, my voice raspy with need.

"You always have a choice, Tatum. Always."

He's right. I know he is.

I could have said no in Dad's office and walked away from everything.

I could have said no on that deck and turned my back on this arrangement, on Kingston.

I could still do it now.

But I already know I'm not going to.

Despite all the reasons I should be doing the very opposite of what I am right now, I can't find it in myself to do it.

There is something here. Something I can't help but want to explore.

It's going to hurt. I know it will. But still, something tells me that the high will be worth the pain.

"King," I moan when his teeth drag across my collarbone. My nipples harden, pressing against the thin fabric of my tank.

"Right here, baby. Tell me what you need."

"For you to stop being an asshole."

He laughs as he pulls the thin strap of my tank over my shoulder. "I don't want to make promises that we both know I can't keep."

In a flash, he has the fabric of my tank around my ribs, my bare breasts exposed to him.

"This isn't—" My words are cut off when he sucks one of my nipples into his hot mouth.

My head falls back against the wall with a small thud, but I've had far too much tequila for it to hurt.

He laves at my sensitive skin, his tongue teasing the tip before he sucks harder, his teeth nipping at me.

"Oh my god. I shouldn't be letting you do this."

He smirks. I don't need to look down to see it. I can feel it.

"I think this is the perfect way to end our nights, don't you? With a reminder of who we should end all our days with."

I glance down to find him staring up at me.

I'm assuming that's his way of reassuring me that there wasn't anything between him and the woman he was photographed with earlier. But it's never going to be enough to stop me from asking.

Their contact was too familiar. The way he touched her...

I gasp as a bolt of pain from his teeth on my nipple shoots straight to my clit.

"Fuck, Kingston."

"Tell me," he demands, his dark green eyes blazing with desire. "Tell me what you need."

"I-I—" I stumble over my words, getting lost in his eyes, in the promise of all the things he can offer me. "I want..." His eyes widen, urging me on. "Eat me. Make me come all over your face. Then I'm going back to bed," I add.

If he thinks he's getting anything out of this, then he's seriously going to need to reconsider.

"I can live with that," he mutters, tucking his fingers into my panties and dragging them down my legs.

Pressing his nose against me, he inhales deeply and groans.

Fuck. It's filthy.

So fucking dirty.

I love it.

Grasping my ankle, he lifts my foot from the floor, giving me little choice but to open up for him.

He stares at my pussy like it's the best thing he's ever seen, and fuck if it doesn't flood with heat.

"King," I whisper, the one leg I'm standing on already weak just from the way he's looking at me.

"Want to end every single day like this."

My head spins at his confession, but I don't have time to try and decipher if I believe him or not, because he latches onto my clit and sucks until it's all I can do not to come right then and there.

Fuck. Why is it so good with him?

Why couldn't it have been like this with the others? The nice ones. The decent ones.

You haven't been with any nice or decent ones, a little voice says.

Those thoughts are banished when Kingston pushes two fingers deep inside.

"Oh fuck. Yes. Yes," I cry, throwing my head back and bashing it against the wall again.

"Look at me," he mumbles, the vibration of his deep voice rocking through every inch of me. "Watch as I make you come."

Oh, sweet baby Jesus. This man.

This fucking man.

Dropping my chin to my chest, I watch every single second of him working my body, until I'm gripping his hair so tightly, I'm amazed I don't pull chunks out.

My voice is hoarse as I scream out his name. Wave after wave of pleasure washes through me, and he doesn't stop until I'm spent.

He pulls away, pressing a kiss to my mound and then on each of my hip bones before he sits back on his haunches.

Movement by the door catches my eye, but it doesn't bother me. I know what—or should I say, who—it is.

Kingston stills the moment he sees the movement, but it doesn't register for a few seconds.

"What the fuck?" he bellows suddenly, jumping to his feet as he glares pure death at Griz.

"Your pussy really shouldn't be watching me eat your pussy, Tatum. That's just fucking wrong," he states, placing his hands on his hips.

The movement drags my eyes to his wound.

"Oh shit," I breathe when I find more blood than I was expecting covering the lower half of his stomach and thigh.

"It's fine," he waves off, turning his back on Griz as if he's worried she's about to start using his dick like a toy. "Why is it still staring at me?"

"Stop being such a little bitch about a cat. She's sweet. Come on," I say, taking his hand after pulling my blood-stained tank from around my middle. "Sit," I demand, shoving him onto the closed toilet.

"She is not sweet," he mutters as I pull the drawer open and find the first-aid kit he mentioned.

Dropping to my knees between his thighs, I grab what I need while King has a stare-off with Griz.

Leaving them to it, I begin cleaning at his scratches with a wipe.

"Holy fuck. What the hell is that?" he practically screeches as he tries to scramble away from me.

"It's an antiseptic wipe, you baby. Jesus, sit back down."

"Just stick a bandage on it or something," he demands.

"We need to make sure it's clean first. You don't want it to get infected."

"If there is any chance of that thing infecting me, then I'm sorry, but it needs putting down."

"Kingston," I snap. "You lay a finger on Griz and you will wake up to find your dick has been unattached from your body," I warn darkly, making his eyes widen.

"You wouldn't."

"Care to test the theory?" I ask, pressing the wipe against him again. This time he only hisses in pain. Wimp.

"You love my dick too much to cut it off. You'd miss it."

"I can find a replacement easily enough. Yours isn't anything special," I lie.

I don't look up at him. I can't. He'll be able to see the truth in my eyes, clear as fucking day.

"Whatever," he mutters, finally relaxing and widening his thighs a little more.

Every time I move, his hard dick brushes against my bare breast.

Neither of us mentions it, but the air around us is buzzing with electricity.

The sound of claws on the countertop hits my ears before they move closer.

"It's looking at my dick like it wants to eat it."

"Then maybe you shouldn't be too worried about me cutting it off after all. My pussy might get to it first."

"This isn't funny," he snaps.

I glance over at Griz and find he's right. She is staring right at King's dick.

"Probably just hasn't seen one so small before."

His stomach muscles clench at my taunt, but he chooses to ignore it. "She always watches you hook up, huh?" The roughness in his voice gives away his jealousy, and I can't help but smirk.

"Well, she is my cat, after all."

After pressing a dressing to his stomach, not that I actually think it needs it, I finally sit back on my haunches and look up at him.

He stares down at me between his thighs before glancing at Griz.

"She looks bored."

I raise a brow and look over.

"Looks fine to me."

"Nah, she definitely came in here looking for more entertainment than you attacking me with a death wipe."

"Kingston, are you suggesting that my cat wants to watch me suck you off?"

He shrugs one shoulder.

"I've no idea. She's your cat, not mine."

His dick jerks and my mouth waters.

I shouldn't do it.

I already told him that he was getting nothing out of me tonight.

I blame the tequila.

Totally the tequila's fault that I lean forward and lick up the length of his shaft.

The second his taste floods my mouth, I throw any kind of caution I might have had to the wind and take him to the back of my throat.

His hips thrust, his ass lifting from the toilet seat as I deepthroat him.

"Holy fucking shit, Tatum. You're fucking perfect."

And with his praise filling the air—and my cat watching—I work him to a fast yet intense release.

47

KINGSTON

I wake clinging to the edge of the bed with my ass sticking out of the covers.

The fuck?

Opening my eyes, I reach for my cell, killing the alarm before glancing to the other side of the bed.

It's empty.

"Fuck," I breathe as memories from the night before come back to me. Although I must admit, some of it is hazy.

I try to shift farther onto the bed, but something stops me.

Looking down, I find that one part of my night was very real.

A curled-up cat is sleeping where my legs should be.

"You have got to be shitting me," I complain.

As if the thing has been waiting for me to wake up and find it, one eye opens slowly. She glares at me, almost as terrifying with one eye as she is with two, before closing it again as if she's bored of me already.

"Fucking cat," I mutter as I slip out of bed and march toward the bathroom.

I glance at the wall where Tatum was last night as I dropped to my knees for her, and then at the toilet where she patched me up and sucked me dry.

Fuck me, that was good.

The end of my night was unexpected. I might have stumbled in here desperate for her, but I was sure we were in for a fight.

I guess I have the stupid cat to thank for that.

Her appearance certainly was a distraction, although I'm not sure if it was a good one or not.

I love fighting with Tatum, and I certainly had a lot of things to say after everything that went down yesterday.

I put myself through the shower and freshen up before selecting a suit and then following the scent of coffee that wafts through the apartment.

It's not a smell I'm used to experiencing here, but I can't say it's one I dislike.

I might want her to think more about what she puts in her body— seriously hypocritical after the amount of whiskey I drank last night, but whatever—but even I can appreciate good coffee when I find it.

The apartment is still in darkness as I descend the stairs, and my brows pinch. Surely she hasn't left, abandoning Satan in bed with me?

It's not until I hit the bottom step that I realize she is here. She's sitting with only her cell screen for light at the kitchen counter with a coffee mug before her.

"Good morning, ba—"

"Who is she?" she demands before I even get my first sentence out.

"Uh...who is what?" I ask, confused.

Moving closer, I find that Tatum is on Google, and almost all of the photographs she's scrolling through are of me and a woman.

Some I recognize, many I don't. Internally, I cringe.

"What are you doing?" I ask, although, I think it's pretty obvious.

"Trying to find her," she explains as she keeps scrolling.

"Good luck with that," I muse, walking around her to the refrigerator to get my juice.

"Who is she, Kingston?"

I smirk. I can't help it. Hearing the jealousy in her tone does things to me.

"Who is Cory Denham?" I counter.

In all honesty, I know the answer. That went to the top of my to-do list pretty quickly after watching the way they were dancing together.

"A friend," she explains.

"A friend who wants to fuck you," I add, feeling the same green-eyed monster growl in my stomach that infiltrated her voice a few seconds ago.

"Kingston, the whole city—hell, the entire fucking country—knows that I'm wearing your ring. I don't think you need to worry that—"

"I'll always worry," I blurt without thinking.

Her eyes widen in surprise.

"You're mine, Tatum. And last night you went out and got drunk with another man." Her eyebrows shoot up.

"Oh no, you do not get to stand there and say things like that when you did exactly the same thing," she argues.

"You don't need to worry about Aubrey. She doesn't want to fuck me. Unlike your little friend."

Her nostrils flare as she glares at me.

"There was no chance of that happening," she seethes.

"Good to know," I state, twisting the top of my juice bottle off and lifting it to my lips. "But you have fucked him, have you not?" My voice is cold and hard. It tells her all she needs to know about my understanding of this subject.

She wants to lie. I can see it in her eyes.

"Yes," she finally confesses. "I've slept with him. Is that what you wanted to hear?"

"No, Tatum. It is the opposite of what I want to hear."

"So?"

"So what?"

She fumes. Her eyes narrow and her cheeks redden. It's so fucking hot it's amazing that I manage to refrain from bending her over the counter and fucking her right here and now to prove my point about who she belongs to.

Reaching down, I adjust my hardening dick.

"Who is she, Kingston?"

"Aubrey Kendrick," I explain, holding her eyes so she can see the truth in them. "She's...a mercenary."

Tatum rears back in surprise.

"A mercenary?"

"Yes. We met at an event a few years ago. She's a useful contact to have. Knows a lot of people."

Tatum's mouth opens and closes, but no words spill free.

"She's good people."

"She kills people for money."

"Bad people," I correct. "Mostly men. She seduces them, makes them think they're special, and then, well...ruins them, mostly."

"And you're going to try to convince me that you haven't slept with a woman who seduces men for money?"

"I'm not trying to convince you of anything, Tatum."

"So you have slept with her."

"A long time ago, yes. Once. We've had a platonic friendship ever since."

She shakes her head. "You're so full of shit I'm amazed it isn't spilling from your ears."

"I'm not lying to you, baby."

She hops up from the stool and angrily shoves it under the counter.

"Do you know what? I don't give a shit. Do what you want, Kingston. That's what our contract states, doesn't it? You can go out there and get your rocks off with anyone you want while I've got to sit here playing the part of the good little wife. It's only a year. I can cope.

"I don't need your shit, your dick, or your fucking attitude problem. I've got everything I could need. My life was perfectly fine before you forced your way into it."

She storms toward the stairs, a loud huff of irritation trailing behind her.

"You don't have everything though, do you, Tatum? That's why you agreed to this," I helpfully point out.

"Get fucked, Kingston," she hisses as she begins climbing.

"Don't take too long. We have an appointment in forty-five minutes."

"I have meetings all morning," she calls back.

"No, you don't. They have been rearranged to fit in the appointment we should have had last night."

A cry of frustration floats down to me before the bedroom door slams hard enough to make the walls shake.

Well. That went well...

"Why are we here?" Tatum demands as Lewis pulls up in front of The Broadway.

"Come on," I say, pushing the door open and then helping her out.

With our fingers entwined, we make our way to reception. There are more than a few interested sets of eyes that follow us as I lead her toward the elevator.

We step inside with a handful of others. which stops her from demanding answers to all the questions I see spinning around in her head.

If it weren't for her stunt yesterday, she'd know exactly what was happening. But seeing as she fucked up our first meeting before dismissing me as if I'm nothing to her, keeping her in the dark for a little longer doesn't bother me.

In only minutes we approach the room I have booked, and after knocking once, I push the door open and gesture for her to enter.

"Ah, Miss Warner, Mr. Callahan. It's so wonderful to meet you," a woman of a similar age to our mothers greets as she pushes to her feet and holds her hand out for us to shake. "I'm Mia Simmons, and I'm your wedding planner. I'm so excited to finalize the details and make your day everything you've been dreaming of."

Tatum shoots me a death glare, but I don't turn to look at her. Instead, I gesture for her to sit on the opposite couch to Mia before taking my place beside her.

"Would you like tea, dear?" Mia asks, lifting the teapot between us.

"Um...sure," she agrees.

"Mr. Callahan."

"Thank you," I say with a smile.

She makes quick work of pouring our drinks before setting her eyes on Tatum.

"Now, I will say I've been given some deadlines in my time, but I think this one might be up there with the most challenging."

Tatum's brow wrinkles as she tries to figure out the woman's words.

"But I have every confidence in my suppliers. You will both have the most incredible day next Saturday."

"Next Saturday?" Tatum blurts, her ass lifting from the couch as if she has every intention of running away.

My grip on her hand tightens, a silent warning to play the game.

She shoots me a look, one that might make a lesser man cower, but not me. I'll stare her down all day long quite happily.

"Oh my goodness," she finally whispers. "I just can't believe it's only next week. Crazy, right?"

The wedding planner wants to agree; it's right there in her eyes, but she wisely keeps her mouth shut on the subject.

I haven't hired the best for no reason.

"It's exciting," she says instead, with a wide smile.

"Okay, so Mr. Callahan--"

"Kingston, please," I say softly.

She nods, smiling at me. "Kingston has already explained some of your wishes, and I'd like to go over those now along with the finer details of the day."

"Of course," Tatum says through gritted teeth, her grip on my hand tightening, her nails digging into my skin in punishment.

We sit there for an hour talking about flower arrangements, colors, bridesmaid dresses, groomsmen suits, cakes, and what feels like a million other things I've never cared about in my life.

Due to the fact I blindsided Tatum with this and she now wants to punish me in any way possible, I'm forced to give way more input than I'm sure most soon-to-be grooms would. But that's okay, I'm happy to take some of the weight.

"Okay," Mia says flicking through her notes one last time. "I think that's everything for now. I will get you an appointment for dress fittings and I'll email that over to you before the end of the day. And then I'll be in contact to confirm everything we've discussed here." She pauses and looks between the two of us with a soft smile playing on her lips and a glint in her eyes. If I didn't already know it from her job, it's now more than obvious that this woman is a sucker for a wedding. "This is going to be a truly beautiful day for the two of you. I can see how excited you both are."

I almost bark out laughing at her blatant lie. Tatum has not been the excited bride-to-be that I'm sure she's used to experiencing, that's for sure.

In truth, she was probably more enthusiastic planning her father's funeral.

"Thank you so much for rearranging at short notice," I say as we rise to say our goodbyes.

"No problem. Have a wonderful day both of you. I'll be in touch."

Without another word, she slips from the room. The second the door closes behind her, Tatum turns her furious stare on me.

"Next Saturday. Are you serious?"

I hold her stare. "We have to be married for one year to meet the terms of your father's will, Tatum. The longer we wait, the longer we've got to be together."

Her expression falters for the briefest moment, it's so fast, I almost question whether I saw it or not. But I definitely did.

"And we don't want to extend that any longer than necessary. I need to get to work, Kingston. I have a life outside of becoming your wife and I'd like to return to it."

Forcing a smile onto my face, I gesture toward the doors. "My pleasure, baby."

"Don't," she hisses, jumping forward and out of reach the second I press my hand to the small of her back.

My smile grows.

Oh, how I missed my defiant little brat.

48

TATUM

"Good evening, Tatum," Judith says with a wide smile as I spill out of the elevator long after everyone else in the building has left for the night.

"Hi. Isn't it a little late for you to still be here? He's not working you too hard, is he?"

"Miles?" she asks with a laugh. "Never. That boy is far too sweet for that."

"Sweet? Are we talking about the same Miles?"

"I'll be heading out in a few minutes—just finishing off a couple of things." She pushes her keyboard aside, turning her whole focus on me. "How are you doing? Things have been a little...intense."

I deflate under her caring gaze.

"You could say that," I mutter. I've no idea how much she knows. We haven't had much contact after the funeral plans were in place, but she's been here for Miles no doubt in the way our mother should be, so something tells me that she's aware of everything that's going on in my life right now.

"You look exhausted," she says softly.

I smile, trying to ignore just how true that statement is. "I'm okay," I lie.

After the relaxing weekend we had, I should be refreshed and ready to take on the world. But yesterday ruined all the good gained from our little getaway.

I might have been wasted last night, but not even the tequila could help me switch off.

After stupidly falling back into Kingston's trap in the bathroom, I took myself to bed and then just laid there, staring into the darkness.

Kingston fell into bed a few minutes later, and I swear he almost immediately started snoring.

Good to know that everything was all right in his world while mine felt like it was spinning out of control.

All I could think about was the woman he was with last night and the terms of the contract.

He's allowed to see other women. He's allowed to do more than touch the small of her back, a move that I didn't realize I liked quite so much until I saw him do it to someone else. Nothing about what he did last night was wrong, no matter how it felt to me.

Hell, nothing I did was wrong either, but I'm aware of how it looks.

But surely, agreeing to marry Kingston shouldn't mean I have to kiss goodbye to friendships with men.

Sure, Cory and I have been intimate a handful of times, but it was only a means to an end. There's nothing between us romantically, and there never will be. We both friend-zoned each other a while ago. We just also enjoy the benefits when we're both single and lonely. There is nothing wrong with that.

"Tatum, you need to look after yourself. That's the most important thing," Judith chastises.

"I am," I lie again.

She stares at me, not believing a word of it. We never could pull the wool over her eyes.

"Is Miles still here?" I ask, changing the subject.

"Of course. I swear he's barely left this building since your father passed. You're not the only one feeling the pressure of all of this."

Guilt knots up my insides that I haven't been a better sister. I'm not the only one who's had their world thrown into chaos.

"Things will get better," I assure her.

"Everyone is worried about this merger," she confesses.

"It'll be okay. Kingston and Miles won't do anything stupid."

"I trust them. But a lot of people only know Kingston as the cut-throat COO at Callahan."

"No one is going to lose their jobs because of this." It's not my place to promise anything. I'm merely one of the employees at Warner Group. Hell, my job could be on the line just as much as anyone else.

"Everything will work out as it should," Judith says with a smile. "He'll be pleased to see you," she adds, her eyes drifting down the hallway toward where my brother is hiding out.

"He still hasn't moved into Dad's office?"

She shakes her head. "All the adjustments will take time," she whispers.

I guess it's easy to forget that Miles didn't have the same kind of relationship with our father as I did.

I take a step back and look over my shoulder, wishing there was something I could do to make all of this easier on everyone.

"Enjoy your evening," I say as I continue retreating.

"You too, sweetie. Get some rest, yes?"

"You got it."

I let out a long sigh as I stand before Miles's office door.

I know he can do this. Both he and Kingston are more than capable of taking over this business. I just wish he didn't have to do it so suddenly, without our father here to lean on when he needed it.

Sure, he has Michael, but it's not the same as the man who has lived everything Warner Group since the day he was born.

Miles wants to make our father, grandfather, and those who came before them proud. And he will—I have every confidence in him.

Lifting my hand, I knock three times and wait for him to call me in.

Pushing the door open, I poke my head inside the darkened room.

"Hey, it's only me."

It takes a couple of seconds for Miles to pull his eyes from his computer in favor of me, and the second I look into them, I gasp in shock.

I've never seen him so...stressed.

"Hey, stranger," he says, forcing a smile onto his lips. "Come in."

Closing the door behind me, I move toward his desk and take a seat.

"You want a drink?" he asks, pushing out of his chair and stalking toward his beverage cabinet.

I watch as he pulls out a bottle of whiskey and pours himself a generous measure.

"No, I'm fine. Thank you." I had enough tequila last night to last me a good few days.

Lifting the glass, he swallows the contents without so much as a wince.

He immediately pours himself another. But this time, he doesn't drink it straight away. Instead, he stares down into it like it might hold the answers to all his problems.

Finally, he lifts the glass to his lips, and he's just taken a sip when I blurt, "Did you know I'm getting married next Saturday?"

He coughs, spraying top-shelf whiskey all over his walnut furniture.

"Shit. Sorry."

Wiping his mouth with the back of his hand, he returns to his chair and places his drink on the desk.

His eyes meet mine, and I get my answer.

"Of course you knew. Is there anything else about my life that everyone else knows about but me?"

"Tate," he breathes, tugging at the tie around his neck and undoing his top button.

"It's okay." It's not. Nothing about this is okay, but I don't want to put any more weight on his shoulders. "I'll do what I need to do and then..."

"And then?" he asks when I trail off.

I shrug. "I guess I'll figure that out at the time."

"You mean there's a chance you're not going to go running straight to England to start over?" he asks hopefully.

It's no secret that Miles doesn't share or even understand my dream of leaving not only Chicago but also America to embark on a new life across the Atlantic.

For as long as I can remember, it's been the location of all my dreams about the future. But suddenly, everything I always thought about isn't quite so clear. Everything is a little fuzzy, my future unsure and unplanned for the first time in my life.

"Yeah, maybe. I don't know. Everything is just—"

"A mess?" he finishes for me.

"Yeah," I agree sadly.

His eyes are ringed with dark shadows, and I'm sure he's gained a wrinkle or two since I last saw him.

Questions about the company and what has him so stressed dance on the tip of my tongue, but while I'm trying not to put more weight on him, I also don't want any more on me. And I fear that if I know the truth about what's going on here, the potential mess that Dad left behind, then I won't be able to forget about it.

Instead, I make a U-turn and focus on the other reason I came up here to see my big brother.

"Miles?" I ask once he's drained his second glass and set it back on the table.

"Yeah, T."

"Will you..." My eyes hold his tired ones. "Will you give me away next Saturday?"

He sucks in a sharp breath, and then I'm pretty sure he stops breathing altogether.

"Miles?" I whisper when he doesn't respond.

He scrubs his hand across his face. "Shit, T. I don't know what you expect me to say to that."

"Well, yes would be nice."

"Fuck, yeah. Yes. Of course I will."

Pushing to his feet, he rushes around the desk, pulls me out of my seat, and crushes me against his chest.

He presses a kiss to the top of my head, making me feel like a little girl all over again while I fight the tears that threaten once more.

He releases me, allowing us both to retake our seats before he groans and slumps back.

"I can't believe you're getting married."

"I—"

"To fucking Kingston," he adds, cutting me off.

"Not by choice," I mutter.

"Those photos of the two of you in Kohler..." He trails off, lost in thought before focusing on me again. "They looked very...real."

My heart constricts.

There are only a couple of people in the world who would be able to see the truth in those photos. One of them is staring me dead in the eyes right now, and the other I met for lunch again this afternoon, although that was more so she could bitch about her shitty boss instead of dissecting my life. It was a refreshing change after the past few days.

I shrug, not wanting to confess to my brother just how real the weekend felt.

"Just doing what we've got to do."

"Tate," he starts before scratching his rough chin, then sitting forward and resting his arms on his desk. "You don't have to do this."

"Miles," I warn.

"Let it all go. I'll buy that cottage for you when it goes on the market. I'll give you whatever you need. Fuck the will and the contract and—"

"I'm not letting you do that."

"But—"

"It's a year. Twelve months. And honestly, he might be a jerk,

BY HIS VOW

but it could be a hell of a lot worse than Kingston. I mean, you've put up with him this long, so he can't be all bad."

It's such bullshit. I know he's not all bad. I've seen some of the good, and it's really fucking good.

Shame it's all an act for him to gain control of Warner Group.

Miles nods but doesn't say anything.

"I'm going to need your measurements for your suit. You and King will be matching. Lori is my maid of honor and only bridesmaid."

"Mom?"

"Can be as involved as she wants to be. Hopefully, this won't be the only wedding of mine she gets to attend, but just in case it is..." I trail off as the thought of this being my only shot settles around me.

What if I'm destined to live the rest of my life as the woman who married and divorced the almighty Kingston Callahan and then die a spinster with my cats?

At least I'll have my cottage, the roses, the English countryside.

Things could certainly be worse.

"I guess I should leave you to it. Invitations will be sent tomorrow, but I'm assuming you already know the time and place."

He gives me a sad smile, confirming my suspicions.

"Well, if you think of anything else I should be aware of, please, call me, yeah?"

"I just want the best for you, you know that, right?"

"Yeah," I agree before pressing a kiss on his cheek and letting myself out.

"Tate," he calls before I get a chance to shut the door.

"Yeah?"

"You know, all you've got to do is say the word and you can be up here with me. Whatever job title, whatever salary, it can be yours."

I smile at him.

To many, I'm sure it would mean the world and would be the opportunity they could only dream of.

But for me, not so much.

"Thank you. I appreciate it but—"

"I love you, T. Enjoy your evening. Although not too much," he adds quickly just before I close his door.

I let out a sigh as I move through the silent top floor of the building toward the elevator.

I'm not sure at what point my big brother learned to read me like a book, but he can.

He saw through those photographs, and it makes me wonder what else he can see when he looks at me.

Can he see the truth that I'm desperately trying to ignore?

49

TATUM

Bubbles explode on my tongue as I take another sip of champagne.

"Where the hell is she?" Lori asks, her gaze locked on the front door of the exclusive bridal shop we're inside while she elegantly holds her own glass of bubbles like she's been doing it her entire life.

"She's not coming," I state flatly.

Lori looks over at me, her expression softening.

"It's fine," I assure her, my chest aching with the truth.

Did I hope that Mom might be able to leave her grief behind for an hour so she could be here to see me try on wedding dresses? Yeah, there was a part of me that did. But there was another part that knew she wouldn't, that it would be too much for her.

Pain lashes at my insides, but what can I do about it? Drag her out of the house kicking and screaming? She probably hasn't even pulled herself out of bed yet, let alone attempted anything else.

I went over there on Wednesday night with a wedding invitation for her. I'd regretted the decision to try before I even stepped a foot inside. All the curtains were drawn. The whole aura around the building was depressing, and it only got worse when I entered.

Mom was drunk—that much was obvious the second I looked at her. The house was a mess. Hell, she was a mess. But she refused to accept any kind of help, just like I knew she would, and after spending half an hour with her, she basically told me to leave, so I did.

I want to help—I do; she's my mom. But I'm also not going to force it on her. If she's not willing to help herself, then I'm not going to put myself out, not when I've enough of my own issues to deal with right now.

"It's not fine, Tate. She's your mom; she should be here for this," Lori argues.

For someone who has an interesting relationship with her own mother, she sure has high expectations of mine.

Plus, Kingston's Mom isn't even coming. At least mine will see the ceremony.

"The only person I need is sitting right beside me," I assure my best friend.

The tapping of heels fills the room before one of the assistants appears before us.

"Okay, are we ready to get started?" she asks excitedly.

Her passion for her job is as clear to see as the wedding planner's. However, I must admit that I'm feeling a little more excited about this than I was at our surprise meeting on Tuesday morning. I mean, we're surrounded by beautiful gowns. Who wouldn't be excited to try them all on?

"Yes," Lori says excitedly. "Can we start with the biggest one you have in the store?"

"I don't need a big dress," I counter.

"I never said you needed one, but you definitely need to try one on." She laughs, happiness shining in her eyes.

"We have time to try anything you like," the assistant says, reminding me that Kingston insisted they closed early and stay until I've found "the one."

As much as I hate to admit it, he's been the perfect fiancé this week.

I've no idea if he's trying to make up for the leaked

photographs or just trying to pacify me so that I don't set Griz on him again, but he's been caring and attentive. He's been involved with Mia regarding the wedding plans instead of leaving it all to me. I mean, sure, he's got a vested interest in making sure the wedding happens, but I can't help feeling like he's even more invested than he needs to be. Almost like he's excited for it, like he actually wants it. Wants to be married.

I've told myself over and over that I'm just kidding myself. That he's just playing the part everyone is expecting of him.

Pushing to my feet, I begin looking at my options.

White, ivory, silver. Beads, pearls, diamonds. Lace, satin, tulle. My mind spins with the variety.

I know my style and what suits me, but I've got this niggle I can't ignore that I want something different. I don't want to choose the style that everyone would expect from me. I want to wow.

This wedding and marriage might be totally out of my hands, but this...this I can control.

"Oh my god, Tate. This one." Lori gasps from the other side of the store.

Abandoning the dress in front of me, I walk over as she pulls it free.

"Oh my god, that's—"

"The one," Lori gushes.

"I was going to say massive."

"It's beautiful, and it'll look so incredible on you."

"It's a bit much," I say, running my eyes down the ivory dress and the intricate lace that covers it.

It has a sweetheart neckline and off-the-shoulder straps and the skirt...wow. It really is stunning but—

"Try it on," Lori urges. "Please."

The assistant moves closer before she begins explaining all the details about the dress.

Most of it passes me by; I don't care about the designer or how many diamonds or pearls it has. I'm not the kind of bride who is going to be bragging about the cost of a dress. It could be twenty dollars from a thrift store so long as it makes me feel like the most beautiful woman in the room on the day. The cost is meaningless in the grand scheme of things. Happiness is way more important.

"Okay," I concede, making my best friend beam.

The assistant takes the dress from her and carries it toward the back of the store where the dressing rooms are, leaving us to keep looking.

Only ten minutes later, I have three other options lined up.

All three of them are much more...me. Slimmer cut than the first one, straps, less...well, everything. And totally the opposite of the out-of-the-box dress I told myself I was going to look for. I guess old habits die hard.

"Well, I know which one I'm gunning for," Lori says as we both look at my options.

"Oh yeah," I deadpan.

"We'll give you a few minutes," the assistant says before closing the heavy curtains and leaving me alone with the dresses.

I let out a sigh as I look at each one, my heart threatening to pound out of my chest.

This doesn't feel real.

Me trying on wedding dresses...

I shake my head, trying to make sense of it all.

Stripping out of my work clothes, I stand in a set of lingerie Kingston bought for me.

He has no idea I'm wearing it, and even if he asked, I'd lie, but I couldn't stop myself. I needed something special today, and to be fair to him, he has very good taste.

We haven't been intimate since our drunken debauchery in the bathroom on Monday night, and as far as I'm concerned, it's going to stay that way for the foreseeable future. Sex changes things. It clouds our judgment and makes things even more complicated than they already are. At least for me, it does.

It was the addition of our physical connection that resulted in me convincing myself that we were more than a business deal. It led me to the pain that Monday caused, and if I can safeguard myself from that again, I will.

Everything is hard enough as it is. I don't need any extra complications.

Going for the safest option first, I pull the heavy yet feather-soft satin up my body and slip the straps over my shoulders.

I look at myself in the mirror, my hands trembling as I hold the too-big dress against me.

It's pretty. Beautiful, in fact. But it doesn't make me feel like I thought it would. It feels wrong, and it makes my pulse pick up speed.

It's just a dress. Not *the* dress.

But then this isn't *the* wedding, so maybe it isn't meant to feel like they tell you it does in the movies.

"Come on, let us see," Lori calls impatiently, making my heart skip a beat.

I should be excited doing this. I should want to step out there and show my best friend.

But I'm terrified.

Taking in a deep breath, I turn toward the curtain and awkwardly slip out.

"Oh." Lori's face falls the second she sees I'm not in the dress she was hoping for. "It's beautiful," she says, trying to recover quickly.

Basically, she mirrors exactly how I'm feeling.

"Okay, come and stand up here and we'll get it fitting like it should so you can see the true look," the assistant says, pointing to a raised platform.

Swiping my glass of champagne on the way, I swallow it down fast in the hope of squashing the unease that's bubbling up inside me. I stand there and let her do her thing, watching the dress transform before my eyes in the mirror.

It looks better, sure, but it still doesn't feel special.

It still doesn't feel right.

"I like it," she says when she finally takes a step back.

Like...

Yeah, like it's really how you want anyone to describe your wedding dress.

My heart begins to pound harder as claustrophobia seeps in.

It feels like the dress is shrinking, stopping me from breathing.

"Can you release it? I need to take it off," I ask in a rush, my temperature soaring higher with every increased beat of my heart.

"Oh yes, of course."

"Tate, are you okay?" Lori asks, concern laced through her voice.

"Uh-huh."

The second the dress loosens enough for me to be able to escape from it, I dart back behind the curtain.

"Fuck," I breathe.

I really shouldn't have had that champagne.

"Tate?" Lori calls.

"I'm okay. I just need a minute."

I let the dress fall to my feet before turning to look at the other three, but my eyes zero in on one of them and my heart continues racing for an entirely different reason.

Everything about it feels different from the moment I lift it from the hangar.

My skin prickles as I slide it up my body and pull it into place.

It's not as big as the first one, and it fits as it is.

I look down at myself, my breath shaking. I don't look in the mirror this time, so I've no idea how I look, but I know how I feel.

Closing my eyes, I find that it's easy to imagine myself wearing this and walking toward Kingston. It's such a vivid image that it knocks the wind out of me to the point I have to reach for the wall to steady myself.

Taking in a few deep breaths, I roll my shoulders back and move toward the curtain.

Both women turn to me the second I emerge. The assistant's expression softens, but it's Lori's reaction that fully steals my attention.

"Oh my god," she sobs, tears immediately filling her eyes. "That's it. That's the one."

Without needing to be told, I step up onto the podium and lift my eyes to the mirror.

What I find staring back at me knocks the air straight from my lungs.

Lori is right.

This is it. This is the dress that I'm going to marry Kingston Callahan in.

50

KINGSTON

A knock sounds on my hotel suite door and I make my excuses to end the call I'm stuck on before heading to open it.

Kian and Miles haven't left the office yet, so that means it can only be one person.

I don't bother looking through the peephole. Instead, I pull the door wide open and drag the man standing on the other side into a tight hug.

"Fuck," he grunts when we collide. "Who the fuck are you, and what have you done with my big brother?" Kieran asks as I thump him on the back.

"Missed you, you little shit," I confess before releasing him and inviting him in.

Little might be pushing it these days. Our scrawny little brother is now both taller and wider than both of us.

"Jeez, someone is feeling a little sappy. I guess that's what happens when you fall under the spell of a feisty woman." He flops onto the couch as if he owns the place, spreading his legs wide and resting his head back. "Is that it? Has Tatum Warner broken you already? Kian and I said that—"

"The fuck have you two been talking about behind my back?"

I bark. The two of them were always closer growing up. Kian loved playing football, although he was shit at it, while I was always too busy with my head stuck in a book, trying to figure out how to take over the world, one vacation resort at a time. But since Kieran ran off into the NFL sunset as it were, leaving Kian behind to play with numbers, we've grown closer. Kieran might be based in Chicago still, but we don't get to see him much. He's too busy with football, endorsements, and his foundation. I get it—I'm just as fucking busy. Doesn't stop me from missing the times the three of us used to spend together.

"Just taking bets on how long it'd take for you to end up pussy-whipped by your new wife."

"Fucking morons," I mutter, grabbing two beers from the refrigerator and throwing one in his direction. He catches it with ease before twisting the top and lifting it to his lips. "So, what's new?" I ask, mimicking his position on the couch opposite.

"Nah, not much. Just got back in from New York this morning. Had a photoshoot for some aftershave."

"Is that why you smell like you've stumbled out of a brothel?" I tease.

"How the fuck would you know what a brothel smells like, Bro?"

"Kian told me about it," I shoot back. "He goes most weekends," I deadpan, making Kieran bark out a laugh.

"Pfft, there's no fucking chance that motherfucker has paid for pussy. He's too fucking tight."

"Ain't that the fucking truth."

I stopped in on Mom. She told me to send her love and apologies for not attending," Kieran says cautiously.

Anger knots my stomach.

"That's great," I lie.

"You didn't even invite her, did you?" Kieran studies me, able to read the answer in my eyes.

"She doesn't want to be a part of this," I mutter.

Kieran's mouth opens and closes to argue, but he wisely decides against it and changes the subject.

"So, how are things with the little lady then?"

Draining my beer, I place the bottle on the coffee table between us and stare him dead in the eyes.

"Women are a fucking head fuck."

His eyes twinkle with amusement.

"Sweet little Tatum giving you the runaround?"

"Sweet? There's nothing fucking sweet about her."

"Oh," he breathes. "Do tell." He rubs his hands together in interest.

"I don't know whether I'm coming or fucking going. One minute, things are..." I trail off, thinking of our weekend at the cabin. "Awesome. She's smart, funny—really fucking funny—and—"

"Hot?" Kieran asks. "You forgot hot."

I quirk a brow. "Bro, have you got the hots for my fiancée?"

"Dude, do not tell me that you don't remember her hanging out in that red bikini when we were kids."

"You were a kid," I point out. "You shouldn't have noticed."

His smirk grows. "You did though, didn't you?" He chuckles. "Miles was such a fucking idiot for thinking she was safe with you. He thought you hated her, but the truth of it was that you were jerking off over her every night.'

"The fuck?" My temperature spikes. I want to say that it's out of irritation. The fucking audacity of this fucker. But in all honestly, it's because he's fucking right.

"I wonder what happened to that itty bitty red bikini. I bet she'd fill it out good now."

"I can uninvite you," I remind him.

"Aw, Bro. Did I touch a nerve? Don't tell me you keep the panties of that swimsuit in the drawer of your nightstand so you can sniff them before falling asleep?"

"You're a fucking asshole." They're in my wardrobe, and I haven't sniffed them for years. Not since her scent faded.

"Yeah," he agrees. "You love me, though. So, what's the plan? We're not actually staying in your suite for your bachelor party, are we? That's fucking lame, man, even for you."

"I'm getting married tomorrow," I remind him. "I'm not doing it with a hangover."

Kieran raises a brow at me, clearly unimpressed with my plan.

"It's not even a real fucking wedding. Who gives a shit if you turn up half-cut?"

Anger bubbles inside me. "I do. I fucking care."

Kieran's eyes widen. "Oh shit, Bro. Have you fallen for her?"

I force out a laugh. "No, I haven't fucking fallen for her. Tatum War—"

"Callahan," he corrects like the smug asshole that he is.

"Tatum is the bane of my fucking life. Did Kian tell you about her cat?"

"Her cat?" he echoes.

"Yes, her fucking cat. She moved it into my apartment."

To be fair, he attempts to hide his amusement, but it doesn't last very long because his lips twitch and then he throws his head back and laughs.

"You hate cats."

"You don't need to tell me that," I complain.

"We need more beer for this," he says, pushing to his feet and marching toward the fridge, pulling out four bottles.

"Fucking thing made me bleed," I say, lifting my sweater so he can see the healing wound.

"Oh shit. I hope you made her make up for that." I don't react. Or at least, I don't think I do. But something gives me away. "Oh, Bro. You are so fucked. I bet she's fucking wild in bed. She's got that glint in her eye that screams 'I love it hard and dirty.'"

Kieran is getting too excited by his possible discovery to notice that the main door to the suite has been unlocked, or that we've been joined by two others. That soon changes when something heavy goes flying across the room. It brushes past my head, a beat before it collides with Kieran's.

"What the fuck?" he bellows, letting the box of tissues drop into his lap.

"That's the fucking least you deserve talking about my sister like that, asshole," Miles sneers.

"Oh Jesus, give me strength," Kian mutters, throwing his small suitcase and overnight bag over the end of the couch.

"I have beer," I offer as a substitute.

"I'm gonna need something stronger if these two are going to bicker like little girls all night."

"Apparently, we're not allowed adult drinks tonight because they would be too much fun for the old man here before his big day," Kieran deadpans.

"Yeah, no. Fuck that," Kian mutters. "I'm not putting up with you lot sober. It's just not happening."

He marches over to the drinks cabinet and searches through the options.

"Who the fuck stocked this, our grandmother?"

"Our grandmother is dead," I point out.

"Exactly," he spits before picking up the phone and dialing for room service. "You need to get on to whoever is in charge of this shit. It's not good enough, Kin—Oh yeah, please could we have two bottles of Macallan brought up?" He listens for a moment. "Yes. That's great. Thank you. Uhh...two hours?" he tags on suspiciously. I narrow my eyes at him. "Perfect. Thank you."

"What have you done?" I ask before he's even put the phone down.

"Me?" he asks, pointing at himself as he marches over and swipes one of the bottles of beer from the table. "Nothing, Bro. You wanted a quiet night; I've just followed orders," he agrees before winking at Miles and Kieran.

"I knew Miles should have been my best man. He wouldn't pull this kind of shit."

"He's too busy walking his filthy sister down the aisle," Kian mutters, earning a scowl from Miles. "And anyway, Miles has never listened to you. If he were in charge, you'd already have a stripper grinding in your lap."

"He doesn't want a stripper," Kieran pipes up, understanding for once. "He wants Tatum naked and—fuck off," he complains when Miles slaps him.

"Cut it out. It's an arranged marriage. They don't even like each other."

"Doesn't mean they're not bumping uglies," Kieran points out.

"Bumping uglies?" Kian asks, his eyes wide with horror. "What the fuck kind of bullshit are they teaching you in the NFL?"

Kieran smirks. "All the fucking good stuff, Bro. You should see the jersey chasers. Fucking epic, I'm telling you."

"We're more than aware," Miles points out. "Enough of them have shared your intimate secrets all over the socials."

"You don't have to read it, you know. But I appreciate the support all the same," Kieran says, blowing Miles a kiss.

There's a knock at the door and Kian hops up, pulling his tie free and undoing the first few buttons of his shirt as he goes to answer it.

"Oh hey," he starts, turning the charm up to max when he finds a girl on the other side.

"Leave her alone, Ki," Miles calls at exactly the same time Kieran shouts, "Stand well back; he's got crabs, and they can jump."

I scrub my hand down my face. What the fuck was I thinking, inviting these three to spend the night with me before my wedding?

Once Kian has pulled himself away from temptation, he grabs four glasses, lines them up on the coffee table and sloshes the tempting amber liquid into them.

After handing them out, he holds his in the air.

"To my big brother. The guy I've been forced to look up to all my life. The man who's taught me everything after I've watched him make every mistake in the book. I hope this arranged marriage brings you wealth, happiness, and most importantly, sleepless nights due to all the dirty fucking." Miles groans as Kian and Kieran hold their glasses out and clink each other's.

"To dirty fucking Miles's sister," Kieran agrees.

Miles punches him in the shoulder, but the fucker is so massive now, I doubt he even feels it before turning his eyes on me.

The warning within them is as clear as day. Hurt my little sister, and I'll hurt you.

We might be best friends, but even that has its limits. And apparently, it's Tatum's heart that has the power to break us apart.

"Bottoms up, baby," Kian calls before the three of them lift their glasses to their lips and down their drinks.

I hesitate, serious about not being hungover when I say my vows tomorrow. But then, all eyes turn on me and I begin second-guessing myself.

Tipping the glass up, the rich alcohol coats my tongue before sliding down my throat like silk.

Meh, what harm is one, anyway?

51

TATUM

"If I would have pictured your bachelorette party, this wouldn't have been what I had in mind," Lori says as she sips on her pornstar martini while relaxing back in a lounger with the sound of running water and soft music in the background.

"No, me neither." But even as I say the words, the thought of being out in a hot and sweaty club right now doesn't appeal.

This night might not be what we would have planned, but I can't help but feel like it's perfect.

Things since Kingston released those photographs to the press have been crazy.

The thought of going out and having the press follow me around, wanting to capture my every movement, doesn't fill me with the warm and fuzzies.

The reality is that being enclosed within the safety of the Broadway Hotel, with the paparazzi restricted to the outside, is what I need.

"We should sneak out," Lori whispers as if someone is listening to us.

I chuckle, assuming she's joking.

"You packed a sexy dress, right?"

"You're being serious," I state.

"Of course I am. It's the night before your wedding; you deserve to have an epic night."

"Umm, I am," I say, lifting my cocktail to my lips and taking a sip.

Jackie, Kingston's stepmom, came down for an hour and had her nails done. My mom was meant to join us, but I'm pretty sure she's hit the minibar in her room and is probably already asleep. Kingston asked if I wanted to have anyone else here. But honestly, I don't.

I've never had a huge circle of friends. But right now, I need people I trust completely around me. We're already lying to enough people about this wedding. I don't need to turn it into an even bigger show than it already is.

"Hanging out with your soon-to-be mother-in-law while in a basement spa doesn't really cut it, Tate."

"Well, when you get married, we can do whatever your heart desires to make up for it. The only place I'm going tonight other than right here is to bed."

She stares at me in disbelief.

"You're not joking, are you?" she asks hesitantly.

"No. My face has been all over the media for the last two weeks. I really don't need to add more. I also don't want to be hungover tomorrow."

"But—"

"There are no buts here, Lor. This is how it's going to be."

"Fair enough," she says, draining her glass and placing it on the side. "We do need more drinks, though."

She presses the button on the little remote control we were provided with earlier to call a server before sitting back on her lounger.

"I've had worse Friday nights," she finally confesses before lifting her cell and opening up Instagram.

Laughing, I reach for my own cell and lose myself in some mindless scrolling.

"You seen them?" she asks, leaning over to show me a photo.

My eyes immediately lock on my soon-to-be husband's smiling face. My heart rate picks up and my temperature spikes.

It is not the reaction I should be having to the man I'm only marrying because of a business deal. But it's the one I have all the same.

She swipes to the next image and I find Miles and Kieran with him, all three with tequila shots lined up before them.

"On three," Kieran says, winking at the camera, which I assume Kian is holding, seeing as he's missing from the line-up. "Three," Kieran suddenly barks before licking the salt from the back of his hand.

Kingston and Miles quickly follow suit, but Kingston is the only one I focus on as he throws his shot back and then bites down on a slice of lime.

"Jesus," Lori breathes. But when I glance over, I don't find her watching the screen. She's looking at me, and there's a weirdly sappy look in her eyes.

"What?" I mutter.

"You want to be that lime so badly right now," she sings.

My chin drops at her insinuation.

"N-no, I—"

"Jesus, you really have been punishing yourself as well as him, haven't you?"

The second the words are out of her mouth, I regret telling her that we haven't been together since that night in his bedroom.

"Fucking complicates the situation," I argue, sticking to the story I first told her when I explained my sudden vow of celibacy.

"Fucking is a massive benefit of marrying an asshole," she counters.

The hurt I remember all too well the moment I discovered he'd shared what I thought was our private moment together at the cabin edges in.

"I can't do it, Lor. That weekend, it—"

"Tate," she says, abandoning her cell on her lounger and taking my hand. Her eyes bounce between mine as if she's trying to find a way to deliver her next words delicately. I narrow my eyes, silently telling her to hurry the fuck up, but the second the words fall from her lips, I regret it. "You're falling for him, aren't you?"

"What?" I gasp. "No, of course I'm not. I can't stand him. He's —" A door closing behind us cuts off my argument before the click-clack of heels moves closer.

Assuming it's the server coming to supply us with new drinks, I don't bother turning to look.

A shadow falls over me and Lori's eyes lift to the person standing beside me.

Glancing over, I have to do a double take when I find a beautiful young woman looking down at me with a soft smile playing on her lips.

"Could we please get two more pornstar martinis?" Lori asks, clearly not getting the memo from what she's wearing that this woman isn't our server.

Her smile grows. "Cute," she whispers, briefly glancing at my best friend before turning her eyes back to me.

Suddenly, she thrusts her hand out for me.

"Tatum, I'm Aubrey Kendrick and I've—"

"Fucked my husband," I blurt.

Lori gasps beside me, jumping to her feet so fast I'd be surprised if she didn't get a head rush. In contrast, Aubrey doesn't so much as flinch at my cutting statement.

"You two have spoken about me, then?" she says before walking around my lounger and taking a seat on the end of Lori's abandoned one.

My best friend watches Aubrey like Griz does before pouncing on a toy.

It's cute, and her need to protect me makes my heart swell with love.

"It's okay, Lor. You can stand down."

Aubrey shoots a look up at my bikini-clad security guard and smirks. If what Kingston told me is to be believed—and honestly, why would he lie?—then I hardly doubt she's fazed at all by Lori. She's hardly scary.

Focusing back on me, she smiles. This time, it's a lot more genuine.

"It was a long time ago. We've been friends—platonic friends —ever since."

"Right," I mutter.

I don't want to like this woman. But there's also something about her that I can't help warming to.

Kingston doesn't have a big network. He keeps his friends close, so the fact he's let Aubrey in, and they've stayed connected for quite a few years, makes me want to believe that she's a decent person.

"Why are you here?" Lori blurts, the martinis loosening her tongue more than usual.

"Kingston mentioned you were having a small bachelorette down here so..."

"You thought you'd invite yourself," Lori continues.

"I can go. It's no big deal. I just wanted to meet Tatum. Kingston seems pretty smitten."

I scoff. "If you're talking about growing his empire and reputation, then yeah, he's totally smitten."

The door closes again, and this time when a pair of footsteps appears, it's our server, ready to take our order.

"Two more pornstar martinis, please," Lori orders.

"Aubrey?" I offer.

"Are you sure?"

"Of course. We're not exactly filling the place up down here."

She nods once, accepting my invitation before looking up at the server. "I'll have the same, please."

"You're right, by the way," Lori says once we're alone again. "Kingston is totally smitten with my girl here. I mean, why shouldn't he be? Look at her."

"Lor," I complain when she waves her hand up and down, gesturing to my body.

"What? If you ask me, he's the one who lucked out with this arranged marriage bullshit."

The three of us fall into an easy conversation about Kingston before we divert off in a million different directions as the drinks continue to flow.

It turns out that Aubrey was pretty confident about her invitation to join us, because when Lori suggests we relocate to the sauna, she quickly peels her oversized t-shirt and leggings off to reveal a bathing suit that I'm sure would drive every single member of the opposite sex—and more than a few of the same—crazy with desire.

It doesn't take much imagination to understand why she's so good at her job. A job we only briefly managed to scratch the surface of despite my and Lori's piqued interest.

By the time Lori and I stumble back to our fancy suite on the top floor of the most prestigious hotel in the city, my plan for not getting drunk seems to have flown right out the window.

I'm flying high on the martinis, and so is Lori as she weaves back and forth in her attempt to find the bedroom.

"You are getting married in the morning." She sings at the top of her lungs as she spins around to look at me. "Ding dong, the bells are going to chime. Or they would if you were innocent enough for a church." She falls about in a fit of giggles before stumbling on nothing and going flying backward.

She reaches out and snags my hand a beat before she crashes to the floor, dragging me with her.

We land with loud squeals before an eruption of laughter spills free as we roll around together.

And just like that all the stress and worry of the past few weeks melts away as I finally let go of everything and just...laugh.

The pressure of building a fake relationship, the lies I've been telling myself about my unwanted growing feelings for King. Everything just vanishes.

It is the best medicine for my shitshow of a life right now, and I embrace it with both hands.

"Oh my god," Lori squeals as she manages to get to her feet before stumbling into the dresser. "Tomorrow is going to hurt."

"No," I cry. "No talk about tomorrow. Here and now. Me and you."

"Me and fucking you, baby," Lori promises before shoving her sweats down her legs and attempting to pull them from her feet.

She's still fighting with them once I'm up and leaning against the wall to ensure I stay that way.

The second she frees her feet, she crashes onto the bed face-first.

"Love you, Tatum Warner," she mumbles. "Fucking love you."

I stare at my best friend with her panty-covered ass on display with a sappy smile on my face.

"I love you too, Lori," I whisper, aware that she's already passed out.

Tears burn my eyes, and a thick, messy ball of emotion crawls up my throat as I think about my new life with Kingston in his penthouse.

I'm not ready to leave my apartment. My girl.

I need water before passing out in the hope it helps to clear my head for tomorrow. It could be wishful thinking; I may well be too far gone at this point.

I pull a cold bottle from the fridge in our small yet fully functioning kitchen before twisting the top and swallowing down mouthful after mouthful of ice-cold water.

I'm halfway through the bottle when exhaustion hits me out of nowhere. I stumble back until my calves hit the edge of the couch and I flop down.

My eyes get heavy as the room continues to spin around me. I glance back at the bedroom where Lori is sleeping and then down at my engagement ring.

I'm getting married tomorrow.

Married to a man I hate.

Or do I?

Everything is so fucked up. So confusing.

Slumping down on the couch, I nuzzle into the cushion as thoughts of Kingston play out in my mind.

Kingston, the hard-ass businessman.

Kingston, the player.

Kingston, the sweet guy who took me away for the weekend and let me see who he was.

Kingston, the sex god...

And it's those thoughts I drift off to sleep thinking about.

His touch. His kiss. His dirty words.

52

KINGSTON

I sit with Kian and Miles, watching as Kieran entertains his harem.

If I thought I attracted females when I stepped foot outside my penthouse, then I really need to reconsider, because our little brother is on another level.

Jersey chasers.

They are persistent and very focused on their end goal: snagging a hot night and the chance of more with one of their beloved players.

This is why I wanted to stay up in the suite. It would have ensured we got to spend some time together without being hit on every five seconds.

"He's way too ugly to attract that level of attention," Kian mutters beside me before swallowing down what's left in his glass.

"Those girls don't care what he looks like," Miles points out. "They just want a night with an NFL god."

"Jesus, don't call him that to his face. His head is already big enough," I tease.

"Because you're so modest," Miles pipes up.

"Nah, he's just pissed that his days of hooking up on a night out are over," Kian points out.

"Says who?" I ask, aware that a comment like that will earn me a death glare from Miles.

"His wife's older brother, that's fucking who."

"From what I heard, there was no stipulation about KC being faithful, and it's not like you want him tapping Tate, so..."

Miles scrubs his hand down his face. If it weren't so loud in the hotel bar then I'm sure we'd hear him groaning.

He's struggling with this. I get it, I do. But he knows as well as I do that Tate doesn't really have any other option.

Yes, he'd ensure she's taken care of if she were to walk away, but he also knows that she's too stubborn for that.

"I won't be unfaithful to Tatum," I assure him, needing him to know that he can trust me—up to a point—with his little sister.

"I'm not sure if that makes me feel better about all of this or not," Miles confesses.

"I'm not going into this intending to hurt her, man. If I have my way, we'll make it through the next twelve months happily before embarking on the next stages of our lives."

Kian studies me closely. My stomach knots as I wait for him to say whatever is on his mind. We've already had way more to drink tonight than I intended, meaning his tongue will be looser than usual.

"Is that really what you want, though?" he asks.

"Of course. We want Callahan and Warner to finally be joined. That's the end goal here. Together we can take over the fucking world." Slight exaggeration.

"That's not what I meant and you know it," Kian says, happily accepting another round of scotch from our server.

"That is what this is about. It's a business deal," I state, reaching for a fresh drink.

"Is that why you look at her with those sappy eyes? Because she's a business deal?"

"Jesus Christ," Miles complains, downing his drink, and then Kieran's—he's way too busy to even notice it's here.

"She is," I argue, although from the way Kian's eyes narrow, I'm not sure he believes me.

"I'll put a thousand dollars on you two not getting divorced in twelve months."

"Don't be an asshole," Miles spits.

"What? Do you really think Kingston isn't going to fall in love with Tate? She's beautiful, funny, intelligent. If KC had a type other than desperate, she'd be it and you know it."

"That's not my type." I scoff.

"Oh, come off it. As long as she's willing, you'll tap it," Kian argues.

"Because you're so different."

"I'm more than happy to share the love. But this isn't about me, and that's not the point. You are going to fall in love with her, and there is no way you'll let her go and allow someone else to have her after all this."

***

I tried to argue with him, I really did. My mouth opened and closed several times, but I couldn't find the words.

I've had two weeks with Tatum so far, and we're on the eve of our union that kickstarts the timer on our relationship. Already, she's turned my life upside down, made me feel things that I'm not sure I have before, and I don't just mean impossibly high levels of irritation at her constant defiance.

What's it going to be like a year from now?

Will I be able to consider a life without her in it, or will she have become such a huge part of my days that it'll be impossible?

Predictably, Kieran disappeared with a jersey chaser on each arm a while ago. And despite his teasing about our little brother's antics, Kian just walked out of the bar to do exactly the same, although there was only one woman on his arm.

I let out a sigh, pushing my empty glass back.

"No one catching your eye tonight?" I ask Miles as he scans the bar.

Shaking his head, he turns his eyes back on me. "Got bigger things to worry about than getting my dick wet." He scoffs.

"Who are you and what have you done with my best friend? I remember a time not so long ago when that was the only thing to worry about."

"Yeah, well. That was before I took on a company on the brink of bankruptcy and was having to hand my little sister over to the big bad wolf."

"Aw, you love me."

He does, I know he does. But this is pushing our friendship right to the max.

If it's possible, his expression hardens further.

"Did you mean it?" he asks, making me frown.

"Mean what?"

"That you don't have any intention of hurting her?"

I slump back, keeping my eyes on my best friend.

"I know I'm a bit of an asshole, but I don't go out intentionally to hurt people. Women."

"Shit, I know. I just—" He scrubs his hand down his face.

He's stressed; I can see it in the darkness of his eyes and the fresh lines around them. I hate it, but there is only so much I can do.

Together, we will fix Warner Group. It might mean making some very tough decisions, but we will not let it go under.

"Fuck, KC. She's my little sister, man. She deserves the fucking world and—"

"I'll give her it," I promise before I have a chance to think about what I'm saying. "Whatever she wants for the next year of our lives, it's hers."

I hold his stare strong, letting him see just how truthful those words are.

"And what if Kian is right?" My heart begins pounding harder as his words repeat in my head.

"You are going to fall in love with her, and there is no way you'll let her go and allow someone else to have her after all this."

I scoff, trying to play it off. "I think you know me better than that, Miles."

He doesn't say anything, yet his silence says a thousand words.

"I'm gonna call it a night," he finally says, pushing his chair back from the table. "Big day tomorrow." He grips my shoulder and squeezes hard in another warning.

"She deserves to have the day she's always dreamed about."

"Bro, this is Tatum we're talking about. She doesn't dream about stuff like that."

He narrows his eyes. "If you say so. I'll see you in the morning, yeah?"

I nod once and he takes off, marching through the bar and stealing almost every female's attention.

If he wanted to hook up tonight, he could.

It's your fault he's going to bed alone, a little voice pipes up.

My skin tingles with awareness as eyes turn on me now that I'm sitting alone.

Unwilling to talk to anyone, I push my chair out and follow Miles's lead.

The ride in the elevator to the top floor of the hotel takes longer than it ever has before, I swear. And by the time I get to the top, my muscles are tight and my head is spinning with the events of the night.

Kian's words still float around my head, along with Miles's warning and my promises.

"Fuck," I grunt, combing my fingers through my hair and dragging it back from my face.

As I make my way toward the best suite in this hotel, the suite that Tatum and I are going to share on our wedding night, I find that my focus is elsewhere. On another door that's closer, more tempting than my own.

My footsteps slow as I approach, the key in my pocket burning with temptation.

I have no idea what the girls have done tonight other than spend time in the spa. I told myself that I'd give them the freedom to enjoy their time, no matter how much it would kill me not to spend the night watching Tatum on the security footage.

Fuck.

I'm fucked.

So fucking fucked.

Unable to talk myself out of it, I pull the key from my pocket and tap it on the panel beside the door.

It's late; they should be asleep.

I'll just slip in, check on her and then disappear as if I were never here.

Easy. Simple.

She'll never even know.

I pause with the door open, listening for voices, and when I don't hear any, I step inside, quietly closing the door behind me.

The second I step into the living room, my breath catches as I find my girl passed out on the couch with a bottle of water ominously dangling from her fingers, ready to drop.

I stalk over before plucking the bottle from her weak grip and placing it on the coffee table.

Dropping to my knees beside her, I reach out, tucking a lock of her messy hair behind her ear.

"King," she whispers the second our skin makes contact, and fuck if it doesn't make my dick instantly hard.

"Are you dreaming about me, baby?" I whisper so quietly, the words are almost non-existent.

Unable to stop myself, I carefully drag my knuckles down her cheek, desperate to feel the softness of her skin.

I fucked up after our weekend away. I knew it the second I hit send on those photographs, and I know it even more after ten days of being unable to indulge in this incredible woman.

She showed me heaven, only to snatch it away again.

Every single day, I've been hard and aching for her, but she's proved just how strong her stubborn streak is by keeping herself at arm's length.

I'm dying. Fucking dying without having a taste of her.

When I get to her chest, she moans again, rolling onto her

back, letting the blanket she'd haphazardly pulled over herself float to the floor.

"Jesus Christ, baby," I groan, running my eyes down her body and taking in the thin tank and tiny pair of panties she's wearing. "You don't play fair."

The air turns thick with desire as I stare at her incredible body, listening to the sound of her shallow breaths in my ear.

Is she as desperate for me as I am for her?

"Kingston," she moans, answering my question as if I asked it out loud.

I should push to my feet. I should walk out the door and resort to jerking off in the shower like I have all week.

"Please," she whimpers, spreading her thighs wider, letting me see the damp patch on her panties.

"Fuck."

My mouth waters and my fingers twitch.

Would she wake up if I were to pull the fabric aside and take what we both need?

With my eyes locked on her face, I tuck my fingers beneath the soft lace and slowly tug it away.

She moans and her hips lift from the couch, but her eyes don't so much as flicker with awareness.

My heart pounds and my chest heaves, a potent rush of desire flooding through my veins.

Lorelei is here somewhere. She could walk out any minute and find me on my knees for my wife.

It should probably be enough to stop me, but it isn't.

With my mouth watering, I lean forward and take what I desperately crave.

53

TATUM

"Oh god."

Kingston's tongue licks up the length of my pussy, making my hips lift from the couch in my need for more.

More.

I always need more.

The weekend at the cabin was nowhere near enough.

I've missed this.

Missed this so much I want to sob in relief as he sucks on my clit, swirling the tip of his tongue around the swollen, sensitive bundle of nerves.

Heat seeps through my limbs as my release makes itself known all too soon.

I'm not ready.

More. I need more.

"Open for me, brat," he growls when my thighs clamp tight, pinning his ears.

A rush of desire heads straight toward my core at his demand and my legs fall open, giving him the space he needs to work.

Reaching out, I thread my fingers through his hair and pull tight, ensuring he isn't going to leave me high and dry.

"Fuck. Kingston. Yes," I cry, my back arching off the couch when he pushes two fingers deep inside me.

My pussy clamps down on those digits, desperately trying to suck them deeper.

More.

With my free hand, I drag my tank down and cup one of my heavy breasts.

Kingston's eyes widen as he watches me, his pupils almost black with desire as I pluck my nipple, adding to the overload of sensation he's delivering with such precision.

"Perfect. So fucking perfect," he groans against me. "Addicted to this pussy, baby. Fucking addicted."

His words and the vibrations his deep voice sends through me push me even closer.

"Fucking need you, Tatum. Been so fucking hard all week."

Another surge of heat rushes to my core.

"You like that, baby?" he asks, pulling back slightly, ensuring the point of no return is just out of reach. "You like hearing how hot you get me?"

"Yes, yes," I cry, lifting my ass and trying to force his mouth back on me.

"Dirty girl," he mutters before diving for me as if he needs the taste of my pussy on his tongue more than he needs his next breath.

He shifts between my thighs, and for a moment I think he's going to sit up and slide that beautiful cock inside me, but then I realize that he's not releasing me. Instead, he's working himself.

Oh god.

The image of him with his hand wrapped around his hard dick fills my head and my body quakes.

"Not yet," he growls. "You come when I tell you that you can come."

"Oh my god," I cry, both beyond turned on and desperate as I am frustrated. "Please, King. Please," I whimper, hoping he'll take pity on me.

"When I say," he repeats firmly.

My grip on his hair tightens and my hips roll against his face.

The length of stubble on his jaw is perfect.

Everything is fucking perfect.

His body moves faster, his tongue keeping pace with the way he works his dick, and before long, I hit that magic moment where he pushes me over the edge.

"Kingston," I scream as I free-fall, my body trembling and convulsing.

He works me through every second of it, his mouth and fingers not stopping until he's wrung every ounce of pleasure from my body.

Once he's confident he has, he climbs onto the couch between my legs and hovers over me as he continues to stroke his cock.

"Fuck," I breathe, aftershocks from my release tingling my nerve endings from simply watching him.

"You're mine, Tatum. Mine," he groans before his cock jerks in his hand and he spurts hot jets of cum over my exposed breasts.

"Fuck," he breathes, staring down at the mess he made. "Fuck, I missed you, baby." His eyes jump to mine and my heart stutters in my chest at the emotion I find staring back at me. "I didn't think it was possible to need someone as much as I need you. I'm fucking addicted, Tate."

Before I get a chance to respond, he ducks low and steals my lips in a filthy kiss, letting me taste myself on his tongue.

Fuck. It's hot.

So fucking hot.

"Oh god," I groan as I come to and fully experience the severity of my hangover.

This is not good.

I roll onto my side and snuggle into the softness of the blanket wrapped around me.

I want the couch to suck me in and never let me out.

But that's beyond impossible.

I'm getting married today.

Married.

My stomach rolls and my mouth waters.

Oh my god, I'm going to be sick on my wedding day.

I'm on my feet and racing toward the bathroom before I've fully registered my thoughts. My knees hit the tiles and I vomit.

Once I'm confident I'm done, I sit back on the warm floor and wipe the back of my hand across my sweaty forehead.

Closing my eyes, I rest my head back and just breathe, wishing the hangover away with nothing but willpower alone.

Surprisingly, it does fuck all, and when I gingerly climb to my feet a few minutes later, the room spins much like it did last night.

I wash my hands and splash my face with water, but it does very little to make me feel better.

Needing to at least brush my teeth, I rip the door open and stumble toward the bedroom where all my stuff is.

My steps falter when my eyes land on the couch and a memory of Kingston slams into me with the force of an eighteen-wheeler.

"You come when I tell you that you can come."

I squeeze my eyes closed, desire pooling between my thighs as I hear those words as clearly as if he just whispered them in my ear.

It was just a dream.

Shaking my head in an attempt to clear the vivid images, I continue forward.

"Jesus, Lor," I mutter as her loud snore bounces off the walls the second I stumble into the bedroom.

She's lying flat on her back, her curly hair like a halo around her head with her lips parted and the most unladylike sound erupting from her throat.

Sleeping on the couch was probably the right thing to do last night.

"Lori," I hiss, unable to speak any louder due to the incessant pounding of my head. "Lori."

When she doesn't so much as stop snoring, I reach out and shake her.

"No, Mom. I'm not going to school today," she mutters, making me giggle.

"Lori, you're a grown-ass woman. You no longer go to school."

Her eyes flicker.

"Lori, I'm getting married today and I'm hungover as fuck."

Those words are what she needs to bring her to, because her eyes pop open and she sits up in a rush.

For a second, I'm impressed by how fresh she must feel, but then her hand darts up and she grabs her head as if it's at risk of exploding.

"Fuck, Tate. I think I'm dying."

"Yeah, join the fucking party."

"What time is it?" Lori asks, still clutching her head.

I glance at my watch and my heart sinks.

We're getting married at 11 a.m.

"Fuck. It's almost eight o'clock."

"Hair and makeup?"

"Will be here in less than ten minutes."

"Oh, Christ."

"I told you not to let me get drunk last night," I say as I rush into the bathroom.

She doesn't respond, and something tells me it's because she's fallen back onto the bed and immediately passed out again.

I've just finished ordering coffee and breakfast to the room when a knock fills the air.

Drawing in a deep breath, I walk across the living room, attempting to look composed and ready for the day.

I snort a laugh.

Composed and ready. What a fucking joke.

I'm halfway across the room when the couch captures my attention again.

"Addicted to this pussy, baby. Fucking addicted."

My heart begins to race and my core clenches.

It feels so real.

But it couldn't have been. He wasn't here.

Was he?

It isn't until another knock rips through the air that I'm dragged from my desire-filled trance and remember what I was doing.

"Good morning. I'm Marissa," a fresh-looking young woman sings the second I pull the door open. "It's your wedding day. Are you excited?"

She beams at me, her eyes twinkling with excitement.

It takes a good ten seconds before she realizes that I'm not about to join in with her over-the-top show of enthusiasm.

"Oh, well, um..."

"Come in," I say, taking a step back and opening the door wider for her and her team.

"Set up wherever. I'll go get Lori," I say before rushing toward the bedroom. She was awake when I left, but there's no telling if she actually rolled out of bed.

Thankfully, the second I step into the room, my eyes lock on my tired best friend's.

"What's wrong?"

"The woman in charge out there brought a level of excitement I can't deal with yet," I confess.

Lori winces before looking over my shoulder.

"We could send them away and just do it ourselves," she offers, just like I did to Kingston when he suggested booking a team to ensure we look and feel our best today.

I shake my head, aware that even if I begged, they wouldn't leave. They're under Kingston Callahan's orders. Nothing I say or do will make them budge an inch.

"It's fine. The coffee will be here soon and maybe she'll calm down."

Lori raises her brow.

"The coffee will help."

Reaching out, I catch her hand and drag her back out with me.

If I have to face the hairbrush and lipstick-wielding firing squad, then so does she.

Besties for life and all that shit.

"Ah, and you must be the bride's maid of honor," Marissa says excitedly, letting me know that she hasn't come down from her high yet. Her smile as she looks between the two of us is borderline manic.

"Holy shit, what has she taken?" Lori asks without trying to move her lips.

"If it's okay with you, we'll start with our maid of honor—"

"It's Lori," my best friend grumbles.

"Have you already showered?"

Silence falls, giving Marissa the answer she didn't want.

"Well, what are you waiting for? The altar and your soon-to-be husband are waiting."

Thankfully, there's another knock on the door. One of Marissa's much quieter sidekicks opens it for us and I almost sob in relief when coffee and breakfast are wheeled in.

"We'll shower in just a few," I say as we descend on the tray.

"Okay. We do need to be ready by ten thirty, though," Marissa points out.

"We're not getting married until eleven, it's fine."

Marissa orders her team around before leveling me with an unimpressed look.

"It's just the two of us," I point out. "We don't need that much work."

Marissa doesn't say a word, but the way her brow lifts tells me all I don't need to know about the level of hot mess I'm rocking right now.

Thankfully, the coffee and the strong painkillers I found in my toiletry bag begin to kick in and I throw my ass into the shower before Marissa strangles me with the cord of her hairdryer.

I've no idea if Marissa just wants to prove that we need a lot of work to be presentable, but she and her team work relentlessly over the next two hours, preening and perfecting everything.

By the time they take a step back, our hair has been styled

within an inch of its life and our makeup has been applied to perfection.

I have to admit, I look incredible. It's just a real shame that I feel like a warmed-up bag of shit. And from the look in Lori's eyes, I'm pretty sure she still does, too.

"Okay," Marissa announces happily, clapping her hands together as if she's applauding herself for overcoming such a huge feat. "I think we are done here. You both look..." She makes a show of kissing her fingers. "Your groom isn't going to know what's hit him," she explains. "And I'm pretty sure the groomsmen are going to be just as enthralled with you," Marissa says, turning to look at Lori.

I can't help but laugh at the way her lip curls in disgust at the thought of either of Kingston's brothers, or mine, hitting on her.

"I think I can live without that," she mutters before turning toward the bedroom where our dresses are waiting.

After thanking Marissa and her team, I see them out and quickly follow Lori.

I find her standing before my wedding dress, and a massive lump crawls up my throat at the thought of pulling it on.

Holy shit.

I'm getting married today.

54

KINGSTON

My cell buzzes in my pocket, but I ignore it, fully aware of who it is as I tighten my tie and take a step back, looking myself up and down.

Forcing thoughts—guilt—over not having my mom here today, I focus on the task at hand.

I'm getting fucking married today.

To Tatum Warner.

I shake my head, a soft smile playing on my lips.

Not in a million years could I have predicted this, but standing here knowing that in less than thirty minutes I'll be sliding another ring onto her finger and making her mine, I can't help but feel that everything is falling into place.

I'd thought I'd be panicking, mourning the loss of my previous life. But I'm not. Not once have I missed it.

Watching Kieran, and then Kian flirting with random women last night, all I could think about was how much more fulfilling it would be to throw Tatum onto the bed and fuck her senseless instead of some nameless, faceless woman who only wants to fuck us to boost her social status and follower count.

Those...transactions are empty.

Sure, there's pleasure, but I can admit to myself that it's nowhere near as earth-shattering as sinking inside Tatum.

Fuck, her pussy is spectacular. Hell, so is her mouth, her hands, her everything.

My cock stirs in my slacks. Fuck, I need to slide into her tight heat almost more than I need to drag in my next breath.

She's holding out to punish me. I get it. But fuck...it's working.

I lift my hand to comb my fingers through my hair but stop just before I make contact.

Fuck, I'm antsy. I need to do something. Order someone around, shout at someone, fuck my girl.

As if someone hears my thoughts, there's a knock on my suite door before the lock disengages and deep male voices fill the air.

"Do you reckon he did a runner in the middle of the night? Too much of a pussy for the ball and chain?" Kieran jokes.

"Nah, he's already too pussy-whipped for that. I bet the motherfucker snuck into her suite last night to remind her why marrying him is such a good idea. Ow. The fuck, man?"

"Stop talking about KC fucking my sister," Miles complains.

"Boys," Dad chastises.

"I didn't say anything about fucking. They probably pulled up Disney+ and watched *Beauty and the Beast* to remind Tate that there is always hope that KC might not always be an ugly motherfucker."

A laugh punches from my chest as I listen to them bicker.

Giving myself one final look, I turn toward the door and walk out to find my boys.

"Ah, here he is," Dad says, watching as I move across the room.

We're all wearing matching suits, and I have to say, we look fucking good.

"How are you feeling?" Kian asks, a smirk playing on his lips.

"Yeah, good. Ready to get this done."

"Bro," Kieran says, backhanding Miles in the chest. "Lil sis is so lucky—you hear that enthusiasm?"

"Fuck off," Miles grunts, long over the mocking about Tatum.

"Here," Kian says, holding out a full bottle of Macallan between us. "Hair of the dog?"

I stare at it, my stomach swirling from the amount of it we drank last night.

"No," I state. "I want to go into this with a clear head."

He nods once before twisting the top and swallowing down a shot, then handing it to Kieran, who offers it to Miles.

He eagerly takes it and swallows down a couple of shots before slamming it back into the center of Kieran's massive chest.

"Okay, I need to go and get Tate," he says, his eyes locked on mine.

I nod.

"We'll see you down there," Kian says, clapping Miles on the shoulder.

As I watch him leave, an unnecessary and unwanted belt of nerves hits me.

What if she changes her mind at the last minute?

What if she's already run?

I've no idea where the thoughts come from, or why I allow them to fester, but now that they've made themselves known, the initial fluttering in my stomach only gets worse.

"You okay, Bro? You look like you're about to hurl," Kian says.

"Probably just realized that he's about to be related to Miles," Kieran points out.

"You've got nothing to worry about," Dad says, stepping closer to steal my attention. I guess he should be the one to understand how I'm feeling—he's been married more times than I care to count. It's like a hobby or some shit at this point. I'm just unsure if he's collecting the brides or the rings. Or something else entirely. The whole thing seems like a lot of effort when each one only ends in divorce in a few short months or years. I guess he's keeping our lawyers busy.

Squaring my shoulders, I look him dead in the eyes. "I'm not worried. It's the first day of a whole new start for all of us."

Dad smiles, pride washing through his features as he stares back at me.

"Right, well. Shall we get this show on the road then?" he asks, refusing to say the words that are balancing on the tip of his tongue.

It's fine. I'm used to imagining praise from him at this point.

The second we get down to the grand ballroom where the service is taking place, Dad slips off to find Jackie and greet several associates he invited.

Tatum and I kept our invitation list relatively modest, only wanting our closest family and friends here, but Dad—unsurprisingly—had other ideas. And thanks to him, our small, intimate wedding has taken on a life of its own to allow him to show off.

It's not necessary, everyone already knows that he's one of the wealthiest men in the state, but he's never one to miss an opportunity to show off.

"This is fucking bizarre, man," Kian says after Kieran has wandered off in favor of a woman in a short pink dress I've never seen before in my life.

"You're telling me," I mutter as we walk down the aisle together.

Our guests turn to look at me. Every single one smiles widely as I approach the front.

The only person I notice who doesn't turn around is Helena, Tatum's mom. Instead, she sits in the front row with an empty seat beside her with her head down.

"It'll be you one day," I point out, ripping my eyes away from her to focus on my brother again. She wants attention, and she's going to be disappointed if she thinks she's going to get any from me. Don't get me wrong, she's not a bad person. But watching how she's failed to support both Miles and Tatum over the past few weeks means I have very little time for her.

Slowly, all the seats in the rows before us fill with people, and Mia, our wedding planner, emerges from behind a huge decorative tree to the side of me, barking orders into a headpiece and clutching a clipboard like it's the oxygen she needs to breathe.

"Oh good, you're already here," she says, staring up at me with a frantic look in her eyes.

"What's wrong?" I ask, my heart skipping a beat as my fear of Tatum changing her mind comes back to me.

"Oh, n-nothing. The flowers were a little late. And then there was a kitchen issue. Nothing to worry about," she says, suddenly producing two buttonholes from out of nowhere. Without asking for permission, she immediately begins putting them into place on our jackets before stepping back and admiring us.

"Very good. Your bride should be leaving her room in less than ten minutes. She looks incredible. You're a very lucky man."

My heart stutters again but for a very different reason.

I've no idea what kind of dress Tatum has. Sure, I can use my imagination based on the kind of things I've seen her wear in the past. But something tells me that she isn't going to be that predictable. She's probably chosen something out of left field like a black dress to mourn her life as a single girl or something. It's exactly the kind of thing my little brat would do.

A smile tugs at my lips as I think of her putting her middle finger up to the world and doing this her own way just to try and grasp some kind of control over the situation.

"Fucking hell," Kian whispers. "You're really fucking gone for her, aren't you?"

"No idea what you're talking about," I mutter, my smirk still firmly in place.

"I was right earlier, wasn't I? You totally let yourself into her suite last night."

I shrug one shoulder, neither confirming nor denying. "I don't kiss and tell, Bro.'

"Oh, fuck off, don't you." He scoffs.

"How was your night? You look a little too well-rested for it to have been any good," I tease.

"That would be because it was so good. I slept like a fucking baby after she was done with me. Don't even remember her leaving."

"Said like a true gentleman," I tease.

"Pfft, because you're so much better."

I smile but don't respond. I fucking wish I'd passed out after an epic night of fucking my wife last night, but alas, I was forced to resort to my own hand. Again.

With only a minute until Tatum is scheduled to arrive, everyone is in place. Kian stands beside me and the officiant before us, patiently waiting to do his job.

"You ready for this?" Kian whispers.

"I was born ready, asshole."

Suddenly, the music changes and my heart jumps into my throat.

Kian moves beside me, turning to look as Tatum and Miles enter the room.

Soft gasps of delight fill the air, and I squeeze my eyes closed in preparation for seeing her.

"Damn," Kian mutters. "You lucky motherfucker."

My fists curl at my sides, my short nails digging into my palms.

I told myself that I wouldn't look back, that I'd wait for her to get here. I've heard the whole thing about women not looking at the bride and instead the groom so that they can experience the moment he sees his woman and the look on his face. Honestly, that is what's terrifying me the most about this whole thing. If I were to turn around, what would everyone see on my face?

My heart pounds harder, and despite my better judgment, my need to see her gets the better of me.

Without permission from my brain, my body turns, and the second my eyes lock on her, I swear the world around me stops spinning.

55

TATUM

My heart is beating so fast I'm sure I'm about twenty seconds from passing out halfway down the aisle.

I guess that's one way of defying my father's wishes. Although, knowing the men I'm surrounded by, they'd probably bring the officiant to the hospital to continue the service there.

Lori moves to the side, allowing me to fully see the back of the man I'm being forced to marry.

Although, that feels like a bit of a joke. No one is forcing me right now. No one is holding my hand and dragging me toward this man and putting words in my mouth. I'm choosing to do this.

My grip on Miles's arm as he guides me toward his best friend tightens. I feel him look down at me with the same concern he did when he first entered our suite. But just like I did then, I ignore it.

He doesn't like this, I'm more than aware of that. But I've made my decision.

Just one year.

Twelve months.

We can endure each other for that long.

It might not be easy, but it'll be worth it.

I hope.

Rolling my shoulders back, I stand tall as every set of eyes, but the ones I secretly want, burn into me.

Turn around, I silently beg, desperate to see his reaction to my dress.

I thought Miles was going to burst into tears when he first saw me earlier. It might be wishful thinking to believe Kingston will react so viscerally, but still, I want to see it.

His entire body is locked up tight, and not a second later, his fists clench.

I'm barely halfway down the aisle and already, I'm affecting him.

I'm not sure how I feel about that.

There is a part of me that loves it, but that's the foolish part of me that allowed me to believe the weekend at the cabin was more than what we are. It's the part that is going to get me hurt.

I need to focus on the other part. The logical part. The part that is going to keep me safe and ensure I come out of this business deal in one piece.

Just a business deal.

Just a business deal.

Then, as if he heard my silent mantra, he looks over his shoulder.

His expression is hard, cold even, but then his eyes lock on mine and everything changes.

His eyes widen at the same time his chin drops and something powerful crackles between us. His eyes fall from mine to take all of me in, and his expression changes again to what I can only describe as awe.

My heart pounds, slamming against my ribs as I move closer to him, my body begging for me to walk faster, to take my place by his side.

"Jesus," Miles grunts, having also seen his best friend's reaction. "Maybe it isn't your heart I should be worried about."

"W-what?" I whisper, unable to decipher his words.

"Nothing."

In only seconds, Miles delivers me to his best friend before kissing my cheek and whispering, "I've got your back, Tate. Always. You need anything, I'll be right there."

"I love you," I whisper. I don't tell my big brother how much he means to me often enough. I hope he knows how important he is, though.

"Love you too, sis."

With a supportive squeeze of my hand, he steps away.

He has so much more that he wants to say, but he knows it's too late, and even if it weren't, I wouldn't listen.

I've made up my mind. This is happening.

Turning to Kingston, my breath catches as our eyes collide.

Memories slam into me with enough force to make me take a step back—not that anyone can see with the size of my dress.

"I didn't think it was possible to need someone as much as I need you. I'm fucking addicted, Tate."

"It wasn't a dream," I whisper, a deep frown creasing my brow and desire building beneath my waist as I remember more and more of what I thought was a dream.

"Baby," Kingston groans, moving a step closer to me. "You look incredible."

"You came to our suite last night, didn't you?"

His lips don't move to answer me, but his eyes flash with hunger and his tongue sweeps across his bottom lip as if he's remembering having my taste there.

"Good morning, ladies and gentlemen. We are gathered here today to witness the union of Tatum Grace Warner and Kingston Michael Callahan. We've come together to honor and celebrate the love shared between these two people as they embark on their new life with a solemn vow, surrounded by their closest family and friends."

I thought I'd be nervous in this moment as the farce of our relationship hits fever pitch, but as Kingston reaches for my hand and stares into my eyes, I feel as calm as I've ever felt.

Nothing about this feels wrong.

In fact, everything feels right.

Too right.

The officiant continues talking about the importance of marriage and the vows we're going to give today, the promises we're going to make to each other.

My breathing is slow, my heart pounding steadily in my chest.

Kingston stares back at me like any groom does his bride, his eyes filled with emotion.

"Tatum, could you repeat after me?"

The officiant's voice doesn't register; I'm too lost in a set of mesmerizing green eyes.

"Tatum?"

Kingston smirks, more than aware of what's distracted me.

He squeezes my hand as the officiant says my name again.

I startle and turn to him.

"I'm so sorry."

He starts again, and I repeat his words, making my promises to Kingston.

I have to keep them for a year, just one short year, but as I say the words, I can't help but feel like they're more than they should be, that I'm promising so much more than the contract I signed, the terms I agreed to.

"Kingston," the officiant says, before I listen to him repeat the same words.

With each one, my heart pounds harder and my hands begin to shake more violently.

The calmness I felt earlier ebbs away as the reality of this situation finally dawns.

This is serious. We're really doing this.

And what's worse, I'm not hating every second.

Everything is a blur as we say our vows. Everything feels like it's spinning out of control. It's all I can do not to fall into a full-blown panic attack—something I haven't experienced since my parents first shipped me off to boarding school. The only thing that calmed me was Miles's presence.

But while he might be in the room, he's not going to help me now.

"Ladies and gentlemen, please join me in congratulating the new Mr. and Mrs. Callahan," the officiant says, earning a loud round of applause from our small audience. "Kingston, you may now kiss your bride."

Without missing a beat, he closes the space between us and takes my face in his hands.

Resting his brow against mine, he stares down into my eyes.

Instantly, I'm a little calmer.

"Breathe, baby."

"King," I whisper, my eyes bouncing between his.

The air is charged, and despite the words we've just said to each other in front of our closest friends and family, there are so many more that go unspoken between us.

"Mine," he breathes before finally pressing his lips against mine.

It starts innocent, but then his hand drops to my waist and he tugs me against him, or at least the best he can with my dress trying to keep us apart.

I gasp when his grip tightens on me. It gives him the opening he was obviously gunning for and his tongue plunges past my lips, kissing me the way I've been dreaming of since last Monday.

There are a couple of rumbling cheers, which I can only assume belong to Kian and Kieran, before Kingston finally lets me up for air.

"Missed you, baby," he whispers, his eyes sparkling with a potent mixture of excitement and desire. "Can't wait to make this official."

"Pretty sure that's what we just did."

He chuckles. "For them, yeah. What I'm thinking about is a much more private affair."

Heat pools between my thighs as my mouth opens to argue, to attempt to keep a level head.

"I know you need it as badly as I do, so don't even try to argue."

Before I manage to get a word out, he grabs my hand and turns me toward our smiling audience.

I knew they were there, but suddenly seeing them all staring back at me makes my stomach flip-flop.

They believe it. They actually think that what Kingston and I have is real, pure, true.

"Come on, I need a few minutes alone with my wife," Kingston says before we embark on my second trip down the aisle, only this time, I'm not walking toward the man I'm willingly giving myself to for a year of my life. I'm walking hand in hand with my new husband.

What the hell have I done?

K ing swings the door open with so much fervor, it crashes back before slamming closed only two seconds later.

"Oh my god," I cry when my back collides with the wall and King's forearms cage me in.

"Did I already tell you how incredible you look," he says, nothing but sincerity in his voice.

My cheeks heat as he stares at me so deeply, I swear he can see straight down to my soul.

"We're married," I squeak like a moron, the weight of the addition of my wedding ring heavy on my left hand.

"Fuck. You're my wife," he says in awe, as if he's only just realized what happened out there. "Mrs. Tatum Callahan."

My stomach somersaults.

Why does that sound...right?

"King, I—"

Honestly, I have no idea what I was going to say—my head and my heart are too busy battling it out for supremacy over this whole situation to form any rational thoughts.

I'm not sure if it's a good thing or not that he steals my lips in a slow, sensual, and all-consuming kiss, ensuring that all those jumbled thoughts fly right out of my head. All sense of rationality drifts away, and all I can do is give myself over to him. My husband.

He slides his hand around the back of my neck, his thumb gently directing my jaw so he can position me exactly how he wants me as his tongue sweeps into my mouth.

My hands find his waist and his muscles jump the second I connect with him, letting me know that he feels this...this intensity between us as well.

"I can't get you out of my head, baby. These past ten days... fuck. Fucking torture," he confesses against my lips, unable to pull away now he's reclaimed them.

"That was the idea. You hurt me, King. Releasing those photos without so much as warning me."

"I know. I'm sorry. Fuck. I'm so sorry. I know it's a shitty excuse, but I'm not used to thinking about anyone but myself. I make decisions that will benefit me or the company, and I just do it. I'll do better. I swear."

I stare up at him, desperately wanting to believe him, but also trying to understand why it's all so important to me.

It's just a year. So what if he thinks about himself and his future? I know that's what I'm doing.

I'm being a hypocrite, asking him to do one thing while focusing on something else entirely for myself.

His eyes bore into mine, the green intense and hungry as he begs me to believe him.

I want to, I do. But also, does it really matter?

I shouldn't expect anything from him. That is not what this is.

When it becomes clear that I'm not going to respond, he leans forward and takes my lips again.

His kiss is hungry and desperate, and I make him move for more.

Dragging his lips across my jaw, I suck in deep breaths in the hope of getting my body under control. It's burning hotter than it should, seeing as we've got a whole host of people on the other side of the door waiting for us.

He moves to my ear, his warm breath rushing over the

exposed skin of my shoulder, causing goosebumps to erupt across every inch of my body.

He groans deeply before confessing, "I can still taste you on my tongue."

"Oh god," I whimper. "It was real."

He chuckles. "Baby, no dream is that good," he mutters arrogantly. "Just a taste of what's to come tonight. I have every intention of ensuring you don't regret anything about what we've done today."

I blink, trying to clear the cloud of lust that's descended over me.

"We're going to have so much fun." His fingers grip my jaw and he turns me to face him, his lips attacking mine once again.

I'm vaguely aware of a knock filling the room, but I'm too lost in Kingston's kiss to pay much attention.

I'm given little choice but to focus though when my best friend's amused voice hits my ears.

"Well, well, well, what do we have here?" she teases.

56

TATUM

The rest of the day is a blur of disbelief, graciously accepting everyone's congratulations and well wishes for the future, and being teased within an inch of my life.

I thought I was needy for Kingston when Lori interrupted our heated make-out session in one of the hotel's offices, but that was nothing. Since the moment we were announced as husband and wife, Kingston seems to have made it his sole mission to have my entire body vibrating with desire.

All the way through having our wedding photos taken, he was whispering filthy things in my ear, ensuring his seemingly innocent and romantic touches drove me to the brink of insanity. Any second we've managed to steal for ourselves, he's pushed me against a wall or a desk or anything he can find and kissed the living daylights out of me, all the while telling me how incredible I look, but also muttering about how much better my wedding dress will look on the floor of our suite.

By the time we're instructed to take to the stage for our first dance as a married couple, I'm about ready to claw my own skin off with my need for his touch.

With all eyes on us once again, Kingston leads me toward the dance floor. My entire body trembles as we take our places. If anyone can see it, they probably assume it's nerves. Well, anyone but Lori and Cory. They have both delighted in teasing me relentlessly all day. They know me well enough to know why I'm so antsy, and it is not helping the situation.

Kingston's hand grips mine tightly while the other slips innocently around my waist, tugging me harshly against his body.

"Been waiting all day for this," he whispers the second his cheek presses against mine.

"Really?" I deadpan as the music wraps around us.

While I'm in his arms, protected by this enigma of a man, it's easy to think it's just the two of us, that the rest of the world ceases to exist around us.

"What? Did you think there was something else I've spent all week fantasizing about other than dancing with my wife?" he mocks.

"Dancing, sure."

"I was just picturing it without clothes and definitely with a few fewer eyes on us," he confesses as we move together as if we've been doing it all our lives. Dancing with him is effortless in a way that I'm not sure life with him is going to be.

We might find this calm moment where we can just be, like the weekend at the cabin. But they're only the calm in the storm. The rest of the time, we're bickering and driving each other crazy with our stubbornness and unwillingness to bend.

With his lips against my ear so that no one can hear or even lip-read, he continues. "I'm going to undo each of these little buttons running down your back," he explains as his fingers bounce over them. "And then watch as your dress sinks to the floor around you."

Oh my god.

"Your breasts are already heavy with need. I can tell without having to remove your clothes, and I already know how fucking incredible they'll look with your nipples hard and begging for my mouth."

My thighs clench and my eyelids lower as I imagine him wrapping those lips around me.

Desire floods my core, ensuring that my already ruined panties are damp again.

Damn this man.

He shouldn't have this potent effect on my body with just a few words and an innocent touch.

"Then, when you can barely catch your breath, I'm going to wrap my hands around your waist, lift you from your dress, and throw you onto the bed, watching as you bounce."

"You need to stop," I beg, already breathless.

"Never," he whispers. "I'm not stopping until neither of us can take any more. You're my wife, Tatum. I'm your husband. It never—"

"For a year, King. I'm your wife for a year." I've no idea why I feel the need to remind him of that right now, but the words tumble free regardless. The second he hears, his entire body stills and he pulls back, his eyes locking on mine.

Something crackles loudly as a bolt of electricity shoots down my spine, rocking my foundation.

"I don't give a shit about our expiration date, Tatum. Right now, you're mine. And I have every intention of treating you the way every wife should be."

It's all I can do to nod in agreement as he continues to stare at me. With nothing but a powerful look, he renders me useless and strips me bare.

"When this song is over, we're getting out of here," he explains, leaving no room for argument.

I swallow thickly, thinking about how it'll look to our guests if we walk out of our own wedding reception.

Real...it looks real.

My heart flutters and my stomach somersaults.

Right here, right now, it feels real.

Too fucking real.

As if someone hits fast forward on the clock, the song changes and other couples flood the dance floor.

"I need you naked now, Tatum. Are you going to be a good girl and give your husband what he wants, or are you going to be a little brat?"

The need to defy him, to demand that we enjoy the rest of our wedding burns through me, although I don't think for a second that he'd ever agree, no matter how much I argue.

"Which option do you think is more fun?" I ask, cocking my head to the side.

He smirks, happily playing along as his hand brushes up the side of my body until he can grip my chin.

I'm sure there are plenty of guests who are watching, judging even, but I couldn't give a fuck.

"I know which I prefer," he finally says, his face set in determination.

He moves faster than I can compute and a shriek rips from my lips as my feet lift from the floor.

I land over his shoulder with his arm wrapped around my thighs —not that he can get anywhere close with the size of my dress.

"Oh my god, Kingston. You can't do this. Everyone is watching," I cry as he begins marching across the dance floor.

I don't look up, but I don't need to, to know that more and more people are turning to look at us.

My face burns bright red, and it's not just because all the blood in my upper body is racing toward it.

Every single person in this room knows exactly what he's carrying me away to do.

Fisting my hands, I rain them down on his solid ass, surely hurting myself more than I am him.

His steps don't so much as falter as we finally leave the room we've spent most of the afternoon and evening inside with our friends and family.

A door closes behind us, and the music we were just dancing to fades away.

My ears ring and my face continues to burn.

"Was that necessary?" I bark.

"Shouldn't have taunted me then, should you, brat?"

I fume over his shoulder.

"You can put me down now," I spit the second he steps into the elevator.

The doors close behind us and we immediately begin climbing through the building toward the top floor. At some point today, the small bag I packed on Friday morning was moved from the suite I stayed in with Lori last night to the one I'm going to be spending tonight in with my new husband.

Butterflies flutter wildly in my stomach, but his grip on my legs never loosens.

"Kingston," I warn.

"If I put you down, I can't be held responsible for my actions."

His words echo through the air, the meaning behind them making it hard to suck in my next breath.

Thankfully, only minutes later, the elevator chimes and the doors open on our floor.

"Thank fuck," he mutters under his breath before marching out and then down the hallway to our suite like his ass is on fire.

Excitement tingles wildly inside me, the anticipation of being with him after brushing off all his attempts for days.

I was meant to be punishing him, but I'm more than aware that I've been punishing myself right alongside him. I can't help but wonder if it was all because I wanted tonight to be special. I don't believe in the whole no-sex-before-marriage thing—obviously—but there is something special about this moment, this "I must have you now and nothing else matters" moment. It's a serious rush. And if it's the result of withholding for almost two weeks, then I'm down.

We fly through the door the second King has it unlocked, and then he blows through the suite with me still hanging over his shoulder like a sack of potatoes in a very pretty dress.

But the moment we step into the bedroom, he finally lowers me to the ground, and much to my surprise, he takes a huge step back and just...watches me.

"King," I breathe with my heart in my throat.

"Fuck, Tatum. Do you have any idea how incredible you look?"

I swallow thickly as my eyes drop down his body.

He's wearing a navy-blue suit to match our ivory and navy color theme, and he looks edible.

His hair is no longer styled how he wanted it this morning, but messy, like he's spent the whole day dragging his fingers through it. His eyes are dark and hungry, his lips full, his jaw has the perfect amount of scruff on it, and the suit…well, it looks like it has been tailored to fit his body to perfection, and I can't wait to peel it off and discover what's waiting for me beneath.

"Please," I whimper, unable to say anything more eloquent in this moment.

I love my dress, it's beautiful, but it's also restrictive as hell. I'm ready for it to hit the floor. I'm ready to embark on the next part of our big day.

He steps forward and his face immediately tucks into the crook of my neck, kissing, licking, and nipping, driving me to the brink of insanity while we're both fully dressed.

He knows what he's doing; he's the master at it.

"Turn around," he finally whispers, sending a new wave of tingles shooting down my spine.

Slowly, I do as I'm told and give him my back. His kisses don't stop, leaving my body craving more. More of his touch, more of him, more of everything.

As he described downstairs, his fingers reach for the small satin button between my shoulder blades.

It took forever to get me fully into the thing. I dread to think how long it's going to—

"Oh," I gasp, as the unforgiving fabric begins to release around me, allowing me to breathe properly for the first time in a lot of hours.

Kingston's lips follow his progress, kissing down my spine until he gets to the final button, allowing the dress to descend. The skirt is so massive, it stands up all by itself. I look a little like the weird toilet roll cozy thing my aunt had in the cottage. It always baffled me, but she seemed to love the ugly thing all the same.

I stand there with my dress covering my legs still, and only wearing a small ivory lace pair of panties and a garter. There were just some traditions I couldn't ignore, and watching King remove this from my body was one of them.

As he drags his knuckles up my sides, I groan in desperation, my nipples puckering even tighter.

"Beautiful," he whispers in my ear, making me shudder. "Now turn around. Let me see my wife."

My stomach knots.

His wife.

Fuck. Why does that make me want to drop to my knees like a good girl who does very, very bad things?

57

KINGSTON

M y suit feels too small for my body as I stand there staring at my wife in only her sexy panties and garter.

She's blown me away today in so many different ways. Everything about her has been perfect. From the way she looked as she walked down the aisle toward me, to her desperation for me when I backed her up against the wall in the office, to the way she gazed up at me as I made my speech—a speech that was nowhere near as full of bullshit as I feared it would be when I first thought about having to write it. Every single word I said about my bride was true. Painfully true. And then the way her body moved so perfectly against mine as we danced together only moments ago...

For a fake wedding, it's been very fucking real.

And as I stand before her now as she bares herself to me, it feels even more authentic than ever.

My heart pounds erratically in my chest, my hands tremble, and my cock throbs.

My need for this woman is growing by the day and I fear that no amount of time, or rounds in bed, will sate it.

"King," she whispers almost nervously as all I do is stare at her.

Fuck. I'm so fucking enthralled by her right now.

Her breath catches as I take a step forward, my shoes brushing against the billowing fabric of her dress.

The image I painted for her as we danced earlier plays out in my mind, and before I know what I'm doing, I have my hands around her waist and I'm lifting her from the floor.

"Kingston," she squeals as I launch her onto the bed.

She bounces, her tits jiggling before she settles right in the middle like a fucking offering.

Planting her feet on the comforter beneath her, she spreads her thighs. She's still wearing her heels, and it's the first time I've seen them thanks to the huge dress. But fuck...they can stay.

"Fuck," I breathe, my eyes dropping between her legs in favor of the scrap of lace covering her pussy.

"See something you like, husband?" she taunts. There isn't an ounce of hesitation. She owns her sexuality completely, and fuck if it isn't the biggest fucking turn-on.

I rub my jaw, doing anything I can to stop myself from jumping on her and taking exactly what I need.

To be fair, I don't think she'd complain if I did. But she deserves more than a quick but explosive fuck for her wedding night.

It should be the best fucking night of her life.

"Yeah," I confess, letting my eyes roam over every inch of her before pausing on the garter. "I see a lot that I really fucking like."

"Seems a little one-sided right now, don't you think?" she asks before her eyes drop to my fully-clothed body.

"Pretty sure you can see perfectly well what you're doing to me," I confess, palming my cock through my pants.

I'm so fucking hard it's not even funny.

"Not good enough. I want to see what I got out of this deal. Show me the goods, Mr. Callahan."

Unable to refuse her orders, my hand lifts to the tie around my neck and I pull it free before dropping it to the end of the bed. Who knows, that just might come in handy later.

An image of my girl on her knees with her hands bound

behind her back by the tie I was wearing when she gave herself to me pops up and does all kinds of unspeakable things to me.

Slowly, I make my way down the buttons on my shirt, exposing an inch of skin at a time.

She hungrily eats it all up, her eyes wider with each bit of progress I make.

"You always have been an infuriating motherfucker," Tatum scoffs, unimpressed with my speed.

I smirk, making a show of ripping my waistband open.

"Kingston," she warns.

I've never really been into delayed gratification. But there is something very, very amusing about building Tatum up until she looks like she's going to explode. I've never considered myself a stripper, either, but it seems I might be doing an okay job of that too.

After toeing my shoes off, I tuck my pants from my feet and stand at the foot of the bed in just my boxers.

"More," she demands. "Let me see what I've got to work with."

"Oh, I think you'll be more than satisfied," I muse as she pushes herself up until she's sitting before me.

Her eyes drop from mine in favor of my body, and the second she locks her gaze on my dick, it visibly jerks.

Before I get a chance to push my underwear from my hips, she reaches out and does it for me.

My cock bounces free, hard and desperate. The tip glistens with precum, and it only gets worse when Tatum licks her lips.

"Baby," I groan. This wasn't what I was planning.

I should be focusing on her. But—

"Oh fuck, you little fucking brat," I bark when she drags her tongue up the length of my cock before sucking on the head like it's her personal popsicle.

My head falls back as pleasure rockets through me. My cock jerks violently in her mouth, my balls already threatening to draw up.

On autopilot, my fingers sink into her hair, instantly ruining her pretty updo.

"Jesus," I grunt when she takes me right to the back of her throat. "I married a filthy whore, didn't I, baby?"

She stares up at me with wide, watery eyes. I'm pretty sure she'd nod if she could.

While one hand helps work my cock alongside her mouth, the other grasps my ass tightly, her long, manicured nails digging into my skin and sending a bolt of pain right to my balls.

"Anyone would think you want my cum, Brat."

She releases me for a beat, sucking in a deep breath before she takes me again. But before she gets a chance to wrap those pretty lips around me again, I tighten my grip on her hair and drag her back, leaving a trail of saliva connecting us. My stomach flips at the sight of her pouting because she wants my dick.

Fuck. This. Woman.

"Later," I growl, although it's fucking painful to do so. I'd happily spend the rest of the night with her bobbing up and down on my dick.

I release her with a gentle push, and she falls back onto the bed.

"Beautiful," I muse before crawling onto the edge and reaching for her panties.

Tucking my fingers under the delicate lace, I drag them down her thighs, over the garter, and then off her feet.

Bundling the scrap of fabric in my hand, I lift them to my nose and inhale.

"Delicious," I mutter, keeping my eyes on her heated ones.

"Kingston, please," she begs. It's like music to my fucking ears.

With a smirk, I drop her panties to the bed and spread her legs wide, taking in the sight of her swollen, glistening pussy.

My mouth waters, but I don't immediately dive for it like we both want. Instead, I descend on her lips, licking into her mouth like we've got all the time in the world.

She trembles under my touch, and it only gets worse as I move down her body.

Her moans and mewls, and her demands for more, get louder and more insistent as I circle her nipples, driving her crazy before I finally suck one and then the other into my mouth.

Her fingers thread through my hair, her grip tight as she tries to take control, to force me where she wants me, but she isn't very successful.

I'm the one in charge, and I will tease her until I'm ready to give her more.

I glance at the headboard, regretting not asking them to switch it out so that she'd have something to hold onto. I consider the tie, but that would mean stopping, and like fuck am I stopping right now.

Her skin is too sweet, too soft, the scent of her arousal too addictive. Nothing could rip me away from my woman right now. Hell, the entire place could go up around us and I'm pretty sure I would just let it happen.

"Kingston, please. I need you to touch me," she cries, her back arching off the bed, her heels digging into my ass hard enough to make my breath catch.

"I am touching you," I say, letting my lips move across her stomach.

"Fuck. You're a pain in my ass."

"No," I counter. "I'm pretty sure that's you right now." Her heels dig in harder. I wouldn't be surprised if she's drawn blood.

Fucking bring it on. I'll wear her marks proudly.

"For all the good it's doing," she mutters irritably, making me laugh.

"What is it you really want, baby? Tell me, and I might just give it to you."

I glance up her body in time to see her lips pursed in frustration.

My little brat is used to getting her way, although something tells me that her pussy is wetter because she's not.

Reaching behind me, I unhook her ankles. Placing one over

my shoulder, I press a kiss to the other, loving the way she squirms as my lips connect with her heated skin.

"God," she moans when I continue kissing down her leg.

Her hips roll and her hands fist the sheets beneath her.

So fucking sexy.

And all fucking mine.

I take my time working all the way down one leg, letting her think that she's close to getting what she wants before I sit back up and start on the other.

"Fucking tease," she snaps.

"It'll be worth it," I promise before repeating the kisses, licks, and nips I treated the other leg to.

By the time I'm at her thigh, she's trembling violently beneath me.

"Oh god yes, please, please," she breathes when I drop to my stomach between her legs and take a deep breath.

My mouth waters, ensuring my time holding back is shattered as I lean forward and suck on her swollen clit.

Her taste floods my mouth and my cock weeps for her.

"Yes, Kingston," she screams as she bucks against my face, riding me and trying to get more.

Wrapping my hands around her hips, I hold her tightly, taking control back from her again.

I eat her until she's trying to rip my hair from my head and my self-control is at the breaking point.

"Kingston," she sobs, when I pull back from her, not letting her fall again. "I'm going to kill you if you don't give me what I need," she hisses.

Chuckling, I give her exactly that, finally letting her fall and delighting in the sound of my name bouncing off the walls around us as she does.

I work her through her release before climbing to my knees and settling with her legs wrapped around my waist.

After making a show of licking her taste from my lips, I grab my cock and run it through her slick pussy.

The second I push the head inside her, her muscles ripple, desperately trying to suck me in.

"Fuck me, King. Please, fuck me."

"Jesus, Tatum," I grunt before punching my hips forward and giving her exactly what we both need.

I clench my jaw as her wet heat takes me so perfectly.

Pausing deep inside her, I circle my hips, ensuring I hit all the spots that make her cry out again.

"Fuck, you're perfect," I blurt.

This might have been designed as a business transaction, but right now, as her body molds to mine in the most perfect way, it feels so much more like that.

To stop me from confessing anything else that I'm not going to be able to take back, I plant my palms on either side of her head and steal her lips, letting her taste herself on me and licking deep into her mouth, claiming her as mine in every way that I can.

58

TATUM

I wake with my entire body burning up, and it doesn't take long to discover why.

Kingston is wrapped around me like a fucking koala.

Sure, I've fallen asleep wrapped in his arms, but it's a whole other thing to wake up like it. Like he needed me in his sleep.

The thought makes my head spin.

It was just the incredible sex, I tell myself as I do my best to slide from beneath his arm without waking him. He doesn't actually want me; it was just the insanity of the day before.

It takes longer than I thought possible, but I finally manage to climb from the bed, leaving him still sleeping behind me as I pad naked across the colossal bedroom.

My steps falter as I round the bed and find my abandoned wedding dress exactly where we left it last night.

I glance back at the giant bed where Kingston continues to sleep in the middle, his arm outstretched as if I'm still there.

My heart clenches, as does my tender pussy.

It's a reminder I don't need about everything that happened after he carried me in here last night.

If I thought things were intense between us at the cabin, then I really underestimated the situation.

Last night...

Fuck.

Easily the hottest sex of my life.

It's probably exactly what every other newly married couple dreams of.

But we're not every other married couple.

We're not wildly in love and planning to spend the rest of our lives together.

We barely even like each other.

And yet...

"Tatum."

My heart seizes in my chest as his deep voice lingers in the air.

I keep my eyes on him, but he doesn't move.

He's dreaming about you...

Fuck.

Ripping my gaze from him, I rush across the room and lock myself in the bathroom before freaking out.

My breaths come faster, and the room spins around me.

I'm married to Kingston Callahan.

I'm going to be his wife for the next year.

Lifting my hand, I stare down at my rings, my heart continuing to pound in my chest as reality settles on my shoulders.

It was easy to forget about it all last night after more than a few glasses of champagne and the fog of lust surrounding us.

But now, in the cold light of day...

"Fuck. What have I done?"

Spinning around, I press my palms against the granite countertop and stare at myself in the mirror.

My hair is wild, any hint of the pretty updo Marissa and her team did yesterday long gone—and so is the makeup, other than the smudged black eyeliner and mascara making me look even more tired and stressed than I really am.

Seconds and then minutes tick by as I continue to silently freak out. My thoughts flick erratically between memories of my time with Kingston over the past few weeks, our wedding day, and my time at the cottage with Aunt Lena.

I can remember every room as if it were my own home. The whole place is filled with laughter and happiness. Nothing like the home I grew up in.

A pained sigh spills from my lips.

It's always been my happy place. A place I've retreated to when life got too hard. A place of solace and peace. A place where all my troubles ceased to exist for the days and weeks I was there.

Losing Aunt Lena a few years ago was hard. I hate to admit it, but it was harder than losing my father has been.

She was like a grandmother to me.

She was fifteen years older than my father. My grandfather's illegitimate child when he was a teenager. She was a huge part of my father's early years. His nanny, almost. She may have married an English man and moved across the pond, but she never forgot about me and Miles. She was like the grandmother I never had. Okay, sure, I did have grandparents for the first few years of my life, but they weren't exactly involved.

Aunt Lena, however, never forgot us.

Every month, she'd send us a goodie box of all the incredible things that were only available in England. Chocolates, candy, and so much more.

The days that box was delivered were my favorite. The excitement that bubbled inside me as we unwrapped them was beyond anything else I experienced.

I'm so lost in my memories of years gone by that I don't hear the door opening, but the second Kingston's eyes land on me, a violent shiver rips down my spine. My eyes lift.

Instantly, our gazes connect in the mirror, and I swear the world shakes beneath me.

"You ran," he says, his voice rough with sleep.

"I needed to pee," I lie.

"So why are you staring at yourself in the mirror like you're regretting every single one of your life choices?"

Any words I might have shrivel up and die on my tongue, the air turning electric as he continues to move closer.

I can't see beneath his waist, but I know he's naked, and that's only confirmed when he presses himself against me.

His cock is hard, and fuck if my pussy doesn't flutter with the thought of him pushing inside me again.

It's wrong.

I shouldn't want him as fiercely as I do after the night we just had together.

I should have had my fill.

It should have been enough.

But I can't help but feel like we've only scratched the surface of what we could have together.

"What's wrong?" he demands, his hand sliding from my hip up to my waist, pinning us together.

We fit perfectly.

Too perfectly.

"Nothing."

"You're lying to me," he states. "Is that really how you want our marriage to begin?"

A weird blend of fury and confusion shoots through my veins and I run my mouth before thinking.

"This isn't a marriage. It's nothing but a fucking sham."

His hand moves faster than I thought possible, and I gasp as it wraps around my throat.

"Kingston," I moan when his fingers flex in the most delicious way.

He doesn't cut my air off, but the warning is there, and my body reacts.

"You like that, baby?" he asks when I grind my ass back against him.

I swallow, letting him feel the answer as my pulse continues to race.

"Now, let's try this again. What's wrong?"

His eyes bounce between mine as the heat of his body once again sears through me, making my blood boil.

"W-we're married," I whisper.

"Right?" His voice is calm, thoughtful, as if this whole thing hasn't affected him or his life in any way. It's not true. I know it's not. I've seen his moments of vulnerability. His concern over letting me into his apartment and sharing his life with me. I swear I have.

"Doesn't this...terrify you?" I ask, hating how open and vulnerable I feel.

"Why should it? It's just a year, right? We do our time, and then we return to our lives as we know them."

My brows pinch.

"And you're okay with that?" I ask.

"Of course. I wouldn't have agreed otherwise."

"Right. Yeah," I mutter, feeling like an idiot.

Of course, none of this really means anything to him.

It's just a business deal.

"We should probably get ready. They're expecting us for breakfast. We already ducked out of our reception early."

"They can wait," he rasps.

The hand that's not around my throat drops to my hip once more and he pulls me back from the counter, positioning me exactly as he wants me.

He releases me in favor of rubbing his hardness through my folds, testing to see if I'm ready.

"Tatum," he groans.

I should be ashamed of how wet I am for him. But I'm not.

We might be the unlikeliest of couples after we've spent most of our lives hating each other, but something magical happens when we collide. Something I'm quickly becoming addicted to.

Happy that I'm ready for him, he pushes just slightly inside me.

I gasp at the intrusion. As always, it feels incredible, but it also stings.

We really went for it last night and my body is feeling it. I just hadn't realized how much until this moment.

"Are you okay?" he asks, his lips brushing against the shell of my ear.

"Y-yeah."

"Liar," he hisses before biting down on my earlobe and sending a rush of heat to my pussy.

"Isn't going to stop you though, is it?"

He chuckles as he pushes deeper inside me. "You know me so well."

He fucks me slowly—so fucking slowly it makes my head spin and my body yearn for more.

Fuck being sore. I need him to unleash on me just like last night.

"Please," I whimper, my grip on the granite counter so tight my knuckles are white.

"Please what, baby?"

"Fuck me, please. I need more."

Our eyes hold in the mirror as I silently plead for him to give me what I crave.

His fingers twitch around my throat before he releases me, and disappointment floods through my veins. But then he wraps a hand around one of my wrists and then the other, plucking them from the counter and pulling them behind my back.

My body tenses to stay in position, and Kingston groans as I grip his cock tightly in the process.

"Damn, Tate," he mutters, holding both of my wrists behind my back in one hand before the other returns to my throat. "Fuck, you just gushed," he gasps in surprise. "You like that?"

I nod—not that it's necessary.

"Dirty, dirty girl," he muses darkly, nothing but unfiltered heat and awe in his eyes.

My lids lower as he circles his hips, hitting me so deeply I feel it in every inch of my body.

"Eyes on me, Brat," he demands. "Watch as your husband fucks you."

"Oh god," I whimper, forcing my eyes open.

His grip on my throat tightens as his powerful thrusts pick up pace.

My release surges forward, my greedy pussy trying to take him deeper.

More.

I need more.

I always need more. And that's a real fucking problem where Kingston is concerned.

I can't have it.

All I can have is this.

A year of this, and then he's going to cut me free.

Send me back out into the world as if the previous twelve months didn't mean anything.

I stare into the dark green depths of his eyes and my heart seizes in my chest.

It's been three weeks and already I'm feeling things I told myself I wouldn't. I'm being swept up by this man and his magnificent cock.

Already, the thought of walking away at the end of this makes my heart race, and not in a good way.

How the hell am I going to do it after a year?

A year of him worming his way under my skin?

I want to say that he'll annoy me so much that it'll never happen. But it already is.

It already has.

And I already know I'm not going to survive it.

59

TATUM

U nsurprisingly, we're the last people down for breakfast.
I'm a mess as we walk in, my emotions all over the
place, my body tender, my eyes sore from lack of sleep.
Having everyone's eyes turn on me the second Kian helpfully
announces our entrance to the huddle of tables waiting for us only
makes the war carrying out inside me worse.

"You okay?" Kingston whispers, noticing my hesitation.

Forcing a smile onto my face, I hold my head high and
continue walking forward.

"Of course," I lie, moving toward the empty chairs waiting
for us.

I'm confident that I'm hiding how I'm truly feeling—until I
meet my best friend's eyes.

She frowns, the smile on her lips faltering as she reads the
truth in my expression.

"You okay?" she mouths, echoing Kingston's question. Only,
when I nod in a pathetic attempt to pacify her, she doesn't believe
it. She knows me better than that.

So does my big brother, who looks at me with a similarly
concerned expression.

I don't meet his eyes. I can't. Not after what I did with his best friend in our bathroom less than an hour ago.

Can he see the marks around my throat from where Kingston's fingers were?

My cheeks blaze.

I'm not a prude—I'll happily wear my sexuality with pride—but I also don't want my big brother to know everything.

"Would you like a coffee?" a server says, having rushed over with a coffee pot.

"Yes," I cry, immediately reaching for the mug that's waiting to be filled with some liquid gold. "Thank you."

"Sir?" she asks, turning to Kingston.

"No, thank you. I'll take a green tea."

Someone scoffs on the other side of the table, and when I look up, I find Kieran mocking Kingston's morning drink of choice.

I always liked Kieran. It was obvious from a very early age that he was going to be the rebel of the family.

I guess if you'd have made me predict which Callahan brother I might have ended up marrying, I'd have said him.

He's always been the most easygoing, fun brother. And much like me, he's put his middle finger up to the things expected of him and followed his own path instead of the one laid out for him.

While I respect Kingston and Kian for everything they've achieved, I have a special level of respect for Kieran.

"Right? What kind of monster did I marry?" I mock, happy to turn the attention to my new husband in the hope of surviving this breakfast unscathed.

Or at least that is my intention until Kian announces, "You should know. I assume he's the one who left those marks on your throat."

"Kian," Kingston snaps as Michael's wife gasps in shock and my mom drops her fork. The knot in my stomach gets even tighter as I focus on my coffee. "Not the time or place."

Kian doesn't so much as cower under Kingston's burning stare. It's probably not the first time, or the last, that he'll experience it.

430

"It was your wedding night," Kian says simply. "If you can't indulge then, what's the point in the wedding at all?"

"Romantic," Lori scoffs from a few seats down.

Kian shoots her a glare but doesn't say anything further.

Thankfully, everyone begins to return to their previous conversations as the server comes back to take our orders, but that doesn't mean I lose the attention of Miles or Lori.

Once we've finished, most of our guests begin to bid us farewell and check out of the hotel.

By the time it's only Kingston's brothers, Miles and Lori left, I'm exhausted.

There have been many times in my life when I've been forced to pull on a mask and pretend that everything is okay. Hell, I used to wear it every time I was in my parents' house, but it's been a while since I've had to wear it for quite so long.

I'm sure most brides want to drag out every second of their wedding—even those who are lucky enough to be heading off somewhere exotic to celebrate with their new husbands. But all I want to do is go home, crawl into bed, and hide in the dark under the covers for the foreseeable future.

But I can't.

I don't get to go home, because it's no longer where I live.

Home is now Kingston's fancy penthouse.

Sure, he's tried to make it nice, and a little less like a billionaire's bachelor pad. But it'll always be his home, not mine.

I'll always be on edge, worried that I'm going to break something or move something I shouldn't touch.

All I want to do is kick back and relax before the insanity of the week ahead of us begins.

While we know about my father's wishes where the future of Warner Group is concerned, nothing has been announced yet.

Kingston and Miles decided—rightly or wrongly, I'm not sure —to wait until the wedding was done before they made a public statement about the merger.

I've tried to keep to myself at work and encouraged my team

to focus on their jobs, but I'm not naive to think that the gossip isn't rife.

The employees of Warner Group may not predict the merger, but Kingston, Kian, and Michael have spent a lot of time in meetings on the top floor of the building since Dad passed, so it's obvious that something is happening.

I don't know the details, and as much as I might want to hope there won't be huge changes to Warner Group in the coming weeks, months, and years, I fear that might be wishful thinking.

Dad wouldn't have handed the company over lightly.

I'm sure he put much more thought into that than he did handing me over.

I shake my head, forcing the thoughts out. No good comes from those kinds of thoughts.

There is something bigger at play here than him wanting to hand over his company to his oldest and closest friend. I'd put everything I have on it.

I'm still not interested enough to ask or dig, though.

It's not my issue, or my problem to try and fix.

My time following my father's orders now has a timestamp on it. Twelve months from today, I'll be free, with the only thing I've ever wanted in my possession.

I don't get a chance to talk to Lori or Miles before Kingston and I retreat to our suite to pack up our things. I decide that's a good thing for now.

The less I'm forced to attempt to vocalize how I'm feeling, the better.

I pack up my things in a daze, and the journey back to Kingston's apartment is a blur.

He attempts to make conversation with me, but most of his questions go unanswered.

We walk through the front door and find our wedding flowers, and more gifts and cards than I can even comprehend, waiting for us in the living area. Ignoring them, I scoop Griz up from the couch and carry her up to the bedroom with me.

Kingston watches me go without saying a word, although that

doesn't mean I can't feel the weight of everything he wants to say hanging in the air around us.

The second I've closed the door behind me, I press the button to lower the blinds, plunging the room into darkness. I walk blindly toward the bed and climb on with Griz still in my arms.

"Have you been a good girl?" I ask as I lie down with her.

She's the one part of this place that now feels like home, and I need that right now more than I ever have.

Griz purrs and nuzzles into my neck, letting me know that she missed me as much as I had her.

With her warmth against me, it doesn't take long before I drift off to sleep. Although, it's not as peaceful I as would hope for. Instead, it's full of fanciful images of a future I'm not going to get.

Soft and sweet child's laughter fills the air as the warmth rushes over my skin. The scents of summer float around me as I sip on a cool drink while staring out over the lush English garden.

Flowers of all varieties and colors fill beds and hanging baskets.

It's the perfect summer haven.

The sun continues to warm my skin, turning my usually pale complexion, a rich golden color I love.

Footsteps move toward me, and I look over in time to see Kingston emerge from the cottage wearing only a tan pair of shorts. His torso is bare and delicious, sending an entirely different wave of heat through me.

"Everything okay?" I ask. He disappeared a little over thirty minutes ago to take a call from Kian.

"Yeah, nothing he can't deal with," he says before ducking down to kiss me.

With the squeals and laughter far enough away, he doesn't immediately pull back. Instead, his tongue teases the seam of my lips, seeking entry.

The second my mouth opens, he groans, eagerly pushing his tongue past my lips in search of my own. His hand wraps around the back of my neck, angling me exactly as he wants me.

For long, blissful minutes, I lose myself in my husband while our children play happily.

There's a bark, our pup playing with them before a loud scream brings our kiss to an abrupt end.

We're both on our feet in a heartbeat and running toward the end of the garden to discover our daughter climbing to her feet, having obviously fallen from the monkey bars of the play set they love.

I hang back as Kingston rushes toward her and sweeps her off her feet, checking her over as if she's the most precious thing in the world.

"I told her she couldn't reach," our boy points out. I glance over, meeting his green eyes and smiling.

"Sometimes we have to make our own mistakes." Or at least, headstrong girls like us do.

When I wake a few hours later, the images from my dreams continue to linger despite my best attempt at banishing them.

Thinking about a future where Kingston and I are still together and have brought children into the world is as terrifying as it is unrealistic.

My destiny may well be that cottage and being able to watch my kids grow and play in the garden, but it won't be with him.

A year from now our time will be over, our commitment to each other fulfilled. He'll continue to focus on building the Callahan and Warner brand and I'll...well, who knows.

Maybe I will get on a plane and start over in England, or maybe I'll hang around here for a while longer. I guess only time will tell. But one thing I know for sure is that whatever we do, it won't be together, no matter how much it hurts my heart to think about it.

"How do you feel about opening an obscene number of

wedding presents?" I ask Griz when she looks up at me with her large, dark eyes. "No. I don't really feel like it either."

Leaving her in bed, I pad through to the bathroom to clean up before mustering as much courage as I can and heading downstairs.

No sooner have I pulled the door open does my stomach start growling. The scent filling the air is out of this world, and it ensures I take the stairs a little faster than I was anticipating.

"Oh my god," I gasp when I find Kingston standing in the middle of his kitchen, surrounded by an array of home-cooked Mexican food.

He spins around at the sound of my voice, his eyes softening the second they land on me.

"Hey, did you sleep well?" he asks.

I shrug one shoulder, unwilling to lie to him, although I have no intention of telling him the reason for my fitful sleep. The fact I remember so vividly is bad enough.

"Well, I hope you're hungry. I wasn't sure what you'd want, so I made a little bit of everything," he confesses, and I swear there's a little shyness in his expression I've never seen before.

"It looks amazing. When are the rest of the guests arriving?" I tease.

"Just you and me, baby. Our first night in our home as a married couple." The smile that follows his words is so genuine and sincere that it makes my heart seize in my chest.

"You don't need to do that," I mutter as he pours me a glass of wine.

He pauses and looks back. "You don't want—"

"Oh no, I do. I meant you don't need to pretend that the rings on our fingers change anything between us when we're alone."

Wine sloshes ungracefully from the bottle as my words hit him before he puts it back on the counter, taking a moment before he turns his focus back to me.

"No, I guess we don't," he mutters almost...sadly.

No more words are said between us as we take a seat at the

kitchen counter and fill our plates with his incredible food, although the atmosphere between us is anything but relaxed.

Does he...does he want us to play the part of loving husband and wife, even when we're in private? And if he does, why? He can't stand me. Why would he want to put that much effort in?

60

KINGSTON

The tension in the room around us is thick, the fear and anxiety of the people staring back at us palpable.

I get it, I really fucking do.

I wish we didn't have to do this.

I wish there was a way that we could move Warner Group forward exactly as it is and turn it around with very few changes. But that's not the position that Jonathan left us in.

The truth of it is that Warner Group is in trouble, and only swift and drastic action is going to save it. That and a massive cash injection from Callahan Enterprises.

Unfortunately, it's going to mean job losses and reconfiguration.

It's going to mean a lot of hard work, long days and nights, and a lot of fucking stress. But I have no doubt that it'll be worth it.

Miles has solid ideas for where he wants to move this company, and I'm right along on that journey with him.

We might finally be under the same umbrella, playing for the same team, but this place will always be Miles's baby, just like Callahan is mine.

I could insist on swallowing Warner whole and spitting it back out as a newly-born Callahan baby with the flashy branding and all.

But that isn't Warner. It's not what its clients want. It's not the direction they should be moving in.

We're going to embrace the vision of the Warner men that came before Miles and Jonathan, and while we focus on moving the corporation fully into the twenty-first century and take it places that they never could have imagined, we're going to keep the integrity.

Warner Group isn't Callahan Enterprises. Warner Group is our little sister, and we're going to nurture her to make her own path in life.

Images of Tatum flicker in my mind, but no sooner have they appeared, than I shoot them down.

Now isn't the time to obsess over my new wife.

Now is the time to focus on her legacy, even if she doesn't want it.

Over the past few days, I've tried to talk to her, to warn her about what's coming her way, but she's shot me down every time, claiming that she's just a manager at Warner Group and should find out what's happening alongside all the others.

She wants to be an employee, a number.

But Tatum Warner never has been and never will be that insignificant.

This is her company, her future, just as much as it is Miles's, and I will do anything I can to ensure she benefits from it in the way she deserves.

I've mentioned job losses and changing roles in the hope of hooking her in, of making her concerned enough for the members of the team that she'd ask. But she hasn't.

She's completely shut down.

I've watched it happen as the days have passed. It started when I stupidly released those images of our engagement, and it's only gotten worse since.

I hoped that the distraction of the wedding might have pulled her out of it. Hell, I'd prayed that I could have fucked it out of her on our wedding night. But despite it being fucking incredible, I wasn't able to bring back the girl I spent the weekend with at the cabin.

I broke her trust, and I'm fucking terrified that I'm never going to get it back again.

In just a few short weeks, she's become such a huge part of my life, but I fear I'm going to have to live the next year of my life with this closed-off version of her.

"Good morning." Miles's deep voice rumbles through the air, successfully halting any quiet conversations that were previously floating around the room.

All eyes turn on him as he stands beside me at the head of the massive conference table.

All Warner Group managers stare back at him, waiting with bated breath for what he's about to say.

I scan the faces, taking in their expressions that range from mild curiosity to abject panic.

"Thank you all so much for being here."

Officially, the workday hasn't started yet, but we need to lay this out before our press release hits in a few hours.

Warner Group shares are already on shaky ground, and we've no doubt that in a few hours, they're going to plummet.

It's going to be a blip, though.

A blip we're going to work through before coming back stronger.

"I'm sure you're all concerned with the direction the company is going to take after the loss of—" Miles's voice cracks and his eyes land on Tatum, who's doing her very best to hide at the back of the group. "Our father," he continues, making her chin drop in surprise.

She only lets her shock show for a second before she locks it down as if it never happened.

Her eyes very briefly shoot to mine before she looks down at her feet, refusing to be dragged into this.

"I wish I could stand up here and assure you all that everything is great. That we knew what was coming our way and that we had a plan. I'm also not going to lie to you all and pretend that is the case.

"The truth is, our father's death was as much a shock to us as it was to you. But it appears that his failing health wasn't the only thing that he was hiding.

"Right now, the future of Warner Group isn't clear. As per our father's will, Warner Group is to be taken over by Callahan Enterprises, and together, Kingston and I will take over as joint CEOs."

Assessing eyes turn on me, but I hold strong, refusing to show an ounce of weakness.

Yes, the future of Warner might be unsure, and some of the people staring back at me may no longer be employed by us in the coming months, but that does not mean that we will fail.

Warner Group might be in trouble, but it will not fail.

There is no fucking way that is happening.

I might not be able to offer my wife much, but I will solidify her future, her legacy.

I will give her a reason to remember our time together—me—with fondness.

I refuse to allow all of this bullshit and stress to be for nothing.

"Mrs. Callahan, can you wait, please." My demand rips through the air as the rest of the Warner Group management shuffles out the door.

We knew that what we had to tell them wouldn't relieve any of the stress they felt walking into this meeting, but if anything, the expressions on their faces are now worse.

My stomach knots as I consider how they're feeling. The thought of them having to go home and tell their partners that their jobs might not be secure, of them looking at their children and worrying about providing for their families.

It's wrong. All of it is so fucking wrong. But what can we do?

This is the shitshow we've been left with, and we have to make the best of it.

Tatum startles, but she doesn't look up. For a moment, I don't even think she's going to follow my order, but then Miles adds, "Tatum, please. We just want to talk."

She's never been able to defy her big brother in the same way she does me, and slowly her movements falter and she steps out of the stream of people heading for the door.

The silence is painful, but none of us attempt to shatter it until the last person has stepped out of the room and closed the door behind them.

Tatum ignores me and turns to Miles. "I know that was hard, but you did a fantastic job," she assures him, a small smile playing on her lips. "I also want you to know, that if you need to lose marketing managers, then lay me off to secure everyone else's positions. You don't even need to pay me a severance package."

"No," I bark. "That's not fucking happening."

Tatum's shoulders tense but, still, she doesn't look at me.

"Miles, this is about the company's future. That is what's important here. I refuse to stand in the way if I can help."

"Stepping away isn't helping," I spit, anger fueling my words. "We need you here with us. You deserve to be standing here with us right now."

I don't know what it is, which words I say that spark something within her, but she finally turns her light blue eyes on me.

My breath catches as our connection causes sparks to flash between us.

"I will help wherever I can, but I am not stepping up beside you. My position within this company has been made more than clear all of my life."

"Fuck that, Tate. Dad's gone," Miles says, pain lacing his voice at the loss of his mentor. "What he wanted doesn't matter. We're in charge and we want—"

"Success." She cuts him off with that one single word and a

hard glare. "I am not prepared to commit my life to this. To you," she says, her eyes finding mine again.

Ouch.

"Excuse me. I have a team to talk to. If I can be of any assistance, or you'd like to discuss my offer, then you know where to find me. Other than that..." She takes a step back and looks between the two of us. "Have a good day."

We stand there side by side, shocked into silence as she spins around, her long, dark hair following a beat later and falling like a thick curtain around her shoulders before she marches out of the room.

It's long after the door has closed behind us that Miles lifts his hands to his hair and breathes, "Fuck."

"She'll come around," I say, although there isn't a lot of conviction in my voice.

"Fuck, KC. You're even more fucking delusional than she is."

I stare at him with my brows raised in question.

"This is where she belongs. Why can't she see that?"

"Because she's lived her entire life being told the opposite. Just because Jonathan is gone, it's not going to change all the years of her feeling like she isn't a worthy or deserving member of your family."

He visibly deflates at my words.

"Look, I'm not arguing with you. I agree, she belongs here. Do you have any idea how fucking good she is at her job?" His expression wavers. He wants to say yes, to say that he's paid attention, but the truth is that he doesn't have a clue. He's been too lost in his own world to pay all that much attention to hers. "But as much as I hate to say it, you're not going to reel her in like this. You aren't going to be able to change her thoughts and feelings about her place here overnight. It's going to take time. Possibly a lot of it."

His eyes bounce between mine as he tries to read between the lines.

"What are you saying?"

I swallow thickly. I haven't said the words that he knows are coming, but I already feel the regret.

My stomach knots up and my fists clench at my sides.

I always knew that holding Tatum close was going to be akin to keeping a handful of sand intact.

She slips further away every single day.

Away from her family, from her unwanted responsibilities here, from Chicago.

From me.

My heart pounds as I roll my lips between my teeth.

"You need to let her go."

All the air rushes from Miles's lungs and he stumbles back.

"No. I can't do that. I've already lost Dad. Mom is..." A fucking disaster. "I can't...I can't lose her too."

My heart bleeds for him, it really fucking does. But I don't know how else he's going to achieve what he wants here.

Right now, with her father's legacy still lingering in the air around us, she'll never agree to step into her rightful position.

She may have agreed to marry me, but only as a way to get what she really wants.

To leave.

She doesn't want to be here.

She doesn't want to be a part of Warner Group's reincarnation.

She doesn't want me.

They're just facts we're going to have to learn to deal with.

61

TATUM

"**T**here you are," Lori cries when she spots me walking through the bar toward the table she's claimed at the back.

As if I've got the weight of the world on my shoulders, I drop into the chair with a loud sigh and let my purse crash to the floor.

"Here," Lori says, pushing a pretty pink cocktail toward me.

Without any hesitation, I lift it from the table and take a massive sip. Sweetness coats my tongue and I groan in satisfaction as the strong liquor burns down my throat.

Fuck. This is exactly what I need. Alcohol and my best friend.

"Oh my god, that's so good."

"Right?" Lori agrees before taking a sip of her half-empty drink, her eyes focused on me over the rim.

"So?" she starts, prompting me to begin talking.

We've chatted briefly this week, but we've both been too busy to spend enough time together to dive into the shitshow that is my life right now.

Resting my elbows on the table, I drop my head into my hands.

"Oh, sweetie," Lori soothes, reaching over to squeeze my shoulders.

"It's awful, Lor. No one knows what's going on. Everyone is freaking out. I...I hate it."

"How many job losses are there going to be?"

I shrug. I'm sure that if I'd bothered to ask either King or Miles they'd tell me everything. Hell knows both of them have tried time and time again. But I don't want the details. I don't want to be pulled into their world and end up stuck in a position I don't want to be in.

I am not them.

I'm a marketing manager with a kick-ass team. I am not senior management material.

"They haven't gone into that much detail yet. They're going to begin holding meetings with each department next week. Some will obviously have more losses than others."

"Of course," she muses. "I guess you're safe though, right? I mean—"

"I told them to lay me off to save them having to force someone else out."

"What?" Lori shrieks. "Why would you do that?"

I shrug, sipping another mouthful of my cocktail.

"Why not? I don't have plans to stay there long-term. I don't need the money right now. If me stepping away means that another marketing manager gets to keep their job, then I'm happy to do that."

"Tate, you are..." Her words trail off as she shakes her head. "Why aren't you my boss?" she cries, changing tactics.

"Because you like numbers, and I...do not."

"And my boss doesn't like people, but it doesn't stop him from trying and failing to deal with them."

Guilt eats me up inside that I haven't even asked her how her week has been. Although, history would tell me that it's been awful.

"You need to leave," I say, like I have a million times before.

"I know, Tate. But while he might be an asshole, he also pays well."

"As he should," I mutter before taking another sip. I've barely eaten today. I've been too busy attempting to keep everyone calm while their worlds begin to spin out of control.

I hate it, but I also know that Miles would never do this if there was another way. I also know how much strain all of this has put on him. One look in his dark eyes and I know he's suffering right alongside our employees.

I'm glad he's got Kingston standing beside him. I'd hate to see my big brother go through this alone. If he was, that might just be the thing to force my hand about standing up there with him.

But rightly or wrongly, I trust the two of them to do the right thing. It's going to be hard, beyond hard, but I know every decision they make will be well thought through and with the future of the company and the lives of our employees at the forefront of their minds.

"As soon as I can find something that pays anywhere close that wants me, I'm gone."

I nod, wishing that I could do something to help. Not that she'd accept it even if I did. My best friend is stubborn and fiercely independent. I learned very early into our friendship that she wouldn't accept any kind of help, financial or otherwise. While I respect the shit out of her for it, I just wish she'd let me share the load every now and then.

"It can't get any worse," I point out as she waves down our server to order another round of drinks.

"I need food too," I point out as I reach for the small menu in the middle of the table. "Ooooh, chicken wings." My stomach growls and my mouth waters.

"Deal," Lori says before placing our order. "So, fuck work and all that bullshit. Tell me all about life as Mrs. Callahan," she says, rubbing her hands together in excitement.

A bitter laugh spills from my lips as I shake my head.

"Don't get too excited, I don't have any scandalous stories for you."

"What?" She gawks. "You looked a little like you'd been mauled by a feral beast the morning after your wedding. Do not tell me it hasn't continued."

"Sorry to disappoint. I've barely seen him all week. Most nights he's still been at the office with Miles and Kian long after I've gone to bed."

"I'm attempting to live vicariously through you right now. It's not exactly working in my favor," she sulks.

"Why? What's happening with Matt? I thought—"

"His grandmother died, and his grandad has dementia. He had to go home."

"Oh shit, that sucks."

"Just when I thought things were going somewhere," she complains, slumping lower in her chair.

"He'll be back, and I'm sure you'll pick up where you left off."

"Yeah," she agrees, although I'm not sure she believes it. "He's just been...I dunno, distant, I guess."

"That's understandable given the circumstances," I argue.

"Yeah, I know. I get that his family needs him right now. He's where he should be. I just..." She shakes her head. "Ignore me. I'm being a whiny little bitch."

"No, you're not. If you feel like something is wrong, then you shouldn't ignore it."

We both fall silent, my words of advice hanging heavy between us.

"I miss you, Tate. Griz too."

"Lor," I breathe, my heart twisting up in my chest. "I'm so sorry. All of this is my fa—"

"No, don't do that. You're doing exactly what you need to do right now. You have nothing to apologize for. Oh, have you opened that insane collection of wedding gifts yet?" Her eyes twinkle with excitement for whatever might be in the box I've spotted at the top of the pile with her name scrawled on the gift tag.

"Nope, haven't even started," I confess, cringing.

"Why the hell not? What have you been doing all alone in that huge penthouse?"

"Wallowing in self-pity and the direction my life has taken."

"Oh boo hoo, life is so hard being married to the city's sexiest man while living in a fancy penthouse," she mocks.

"Money and looks aren't everything. Honestly, though, I've no idea what I've been doing. I've been so exhausted I've crashed most nights. All this emotional bullshit is draining."

"It was a beautiful wedding, though," Lori muses. "I can't wait to see the photographs."

"Yeah," I agree. Well, with the first part anyway. I'm unsure how I feel about seeing the images the photographer captured that day.

At best we'll look like we're really in love and ready to spend our lives together. At worst...we'll look like we're really in love and ready to spend our lives together.

Something tightens around my ribs as I remember how I felt walking down the aisle toward Kingston. Of the way my heart fluttered when he said his vows, how my body burned for him when we danced.

It all felt too real. I can only imagine that it looked the same way.

I can't get my head around how it all makes me feel. I'm not sure I'm mentally prepared to see the emotion that I know is going to be as clear as day in my eyes.

"What's wrong?" Lori asks, leaning forward and resting her chin on her hand as she studies me closely. "You had that same look in your eyes the morning after."

I shake my head, blowing out a long breath as I fight to find the right words.

"I..." An unamused laugh tumbles from my lips as I think about her teasing me about my life right now. On the outside, it looks like I've got everything. But why don't I feel like I have anything?

My entire life right now is nothing but smoke and mirrors.

"Tate?" she asks, her brows drawing in, leaving a deep frown between them.

"I don't...I don't know if I can—"

"Chicken wings?" the server says, lowering two fully stacked plates onto our table.

The sweet and smoky scent of the barbeque sauce fills my nose, but I'm not as hungry as I was when we ordered them.

"Thank you," Lori says in a rush. But no sooner has the server gone is she back with fresh cocktails.

Reaching out, I lift my glass to my lips and drink half in the hope it'll help settle whatever is spinning out of control inside me.

Lori watches me, concern filling her eyes, but she doesn't push. She knows that I'll tell her everything when I've found the right words. If they exist.

Reaching for a wing, I lift it to my lips and rip some meat off.

"Oh my god," I moan as the sauce hits my tongue.

"I know, so good," she groans, her eyes rolling back in pleasure.

We demolish half a plate each, barely coming up for air. It gives me some time to try and make sense of my thoughts, and I just feel like I'm getting somewhere when I sense someone behind me.

Lori looks up, and the second her eyes widen, I can predict exactly what's about to happen.

Heat blooms down my side before a very familiar hand reaches out, stealing a chicken wing before his giant body drops into the vacant seat beside me.

With his free hand, he undoes his jacket and gets comfortable.

"Seriously?" I hiss between licking the sticky sauce from my fingers.

Kingston's eyes jump between mine and my lips as he eats my fucking wing.

"Isn't that a little too unhealthy to put into your temple of a body?" I quip, fighting the glare I want to give him for stealing my food and clearly fucking stalking me. But the way he works that chicken wing with his full lips stops me from saying another word. Fuck.

449

I can't help it; I shamelessly squirm in my seat. It's been a long, stressful week. I could really use a little relief right now...

My lips part to demand he leave when another shadow falls over me and the final chair at our table is pulled out.

"Oh goodie, you brought a friend," I deadpan as Kian makes himself comfortable.

He points at the plate in front of Lori before asking, "You mind?"

"Good to know that one of you has some manners," I scoff.

"What's yours is mine, baby," Kingston teases.

"No," I counter. "What's yours is mine, and what's mine is also mine."

I smirk, holding his stare firm.

"Ah, I have the world's best sister-in-law," Kian muses before stealing another wing, much to Lori's irritation.

"Finally," Lori muses. "Something we can agree on."

Ripping my eyes from Kingston, I focus on my best friend, lifting a brow in question.

"Ignore her, she's just bitter that she didn't get to spend your wedding night with the best man."

Lori's eyes almost pop out of her head, making Kingston laugh.

"Okay, did I miss something here?"

"Just the moment Mr. Callahan here got his ass handed to him on a silver platter. Not often you get turned down, is it?"

The air crackles around us and I startle when Kingston's large hand lands on my thigh.

"This was a great idea," he muses. "But I think we need more wings."

62

KINGSTON

I watch Kian as he smirks at Lorelei, knowing exactly what he's thinking.

Pain-in-the-ass, stubborn, know-it-all woman.

And he's not wrong.

Tatum can be a lot to handle. But the two of them together...

Not many men stand a chance. Hell knows that many weaker than us would probably be eaten alive. Pretty sure more than a few have.

These women know what they want, and they aren't afraid to ask for it.

It's equally sexy as it is terrifying.

I know all too well that Kian likes a challenge just as much as I do. But I think he's barking up the wrong tree if he thinks Lorelei will play the kinds of games that are spinning around his head right now. And not just because she's seeing someone.

Looks-wise, she might be exactly his type. But she has way more personality, sass, and intelligence than his usual women. Something tells me that she'd run rings around him and he wouldn't even see it coming.

When the server passes by, I order the girls another cocktail each as well as a scotch for me and Kian, and more wings.

"So, have you had a good day at work?" Kian naively asks Lorelei.

Tatum and I might still have a long way to go to truly get to know each other and those who are important in our lives, but I do know that Lorelei hates her job with a passion and that asking her about it is probably on the same level as asking about her menstrual cycle. Off fucking limits.

Lorelei stares Kian dead in the eyes before flatly suggesting, "Now that you've delivered your brother to my best friend, there is no need for you to stay."

"Oh, burn." I laugh, earning myself a hard stare from both of them.

"He does struggle traveling across the city alone," Kian mocks.

"Not my fault I'm a magnet for all the hot women and you're not."

"Give me strength," Tatum mutters. "I'm going to the bathroom." She pushes out her chair and stands, successfully removing my hand from her thigh, before she leans over. "And don't even think about following me," she hisses before Lorelei announces that she's joining her.

"Women are weird," Kian mutters once they're out of hearing distance.

"You can't call every woman who doesn't fall for your charm weird. It just means they have taste."

"Fuck off. I haven't even tried to hit on her," he argues. "Some of us can abide by the rules, you know."

"The rules?" I ask as he dives into the plate the server delivers, immediately devouring a wing and covering himself in sauce, not unlike what he used to do as a kid. Fucking animal.

"Yeah. You know, don't fuck your boy's sister," he says, raising a brow and then shooting a look in the direction Tatum disappeared.

"Oh, because I chose to go there."

"Don't see you arguing about it."

"Would you?" I ask, immediately regretting the question

when a salacious smile curls at his lips. "Don't fucking answer that."

"Anyway, as I was saying. Your boy's little sister is off-limits, as is your sister-in-law's bestie. Couldn't even go there if I wanted to, man."

"Right," I mutter around a wing. "Because you've always followed the rules."

"Mother fucking Teresa sitting right here, and you know it."

I shake my head, choosing to give the wings more attention than my moronic brother.

"Maybe Lorelei had a point. Why did you feel the need to follow me here?"

He smirks. "Hot girls. Scotch. Wings. Where else would I be on a Friday night?"

"Trying to pull a woman you stand a chance with?"

He throws the bones in his hand at me before reaching for another.

"Why have we never been here before? These are insane."

"You know, Mom was right all those years ago. It is vital to always have a packet of baby wipes when you're around."

I eat a handful more wings while Kian devours a farmful of chickens before Tatum and Lorelei reappear, ruining the possibility of following my wife to the bathroom again like the last time she was on a night out with her friend.

I smirk. Good times.

"Jesus," Lorelei mutters the second she lays eyes on my brother. "I didn't realize they let animals in here. You know what these are for, right?" she asks, thrusting a stack of napkins at him.

He looks up before throwing more bones on the now wingless plate and grinning at her with sauce smeared around his mouth and covering his teeth.

"And girls actually want to go here?" Lorelei asks, wagging her finger in Kian's direction with her top lip peeled back.

"You really should take more time to appreciate who you're sitting with, babe."

"Oh no you didn't," Lorelei sasses, much to Tatum's amusement. "I am no one's babe. And I am certainly not yours."

"Sit down and drink your cocktail," Kian mutters, unamused and unfazed by her attitude.

Lorelei might not follow his orders, but Tatum does.

I lean over as she practically chugs her cocktail.

"Don't get wasted, baby. I have plans for you tonight."

She shoots me a look and electric bolts shoot straight to my dick, although I'm not sure if the look is less desire and more "I will end you with nothing more than a chicken bone if you don't shut the fuck up." To be fair, I'm happy with either.

I just want to spend some time with her. I've missed her this week, but as much as I've wanted to get home at night to hang out with her, work and Miles needed me.

We always knew this week was going to be a shitshow, but it was worse than we could have predicted. And next week is going to be even worse as we begin to roll out our changes.

And it's not just Warner Group stealing time away from my new wife. I might have stepped up to stand beside Miles, but that doesn't mean that my role at Callahan Enterprises has become any less demanding.

I'm being pulled in a million different directions right now when, deep down, all I want to do is go home and fall into bed with my wife, remind myself why all this stress is worth it.

I thought I was all about the business growth and our future. I mean, I wasn't wrong, our arrangement is about our future—but I never thought it would be *our* future. As in, mine and Tatum's, not Callahan Enterprises'.

I stare at my wife as she chats to Lorelei, appreciating her beauty while being totally oblivious to it.

The things I said to Miles yesterday come back to haunt me.

I know what I said was true. In order for her to find her place here, the place she truly belongs, he's going to need to let her go. She'll never find her way back, on her own terms, if she never leaves.

But as true as those words might be, they're also fucking terrifying.

Just a few weeks ago, the thought of her leaving, of turning her back on Chicago, wouldn't have bothered me in the slightest, but in such a short time, she's wormed her way under my skin. And suddenly, I can't imagine my life without her in it.

I've no idea where that leaves us. Deep down, I know what she wants, and it isn't to be here.

I could demand she makes different choices, push her down the route I think is right for her, but it's the fastest way to lose her.

If I'm going to play this game, then I need to think outside the box. I need to control the play from a distance.

When I said my vows last weekend, I meant them.

For better or worse, Tatum Callahan is mine. I just need her to figure that out, and preferably sooner rather than later.

"Whoa," I gasp, catching Tatum before her knees buckle beneath her and she tumbles to the floor. "I've got you," I say, swinging her legs up into my arms to carry her into my—our—apartment.

"I can walk," she snaps, although, with the way she slurs her words, it's not quite as cutting as I think she was going for.

"Why would you want to when you don't have to?"

Her body tenses as if she's about to fight me, to wriggle until I have no choice but to put her back down and watch as she attempts to navigate our apartment looking like Bambi on ice.

But then she changes her mind and she relaxes against me again, her face nuzzling into my neck.

"Why do you always smell so good?" she asks absently.

"Because I want you to sniff me and then rip my clothes from my body so you can get more of me."

Just the thought of watching her slender fingers working their way down my shirt and then impatiently tugging at my waistband makes my cock swell.

"Hmm, I do like you with no clothes on. You're almost bearable when you're naked. You've got a very nice cock for such an asshole."

I laugh. "I'll take that as a compliment."

"As if that big head of yours would let you take it any other way."

I walk us through the living room, past the pile of unopened wedding gifts that are still waiting for us to go through them.

Honestly, I thought she'd have unleashed on them the first chance she got. But like many other things I've discovered about Tatum Callahan, she's surprised me.

With my focus on much more important things than the crystal glasses I'm sure someone has bought us, I turn away from the gifts and carry my wife up the stairs as she impatiently starts working on my shirt.

"Feeling horny, baby?" I ask, my voice rough with desire.

Her hand pushes inside my half-unbuttoned shirt and grazes my stomach. My abs jump at her contact and my cock continues to harden.

"Just remembering the night before our wedding," she confesses. "I can't remember which bits were real and which bits were a dream."

"Baby, all of it was too good to be a dream," I deadpan.

"I'm not so sure," she taunts. "You might need to show me exactly how you did it so I can see if you come close."

"Now that sounds like an offer I can't refuse."

Once we're in our bedroom, I walk her over to the couch and then lower her to her feet.

Her hair is a mess, and her makeup is smeared after a long day at the office and an evening drinking.

"What are you doing?" she asks, blinking up at me with confusion washing through her expression.

"Giving you the full experience."

Tugging her purse from her shoulder, I throw it across the room before pushing her jacket from her shoulders and then spinning her around to pull the zipper of her dress down.

Slowly, I push it from her shoulders and let it pool around her heels.

To keep it authentic, she needs to take them off, which is a damn fucking shame. Hooking my fingers under her bra, I unhook it before pulling it from her arms. She groans as I release her heavy breasts, and my hands twitch to reach for them. But I hold strong.

Keeping her back to me, I shrug out of my jacket and then pull my shirt over my head before tugging it over her body, covering her up.

"Kick your shoes off, baby, and then lie on the couch. Get comfortable."

She instantly does as she's told, and if that doesn't get my dick impossibly hard, I don't know what does.

"Where are you going?" she asks in a panic when I take a step back.

"I won't be long. Relax, baby. You'll get what you need, I promise."

And with those words lingering in the air, I march into the bathroom and take a longer shower than I'd like to while I know she's out there waiting for me.

It'll be fucking worth it, though.

Those moments on the couch in their suite have played out on repeat in my head ever since. Along with the ones we added on our wedding night, of course.

63

TATUM

I wake to a rush of heat pooling between my thighs.

"Oh god," I moan, attempting to squeeze my thighs together to squash the ache.

But I can't

There's something—

"Kingston?" I gasp as I rip my eyes open and find his head between my thighs and his eyes locked on my face.

Fuck.

"Good morning," he growls against me.

"Y-yeah," I mutter like a brainless idiot.

I mean, honestly, what more can he expect when I get woken like this?

He swipes his tongue over my sensitive flesh and my body trembles, fully waking up.

"You fell asleep on me last night, Tatum," he tells me.

My lips part as I try to remember.

I have vague memories of him carrying me into the apartment and laying me out on the couch, but anything after that is blank.

Shit.

His grip on my inner thighs tightens before he pushes them wider, giving himself space to work.

"Oh shit," I gasp as he sucks on me.

"I promised to show you how much better I am than a dream, and you passed out."

His words are teasing, and the deep rasp of his voice only makes the feeling of him down there even better.

"Undo the buttons on my shirt, baby. Let me see those tits."

Without instruction from my brain, my hands move and I pop each button open until I'm able to pull the fabric apart and give him what he craves.

"Fuck, yes. Play with them. Show me how you like it."

My head swims with his orders, the lingering haziness of sleep still holding me in its clutches, but that doesn't matter for my body —it follows orders easily.

His eyes widen, his normally electric green turning almost black as he watches me pull at my nipples, putting on a show as he gently grazes my clit with his teeth.

"I'm not letting you out of this bed until you've come over my face, around my fingers, and finally on my cock."

My chin drops at his words as I palm my breasts harder.

Perfect start to a Saturday morning.

He sucks me hard and my back arches off the bed, pleasure racing through me, making all my nerve endings spark with what's to come.

Kingston might be a lot of things, but he is a fucking god in bed.

No, not a god. A fucking king.

"Yes," I cry as he works me with the perfect pressure and speed.

His grip on my thighs tightens until I know that I'll be rocking bruises in the shape of his fingerprints for a good few days.

I want to hate the idea of being branded by him, of being forced to remember him when I look at myself. But I don't.

I'm already wearing his ring; I may as well wear his bruises.

In only minutes, he works me to my first release of the morning.

He sits up with his face glistening with my juices and a shit-eating grin tugging at his lips.

"Count," he demands, his eyes dropping to my tits before moving down to my pussy and then back up to my eyes.

"One," I whisper, barely able to form words as I continue to ride out the aftereffects of my release.

"Good girl," he praises as he plunges two fingers deep inside me, curling them just so before he embarks on number two.

"Fuck. Kingston," I cry when he rubs at my G-spot. Abandoning my breasts, my fingers twist up the sheets beneath me as he pushes me to a fast and intense release.

Anyone would think he's feeling a little impatient to get inside me.

"Eyes, Tatum. Look at me while I make you come."

Like the good girl that I certainly am not, my eyes spring open and find him.

"I need you to know who's doing this to you, baby."

"I'm unlikely to forget," I sass.

He smirks.

"I guess that's what happens when I'm that much better than all the men of your past."

I scoff, not wanting to feed his ego any more than I already have.

"You don't need to say it, Tatum. I can read it in your body, in your eyes. I can feel it."

My heart pounds harder at his words as the air continues to crackle between us.

"It's never been this good," he continues. "Never."

"Kingston," I scream as he pushes me over the edge into my second release with both his fingers and his words.

"Baby," he growls, reminding me that I should be doing something.

"Two," I gasp as he continues working me through it.

No sooner have I come down from the high than his fingers are gone and he's shuffled forward with his dick in his hand, ready to push inside me.

My muscles feel the thickness of him stretching me open.

It's been a long few days without this.

It's when we're at our best as this fake couple. Nothing else matters when it's just the two of us, naked and giving in to the chemistry that's constantly sparking between us.

It doesn't matter what our surnames are, what our jobs are, who our brothers or best friends are, nor all the reasons why we are completely incompatible.

"Oh god, yes," I moan as he pushes inside me.

"Shit," he groans as my pussy ripples around him, trying to suck him deeper. "I will never get enough of this. Your pussy is fucking insane, Tate."

His eyes hold mine and my heart jumps into my throat at the sincerity and emotion I can see in them.

I shouldn't be able to. There shouldn't be any emotion here.

It's a business deal with benefits, apparently.

That is where the line needs to be drawn.

The line that you've been obliterating for days now?

I banish that thought as fast as it hits, refusing to even consider the reality of this situation.

Just sex. It's just sex with a man I married for nothing more than securing something I want.

It's a marriage of convenience so that we can both gain what we want. Nothing more. Nothing less.

Definitely nothing more...

He rolls his hips the moment he's fully seated inside me, and I cry out as my hands go to his ass in an attempt to get him even deeper.

More. I need more.

No.

Less.

I should want less.

Fuck. I'm so fucking confused.

His hand lands beside my head and his lips descend on mine, his tongue pushing inside my mouth and mimicking what his dick is doing lower down my body.

Forcing myself to stop thinking and freaking myself out, instead, I hold on for dear life and just pray that when this all comes to a head, I'll be able to survive it.

He fucks me with slow, measured strokes. It's nowhere near the hard and fast fucking I really need to clear my head, but at the same time, it builds me higher and higher to the point that when his fingers graze my clit, I explode in the strongest release of the morning.

I clench so hard around him that he has no choice but to fall over the edge with me, his dick jerking violently inside me as he fills me with ropes of hot cum, branding me on the inside just as he has the outside.

I'm fucked.

So royally fucked.

"Fuck, that was good," he pants before dropping to his side and pulling my body tight to his, holding me as if I'm going to shatter into a million pieces as our heart rates return to normal.

I only manage to lie there for thirty seconds max before my head starts spinning with thoughts again and I attempt to roll away from him.

Snuggling in bed isn't helping with anything.

"Where are you going?" he asks as I sit on the edge of the bed and comb my wild hair back from my face.

"I'm not spending the day rolling around in bed with you. I've got things to do," I lie.

"Oh?" he asks. The sheets rustle, and I don't dare glance back. He's going to look like a sex god, I just know it. "Care to enlighten me? Because I don't think there is anything that could be better than spending the day rolling around in bed."

"Don't you have to work?" I ask hopefully.

"Nope. I told Miles I was spending today with my wife. I've neglected her this week, and I want to make up for it."

"Why?" I blurt before I get a handle on my mouth.

"Why what? Why do I want to spend the day with you?" he asks, sounding confused.

"You don't like me, King. Why would you choose to—"

"Tate," he breathes before the warmth of his touch burns down the length of my arm. "I'm beginning to realize that I like you a whole lot more than I probably should."

I hop to my feet and force some distance between us. The second I move, I cringe, feeling the evidence of what we just did leaking down my thighs.

"See. That...That is exactly why we shouldn't be doing this," I say, throwing my arm back to gesture to the bed he's still lying in and what we did this morning. "What you said, the reason why we shouldn't spend the day together."

"Why the hell not? Isn't it better this way?"

"No, Kingston. It is not better this way. Fuck," I breathe, dropping my face into my hands as he moves behind me.

I sense him coming, my skin tingling as he gets closer.

"Don't touch me," I warn, able to predict his moves.

"Fuck that, Tate."

His hands land on my shoulders, and I'm spun around before I get a chance to argue.

My lips part, ready to fire back at him, but then my eyes catch on his and all of my fight leaves me.

"We're married now, Tatum. We don't have to continue fighting each other. It's okay to...be the couple we're pretending to be."

My brows pinch as his eyes bounce between mine.

"But it's not real."

"Says who?"

"The contract we signed," I counter.

His hands move—one of them slides to my neck, and the other drops to my waist before my back presses against the cold wall behind me.

I gasp in surprise, but he doesn't react—not to my shock, at least.

"What about this right now doesn't feel real, baby?" he asks before his lips descend on mine.

He kisses me deeply, stealing away all my thoughts and

concerns and replacing them with nothing but him. His touch, his scent, his unwavering confidence.

Wrapping his hand around my thigh, he hitches my leg up around his waist, letting me feel how hard he is again against my sensitive pussy.

"King," I moan.

"Life is too short to fight what's right in front of us, Tatum. And a year is a long time to deny what we really want."

The mention of our expiration date is almost enough to drag me back to reality, but then his lips find mine again, and my feet leave the floor.

He walks us effortlessly to the bathroom and then directly into the shower. Not once does he release my lips. I've no idea if it's for fear of what might come out of them yet or because he just can't stop.

Both options fucking terrify me.

But I also can't argue.

We put ourselves here; we decided to spend the next year of our lives together. Why shouldn't we enjoy it? Reap the benefits we can give each other?

Because you'll never just be an arrangement with benefits...

Ice-cold water rains down on us, effectively stealing my thoughts and fears at the same time Kingston drops me lower, entering me easily as he backs me up against the wall.

"Can't get enough of this pussy, Tatum. And I know you feel the same about my dick. Stop thinking and just enjoy. Take the pleasure where you can get it."

64

KINGSTON

"Look out, it's a big one," I say in the worst Australian accent imaginable as I heave a huge and heavy box from the back of the pile.

After Tatum's...emotional moment, shall we say, in the bedroom, I haven't given her a second to get lost in her head.

I get it. I really fucking do.

What we've found here together is fucking terrifying. But things could be so much worse. I am married to this incredibly sexy woman who challenges me as much as she makes me laugh. Not to mention that our chemistry is off-the-charts hot. I've never experienced anything like it before. Sure, I've had hot sex, but nothing—and I literally mean nothing—compares to her.

Is it a problem? For right now, no. It's fucking not. But in twelve months' time, it very much could be.

But that's twelve months away. Why can't we just enjoy what we have right now? Anything could happen in that time. A year ago, we certainly never would have predicted that we'd be where we are now, that's for sure.

Everything happens for a reason, right? That's what everyone says.

Maybe Tatum and I are meant to learn something from this

whole experience. Maybe it's going to teach us lessons that we're going to need for the rest of our lives, and we'll be able to always look back on our time together fondly.

"You're an idiot." She laughs as I place it in front of her.

The living room is a disaster. After ignoring the gifts for a week, we're finally working our way through the obscene pile.

I mean seriously, who in their right mind actually thinks we need any of this stuff?

Do either of us look like a Lazy Susan kind of person? We only invited those closest to us; surely, they're aware that we've both lived on our own for a few years? We don't need new sets of glasses or a lace-edged fucking tablecloth. I mean, come on, it's been a long time since nineteen-seventy-freaking-five. The only people who still have lace-edged tablecloths also still have vases of bad fake flowers and those fucking frilly lace things underneath them. Baby tablecloths, if you will.

"You mean a doily?" Tatum asks through peals of laughter as I explain my thoughts about some of the hideous gifts we've received.

Honestly, I thought the people who attended our wedding actually liked us. Clearly, I was very wrong and I shall be reconsidering any future gifts I may send their way.

"Yes. No. What a fucking stupid name is that?" I ask, falling to my knees in front of what I'm sure is going to be another ugly gift.

Sure, I can be an asshole. I'm more than aware of that. But is this everyone's way of letting me know that they really don't like me? By filling my apartment with shit I don't want?

Tatum shrugs. "Aunt Lena used to crochet them. She tried teaching me once."

I drag my hand down my face. "Of course she did," I mutter, totally unsurprised.

"What?" Tatum laughs.

"Nothing. I just can't picture you wielding a knitting needle."

Her brow lifts.

"What?"

"A knitting needle? To crochet?"

"I dunno. It's not like I've ever sat down to do either."

"Maybe not, but you do know you don't paint with a pencil, right?"

"Fine. It's fine. Laugh it up."

She shakes her head, trying to hold her amusement in. "I just thought the great Kingston Callahan knew everything."

"Everything that's important to life. Knitting and crocheting aren't a part of that."

"Well, maybe they should be," she teases. "I can picture us now..." she says, waving her hand out as if the image is appearing like magic before her. "At Christmas, wearing matching Mr. and Mrs. sweaters knitted by none other than you."

I scoff. "Laugh all you like; I bet I'd be a kickass knitter."

"Of course you would, Mr. Everything I Touch Turns To Gold."

"That's not true and you know it."

"Do I?" she deadpans.

"Yep, I touched you a lot earlier and you didn't turn to gold. In fact..." I say, crawling closer to her. "You melted."

Planting my hands on either side of her hips, I get right up in her face, forcing her to lean back to escape me.

"King," she warns breathlessly.

"What, baby?" My eyes alternate between looking into hers and down at her tempting lips.

Reaching out, I wrap my hand around the back of her head before lowering her to the floor and fully crawling over her.

Claws tap on the wood flooring and I groan.

"Not now, Queen Fluffpuff," I complain when the damn cat stalks over like she owns the place.

"Is it a wonder she doesn't like you? Her name is—"

The angry hiss the cat emits cuts off Tatum's words.

"Aw, baby girl. It's okay. Kingston isn't going to hurt me," she coos before reaching out and tickling the thing's chin.

"Seriously?" I ask, still looming over her with much filthier intentions than watching her play with her cat.

"Be nice to her and she'll treat you with respect."

"Or we could lock her in one of the guest rooms while we get busy."

She glares at me.

"Be a good kitty, Fluffpuff, and back off while I take advantage of your owner."

Tatum squeals and thrashes beneath me as I tuck my face into the crook of her neck and suck on her sweet skin.

Everything is fine for about fifteen seconds, but then I feel it.

Four little feet land on my back before eighteen very sharp claws pierce my back.

"Oh, you little shit," I bark before jumping to my feet and attempting to shake her off me.

"King stop," Tatum cries as she rushes toward us, no doubt to rescue the cat.

I'm the one bleeding here.

"Okay, Griz. You got him good, girl," she soothes. "Stand down, yeah?"

It takes a few seconds of sweet-talking the feral creature but finally, she manages to detach her from my back.

"Fuck, that hurts."

"You shouldn't have taunted her."

"I didn't," I argue, knowing full well it's a lie. "Can we lock her in the guest room now?"

"No. You're just going to need to learn to get along with her."

Reaching behind my head, I tug my t-shirt from my body and stare at the back in horror.

"Fucking cannibal," I mutter, shooting the cat a death stare, which she quite happily returns. I'm pretty sure she snarls, too.

"She's trying to protect me," Tatum argues.

I look between the two of them. One I want to fuck, one I want to...probably best I don't go there, even in my head.

"Look," I say, taking a step forward. Tatum's brows pinch as she waits for what I have to say, but before another word leaves my lips, I drop my attention to the cat. "Me and you, Fluff. We've got to put up with each other for the next year. I know it's not ideal, but it is what it is. Do you think we can come to some kind of agreement to allow me to fuck your owner whenever and wherever I want without risking bodily harm?"

Tatum's body trembles with amusement, and when I glance up, I find that she's biting on the inside of her lip to stop from laughing.

"I'll buy you any treats you want. Salmon? Sardines?"

"Doritos," Tatum says.

"W-what?" I stutter.

"Buy her too much fish and you'll likely find it stuffed down the couch to rot."

My eyes widen.

What the fuck is wrong with this cat?

"Doritos?" I repeat, more than happy to buy the thing chips if it means I get one extra one-on-one time with Tatum. "Any flavor?" I ask, secretly thinking about giving her the hot ones.

Her litter tray is in your bathroom. Don't do it.

"Cheesy ones."

"Okay. I can do that," I agree before looking down at the cat again. "Do we have a deal? Let me have access to Tatum and I'll buy you all the Doritos you can eat?"

She continues glaring, but I swear I see a chink in her armor.

"Fantastic. Great doing business with you." I look back up, focusing on Tatum. "Now, where were we?" I ask, gripping the back of her neck and pressing my forehead against hers.

"We were going to find out what was in that box," she says, ignoring what she can clearly see in my eyes.

"Yeah," I muse. "Exactly what I was just thinking about too."

"Come on, Griz. If you're lucky, it might be the world's most over-the-top cat toy."

"I'm not having one of those ugly scratching post things in my home," I warn.

"And yet, you have this beautiful tablecloth," Tatum says, pointing to the offending thing on the top of the pile of open gifts.

"Hmm."

I rip into the paper as Tatum lowers herself and Griz to the couch, watching with interest when all I reveal is a cardboard box.

Reaching for the scissors, I open it and pull the contents free.

"Wow," Tatum breathes. "That's...I'm speechless."

"What even is it?" I ask, taking a step back.

"A piece of modern art, I guess?"

"It looks like a lump of wood on a stand," I point out.

Tatum tilts her head to the side. "That's because it is."

Reaching for the abandoned gift paper, I search for a tag to discover who thought that buying us this monstrosity was a good idea.

"There isn't a tag."

"I guess that saves us writing a fake thank-you note."

"It has to be someone who knows the truth," I muse. "Probably Kian. It's the sort of shit he'd pull."

"I'm sure it would look wonderful in his apartment. Should we deliver it ourselves?" Tatum laughs.

Raking my hand through my hair, I stare down at the mess.

"This is a disaster."

"Grab the one from Lori. She will have got us something decent," Tatum reasons.

"You think so?"

She thinks for a moment before shrugging one shoulder, her confidence draining.

"Here, you can do the honors," I say, passing her the box.

Setting Griz aside, she rips into it.

The second she opens the box, her brow furrows in confusion before the most incredible transformation happens.

Happiness washes through her expression before her lips curl up and a loud laugh erupts.

"Oh my god," she cries, tears filling her eyes.

"What? What is it?"

"I-it's...for you," she stutters, barely able to contain herself enough to speak.

"Me?" I ask, moving closer and taking the box when she holds it out, now wiping tears from her cheeks.

Ripping my eyes from her, I peer in the box.

"What the actual fuck?" I bark, staring down at a...at a strap-on penis?

"Don't you remember?" Tatum roars, now clutching her stomach as she laughs. "You like it dry."

The memory of the night in the Italian restaurant slams into me, although I remember less detail about what happened in the actual restaurant and more of what happened in the bathroom.

"You're not using that," I state, keeping my cool.

"We'll see. You know, they say that it's good for the soul to give up control every now and then. Great stress relief."

"I'm sure they do," I say, throwing the box to the pile of other shit that needs to leave my apartment and stalking into the kitchen for a drink. A strong fucking drink.

65

TATUM

"I'll go," I say when the buzzer rings through the apartment.

The place looks almost unrecognizable. It's as if a tornado has blown through it. There is wrapping paper, boxes, cards, and the random assortment of gifts we've received littering every single surface.

It's only been like this a few hours and already, I swear I can see Kingston's eye twitching in irritation.

It's all the more reason to put off cleaning up.

It's wrong, but I can't help but love seeing this side of him.

The takes-no-shit businessman that everyone else sees is long gone right now. It makes me feel special that I'm getting to discover the real man inside the suit.

My stomach growls as I get closer to the door. I am more than ready to dive into the takeout I managed to convince Kingston to order.

Mr Health-Freak wasn't really for it. But it's Saturday night, and the past week has been hell. He deserves to kick back and relax just as much as everyone else. Hell, possibly more so. And anyway, one night of takeout isn't going to ruin anything.

Eagerly, I pull the door open, more than ready to pull the bag of Chinese into my arms and inhale the tempting scent.

It takes a second for the image to clear enough in my head to discover that the man standing before me isn't delivering our delicious dinner.

Instead, it's my new brother-in-law.

"Good evening," Kian says with a wicked grin that I'm sure gets more than a few women in trouble. "How's the hangover?"

With a glare, I pull the door wider to invite him in.

"I've no idea what you're talking about," I mutter.

"Sure you don't," he says happily as he marches through the entrance hall in search of his big brother. "What the fuck?" he barks the second he lays eyes on the state of the living room.

"Don't start," Kingston snaps.

"You finally opened them then." Kian's voice gets quieter as he speaks, and when I step into the room, I discover why. He's already in the kitchen, pulling a bottle of Kingston's scotch from the cupboard. "Drink?" he asks as if it's his to offer out.

"Sure," Kingston agrees before turning his eyes on me.

"Tate, do you—"

"I'm good with my water," I interrupt, making Kian smirk with accomplishment.

Yeah, okay. I'm still suffering from last night.

"So, what did you get?" he asks, walking back over with two glasses of scotch before dropping onto the opposite couch to Kingston and next to Griz.

I wince, unsure how she's going to react to a man encroaching on her space, and when I glance at Kingston, I find him smirking, clearly having similar thoughts.

"You probably don't want to know. Most of them are ugly enough to convince you to never get married."

"You opened mine though, right?" Kian asks, unaware that he's getting a full body assessment from my cat.

I swear she looks him up and down, studying every inch of him as she makes a judgment.

"If you sent the log on a stick, then yes. We opened it and have already organized a courier to send it directly back to your place."

"Log on a stick?" he asks with a deep frown. "I sent you a coupon for a year's supply of lube."

"Fuck off. You didn't, did you?" Kingston scoffs.

"Well, if you haven't opened it yet, you wouldn't know, would you?" As he replies, Griz gets to her feet and begins stalking closer, sniffing the air around him.

Kingston watches closely, waiting for the moment she strikes.

"Oh hey," Kian says when her movement catches his eye. "Didn't see you there. Aren't you cute," he says, thoughtlessly reaching out, ready to tickle her.

I'm still debating whether or not to warn him that my kitty isn't a big fan of men. But just before any words tumble from my mouth, he makes contact with her ear. I wait for the strike, for the blood and the cry from Kian that will more than likely follow.

But it never comes.

Instead, Griz tilts her head to the side and begins to purr happily.

What the actual—

"The fuck?" Kingston barks, echoing my thoughts.

"What?" Kian asks innocently as Griz leans closer, craving more of his attention.

The buzzer rings again before either of us gets a chance to respond.

"This had better be dinner," I mutter, having visions of Kieran standing on the other side of the door this time instead.

"Oh sweet, you've already ordered."

I narrow my eyes at Kian before spinning on my heels and marching back to the front door.

Their rumbling voices follow me, but I can't make out what they're saying. And everything is forgotten when I pull the door open and thankfully find what I really want.

Food.

Without looking like a homeless person who hasn't eaten all week, I force myself to reach for the bag at a normal speed and politely thank the guy before kicking the door closed and racing toward the kitchen with my goodies.

But I come up short when I find Griz now sitting on Kian's lap.

Little fucking traitor.

"What the fuck are you, some kind of cat whisperer?" I blurt in shock.

Griz doesn't like men. It took months for her to come around to Cory, but even still, she point-blank refuses to go anywhere near him.

This...this is completely unheard of.

"Oh yeah, that's my side hustle in the evenings—find out the secrets of all the pussies in the city," Kian deadpans, making Kingston snort in amusement.

"Good god," I mutter, taking another look at Griz in his lap before continuing to the kitchen to unload my food in peace.

"Kingston let you order Chinese," Kian says, his voice closer now.

Glancing over my shoulder, I find him gazing down at the variety of dishes I've laid out on the island.

"Yep," I say, popping the P.

"Well, I guess it's true what they say. Men really will do anything for the best pussy."

I narrow my eyes at him, refusing to acknowledge that he's got my cat in his arms. In his fucking arms...

I'm way too hungry for this bullshit.

"Kingston doesn't let me do anything. If I want Chinese, I will order Chinese. I'm not some little lady who is going to be controlled by a man, no matter how powerful that man deems himself to be."

Kian stares at me as if I've just sprouted an extra head.

Kingston walks in, giving Griz a wide berth, before stepping up behind me.

"Did you hear that?" he says with what I can only say is pride.

"Uh..." Kian starts.

"My wife thinks I'm powerful."

I don't need to look back to know that he's smirking as he

wraps his arms around my waist and rests his chin on my shoulder.

"That was not what she said," Kian argues.

"It's how I heard it."

"Whatever. Grab me a plate, Bro. This looks amazing."

"Excuse me?" I hiss, folding my arms over my chest. "I didn't order for three."

"No," Kian muses, looking at the obscene amount of food before us. "It looks more like you ordered for ten. I think we'll be fine."

He pulls a stool out before lowering himself into it and then Griz to the kitchen counter.

Kingston tenses behind me.

"What are you doing?" he barks.

"Uh...eating."

"The fucking cat, K. Get it off the kitchen counter."

"Christ, it's no wonder she hates you, man," he says before turning to Griz. "You're okay up there watching, aren't you, my little buddy."

"Jesus fucking Christ," Kingston mutters. "Am I even hearing this right now?"

I chuckle as I twist out of his arms and grab the plate Kian wants.

The second I pass it over, he begins loading it up before offering Griz a prawn cracker, which she eagerly takes out of his hand.

"Unbelievable," Kingston hisses before joining us.

We eat in silence for a few minutes. Kian and I are much more enthusiastic than Kingston, who pokes everything with his fork suspiciously.

"Do you even know how clean the kitchen is of the place we ordered this from?" he asks.

"Dude, will you stop being such a fucking pussy and just eat? Tatum isn't going to poison us all."

He spears a piece of pork and begrudgingly pushes it past his lips. His eyes widen slightly as the sweetness of the sauce, is quickly followed by the heat of the chili exploding on his tongue. He refuses to comment on how good it is, though.

Rolling my eyes, I look at Kian, who's watching his brother with the same amusement on his face.

"Why are you even here?" Kingston asks after swallowing.

"I came to extend an invitation to dinner with our mother tomorrow," Kian explains.

Nothing but silence follows.

Their mom wasn't at the wedding last weekend, although we have opened both a card and a gift from her and her husband.

I only have very fuzzy memories of Elizabeth from when I was a kid. She and Michael had a very ugly divorce while Kieran was still a baby, and despite the years that have passed, they still refuse to be in the same room as each other.

Kingston said he wasn't bothered about her not being there. He also claims not to be bothered about his mother's lack of presence in his life, but I'm not sure either is entirely true.

Kian and Kieran still have a relationship with her. But Kingston was that much older when their marriage fell apart, and he remembers it and the pain that came with it all too well.

"Was she incapable of calling me and asking herself?" he spits, his mood changing in a heartbeat at the mention of her.

"KC," Kian warns. "She just wants to spend some time with you and Tate. Congratulate you properly."

"It's not necessary. If she wanted to celebrate, she could have attended last weekend with everyone else."

An awkwardness falls over us, threatening to ruin my appetite.

"We should go," I say, reaching over to rest my hand on Kingston's thigh.

"Why should we make the effort when she can't?" The words are so full of bitterness, it makes my heart hurt for what he's been through, for how much pain she's caused him over the years.

"Because you're a bigger person than she is," I explain, trying to get him on board.

"I thought you thought that I was a shitty person," he argues.

"Sometimes. Is Kieran going?" I ask, in the hope that I can sweeten the deal.

"He's been invited, but trying to get plans out of him is like trying to nail Jell-O to the wall."

"Isn't everything challenging enough right now?" Kingston asks.

"Look," Kian reasons, "if you really don't want to, I'll tell her no. I won't even lie and say that you're busy. But she's our mom."

Kingston looks at me, searching my eyes for the answer.

I shrug, obviously unqualified to hand out any real advice in the parental department.

My mom is more than likely spending her Saturday night with multiple bottles of wine.

"It's your decision. I'll stand by you whatever you decide," I say honestly. I might be aware of their fucked-up family dynamic, but I refuse to sway his opinion on it.

If he wants to go, I'll smile at his mom and say all the right things. If he doesn't, then I'll respect that.

"I'll think about it," he mutters before pushing a forkful of rice into his mouth as a distraction. "This is really good," he confesses after a few seconds.

Kian smirks. "Marriage looks good on you, man," he says proudly. "It's doing what I've failed to do all these years."

"Oh yeah, what's that?" Kingston asks, intrigued.

"Making you fucking normal."

"Asshole," Kingston mutters before throwing a spring roll at Kian. It bounces off his cheek before landing right next to Griz, who happily steals it.

"See," Kian says, tickling her ear again. "He's not always so bad. Enjoy, buddy."

66

KINGSTON

The warmth of Tatum's palm on my thigh spreads through my entire body.

"We don't have to do this if you don't want to," she says softly.

We're sitting outside the home my mom shares with her husband and their children.

It's a place I've been to countless times, but it never gets any easier.

This is the home where she raised her daughters with her husband. The place she made memories with her...family.

They've always made every effort to let me know that I'm always welcome here, but I can't help but feel that they're empty words said out of obligation more than anything.

Mom left us. We were only young kids, but she turned her back and left in favor of a new life with a new man. She started a whole new family.

Kian and Kieran embraced it. They were younger; they didn't see the ugly side of it all that I did. A side that I was never able to get past.

The heated arguments. The smashed plates. The slamming doors.

The tears. The pain. The heartache.

Dad loved her. He loved her more than I think she ever realized. Or at least, that's what I've been led to believe, seeing as she was the unfaithful one.

She's explained to me time and time again that she never wanted to hurt Dad, but that she was unhappy in her marriage. Dad worked too much, and she was exhausted, lonely, and a whole host of other things.

I got it. Even at a young age, I could see that all the things she was saying were true. Dad was never at home, and they'd had us very close together. I could see it. But that didn't mean that she needed to turn her back on us and replace us with another family.

"It's just dinner," I reason.

I try to accept her invitation twice a year. It's enough to satisfy my mind that I'm making an effort. In reality, it's bullshit. I should want to spend time with her—with them. But I don't. The only thing I feel when I'm here is rejection and not being good enough. And neither of those are things that I need in my life.

"We'll eat and be gone in under two hours."

I kill the engine before a pained sigh spills from my lips.

"King," Tatum whispers.

I glance over, immediately hating the pity I see in her eyes.

"No," I warn. "Don't do that."

"What? I'm not doing anything," she argues.

"Let's just go," I say, throwing the door open and climbing out.

I crack my neck and roll my shoulders back.

Kian and Kieran are already here. I swear, they're the only reason these events are bearable.

I've barely taken a step forward when Tatum's warm hand slips into mine and squeezes in support.

It's...nice. Having her here with me right now is a lot more comforting than I expected it to be.

Before we climb the steps to the front door, I glance down at her. She's wearing a pair of skinny jeans and a simple blue sweater. It's just a touch lighter than her eyes, and it makes them sparkle in the most incredible way. Her dark hair has been braided and rests over one shoulder, exposing her slender neck and the very faint mark I left behind last night.

I bite down on my bottom lip as I remember the way we moved together on the couch after Kian left.

Thankfully, Griz passed out in a Chinese takeout-induced coma, and I was able to have my way with my wife without being skinned alive by the fluffball.

My cock twitches as I vividly remember her sinking down on it. She was so wet and ready for me.

"You're staring," she points out as I navigate the stairs blindly, unable to take my eyes off her.

"You're beautiful."

"Careful, King. Keep saying things like that and I'll start to get ideas."

"Get as many as you like. I'm obsessed with every single thing about my wife."

Her cheeks heat at my words and she averts her gaze, unable to hold my eyes when I say something so heavy. I've noticed her do that a lot in the past few days, as if she can't deal with the reality of what is happening here between us.

"What are you doing?" she asks when I stop at the front door and reach for the bell.

It's stupid. I know that I can just walk in, but for some reason, it just seems wrong. I don't belong here. I'm a guest, so I ring the bell like anyone else would.

I shrug, letting her answer her own question. Thankfully—or not, I'm not entirely sure—the door opens before us to reveal my beaming mother.

I haven't seen her in at least four months, but as always, absolutely nothing has changed about her.

Her blonde hair is styled to perfection, her makeup is flawless, her eyes twinkle with life, and her smile is genuine.

I should feel some kind of warmth and comfort from her reaction to seeing me—her firstborn child—but no matter how excited she is, all I feel is empty.

"Kingston," she breathes, her eyes running down the length of me as if she's looking for the differences in me like I did her. "It's so good to see you." She steps forward and holds her arms open before wrapping me in a hug. "I missed you so much. I'm so sorry I couldn't be there last weekend. We—"

"It's okay, Mom," I say before I'm forced to listen to her excuse. It doesn't matter what it was; the damage has been caused already.

"And Tatum, oh my goodness, look at you," she says, turning to my wife and taking her hands. "So beautiful. And so happy. Married life looks like it suits you."

My heart pounds, hearing Mom say those words. I want to believe that she's seeing the truth, but Tatum is faking it just as well as I am right now.

She might not be miserable at the moment, but I also wouldn't describe her as happy. Terrified, maybe.

"Well, we are only a week in, so..."

"Ah, the honeymoon period. Say no more," Mom says with a wince, making me cringe. "Come on in. Dinner is almost ready. Everyone but your sisters are in the dining room. I'm yet to drag them from their pits."

"Thanks," I mutter, gripping Tatum's hand tighter and stepping inside.

The scent of their house mixed with Mom's home cooking wafts through my nose, but it doesn't settle me at all.

"Is there anything you need help with, Elizabeth?" Tatum offers politely.

"Please, call me Liz, sweetheart. I'd love a hand; it'll save me from trying to drag Neil away from talking football with Kieran. That's if Kingston doesn't mind, of course."

"How badly are you going to interrogate her?" I ask, torn between letting Tatum go and refusing to let her out of my sight.

"Oh, I would never. I know Tate well enough to know that she's strong enough to put up with you."

"Lovely," I mutter as I tug Tatum into my side and lower my lips to her ears. "Please," I beg. "Be good."

She laughs quietly. "Haven't you heard, KC? I'm an angel," she mocks.

"Angels don't suck dick the way you do, baby."

She gasps, but something tells me that it's more from a rush of desire than it is shock.

"Go and play with your brothers. I'll be there soon."

Before she gets to escape, I wrap my hand around the back of her neck and drop my lips to hers.

"I'll just be in the kitchen," Mom says, excusing herself.

"I'm right here, King. All you've got to do is say the word and we're out of that door," she promises once I've released her in favor of staring her in the eyes.

"Thank you," I whisper.

"Anytime. Now, go talk boy stuff."

She spins away from me, and I stand there frozen as I watch her disappear.

No sooner has she disappeared around the corner do I hear giggles from above me.

Hiding my expression, I glare up at the banister and find exactly what I was expecting. Two dark shadows that belong to my half-sisters.

"Karma is a bitch, you know. She'll come back and bite you in the ass."

"We weren't listening," Mackenzie argues as they both step into the light.

"Of course you weren't. I do remember being your age, you know."

"Pfft," Matilda scoffs. "I doubt it. You're like...ancient."

As they descend the stairs, I have to do a double take. With every day that passes, I'm sure they look more and more like Mom. It's unnerving. I'm not sure Neil had any input on their DNA.

"Devil child," I mutter before pulling them both into a hug. Honestly, despite being a royal pain in my ass, they are the best thing about this house.

"Where's Tate? We want to see the photos," Matilda says excitedly, staring up at me with her huge blue eyes.

"Oh, I see how it is," I tease. "She's in the kitchen." They both take off running. "Be nice," I call, but it's too late. They're gone. "Good luck, baby," I mutter under my breath as I make my way to the dining room.

Deep voices rumble long before I get to the door, and they pause the second I step into the room.

"Kingston," Neil says, the same shock he has on his face he does every time I turn up here.

He's not a bad man, the opposite actually. But I'm not sure I'll ever get over the fact that Mom betrayed Dad with him. That he and his daughters have lived the family life we should have had.

"Afternoon," I greet, looking him in the eyes before glancing at my brothers.

"Here," Neil says, offering up a beer before continuing his conversation with Kieran. He's a massive Chicago Chiefs fan, and Kieran never hears the end of it.

"Hey," Kian says, his eyes darting to the door as I drop into the chair beside him. "Tatum not with you?"

"She's with Mom."

"That was brave," he teases.

"It's fine," I lie before taking a pull on my beer. "There isn't anything she can say that will make any of this worse."

He stares at me as if to ask, "Really?" but he doesn't say a word.

As far as Mom knows, Tatum and I had a whirlwind romance followed by a shotgun wedding. Knowing her, she's probably expecting some big pregnancy announcement in the coming weeks to help explain it. Thankfully, she's going to be disappointed. Life is complicated enough right now.

"So, Kingston," Neil asks, having finished his conversation with Kieran. "How's it feel being a married man?"

"Yeah," I say. "It's great. Right, you know?" I add, aware that he'll agree.

"How did Miles take it? I bet he didn't see that coming."

"He wasn't the only one," Kieran scoffs like an asshole.

"He...uh...made his feelings known."

"KC had the bruises to prove it, too," Kian adds.

Neil chuckles. "I remember the first guy my little sister dated," he says getting a far-off look in his eyes as he thinks back. "He was a jerk."

"Didn't she marry her high school sweetheart?" Kian asks. Fucker literally remembers everything.

"Yep. Still think he's a jerk," Neil jokes. "So, I guess it's your turn next then," he says, looking pointedly at Kian.

"I don't have time for that. Too much going on at work."

"Isn't stopping Kingston," Kieran points out.

"And I'm happy for him. But that doesn't mean we all want the same. What about you, little brother? Any of your jersey chasers wife material?"

Kieran scoffs. "You know damn well they're not. I'm not marrying someone who's scored more touchdowns than I have."

I sit back and listen as the three of them banter back and forth. I love seeing my brothers happy, but it's not enough to banish the unease of being here.

It's not long until soft female voices fill the air, and only seconds later, the four of them all appear carrying plates full of food. But while Kian and Kieran comment on the food, my attention is stolen by the woman carrying the potatoes.

Her eyes are alight with happiness and there's a full, beaming smile on her lips, which only grows when she finds me.

"You okay?" she mouths.

My heart seizes in my chest at the sight of her here, and the truth comes tumbling out before I can catch it. "I am now."

67

TATUM

Spending the day with Kingston and his family was...a lot.

I hated seeing him on edge. I've never known him not to be in control of a situation, but long before we even stepped foot inside that house, all he wanted to do was turn around and run.

His anxiety over spending the afternoon at his mom's was palpable, and I hated it. All I wanted to do was make it better, and easier for him. But there wasn't anything I could do. The bitterness he feels toward his mom has been festering for a long time. It's going to take a hell of a lot more than a few words from me to make it go away. And there's a chance it never will. The betrayal he feels might always be there. No one could blame him if it is.

Relationships between children and parents are complex. I know that just as much as he does. Sometimes, people can work through it. Other times, it's just too big an obstacle to overcome. But the fact he still tries says a lot about him and the love he has for his family, especially his brothers.

As soon as we got back earlier, he changed and disappeared into his home gym.

I wanted to stop him, to demand he talk to me and try and get it off his chest, but I knew he needed more than that. So, I let him go do his thing while I poured myself a glass of wine and then ran a bath, needing to kick back before a new manic work week begins.

With the scent of my favorite bath salts filling the air and soft, relaxing music playing quietly on my cell on the counter, I think back over the past few weeks.

But no matter what, my thoughts always come back to Kingston today.

The look on his face, the hard set of his shoulders. All of it felt wrong.

But just like all the other things I've learned about him over the past few weeks, it helped me to feel closer to him. And that's a problem.

I swear, with every day that passes, he's becoming a bigger part of my life, a more important part. One I'm not sure I want to lose anytime soon.

I don't realize that I drift off to sleep until a bang jolts me awake. My eyes fly open as my heart jumps into my throat the moment I discover a shadow looming over me.

"Oh my god," I gasp, my heart beating out of control as Kingston drags his sweaty clothes from his body and moves closer. "What are you—" My words falter the second my eyes meet his.

They're dark and haunted in a way I've never seen before. If I thought that hitting the gym would banish his demons, then I was wrong. Very, very wrong.

"What's wrong?" I ask as he steps into the tub with me.

The water level immediately rises as he sinks down into the water, causing it to slosh over the edge.

"Nothing," he lies. "Come here," he demands before reaching for me and effortlessly lifting me onto his lap.

The second he has me where he wants me, he threads his fingers through the damp hair at the nape of my neck and drags my mouth to his.

His kiss is desperate and full of all the emotion I could see in his eyes.

I feel it all the way to my toes.

Wrapping my arms around his shoulders, I hold him as tight as I can, letting him know that I'm here, that it's okay.

In only minutes, the heavy emotion gives way to desperation, his grip on my hip tightens, and he moves me, grinding my pussy over his length.

"Oh god," I gasp into his mouth.

Without breaking our connection, I reach between us and line him up.

I don't need any more foreplay than this. I'm ready for him.

"Tatum," he moans into our kiss as he pushes inside me.

"Take what you need, King. I'm here. Use me." The words make my chest ache because they're so painfully true.

He thrusts, filling me in one move. I sit up a little to get a better angle and rest my forehead against his.

His stare burns into me, but I don't open my eyes. I can't. I'm scared.

Terrified of what I'll find staring back at me.

"Shit, baby. You've no idea how much I need this. How much you being there today meant to me."

"It was nothing."

"No," he spits fiercely, shocking me enough to force my eyes open. "It was everything."

I can barely inhale in my next breath at the emotion staring back at me. It hurts. I feel his pain as powerfully as he does, and all I want to do is take it away.

"Thank you," he whispers, making me wonder if he has a lump in his throat that rivals mine.

I nod, letting him feel it as we move together beneath the water.

It's slow, sensual, and entirely too much.

Tears prick the backs of my eyes and my nose itches. I fight it. I fight it as hard as I can as my heart threatens to freefall in my chest.

I shouldn't be feeling this for this... this...beautifully broken man.

Yes, he's all the things I always thought he was. Arrogant. Egotistical. An asshole. But there is so much more to him than that. So much that he doesn't let the world see, and I'm becoming more and more addicted with every new discovery I make.

Silence falls between us, leaving just our heaving breaths and the sloshing of the bath water, but the air is heavy with all our unspoken words.

Words that we shouldn't need to say, let alone feel.

"Tatum, I—"

Lifting my hand from his shoulder, I press two fingers to his lips.

"Don't," I beg. "Actions, not words."

I'm not sure if it's relief or disappointment that fills his eyes, but it's gone so quickly, I don't stand a chance of attempting to decipher it.

"Need you," he groans as his hips pick up pace, sending even more water crashing over the sides.

"Then take," I offer. "Whatever you need."

He stares up at me as if I'm something special, someone important, and I have no choice but to close my eyes and block it out.

It's too much.

Just as I suspected, from the moment we walked into the Warner Group building together the next morning, we got swallowed up in the fear vibrating around every office about what the future of the company and everyone's jobs holds.

Thankfully, I was able to lock myself in my office during the day and only had to deal with my team.

I'd already made it very clear to them the week before that despite me being first a Warner, and then a Callahan, I have absolutely no inside information about what was happening, or any sway about who would stay and go. Thankfully, they all respected me enough to leave it at that and focus on their jobs.

The atmosphere around the building was awful. I've always enjoyed my job and never, ever clock-watched, desperate for the day or the week to come to an end, but this week is different. But as much I as I want to leave the oppressive conditions of the office behind, going home brings me even more anxiety.

Visiting Kingston's family this past weekend seemed to crack something inside him. He's been different ever since.

From what I've heard through the grapevine at work, he's the same ruthless asshole we all know and...endure as he and Miles have started putting their plan into place. But at home, he's been even more attentive, gentle, caring.

Every night after work, I expect him to have shaken it off and returned to his usual ways, but every day he returns home that little bit more vulnerable and broken.

It's as unnerving as it is mind-blowing that he immediately seeks me out, wraps me up in his arms, tucks his face into the crook of my neck and uses me as some kind of pillar of support.

The nights he's been home late, I've taken it upon myself to make use of his kitchen and attempt to rustle us up some dinner. Some nights have been more successful than others. But no matter what time he's been home or how awful his day has been, there is always one certainty. We always have sex, and every single night he passes out with his arms wrapped around me.

While I might be exhausted, I haven't been finding sleep quite so easily. Instead, most nights I've been lying there until long past midnight with my mind spinning.

I wish I could stop, but with every day that passes, more questions about where all of this is going crop up.

Kingston hasn't attempted to say whatever it is I felt like he was going to confess on Sunday night, and I'm relieved.

It might have been nothing, but the look in his eye and the pain that was oozing from him made me believe it was a hell of a lot more than nothing. And not just that, but something I am nowhere near prepared to hear.

The feelings floating around are enough, but words...

I shake my head, trying to clear my thought so I can find some rest.

It's Sunday night again, and another work week is looming.

Kingston has worked all weekend. He's exhausted. His eyes are dark, the circles beneath them bruised and swollen.

Miles is the same, and it twists me up inside to know that he's returning to an empty home at night. I wish I could be there for him too, but Kingston is monopolizing my time. I just have to hope that Miles is finding relief from it all somewhere.

I lie there for hours listening to his shallow breathing, relieved that he's managed to get some rest, all the while it eludes me.

I've no idea what time I eventually drift off, but when Kingston's alarm goes off the next morning, I'm nowhere near ready. Nor is he, if the groan he lets out before turning it off says anything.

No sooner has the noise vanished does his arm wrap back around me, holding me tightly.

"Can't we just stay here for the day?" he asks, his voice rough with sleep and sexy as hell.

Despite my exhaustion, my body wakes up at the sound of it.

"If only," I whisper. "Just think, we could have still been on our honeymoon right now."

"Don't," he warns. "I promise, when we go, it'll be fucking epic."

"It better be," I tease.

Silence falls between us and I begin to think that he's drifted back off to sleep when my own alarm starts.

"Okay, okay," he moans before finally releasing me and climbing out of bed.

I roll over and shamelessly watch as he stretches his arms above his head, making the muscles of his back and ass pull and stretch.

Delicious.

Suddenly, he turns around and instead of ass, I get an eyeful of his morning wood.

"Morning, Mr. Callahan," I tease.

"Shower with me, Mrs. Callahan? Send me into the office happy and ready for the day?"

I want to refuse, but then I look up at his exhausted, hopeful eyes and I can't.

He needs me, and I'm powerless but to agree.

Throwing the covers off, I stalk around the bed toward him. I'm wearing a tank and panties, but from the way he's watching me with hunger darkening his eyes, you'd think I was already naked.

The second I'm within reaching distance, he pulls my tank up my body before his mouth descends on an already peaked nipple.

"Kingston," I gasp as his hands skim over my waist and push my panties from my hips.

"You make all of this bearable, baby. I wouldn't be able to do it without you right now."

It's bullshit. Men like Kingston don't need a woman to help them get through. But I appreciate the words all the same.

Once I'm breathless from just his mouth on my breasts alone, he takes my hand and guides me into the bathroom before backing me up in the shower and wrapping my leg around his hip so he can push inside me.

He fucks me so thoroughly that I still feel it over an hour later as we walk into the Warner Group building hand in hand, just like we have done every day this week. And just like every other day, journalists line the streets, barking questions at both of us about the state of the company, if it's true that we're going into liquidation, and a million other incorrect assumptions about what's happening here.

With every question, Kingston's grip on my hand tightens.

"Jesus," he groans as we step into the elevator alone.

"It'll get better," I promise, taking his rough jaw in my hands.

"I know. It'll all be worth it in the end."

Stretching up on my toes, I brush my lips against his as we climb toward my floor where we part for the day.

"You know where I am if you need me," I say, holding his eyes.

"Is that your way of inviting me to fuck you in your office?" he asks, wiggling his brows at me.

I smirk at him before backing away the second the doors open.

"Be good. I'll see you later, yeah?"

But before I can escape, he reaches out and pulls me back into his body.

He stares down at me in a way that makes my heart pound against my ribs.

"Have I told you how fucking incredible you are today?"

"Not with words, but your body did a good job earlier."

"Fuck. Don't send me up to your brother with a boner."

"I'll see you later, sir. Try not to make anyone cry today, please."

This time when I step back, he lets me go. Although not before he makes a show of adjusting himself.

"We didn't think he was going to let you out," Josh says with a laugh as I pass his desk.

Glancing up, my cheeks heat when I discover that every one of my team is watching me.

"Twenty minutes," I bark, refusing to acknowledge what they just witnessed.

"You got it, boss," Josh says, saluting me like an idiot.

Marching into my office, I close the door behind me and rest my back against it.

My eyes are sore from lack of sleep and my muscles ache, but that doesn't mean that desire isn't pumping through my veins from the way Kingston looked at me just now.

I think it's fair to say that he's totally swept me into his web. But while I might be able to admit it to myself now, it doesn't freak me out any less.

Shaking my head, I walk toward my desk and drop into my chair.

My watch buzzes and I pull my sleeve up to glance at the screen. When I do, my heart drops into my feet.

Has your period started?

Track your cycle now.

My hand trembles as I stare at the words.

"Fuck. When..."

Everything has been crazy, I've been so distracted but...

I open the page on this week before flicking back to the previous one.

And there it is.

The little red heart I draw on the day I'm expecting to get my period.

Five days ago.

Tears burn my eyes as I slump back in my chair, desperately trying to remember a time when I was five days late and that everything was okay.

But I can't.

I'm never late.

68

TATUM

I t's stress.

Stress and exhaustion and everything else I've been dealing with for the past few weeks.

That's all it is.

Just my body proving to me that everything has been just a little bit too much.

It has to be.

With my head spinning and panic making my entire body tremble, I manage to get through my morning meetings. But I barely remember a word that was said or what was agreed.

By the time lunch rolls around, I'm a mess.

I want to believe that all the lies I'm telling myself are true.

But deep down, I know they're not.

This is more than stress. More than exhaustion.

It's the reason I haven't felt right. Why I haven't been sleeping, and why I'm so unbelievably tired because of it.

But for as distracted by the turns in my life as I have been, I know that I haven't failed to take my contraception. I'm as confident about taking that as I am that I'm breathing.

It's why I should be able to believe that this is a false alarm.

But I'm also not naive enough to think there still isn't a

chance. A slim one, sure, but this happens to women around the world every day.

I groan, dropping my head into my hands. I should have put up a fight about him not using condoms. I should have kept my head screwed on and put every single kind of obstacle in the way.

I should have...I should have done so, so many things in the past few weeks.

This is up there with one of the biggest mistakes, but so is falling for Kingston. Because that's where I'm at right now.

There. I've said it. Or at least thought it. I have fallen for my husband. For the man who is meant to be no more than a business deal.

Blinking back tears, I push my chair out behind me, throw my bag over my shoulder and hold my head high as I walk toward my office door.

It's still a little early for lunch, and I'm certainly not hungry, but I can't sit here any longer.

I need answers.

Once I know the truth, then I can figure out what I do next.

Thankfully, I make it to the elevator without having to interact with anyone.

The elevator is full of others all heading out for an early lunch, but they all ignore me, too lost in their own conversations and worries to pay attention to me.

It's not until I get to the exit that someone finally speaks to me.

"Are you okay, Mrs. Callahan?" Garrett the doorman asks.

I give him a double take, my brain misfiring at the name he calls me.

"Y-yeah, thank you."

"I hope you don't mind me saying, but you look very pale. Is there anything—"

"I'm fine," I say in a rush. "Haven't eaten."

"Mrs. Ca—"

"Tate," I remind him.

"Go and get yourself something good for lunch, Tate. You've got to look after yourself."

"Thank you," I whisper before blowing out of the building and finally inhaling in a deep breath of fresh air. Not that it does a lot. It doesn't give me answers or make the situation any better.

"Tatum Callahan, can we ask you a few questions about the future of Warner Group? We understand your father left—"

I hold my hand up and keep my head down, letting the lingering reporters know that I'm not interested in talking to them.

I don't look up until they're well behind me, and when I do, I find Lewis lingering in Kingston's car beside me, ready to whisk me away.

"Can I take you somewhere, Ms. Tate?"

Emotion bubbles up my throat, and I almost start sobbing there and then on the sidewalk.

"Thank you," I whimper.

I shouldn't. I should call an Uber, because no matter where Lewis takes me, he'll report back to Kingston.

But I can't stop myself from climbing into the back of the car and slamming the door on the rest of the world.

"Are you okay?" Lewis asks, his eyes on me in the rearview mirror.

"Yeah. Please could you take me to the mall?" I ask.

"Of course. Sit back and relax, I'll have you there as soon as possible."

"Thank you, Lewis. I really appreciate it."

As I get comfortable, I consider how not so long ago I'd have point blank refused to get into Kingston's car or have his driver help me out. But right now, it's everything I need.

When I step out of the car in the parking lot, no one turns to look at me. No one shouts any questions. It's a huge relief knowing that I can just blend into the crowd and do what I need to do without eyes on me.

"Do you know how long you're going to be?" Lewis asks before I take off.

"I don't. You go back in case Kingston needs you. I'll be okay."

He frowns. I know that Kingston has told Lewis to put my needs above his, and while I appreciate it, I also don't need him waiting for me. He doesn't need to witness the fallout of whatever this little trip to the mall is going to result in.

"Ms. Tate," he warns.

"Lewis," I sigh, reaching out to squeeze his bicep. I've no idea if it's appropriate or not, but quite frankly, I don't care right now. "I promise you, I'm fine. I don't know how long I'm going to be. If I need you, I will call you."

His eyes bounce between mine. He's conflicted. I hate putting him in this position, but it is what it is.

"Okay," he finally concedes. "But call me, please."

"I will. Have a good afternoon," I say, forcing a smile that I don't feel onto my lips.

"You too, Ms. Tate."

I wait long enough for him to pull the driver's door open and drop into the seat before taking off.

I should probably wait until I see the car disappear, but I'm too impatient to get my answer.

I've never been very good with the unknown, and now is just more proof of that.

My legs move as fast as physically possible in my heels and before I know it, I'm marching through the doors to the pharmacy.

With my heart in my throat and my hands trembling violently, I find the section I need and scan the shelves.

I've no idea what I want or which is the best.

I've never done this before.

In all my adult years, I haven't once had a serious enough false alarm to have to resort to this. It was something I was fairly proud of, considering that I haven't been any kind of angel.

But I guess all good luck comes to an end eventually.

I finally grab a box that promises the most accurate results on the market—probably bullshit from their marketing department, but whatever—and take it to the cashier.

I don't know what I expected, but the kind, middle-aged woman scans the test through the register without giving me any kind of judgment. I mean, why should she? As far as anyone else is concerned, I'm a grown-ass woman with a ring on my finger.

If only they knew the truth about my current situation...I bet she'd begin judging in a heartbeat if she knew I only said my vows to secure a cottage. And Kingston only agreed until death do us part so that he could take over my family's company.

I shake my head, trying to forget about reality as I tuck the box in my purse and walk back out of the store in search of a place to discover my fate.

I should probably go home.

Home...

Where even is my home right now?

Without thinking too much about it, I find the closest bathroom and lock myself inside a stall.

It is nowhere near the ideal place to do this, but I can't wait to get back to Kingston's apartment.

I need to know if all this freaking out and panicking is for nothing.

Or if...

I blow out a slow, calming breath in an attempt to get myself together before doing this, but it does very little to settle the riot inside me.

Pulling the box from my purse, I rip into the plastic covering and pull out the test and instructions. I scan the text, taking note of the important parts I need to remember before pulling my skirt up around my waist, dropping my panties, and lowering my ass to the toilet.

"Here goes nothing," I whisper to myself as the sounds of other women using the facilities float around me.

You're going to have to tell your unborn child that you did your test in a public bathroom....

Those thoughts do not help my performance anxiety in any way as I sit there trying to do my thing.

It takes longer than it should but eventually, I pee, all the while praying that at least some of it has hit the stick as it should.

Once I'm done, I pull it free, place the cap on it and lay the test on top of the toilet roll dispenser as I clean up. Then I lower the toilet seat and just wait.

I stare down at my watch, refusing to look away from it until the two minutes are up. I don't want any confusion or any false hope if I look too soon and the true answer hasn't developed. I did that with a Covid test before and the disappointment was real. I do not need my emotions put through any more right now.

But as I sit there, all I can see is one answer. And it's not the easy one where I stare at a single line, throw the test in the bin and continue on with my life, having learned a very important lesson—always use condoms. But the one where I do have another life growing inside me.

Kingston is going to be furious.

But that's only the beginning of my spiraling fears.

What if he thinks I did this on purpose?

There is no reason why he would. It's not like I'm trying to steal his money, or his power, or even him as a person. I have everything I could need already, or at least I will after our year of marriage.

But knowing all that doesn't stop the irrational thoughts from coming.

What if he divorces me? Then what?

I'll be left with nothing.

We'll be left with nothing.

No money, no job, no cottage.

No. Miles wouldn't let that happen.

Lori wouldn't let that happen.

But...

The time changes and my heart seizes.

It's time.

"Fuck," I breathe, shaking out my hands and then tucking my hair behind my ears nervously.

I reach out, plucking the upside-down test from the dispenser, and close my eyes.

Just look, Tatum. Discover your fate.

Everything else will fall into place.

Trust the process.

Trust the process...

Spinning the test around, I force my eyes open and stare down at my answer.

My stomach rolls instantly, and before any thoughts hit me, my knees collide with the dirty tile floor and I heave into the toilet.

69

KINGSTON

I stare at the message I sent Tatum hours ago. She's read it, but she hasn't responded.

Concern twists up my insides. She always replies.

It's almost midnight and Miles and I are giving up for the night.

Today was always going to be stressful, but I didn't anticipate just how hard it was going to be to begin letting people go. People who have worked hard for Warner Group for years. But it wasn't just the letting people go that dragged us down today, it was a couple of incredibly important people who came to us to tell us that they would voluntarily leave in the hope of saving others.

Sure, both of them are approaching retirement, but their roles here are vital for the future development of the company.

There is going to be a huge hole without them, but also, saving their generous salaries will greatly help us right now.

Talk about a rock and a hard place.

There are people who can fill the positions. That is not in question. We just don't have the time right now. We need to hit the ground running with this new direction for the company, not hang around while we wait for newly-promoted colleagues to catch up.

"What's wrong?" Miles asks, his voice rough with exhaustion as he catches me staring at my cell for the hundredth time tonight.

"Tatum hasn't replied," I mutter, trying to cover my true level of concern. It's the last thing he needs right now.

"She's probably sleeping like other normal people."

"Yeah," I muse. I'd agree if I'd have messaged her in the past couple of hours. But she saw this message and she didn't reply.

I don't want to be one of those men who jump to conclusions over every little thing, but I can't stop myself right now.

I want to say it's the lack of sleep, but it feels like more than that.

"Start all over again first thing tomorrow morning then?" he asks with a wince.

"Can't wait," I mutter, already regretting our agreed start time tomorrow. Finally, I turn my computer off and pack up my shit.

Miles pushes to his feet and walks toward the door to the office that has been allocated as mine.

We started in his first thing this morning but needed a change of scenery as the day rolled on.

"Don't wake my sister when you get home. Be nice to her," he warns before slipping out of the office.

The thought of waking her and ending the day properly is appealing, but so is just slipping into bed behind her and falling asleep with her body pinned against mine. There's something I never thought I'd be happy with. Cuddling.

Oh, how things change...

I make my way down to the underground parking lot and locate my car that Lewis had delivered for me earlier when I knew I was going to be working into the middle of the night, before heading home to my wife.

For the first time in what feels like forever, a genuine smile plays on my lips.

I never thought I'd be happy focusing all my effort on one woman, but Tatum makes it so easy.

Everything about her—even fighting with her—is effortless.

Just being around her makes me feel like I'm a better version of myself. It's weird. But I like it.

No. I more than like it.

I love it.

Scrubbing my hand down my face, I shake my head, laughing at myself and the U-turn my life has taken.

I wouldn't change it, though. Not for anything.

I thought I was happy before, that I was content with life, with work, with women. If anyone had asked, I'd have confidently said that anyone in a serious relationship was the one missing out. But now, I'm not sure that's the truth.

I don't miss my old life. But if what I've got now was suddenly ripped away from me, then it would hurt. Badly.

I may have agreed to the marriage, but that was only because of what was on offer business-wise. I'm pretty sure I'd have agreed to a marriage with anyone if it meant we got our hands on Warner Group. Tatum was just a bonus.

But now I can't help thinking that Warner Group was the bonus, because Tatum was the main prize in all of this.

Even when she's being crazy and I can't for the life of me figure out where her head is at, she's quite possibly the best thing that's ever happened to me. That realization surprises me just as much as it terrifies me.

The journey home and then the ride in the elevator to the top floor of the building seems to take longer than it ever has before.

Nothing but silence and darkness greet me when I step into the apartment. It's a throwback to before she moved in, and I don't like it. No. I hate it.

Unease trickles through me that she's not here.

But unwilling to put the lights on and wake her, I silently move through the apartment and climb the stairs in search of her.

The second I step into the dark bedroom, I breathe a sigh of relief, because she's curled up in bed with Griz beside her.

I strip and shower in record time before crawling into bed with her.

She doesn't move or say a word, but she doesn't have to. She's here. That's all I need.

I swear, no sooner have I relaxed, do I pass out. I never used to fall asleep this fast, especially after a long, stressful day, but it seems that Tatum might be the antidote I need.

Despite getting a few solid hours of sleep, I feel like a zombie when I walk back into my office the next morning.

Tatum was still sleeping when my alarm went off, and I ensured I was quiet enough to keep it that way as I snuck out of the house.

I left a note, but I hate myself for it. I don't want to be the husband who leaves the house before sunrise and returns long after it's set again.

I've literally lived through the reality of that kind of relationship, and it's not something I ever want to go through again.

I laugh at my thoughts as I drop into the chair behind my desk. Our marriage isn't even real. It's based on lies and forgery. We didn't commit ourselves to each other because of our undying love. We did it because of business.

It shouldn't matter about being a good husband. That isn't what we signed up for. We agreed to put on a good show in public while putting up with each other in private.

Things right now feel very different from how I saw this playing out at the beginning.

Nothing about our marriage or our relationship seems fake. Everything I feel for Tatum is very, very real. Too real.

"You look way too happy considering how little sleep we've had," Miles says, inviting himself into my office.

505

We might both be wearing different suits from the day before, but everything else feels the same.

If it weren't for the sweet scent of my wife that lingers in my nose, I'd believe we never actually left as he takes a seat and we continue from where we left off.

The sun rises over the city, but we're too lost in our plans and forecasting to pay any attention. There's movement outside of the door as the rest of the office comes to life. Judith pokes her head in to see if we want anything before disappearing again with Miles's coffee order.

We don't have meetings scheduled until eleven, and we make the most of every second.

Unfortunately, having to tell people that their positions in the company no longer exist doesn't get any easier, and by the time we take a break sometime after lunch, I'm at my limit.

My need to go home and lock the world out for a few hours is at a level I'm not sure it's ever been before.

It's because you have Tatum, a little voice pipes up. *You never needed it before because this was all you had.*

"You want some lunch? Or maybe a drink?" I ask, pushing from my seat and walking over to the window to stretch my legs.

"Yeah. Give me a few and we'll go," Miles agrees brokenly before slipping from my office and leaving me alone.

Pulling my cell from my pocket, I open up my message thread with Tatum, hating that she still hasn't replied to my message from last night.

> Kingston: Missed waking up with you this morning. I hope your day is going better than mine.

"Okay, ready," Miles says from the door, forcing me to lock my cell before the message has even shown as delivered.

Judith smiles at us as we pass her desk. She might not be involved with the decision-making and hard conversations, but she looks about as stressed as I feel. She's as much a part of the Warner family as Miles and Tatum. She'd been by Jonathan's side almost the whole time he'd been CEO. This place runs through her blood; the people who work on the floors below mean something to her. It's good to see the dedication and the love she has for everyone here. It just goes to prove that we're doing the right thing.

Miles doesn't say anything when I press the button for the thirteenth floor instead of the ground, but the smirk he gives me says everything.

"You've fallen for her, haven't you?" he asks after a few more seconds.

"What?" I ask, feigning innocence. "Of course not."

"Don't lie to me," he warns. "I can see it in your eyes."

"Miles," I sigh, combing my fingers through my hair and dragging it back.

"Just don't hurt her. Please. Don't fucking hurt her."

I stare at him, trying to let him see how serious I am with my next statement. "I'm really going to do my best not to."

"Good. Have you told her?"

"Told her what?"

"Fucking hell. For an intelligent man you're a fucking dumbass, KC," he mocks.

"Oh, I'm sorry, I didn't realize you were suddenly the oracle of relationships."

"Clearly, I'm not. But I know you two, and I know what I see when you're together. Tell her how you feel, man."

"I can't believe you're encouraging this," I mutter.

"It's a bit late to do anything else. You're fucking married and sharing a bed every night." I can't help it, a wicked smirk curls at my lips. "Fuck off," Miles snaps as the doors open and we spill out onto the marketing floor.

There are plenty of people, most of whom look up the second we enter, their eyes going wide with fear like we've come down to lay them off on the spot. But the section where Tatum's team works is suspiciously empty.

"Maybe they've all gone out for lunch," Miles muses. "They

submitted their final campaign ideas to Eric this morning. Probably celebrating."

"Maybe," I mumble, my eyes scanning the empty desks.

Moving closer to Tatum's office, I rap my knuckles on the door three times before pushing it open. But my wife isn't inside. In fact, it doesn't look like she's been here at all. Everything is tidy.

"Come on, I'm starving. You can make all the moon eyes you want at her later."

"I do not make moon eyes," I scoff, following him back to the elevator.

"Sure you don't."

With our meetings done for the day, we spend a little longer at lunch than we probably should, along with having one or two more drinks than are appropriate for a Tuesday afternoon.

By the time we walk back into the Warner Group offices, we've both got a bit of a buzz going on. It should certainly help make the afternoon a little easier to take.

"Good afternoon, Judith," Miles sings happily, making her eyes light up with amusement. "We brought you a gift." He places the cupcake we picked up for her on her desk, and her smile grows.

"Ah, you shouldn't have."

"Just a small treat to let you know we care," Miles explains before we take off again. "I need to grab a few things," he says, ducking into his office, leaving me to make my way down to my new one alone.

I step inside and take a deep breath as I walk toward the windows and stare out over Chicago.

I pull my cell from my pocket, but there is still nothing from Tatum.

My concern continues to grow. Miles is still trying to convince me that she's with her team, enjoying herself. But I don't believe it.

Something is wrong.

A couple of minutes pass before the door swings open behind me, crashing back against the wall.

I spin around, and the look on Miles's face sends dread shooting through my veins.

"What is it? What's wrong?" I ask in a rush.

He holds a piece of paper between us with a trembling hand, his face white and his eyes wide.

"She's gone."

"W-what?" I ask, not comprehending the words.

But then my eyes drop to the letter.

Only, it's not just a letter.

It's a resignation.

Tatum's resignation.

Effective immediately.

70

KINGSTON

"TATUM," I bellow as I race into the apartment.

Coldness engulfs me, letting me know that she isn't here. But it's not enough. I need to see it with my own eyes.

The ground floor is empty, so I make a beeline for the stairs, leaving Miles to loiter behind me with concern twisting up his face.

"TATUM," I shout again, desperate to hear her soft voice call back.

But she never does.

I crash into the bedroom like a madman and scan the space.

But it's empty, cold, and when I move into the bathroom, the sight of the clear vanity finally forces me to accept reality.

She's gone.

Pain rips through my chest as I stand there, feeling like the world is crumbling around me.

I've no idea when her presence in my life became such a huge part of it, but the hole she's just left is bigger than I ever thought possible for one person to leave behind.

I don't realize Miles has joined me until his deep voice echoes off the walls around me.

"What did you do?"

His words cut through me like a knife straight through my chest.

"Me?" I ask, spinning on him.

"Yes. You. What did you do to make her run?"

His expression hardens. There is no doubt in his mind that this is my fault.

"I didn't...fuck," I breathe. "I didn't do anything. I—"

"She wouldn't just leave, KC. All these years, she's put up with all the shit Dad threw at her. She's got almost everything she always wanted. She agreed to this fucking sham of a relationship, for fuck's sake. She wouldn't run for no reason."

I stand there feeling more useless than I ever have in my life before. My chest heaves and my fists curl at my sides.

He's right; she wouldn't just bail. She's been through too much to get this far to throw it all away. But that doesn't mean I did anything to push her to it.

"Everything was fine. I've no idea what—" My fingers thread through my hair and I pull until it hurts, desperately trying to make sense of this.

Sure, I've been working all the hours of the day recently, but she understands why. Hell, she encourages me and supports me. Does all the things a good partner should do when life is stressful. Or at least in my opinion, that's what they should do.

What they shouldn't do is hand in their resignation out of the blue and fucking disappear without any warning.

"I told you not to fucking hurt her," Miles growls angrily.

I stare at his dark, furious eyes and swallow nervously.

I want to argue and tell him that I haven't hurt her. But we'd both know that I'd be lying.

This whole fucking situation I agreed to before Jonathan even passed is hurting her, let alone anything I've done since.

Sharing those images of us at the cabin with the press was a stupid move. And I'm pretty sure it's something I'm going to regret for the rest of my days.

Our relationship might have started as a contract, a business deal, but that isn't how we should be treating it. It's a marriage, a union, two people who have to live together and trust each other.

She's my partner, my other half.

My wife.

She's...

Fuck.

I scrub my hand down my face as my heart continues to race.

"I don't know what the fuck I'm doing here, man. I'm trying. I'm fucking trying."

"You're telling me," he mutters under his breath, not helping the situation in the slightest.

"She won't have gone far," I reason before marching back out to the bedroom, noting the absence of the ball of ginger fluff that's usually taken up residence in the middle.

"Fluffpuff," I say as Miles steps up beside me.

"W-what?"

"The fucking cat," I mutter. "It's gone."

"Griz?"

"Yes. She's taken him."

"Her," he corrects.

"Whose fucking side are you on here? It's a fucking cat; who cares if it's a boy or a girl?"

"Tatum's," he answers, making my brows pinch in confusion.

"What?" I bark.

"You asked me whose side I'm on. I'm on Tatum's, always."

I scoff. "So much for fucking bro code."

"She's my little sister, man. She always comes first."

She fucking does for me, too. It's a fucking miracle, but I manage to swallow that thought before it bubbles out of me.

"So, where's she gone? Home?" Miles asks.

"This is her fucking home," I cry.

He glances at me but refrains from saying a word as he pulls his cell from his pocket and hits call on her name again.

I'm not sure why he bothers; she hasn't answered a single call since he discovered her resignation sitting on his desk.

I move through the home I've lived in for years, but suddenly, it feels wrong.

How can one person have such an impact on another's life in such a short time, let alone make them feel different about the place they come to hide from the world?

My eyes land on the soft pink blanket and the scatter cushions on my couch. My chest tightens to the point it's hard to breathe.

She's changed her mind.

After everything we've been through together recently.

My stomach knots as a mixture of concern, shock, and anger battles within me.

"Bro, you coming?" Miles asks.

The side of my face burns as he stares at me while I pointlessly look at the couch.

But as much as I want to respond, I can't. I can't find any words.

He moves back into the room as images of the two of us curled up right there play out in my mind.

"KC?"

"S-sorry, I-I'm coming." I turn to face him but find him even closer than I had expected.

"You like her, don't you?"

"W-what?" I ask, my head spinning.

His eyes hold mine as he rolls his lips between his teeth. He's battling with what he wants to say, but as much as I want to demand he spits it out, I'm also terrified of having to answer him honestly.

"Tatum. You like her."

"I mean, yeah. She's cool. Less annoying now she's grown up," I hedge.

"Kingston," he warns.

"Fuck. Miles. What do you want me to say here?"

"That you care," he fires back.

"Of course I fucking care. She's Tatum. Your little sister."

"So you're telling me that you look this wrecked," he says, waving his hand in front of my face to highlight whatever it is he's witnessing right now, "because she's my little sister. You've always been a really shitty liar, KC. How about you man the fuck up and tell me the truth."

My mouth opens and closes as I try to find some words that will pacify him. But I fear that the only ones that will work aren't ones I'm willing to admit to myself yet, let alone out loud to Tatum's brother.

"Miles," I finally sigh.

"No. I'm not playing this fucking game, King. You want her, you feel something for her, then you fucking own it. Tate deserves to have a man who's willing to fight for her, not a pussy who isn't strong enough to own his feelings for her."

I stare dumbstruck at my best friend, unable to form words as I consider the possibility that there was some kind of admission within his statement that he's okay with this thing between me and Tatum as long as I own it.

But can I?

Have I fallen for her?

Fuck. Why am I even asking myself that question?

I know the fucking answer. I have for a while.

Miles is right. I'm just too much of a pussy to admit it.

Reaching up, I rub the back of my neck, the words I need to say getting stuck in my throat.

Looking up again, I find his eyes. I never realized how similar they are to Tatum's until recently. They're just a shade darker.

Swallowing down my apprehension, I hold his stare and confess the truth.

"I've fallen for her."

I've no idea what I expected him to do. Punch me again, I guess. But smiling is not where my imagination went.

"What?" I snap, still bracing myself for the hit that should have followed my statement.

His smile grows.

"You're a fucking idiot. Come on," he says, grabbing my upper arm and dragging me across the room.

I let him lead, but only because I'm so fucking confused.

"Let's go and get your girl."

With my heart in my throat, I take back control of my legs and walk out of the apartment with the intention of ripping the entire city apart until we find her.

Miles is right; she can't have gone far. Not that halfway across the world would be too far for me to find her.

She has to know that, too.

She's significantly underestimated me if she thinks I'm going to take this lying down. If she thinks her leaving isn't going to affect every single thing about my life.

You fucked up here, Tatum Callahan.

And the second I find you, I have every intention of showing you just how much of a brat you've been this time.

T he sound of Miles's fist raining down on Tatum and Lorelei's front door echoes down the silent hallway of their building.

"Tate, open up. It's just me," he lies. "Shit," he curses when nothing but silence greets his most recent demand.

"You do know she has a peephole and that she'll be able to see that you're lying if she's looking through it," I point out like an asshole.

"Do you have a fucking better idea?" he snaps, clearly losing patience fast with his little sister's antics.

We should be working. We should be continuing with safeguarding all our futures, but no, we're chasing my little brat.

"Actually, I do," I state, reaching into my pocket and pulling out a set of keys. One of which unlocks Tatum's front door.

Selecting it, I push it into the lock.

Miles's chin drops. "She gave you a key?"

"Something like that," I mutter as I throw the door open and march inside.

"Tatum," I call, my voice hard and demanding.

This time, there is a reply, although it's not the soft, seductive sound of my wife's voice.

It's an angry hiss.

I march into the living area to find the cat standing guard in the middle of the kitchen island with her hackles up and her teeth bared.

"Hi, Fluffpuff, good to see you too."

At my voice, her hissing gets louder and more violent. Her entire body tenses as if she's about to launch herself at me and claw my eyes out.

"Ah, Grizzy, is Kingston being mean?" Miles sings, ignoring the feral look in its eyes and lifting her into his arms.

And she lets him.

What the actual fuck?

"Grizzy?" I ask.

"Hell, yeah. We go way back, don't we?" he asks the fucking cat while tickling behind her ear and making her purr like a sweet little kitten.

"Right. That's just fucking great. Could you ask her where the fuck my wife is, please?"

"She's a cat, KC."

I shrug before taking off in the hope of finding some kind of clue in her bedroom.

I come to a stop in the doorway, immediately struck with not only her sweet scent but with memories of the night I brought her back here after we signed the contract in Jonathan's office.

She was so fucking wasted, she had no idea I'd even picked her up, let alone carried her out of Maxies and got her ready for bed.

The prospect of being married to me drove her to that.

The only way to come was to get fucking wasted.

I might have had her stuff moved to my place, but the room is still full of things and also still looks like a tornado has torn through it. But then, I guess that's just Tatum. It's exactly what she's done to my life. Torn through it, caused chaos, and ensured that it'll never be the same again.

I step farther into the room, my images morphing to those of the next morning when I found her hungover and regretting her life choices. The morning I had my first introduction to her delightful pussy...

I shake my head, searching the counters for something of use.

It's not until I find a pinboard on the wall full of old photographs that I come to a stop.

Miles's footsteps thump down the hallway as I stare at an image of the two of them as children. They're in the most incredibly colorful garden.

My stomach knots and my heart seizes.

"Have you found anything?"

"Yeah," I mutter. "I think I know exactly where she is."

71

TATUM

I wrap my jacket tighter around myself as I walk down the quiet country road.

The weather here isn't all that different from what we encounter in Chicago, or at least that's been my experience over the years. But right now, there is none of the spring warmth I left behind and nothing but a winter chill that makes me want to hibernate in front of the log-burning fire I've got in the rental I managed to secure at the last minute.

But glutton for punishment, no sooner had I dropped my case in the bedroom, I headed back out to come here.

I knew it would hurt, but then everything about what I'm doing right now does.

Stepping into the airport, and then onto the plane was akin to ripping my own heart straight from my chest.

But at the same time, I know I'm doing the right thing.

The right thing for me and...

I press my trembling hand to my stomach, my breathing getting erratic again as I think about my reality.

By leaving, I've sealed my fate.

It's funny, because I thought I did that the day I signed the contract agreeing to be Kingston's wife for a year in my father's office.

I thought that was the thing that would change the trajectory of my life. Well, I guess it has. I can guarantee that I wouldn't be standing here now, dealing with what I am, if it weren't for that moment.

If it weren't for Kingston.

My chest tightens as if someone is wrapping rope around it. It's been the same since the moment I looked at that notification on my watch yesterday.

Fuck. How was that only yesterday?

Being in Chicago already feels like a lifetime ago.

On unsteady legs, I walk around the corner.

I know what is about to greet me, and while I made the decision to do this, to be here, to see this, now it's about to happen, I don't think I'm ready.

How can you be when you know it's goodbye?

I close my eyes before taking the last step around the corner, and when I open them again, there it is.

The little cottage that means so much to me.

All the air rushes from my lungs and tears burn the backs of my eyes as all the memories I have of this place come rushing back.

I continue forward, my legs weaker than ever.

The front yard is overgrown, the roses that grow up the trellis by the front door uncared for, the bushes out of shape and unloved.

Even the bright red front door is faded and chipped. It's a far cry from the house of my memories. But while it might be tired, it still has the same heart. I can feel it from here. The magic still exists inside those old, thick, uneven walls.

I continue forward toward the small play park on the other side of the road and take a seat on the bench.

Miles and I used to spend hours over here as kids. Even long after we outgrew it, we'd just sit under the slide and chat about nothing, play games, do all the kinds of things kids do to pass the time. Time that they think moves so slowly.

Why is it that as kids, all we want to do is grow up, but the second we do, all we want is to return to the carefree lives we used to have as children?

Life is cruel. It's the only explanation.

It's the only reason I've got for why I'm sitting here right now in so much pain.

Not only did I walk away from my husband and the new life we were building together—albeit fake—when I decided to come, but I've also given all of this away.

It's why I needed to come.

I needed to say goodbye.

From the moment I discovered Dad hadn't done as he promised and left this place to me in his will—or at least he didn't without a million caveats—deep down, I knew my dream was over.

Sure, I agreed to his stupid plan with the hope that I might still get it. But I knew then that it would fail. That ultimately, I'd end up without anything.

And honestly, it's fine. I don't need anything from him.

This cottage, it was a dream.

But I don't need a man to create the dream life I crave.

I don't need a man for anything.

Unease flutters inside me.

Kingston sure made things...more bearable, though.

I thought living with him, getting closer to him, getting to know him better was going to be torture.

How wrong was I?

Sure, we've fought. We've butted heads and have some varied differences of opinions, but also...we've kinda just worked.

Fighting with him was fun. Tormenting him and waiting for him to crack was even better. But none of it was as good as when we collided.

Fuck. Together we were electric.

I've never felt like that with anyone else before.

Just one innocent touch turned my entire body to mush. It was as if he held a secret button that I never knew existed, and the second he pushed it, I just melted for him.

Ripping my eyes from the cottage, I stare down at the rings on my finger.

I told myself that I'd take them off once I settled in my seat on the plane.

But I couldn't do it.

I convinced myself that it was because I was still on American soil. That it would be easier once I landed on the other side of the pond. That everything would be different the moment I touched down in England.

But nothing changed.

The pain, the heartache, the confusion, the fear. All of it is still there.

And now that I'm here, in the village I love so much, looking at the cottage I adore, it's even stronger than ever.

The bitter wind whips around me again and I shiver violently, my thin jacket doing little to protect me from the elements.

Unable to sit here any longer, I push to my feet and turn back on myself, walking away from the cottage with my heart in my throat.

I return to my rental with grocery bags hanging from my fingers. I should have called a car to take me to a bigger store to get everything I need, but I don't have the energy for that. It'll also have to involve talking to someone and the less I do that, the better.

I've got what I need for now, and I figure I'll order more for delivery. That way, I can stay locked up inside in the hope of figuring my shit out.

A bitter laugh spills from my lips.

Is it even possible to sort my shit out at this point?

Everything seems impossible.

I know running wasn't the most mature way to deal with all this, but I knew that I'd never be able to think in Chicago.

Sure, I could have stayed in the country and locked myself away somewhere a little more local.

But I don't want to be local. I want to put as many miles between me and all my mistakes as possible.

I hang my head as I dump the bags on the kitchen counter.

Was it all a mistake?

My head spins and my body aches with exhaustion.

I'm six hours behind London time, and I feel it all the way to the tips of my toes.

I consider my options from my recent purchases, all very unhealthy and refined carbs that would give Kingston a coronary, but it's what I need right now.

Unable to wait for the oven to heat up for the pasta carbonara, I instead place it in the fridge and grab the massive bag of chips I bought.

With the huge bag and a bottle of water tucked under my arm, I abandon everything else in search of the bathtub I saw on the rental listing for this place.

There wasn't a lot of choice at the last minute, but the second I saw this property, I knew it was waiting for me.

It might not be Aunt Lena's cottage, but it's close. It's cute, quaint, and so very English.

The ancient staircase creaks as I climb toward the second floor, and I can't help the small smile that appears on my lips. Everything about this place is a world away from my life in Chicago. I think that's why I love it so much. Here, nothing matters. No one cares what my surname is, who my parents are, who I work for, or...a shudder rips down my spine as I lower my goodies to the small vanity in the bathroom...who my husband is.

My stomach twists painfully as I think of the man who's become my everything these past few weeks.

Every single thing about him was unexpected, but almost all of it in a good way.

My breathing becomes ragged as I think about his reaction to discovering me gone.

I want to say that he's bothered, angry even. But there is a part of me, a really fucking terrified part that doesn't think he'll care.

That the feelings I've been growing over the past few weeks have been totally one-sided.

That I'm the naive little woman who caught feelings for the man she was never meant to have.

It was a business arrangement, and I have more than enough experience with how men like Kingston Callahan operate. They will not relent until they close the deal.

Ripping my eyes from the sad and broken reflection of myself staring back at me in the mirror, I turn the bath on and pour some of the bubbles from the side into the running water.

The sweet scent of lavender and chamomile floats into the air, and immediately it makes my stomach roll.

It's not his scent.

As quickly as I can, I turn the faucets off and drain the water, watching the bubbles go with it.

My hands tremble as I lean on the edge of the tub, memories of the baths we shared at the cabin coming back to me before my eyes find my rings again.

Before I know what I'm doing, I've shuffled across the tiled floor and I'm heaving into the toilet, attempting to purge the pain from my body.

But it doesn't work. When I fall back on my ass, sweaty and weak, it's worse than ever.

How is it possible to miss someone you were never meant to have?

But it's not just Kingston I've left behind without warning.

It's Miles. My team. Every single person in my life apart from Lori.

The need to call Lori and let her know that I arrived safely, to hear her tell me that I've done the right thing burns through me. But I don't. I can't.

She doesn't know the whole truth. No one does.

No one but me knows just how serious this whole situation has become.

I wanted to tell her, but she was at work when I called to give her the heads-up and asked if she'd be willing to take care of Griz for me while I sort my shit out. I didn't feel like I could drop a bomb that big on her over the phone. It was already bad enough that I was telling her that I was leaving and that she'd have no way of contacting me.

About thirty seconds after making my decision to book a flight and flee, I also decided that my cell would be turned off the second we took off and it wouldn't be coming back on again.

The temptation to buy another with a new number just so I can be in touch with Lori is strong. But I know how hard it would be to lie to Kingston and Miles when they come for her. And they will, I've no doubt of that fact.

They know that she'll be the one to discover my whereabouts, and they won't relent until they're confident she's handed over every bit of information she has.

So, if she doesn't know anything, she can't hide anything.

It'll make it easier in the long run. For her, anyway.

What would have been easier for me would be rocking up at her office with her suitcase already packed in the trunk of the Uber and dragging her with me. But that also wasn't an option, so here I am: alone and terrified on the bathroom floor.

72

KINGSTON

"I hate to say it, but you're not going to reel her in like this. You aren't going to be able to change her thoughts and feelings about her place here overnight. It's going to take time. Possibly a lot of it.

"You need to let her go."

I swallow thickly as my own words play on repeat in my head as I lie in bed, staring at the ceiling.

It's the middle of the night, but just like every other night this week, sleep won't find me.

It doesn't matter what I do, how hard I work myself at the office or in the gym, or how much I distract myself with thinking about everything in my life but her, I still can't sleep. My head still spins and my chest still aches.

I fucking hate it.

But not as much as I hate the fact I can't do anything about it.

I mean, yeah. There is plenty I could be fucking doing right now. I could be on a fucking Red Eye to London to chase her down and bring her back.

I could have done it already. I could be with her right fucking now with her wrapped in my arms. Hell, I could have dragged her back already.

But as much of a relief it would be, it would also be the wrong thing to do.

Those words I said to Miles not so long ago continue to cycle around in my head.

I was right. I knew that when I said them, and I still know it now.

It's why she's gone.

She's not ready.

She may never be ready...

All she's ever done is dream about leaving this place and starting over in England. She doesn't want a life here; she doesn't want to be a part of the Warner legacy that those who've come before her have worked so hard for.

I admire her for it. There are so many children of successful parents who accept their place in the family just for the fame and wealth. I respect the hell out of the fact that she wants to be her own person, follow her own path, and carve out her own life.

But I also can't help feeling like it's a pipe dream. Something that she thinks she wants, despite the fact that her destiny has been, and will always be, here.

With me...

I blow out a slow, pained breath.

It's not just my chest that feels like it's gone a few brutal rounds with Tyson Fury, but my eyes too. They're dry, scratchy, exhausted.

I need sleep, but I fear that nothing short of medication is going to get me there at this point.

Miles is suffering too, but for as concerned as he might be about his sister, it's not the same as how I'm feeling.

He might be feeling like he's lost his right arm, but I feel like I've had my entire world ripped away.

It's ridiculous. Only a few months ago, Tatum didn't feature in my life all that much.

We drove each other to the brink of insanity whenever we were forced to spend time together, but those moments were becoming less and less frequent as we got older.

But now, she's the only thing I can think about.

Miles thinks he understands, but he doesn't. He can't.

Neither can Kian.

The only person I fear might just look into my eyes and appreciate exactly how I'm feeling is a man I've been avoiding like the fucking plague.

My father.

Am I being a pussy by avoiding his calls and canceling the meetings he keeps putting in my calendar? Yep, abso-fucking-lutely.

But I also know exactly what he's going to say. And I don't want to fucking hear it.

I may not have been privy to the conversations our fathers had about our union, but I know for a fact that my father wouldn't have gone into it expecting me to fall for her.

He's always taught us to go into relationships with our heads, not our hearts.

I understand where his advice comes from. The one time he let his heart lead, it ended up shredded and broken.

Our father hasn't loved since.

Every acquaintance and new stepmother we've been introduced to has been a decision based on his head. Someone who's looked good on his arm, opened up opportunities, and as much as I hate to consider it, probably good in bed, too.

That's what he expected from me and Tatum in this arranged marriage.

He wanted me to keep my head and secure us Warner Group, to ensure we could continue with our substantial growth.

It was a good plan. A really fucking good plan. One I wish I was smart enough to see coming. But I have to admit that I was just as blindsided by the suggestion when Dad brought it to me as Tatum was the day of the will reading.

But I also couldn't have predicted these past few weeks. Nor would I have wanted to.

They've been incredible—I guess everything an arranged

marriage should be—up until Tuesday, when she decided that her inheritance wasn't worth having to endure me.

Pain slices through my chest.

I don't want to believe it.

Tatum Warner isn't the kind of woman who runs from anything. She rolls her shoulders back, holds her head high and stares the problem dead in the eyes.

I've seen her do it time and time again. Mostly because I've been the one she's glaring at.

Unable to stay here lying to myself that sleep will come, I roll out of bed, my body aching like I've never experienced before. Sure, I'd had some serious gym sessions over the years, and there was a time that Kieran wasn't the only one running around on a football field, but I've never, ever felt this fucking broken.

I don't get it. How can one person have such an effect on your life that it physically makes your muscles ache?

I'm starting to understand Dad a little more. I always thought he was a cold, closed-off asshole for the way he treated women. But I get it.

Tatum and I barely had any time together and yet this is the result. How the fuck must it feel after years of marriage and three kids together?

Fuck. It doesn't even bear thinking about.

No wonder he turned his focus to business and fucking women who'd never claim his heart.

Self-preservation at its finest.

It's no way to fucking live your life, though. Constantly scared of being hurt.

I shake my head as I step into the shower, turning it on and letting myself get blasted by cold water.

It's certainly not the fucking life I want to live, that's for sure.

I told myself—and Miles—that I'd give Tatum two weeks, two long-ass fucking weeks, before I did anything.

At the time, it seemed like a good fucking idea.

I was sober and listening to my own advice about her needing time to process. I was trying to be a decent fucking human being and not sweep in and turn her world upside down all over again with my demands.

The second I said the words, I regretted them, and I've questioned my sanity a million times since.

I'm right, though, I know I am.

Doesn't fucking help much when she's the only thing I can think about.

———

With the sun barely peeking above the horizon, I pull my car into the underground parking lot beneath Callahan Enterprises.

I haven't been here since Miles and I began putting our plan into action with Warner Group, and it's not until I step out of the elevator on the silent top floor of the building and breathe in the familiar scent that I realize how much I've missed it.

This place has been my home for almost as long as I can remember.

As a teenager, it didn't matter where we lived, or what school I attended, or what woman Dad was fucking; it was this place where I felt most at home. Apparently, not a lot has changed.

Our assistant's desk sits empty, as I imagine almost every other one in the building does at this time of the morning.

It's peaceful, and I'm not sure if that's exactly what I need or if coming here is the worst decision I've made since giving Tatum time.

Probably the latter.

The windows around my office are dark, not allowing anyone to see inside. It makes me wonder how much my presence has been missed. Up until recently, I spent more time in this office, in this building, than I did in my apartment.

Has anyone other than Kian and my assistant noticed?

I walk into my office, and feel immediately as if nothing has changed. I embrace that moment and try to cling onto it for dear life, but as the seconds tick on, reality returns just as potently and as painfully as before.

I'm doing the right thing.

Grabbing a bottle of water, I fall into the chair that sits behind my desk and power up my computer as the sun begins to turn the city beyond a warm orange.

I've always appreciated the view, but for some reason, today it fully steals my attention and I find myself completely lost in it, as thoughts of what my future might look like once the dust has settled on all of this, play out in my mind. A lot of the images are fuzzy, but one thing is very clear. And that is her.

My wife.

My heart pounds harder as the decision I made days ago only gets stronger in my mind.

I'm going to get her back. And I'm going to do anything and everything in my power to make it happen.

If I only learn one thing from this whole ordeal, it's that Tatum Warner is made for me.

Finally ripping my eyes away, I log into my computer and pull up my emails, cringing at the number of unread ones in my inbox.

I scroll to the bottom and begin working my way up.

The hours pass painfully slowly as I make progress, but at least they pass, moving closer to the deadline I've given myself.

"Well, well, well, look who we have here," Kian taunts when he emerges once the sun has fully risen and the city has come to life before me.

"Fuck off," I grunt, although it does very little to deter him.

"I thought you'd forgotten how to get here," he teases before dropping into one of the seats on the other side of my desk with a smug smirk playing on his lips and a coffee in his hand. The scent of it turns my stomach and makes my fists clench.

It reminds me of her.

"Did you need to bring that in here?"

Kian rolls his eyes. "Seriously, who made you the fucking coffee police? Some of us are normal and need a morning boost."

I glare at him, but he just returns it with his own.

"So what's the latest then?"

I shake my head. "Nothing new."

"Yeah," he muses, "I can see you're still a miserable fucker. She's really done a number on you, huh?"

"Is this fucking necessary?" I bark.

"Looking at your face and those massive fucking bags under your eyes, I'd say yes. Just fucking go to her, man. You know exactly where she is."

My teeth grind in irritation.

Yes. I do know exactly where she is. It took a few days, but Aubrey tracked her down to a rental in the same village her Aunt Lena's cottage is in. Hardly a surprise.

I also know that she's rented it for a month. A fucking month.

I've no idea what she's planning on doing with her time there. Or if she's planning on extending it.

One thing I do suspect is that she's not anticipating that I know every single one of her movements.

She hasn't put her cell on since leaving the country, probably because she thinks I'll track her through it. Which of course, I would. But that's not the only way to find someone, especially when they don't have the first clue about how to hide.

"I can't," I mutter, irritated that I need to go through this again.

"Yeah, so you keep saying, but I still don't fucking get it. You love her, she loves you. Just go and fucking prove it. You're being a pussy, if you ask me."

"I'm being a fucking grown-up. Chasing her isn't—" I cut myself off, fed up with repeating myself. "Haven't you got any fucking work to do?"

Rolling his eyes at me again in a way that only a spoiled middle child can, he pushes to his feet and marches toward the door.

"We've got a conference call in an hour. Can I suggest you remember how to smile, please?"

The sight of his abandoned takeout coffee cup still sitting on my desk catches my eye and before I know what I'm doing, I'm launching it across the room at him. The lid comes off mid-flight and the remnants cover his light grey suit and white shirt.

"You fucking asshole," he seethes.

"Fuck off and do some work," I say before turning my back on him and focusing on my computer again.

I guess misery does love company, and all that.

73

KINGSTON

I sit staring at the images on the screen before me, but I don't see any of them.

I know Dad is there, and Kian, but I don't dare look directly at them. They'll see everything I don't want them to. It's too late for Kian—he saw it all this morning. He can still probably smell the scent of coffee to remind him that he needs to keep his mouth shut in the future.

But I can't let Dad see. I can't allow him to know that I'm crumbling because of a woman.

Their voices float around me, a blur of different accents from both across the states and the world. But I don't know what they're talking about. I managed to focus for about twenty minutes, but it's been the better part of an hour since then and they're still making plans and looking toward the future.

It's a weird dynamic, being a part of one company that's desperately trying to survive while another flourishes.

We've got resorts in all stages of building and renovations across the globe, and we're making new acquisitions all the time. It's certainly a change of pace being back here after focusing my efforts on Warner Group.

All I can hope is that in the not-too-distant future, Warner

Group conference calls sound a little more like this one. Or at least what I assume this once sounds like, seeing as I've fully checked out.

We're not always going to be making hard decisions and laying people off. Get over this hump and I've got every confidence that we'll be growing faster than we can cope with, expanding our team and hopefully our profits right alongside it.

My vision is clear, so is Miles's, but while we might have a lot of work ahead of us to achieve our goals, there is one very obvious thing missing. Or should I say one person?

I shake my head, trying to clear images of her sitting in an office on the top floor of the Warner Group in her sexy pencil skirts and teasing blouses.

Fuck. We could have some fun up there with the windows darkened and—

"Kingston. Have we lost you?" Dad says, his voice as hard and as unforgiving as it always is in meetings.

Dragging myself from the haze of my imagination, I make the fatal mistake of looking at him.

His head might only be an inch or so big on my screen, but it's enough to see the shock on his face when he finally gets a proper look at me.

Fuck.

All the air comes rushing out of my lungs and I deflate in my seat.

I feel like a little boy who's just been caught snooping around in his office when I've been clearly told to stay the fuck away and to mind my own business.

"Sorry, what were you saying?" I ask, praying my voice sounds less broken than I feel.

"We need an update on your project."

My heart sinks. I've got numerous emails sitting in my inbox with questions and queries about the renovation at the retreat, but the subject line alone stopped me from opening them.

How can I when all I see when I think about that place is her?

"Everything is on track," I lie, hopefully confidently.

"Everything?" Dad asks as if he knows differently—which he shouldn't, because he's refused to get involved with it. He's sticking to his guns about it being a bad decision, and honestly, I'm glad because it gives me free rein, and when I'm proved right, it'll feel so fucking good.

"Yes. I have a few minor things outstanding but we're hitting deadlines, and progress is good."

Thankfully, the conversation moves on to something else, something that captures Dad's attention more than my retreat, and I'm able to let my mind drift again.

I hate it. I hate not being focused and fully involved in my job, but there isn't anything I can do about it.

A knock on my door drags me from my thoughts once more, and when I spin around to look, I find Melissa poking her head into the room with an apologetic expression on her face.

'I'm sorry,' she mouths before holding out a manilla envelope.

Pushing from my chair, I reach for it and turn it over.

"Thank you," I say quietly before looking down at my name and address written in beautiful script.

I'm about to throw it onto my desk and return to pretending that I'm listening, but something makes me second-guess that decision.

So, with everyone still chatting on my screen, I tuck my finger under the flap and pry it open.

It takes me a second to register the logo on the paper I pull out, but the second reality hits, the entire world falls from beneath me.

I drop the envelope on the desk and push to my feet, moving away from it as if it physically burned me.

"Kingston? Is everything okay?" Dad asks, although he sounds like he's in a tunnel and getting farther away with every word.

The room spins as I stare down at the paperwork.

She's...

She's divorcing me.

My heart races as disbelief floods through my system.

She was meant to be having some time, some space to figure everything out.

She's not meant to be serving me fucking divorce papers.

"Kingston?"

I'm unaware of each of the screens going black. I don't even register that my knees buckle and I fall back into my chair.

She's divorcing me.

That means...she's sacrificing everything.

I've no idea how much time passes as I sit there staring at the paperwork. It could be mere seconds, or it could be hours.

My office door opening barely cracks through my daze, and a large hand landing on my shoulder scares the living shit out of me.

"Fuck. Dad," I gasp, turning to find his assessing eyes focused harshly on me. "You scared the shit out of me."

"Hmm," he rumbles, ripping his eyes from mine and glancing at the paperwork on my desk.

He doesn't react to it, not that I expected him to. He's got what he wanted out of this arrangement. The only person who is losing anything here is Tatum.

If I sign this, then everything she's ever wanted is going to be taken away from her.

She's going to be taken away from me.

I suck in a ragged breath, unable to properly process what all this means.

Tatum isn't the only one losing here. I feel like everything I've ever cared about is slipping through my fingers like grains of sand.

I watch as he walks around my desk and lowers himself into the same chair that Kian was sitting in earlier. And then he just watches me. I'm not saying a word, but I'm pretty sure he can read my thoughts well enough to know exactly what's going on.

"I'm not the enemy here, Kingston. You can talk to me about this."

Can I?

Isn't he just going to tell me that I'm better off without her, that I've been stupid to let her in and give her even a chance at being able to break my heart?

"Dad, I—"

"Love her," he finishes for me.

"Fuck, that's not—"

"Kingston, lying to yourself isn't going to help right now," he warns, leaning forward and resting his elbows on his knees, his eyes focused on mine.

I slump lower.

"This wasn't how all of this was meant to go," I mutter as I scrub my hand over my rough jaw.

"No," Dad agrees helpfully. "But sometimes, you've just got to embrace these things."

My brows pinch together in a mix of confusion and shock.

"What?"

He smiles at me and shakes his head.

"Why aren't you telling me that I fucked up? That I did exactly what I shouldn't have done and lost focus on business because of it?"

He shrugs one shoulder but doesn't say anything for long seconds, which only makes my head spin faster.

"King," he finally says before gritting his teeth and lowering his gaze for a beat, composing himself. "I know I haven't exactly been the best role model when it comes to women and relationships, but—"

I scoff, thinking of the many, many women who have come in and out of our lives over the years.

"And I know I've told you that you shouldn't fall in love, that it only ends in pain but—"

"But?" I balk, laughing, although it's edged with bitterness. All our lives he's been adamant that we never fall in love.

"King, I loved your mother," he says, his eyes getting glassy as he thinks of her. "I loved her so much. I'm not saying that I was the perfect husband. I'm aware that I was far from that. But what she did, fuck. It still hurts to this day.

"But if I'm being honest, even if I knew how it was all going to end, I wouldn't have had it any other way. My years with her, you three...I could never, ever regret that."

"But you—"

"I know, King. I know. But you and Tatum." He sighs, shaking his head. "The way you look at her. It's so fucking familiar it hurts, King.

"But what kind of father would I be if I tried to convince you to walk away from something that puts that look in your eyes?"

A lump crawls up my throat. I try to swallow it down, but I stand no chance.

I've never had this kind of conversation with my father before. I'm not sure how to take it.

"Tatum's a good girl, King. You could do a hell of a lot worse than her."

My mouth opens and closes as I try to come up with some kind of answer.

"She wants a divorce," I blurt, my mouth saying the words before my head realizes I've made a decision.

"And are you going to give it to her?" he asks simply, raising a brow in question. "Or are you going to fight for what you really want?"

74

TATUM

I sit in the window of the cafe, staring out at the locals and tourists alike wandering around the village center.

I find the place just as magical as I did as a kid. I swear, people are just happier here. They don't walk around with what looks like the weight of the world on their shoulders. Instead, they have their heads up and their eyes wide, taking in the beauty that is around them.

It might still only be spring, but as always, the grass is greener, the flowers are prettier, and the fluffy white clouds in the blue sky are cuter. Okay, yeah, it's still cold as fuck outside, but it's so beautiful, it's easy to forget. And really, there is nothing better than curling up in front of the fire.

Being in his arms is better.

I banish that thought as soon as it hits.

I want to say that it's getting easier to forget about him, about home, but it's not. With every day that passes, I find myself questioning my decision more and more.

But then I remember that he's not here.

It's been over a week since I secretly boarded a plane and hopped across the pond. A week since I've seen him, since I've spoken to him—or anyone, actually. I'd be stupid to believe it's because he doesn't know where I am.

It wouldn't take a genius to figure out that the first place I'd come to was here. Sure, he wouldn't know what house I'm staying in seeing as I don't have access to Aunt Lena's place, but there are only so many places I can hide in this small village.

But as far as I know, he hasn't even tried to find me.

It's been three days since he was served the divorce papers I'd demanded Richard expedite so that I could close this chapter of my life sooner rather than later.

Richard hasn't heard anything, as far as I'm aware. I haven't heard anything—not that I've turned my cell on, of course. But I've been on my emails, and there has been nothing from him.

Lori has emailed me every day letting me know that she's thinking of me and she misses me. She keeps sending me images of Griz and letting me know what my girl has been up to. It makes me smile as much as it makes my heart ache.

I miss them. Miles too. He's reached out more than once, begging for me to respond, even if it's just to let him know that I'm okay.

But I can't. Not yet. I'm not ready to hear whatever it is he might have to say about my resignation. About the choices I've made by walking away from everything.

Lifting my pastry to my lips, I take another bite. It's flaky and perfect, but I barely taste it.

Everything has been the same the past few days. I may as well be eating cardboard.

I've no idea if it's a symptom that I'm going to have to put up with for a few months, or if it's just the result the past week has had on my exhausted body.

Some nights I manage to get some sleep; others I just toss and turn, my head spinning a million miles a minute as I freak out over my future.

I don't need to; I have nothing to freak out about.

I might have kissed goodbye to my trust fund and our apartment, but I have enough saved that we'll be okay.

I'm going to be able to give this baby everything it needs and keep a roof over our heads. Plus, there are a million other jobs in the world. I don't have to work for a fancy marketing department in the city. Hell, I'll deliver freaking papers if it helps pay my way. I'm not fussy. All I want is a life that is my own. One that I get to choose, not one that is dictated by a man.

My man...

Kingston's smiling face as he looms over me in bed, his hair falling into his face and his jaw rough with stubble fills my mind as grief wraps around my chest.

Over the past few days, I've told myself that I'm struggling to let go of everything I thought we had because I never got to properly say goodbye.

I'm pretty sure it's bullshit, but I'm telling myself it regardless.

The truth is, I fell harder than I even thought, and walking away from him, from the life we were building together, has ripped my heart in two.

I was never meant to fall for him. I hated him, for fuck's sake.

But I couldn't help it. Every look, every touch, every whispered dirty word and I lost a little more of my heart to him. Pieces that I don't think I'm ever going to get back.

I've never been in love before. I didn't know what to expect. But I also can't say that I'm surprised that losing it hurts this much. I've listened to enough Taylor Swift songs to understand that it's like a baseball bat to the chest, time and time again.

Dropping the rest of my pastry to the plate, I shove it away, unable to eat any more.

Reaching for my tea—yes, my tea—I take a sip, hoping it'll taste like something.

Nope.

I push that away as well, focusing on the people outside again in the hope of being distracted from my pain.

What did I really expect? That I'd serve him divorce papers and that he'd drop everything and come running?

Yeah, maybe a stupid, fickle part of me hoped that he would.

I may or may not have daydreamed about the doorbell on my rental ringing and him standing on the other side of the door, ready to confess his undying love for me.

A bitter laugh spills from my lips as I think about it.

It's never going to happen. He's more concerned about taking over Warner Group and growing his empire than he is with having me in his life. I was just an easy lay. That's probably the only reason he's realized that I've gone.

My stomach knots at the thought of that being true.

I don't want it to be. I want to believe that something was building between us. But it's easier to try and convince myself that it was all one-sided. It's the only way I stand a chance of getting over it. Getting over him.

Without thought, my hand shifts to my stomach, pressing gently.

I'm never going to be able to get over him. Not since he left a piece of himself with me.

Guilt twists up my insides. I've known for a week. That's a long time in pregnancy terms. He deserves to know what our short time together has resulted in. But the thought of talking to him, of telling him about it terrifies me.

A wave of nausea washes through me and I bite down on the inside of my lip, as if that'll help.

It's just ebbing away when someone outside the cafe's window catches my eye.

Aubrey?

I narrow my eyes and push to my feet.

Before I know it, I've abandoned the little table I've wasted the morning sitting at and I'm out on the street, the cool breeze whipping around me, sending a shiver racing down my spine.

The sidewalk is crowded and I'm forced to stretch up on my tiptoes to try and see.

Darting around all the people, I race in the direction I thought she was going, searching like a mad woman.

But I never find her.

When I get to the end of the main street, I turn around and

scan the village center with a weird sense of unease prickling my skin.

I was so sure that was her. Maybe the lack of sleep and hormones are getting to me.

Deciding that it was nothing more than me losing my mind, I tug my purse up higher on my shoulder and keep walking. I'm halfway toward Aunt Lena's cottage already, so I may as well continue.

I'm only torturing myself by walking past it every day, but I can't help it. Just like always, the draw I feel toward it is magnetic.

I guess I'm just craving a time when life was easier and simpler. When the only thing I had to worry about was what candy Miles and I were going to get on our daily trip to the store and what games we were going to play.

Sounds like the perfect life.

A melancholy sigh passes my lips as I turn the final corner.

Just like every other time I've visited, I think I'm prepared for the emotions to bubble up at the thought of never going inside again, but nothing could have prepared me for what I find.

A sold sign.

All the air rushes from my lungs as if someone just took a bat to my chest.

"No," I cry, wrapping my arms around myself as if they'll hold me together.

I didn't even realize it was up for sale.

My vision blurs and tears fill my eyes before spilling free and cascading down my cheeks.

I stumble forward, sniffling like a fool.

I can't help it.

It's over.

I thought I was okay with him receiving the divorce papers. I thought I had made the right decision and that letting go couldn't be any harder than walking away from Kingston last week.

But I underestimated just how painful it would be to know that he agrees with me. That he doesn't want me.

Maybe he never did.

Maybe it was all an act.

My sobs get louder, and I stand there in the middle of the sidewalk, staring at the house that holds so many of my favorite memories as well as my dreams for the future.

But it's over. It's gone.

The cottage I always hoped that would one day be mine is going to belong to someone else, maybe a family.

My breathing is ragged as I try to be happy for whoever has purchased it.

One thing is for sure, they're going to be so, so happy in that home.

By the time I get back to my rental, the sun is setting, the air is bitterly cold, and my eyes are raw from crying.

It's just a house.

Bricks and mortar.

But it doesn't matter how many times I tell myself that, it feels like so much more.

Dumping my purse on the side table in the small hallway, I march straight past the compact kitchen and climb the stairs on exhausted legs.

I strip down to my t-shirt and panties and then crawl straight into bed.

Shivers rack my body and I curl into the tightest ball I can. The second I pull the covers over my head, plunging myself into darkness, I succumb to the devastation.

My sobs are loud, angry, and unstoppable, but I don't try to stop them.

I need to let it all out. The pain, the fear, the loss.

These past few weeks, from the moment I got the call from Miles to tell me that Dad had died, have been exhausting.

I had no idea that I was holding everything together with a shoestring, but now that it's snapped, I understand just how fragile my life has become. I was holding onto Kingston in the hope of him keeping me in one piece. But that was never his responsibility.

The only person who can help me deal with all of this is me.

And I need to start trying to figure out how to do that so that I can plan my future—our future. It's not just me I have to worry about now.

My hand moves to my abdomen and another loud sob erupts from my throat.

"Everything is going to be okay," I whisper into the silence. "We're going to be okay." But even as the words leave my lips, knowing that we're going to have to do it alone...I don't believe them. And the last thing I want is to be the kind of parent who lets their child down before they're even here.

75

TATUM

Time is meant to be a healer but as the days pass, the pain never recedes. In fact, it only gets worse. So does my guilt over keeping this secret. It grows and grows inside me and my concern over the fact I've done nothing but a pregnancy test to this point is building.

I thought time out here would help clear my head, but so far, I haven't felt anything close to clarity.

Everything is just as big a mess as it was when I left Chicago, only now, I'm alone.

A couple of days ago, I finally replied to one of Lori's emails. I couldn't take it anymore; I needed to talk to someone.

After a few emails back and forth, I finally plucked up the courage to face her and we video-called on my computer.

I cried the entire time.

If I was hoping to convince her that everything was okay, then I failed massively.

I didn't tell her the truth. I wanted to, but she can't be the first person I tell. It has to be Kingston, no matter how painful that experience will be. Facing him will be heartbreaking. Confessing will be agonizing.

She put all my pain down to heartbreak, and she cried right along with me.

I managed to get a little more sleep that night. Unloading at least some of what I'm feeling on my best friend helped, even if only for a few hours.

I haven't spoken to Miles yet, although I have replied to his emails. They were becoming more and more frantic with worry. He already has enough on his plate; I don't need to be added to his stress. Just another thing to feel guilty about.

I'm fucking everything up.

My life, obviously, has gone to hell in a handbasket, but I'm dragging those I love right along with me, and I hate it.

I just want everyone to be happy.

The only one who seems to be rolling with the punches is Kingston.

Lori hasn't seen him; Miles hasn't so much as mentioned his name. So I guess his life is business as usual, as if I never existed.

Finally, the cold spell that was holding part of the country in its clutches seems to have passed, leaving behind beautiful warm spring days that are full of hope for the future.

With a cup of decaf tea in hand and a bag of fresh pastries I picked up on my morning walk, I take myself out to the small courtyard-style garden. It sits at the side of my rental, allowing me to see both the street and the fields behind. Lowering myself into the swing chair that I've moved so it's in the sun, I let out a sigh of contentment as I relax.

There is nothing but the sound of the birds in the trees nearby.

It's the perfect haven, but no matter how peaceful it is, the knot that's been getting tighter and tighter inside me never relents.

I sip my tea, willing it to release, to give me some kind of relief for even just a few minutes, but it never does.

Instead, all I can think about is him.

Kingston Callahan.

My husband.

It's been two weeks since I looked into his eyes and felt his touch, his warmth. While those two weeks feel like a lifetime ago, it also feels like only yesterday. I can still viscerally remember how my entire body lit up when his fingers grazed my skin.

No one else has ever left me with this kind of longing.

I've always been able to separate sex from feelings, and I truly thought I'd be able to do the same with him.

A man I thought I hated.

Really, it shouldn't have been a challenge. But then, I didn't expect to find that hidden side of him. The sweet, romantic side that made me swoon harder than I ever had before.

I shake my head, silently chastising myself for even thinking about him, about the effect he has on me. That isn't what I'm meant to be using this time for.

I'm meant to be putting distance between us, planning my future.

But honestly, I have no idea what my life looks like after Kingston.

Right now, it feels bleak. Lifeless. Unfulfilling.

No man should have the power to rip all those things away from me. It's not fair.

A single tear trickles from the corner of my eye and I swipe it away angrily.

I glance at my tablet that's sitting on the cushion beside me. The urge to call Lori burns through me, but it's too early. She won't be up yet.

Miles will...

Before I know what I'm doing, I've logged into my video chat app and my finger is hovering over his contact.

Nerves assault me out of nowhere.

Will he even want to talk to me?

I was a coward, leaving my resignation on his desk and running.

A strong woman would have handed it over and then walked out with her head held high.

Before all of this, I have every confidence that I'd have done exactly that.

But I'm struggling to grasp the woman I was before all of this. The one who stuck her middle finger up and said "fuck the world". I hate it. I hate being this fucking broken and vulnerable.

"Fuck it," I mutter before tapping my finger against the screen.

Not a second later does the dial tone fill the air as I wait with my heart in my throat to discover if my big brother will answer or not.

I startle when the screen freezes, but then the most incredible thing happens.

Miles's sleepy face fills the screen.

His hair is a wild mess, sticking up in all directions. His eyes are barely open and surrounded by dark, swollen circles, and there is a thick pillow crease in his cheek. He looks exhausted, confused, but kinda cute, in an annoying big brother way.

"Tate," he rasps. "Fuck. Are you okay?" He pushes himself up, letting the sheets fall from his body.

"Ew, dude. Put it away," I tease when his toned torso comes into view.

I immediately feel better being able to tease him.

"You're just jealous because it's hotter than anyone you've ever been with."

"Dangerous territory, Miles," I warn.

"Shit, yeah. I need coffee." He glances to the side and balks. "Do you know what time it is here?"

"I'm sorry, I can go. I just—"

"No, no," he says, propping himself up against his headboard and resting his cell on his knees. "I'm here. How are you?" he asks a little hesitantly.

"Yeah," I sigh. "You know. Processing, I guess."

He stares at me. Really stares at me. It makes me want to recoil and hide.

"You look good," he says, forcing a bitter laugh to spill from my lips.

549

"I don't, but thanks for the confidence boost, Bro."

"No, I mean it. I think the English countryside is doing you some good."

Still unconvinced by his assessment, I change the subject, although not to anything less painful.

"They've sold the cottage."

"Shit," Miles hisses, dragging his hand down his face. "I know, Tate. I'm so fucking sorry. As soon as KC got those papers, everything just—"

"It's okay," I lie. "I knew what I was doing when I instructed Richard to initiate our divorce. It's the right thing to do."

His expression turns sad, reverent even.

"Miles," I warn. "Do not tell me that you're going to argue about this. You hated the idea of us being together."

"Yeah," he agrees. "I did hate it. But then...I dunno," he says with a shrug. "I saw the two of you together and I guess it all just kinda made sense."

A laugh full of disbelief and amazement bubbles up.

"You're kidding, right?"

"No," Miles says firmly. "I saw it, Tate. You really liked him."

Tears burn my eyes as the cold hard truth in his words slams into me.

"Miles, please. Don't do this. Talk to me about—"

"Work?" he asks with wide eyes, already predicting that I'm not going to want to go there either.

"Shit," I mutter. "I'm sorry." I've already said it in the email, but it's not enough. I'm not sure sorry will ever be enough for the way I left.

"I know you are, T. It's okay. I understand."

"Is everything...going okay?" I don't want to know, but also, I do. Warner Group is Miles's entire life now, and I want to know how he's doing, how he's coping.

"It's... going," he says, his chest decompressing as all the air rushes from his lungs. "It's fucking hard, T. I knew it would be, but fuck. Letting people go is really fucking hard. Every day something is changing; it's hard to keep track of everything."

"It'll be worth it," I promise him.

"I wish I had you beside me."

"You've got King, you don't need me."

"Don't we?"

We.

Fuck, if that one word doesn't slice my chest clean open.

"Miles," I whisper, my voice cracking with emotion.

"Sorry, but it's true. I'm not the only one who needs you."

It's the first bit of evidence that maybe King isn't as okay with all of this as I assumed he was. But while I might have thought that hearing he was suffering too would help me, it really fucking doesn't.

I don't want to hurt him.

I don't want to hurt either of us, but I feel like I'm bleeding out right here on the swing seat.

"I-I can't hear this, Miles."

"What happened, Tate?"

I shake my head, closing my eyes and trapping the truth behind my lips.

"It all just got too much. Dad, King, the wedding, work. Everything just—"

His eyes narrow, making me wish I could put a barrier up between us so he can't see the truth playing out in my eyes.

"It's more than that. My little sister can cope with more than what's been thrown at her recently. It takes a hell of a lot more than that to break her."

Emotion bubbles up faster than I can control.

"Shit. No. Don't cry," he soothes.

"I'm sorry. I just...I can't keep it up anymore," I confess weakly.

"I wish I was there," he says sadly. "I hate that you're alone."

Steeling myself, I wipe my eyes and hold his through the screen. "I'm okay. I need to be alone right now."

"But you don't have to be," he says, detecting my lie the second it falls from my lips.

Silence falls between us. It's not uncomfortable, but the

unanswered questions lingering in the air between us ensure I don't fully relax.

"Is there anything any of us can do to change your mind?"

"About King or work?"

"Both, either. Anything. I miss you."

I shrug. "I don't know what I want or where I belong right now."

"Here, Tate. You belong here. You always have."

A sob erupts. I hate how lost my big brother looks.

I want to be there for him. I do. But I can't. It's not my place.

Although, what I just said is true. I have no idea where my place actually is.

I thought it was here. But something is missing.

Miles yawns and guilt rushes through me that I'm stopping him from sleeping when he so clearly needs it.

"I should let you go."

"No, it's okay. I don't need to be at the office for a few hours."

"Then you need to sleep. I'll call you again at a more sensible time."

He stares at me.

"I promise. I might not be there, but I'm still here, Miles. If you need me, no matter what it's for, I'm here." The words fall a little flat considering that I ran from him only two weeks ago with no warning or any way to really contact me, but I lay them out regardless.

"I know. I love you, T."

"I love you too, big brother."

"I'll see you soon, yeah?" he says with more hope glittering in his eyes than I think he should have.

Can I go back to Chicago anytime soon? I'm not sure.

But then, do I want to stay here? No, I'm not certain I want that either.

The cottage has already been sold.

I did this. I made my bed, and now I have to lie in it.

The second we hang up, coldness rushes through me quickly

followed by a wave of homesickness so strong, I think for a second that I might actually vomit.

Abandoning my tablet, I push to my feet and walk into the cottage with my now cold cup of tea.

After using the bathroom and giving myself a talking-to in an attempt to get my head straight, I make myself a fresh drink and head back outside. I'm halfway to the swing seat when I stop dead on the spot.

In the middle of the small outside table is a massive bunch of flowers.

No. Not just flowers.

The exact same ones that were in my wedding bouquet.

Oh my god.

He came.

76

KINGSTON

I told myself that I'd give her two weeks.

The arrival of the divorce papers didn't change that. Nor did my father's words. Although they did confirm what I already knew.

I had the flights booked. I had a plan. The only thing I didn't have was much confidence about how it was all going to play out.

Sure, I know how I want it to go.

I want her to take one look at me, realize her mistake, and run into my arms, to forget whatever scared her off and allow us to continue building a life together.

But that could be a pipedream. After all, this woman literally skipped the country to get away from me. I fear that she isn't going to take my sudden appearance in the way I'd like.

Something serious made her leave me. I have very little hope that she's been sitting around here waiting for me to return and sweep her off her feet. A guy can still wish, though.

My plan was to walk straight up to the front door and announce my presence the second I got to the address of the cottage Aubrey sent me, but as I walked down the street, her voice hit my ears and I was powerless but to hide behind a bush like a pussy and listen to her.

The emotion in her voice as she spoke to Miles threatened to break me. All I wanted to do was pull her into my arms, hold her tight and tell her that everything was going to be okay. That whatever it was, I'd make sure that she was okay.

That's my job after all, as her husband.

But I couldn't. So instead, I gave her space to talk to her brother, all the while letting the softness of her voice wash over me like the warm breeze.

When she hung up, I almost moved and announced my presence, but before I could, she'd hopped up and disappeared.

With more nerves than I think I've felt in my entire life, I invited myself into the small yard she was sitting in and placed the huge bouquet of English roses on the small table in the middle of the space.

I ordered them before leaving Chicago and collected them the second I arrived in the village less than twenty minutes ago.

The second I saw them, I was hit with a wave of nostalgia so strong it almost knocked me to the floor. The image of her walking toward me on our wedding day carrying an almost identical bouquet was so vivid in my mind.

Taking a step back, I tucked myself under an ornate archway that I'm sure will be covered in colorful flowers in the months ahead, and then just waited.

And that's exactly where I'm still standing when she finally re-emerges from the small cottage she's been staying in for the past two weeks.

The sight of her takes my breath away.

Her dark hair is twisted up on the top of her head, loose strands hanging around her neck and blowing in the breeze. She's wearing a knee-length denim dress with a thick knit cream cardigan over the top.

I might only be able to see her from the back, but I already know she looks beautiful. She's Tatum; how could she look any other way?

She manages four steps before noticing the flowers, and when she does, her entire body tenses.

My heart lurches into my throat, making it hard to take in the breaths I need as I wait for reality to hit her. I know the second it does that she's going to search for me.

Who else would have left those flowers there?

Time stops. The world ceases to exist as I wait for her to do something.

Anything.

She can turn around and hit me with the flowers if she wants, as long as I get some kind of reaction. I can deal with her anger, with her hatred—I've done it all before. But what I can't deal with is apathy.

If she even tries to pretend that she doesn't care...fuck. I can't even comprehend it.

Just when I start to believe that she's not going to look for me, slowly her eyes lift from the flowers and she begins to scan the yard.

My heart races and my hands tremble as I attempt to prepare myself for what could come. It could go one of a million ways.

When she doesn't find me in front of her, she begins turning around.

My breath catches, and I don't release it until she's facing me, and then it comes out in a rush of relief.

She's here, standing before me, looking like the most beautiful thing in the world.

Her face is clear of makeup, her eyes are wide and hold a sparkle of life that gives me hope that everything might just be salvageable, and her lips are parted in shock as the air crackles like a livewire between us.

"Kingston," she whispers as if saying it too loud will make me disappear again.

I swallow, refusing to allow my nerves to get the better of me.

"Tatum," I greet, holding myself from rushing toward her and pulling her into my arms where she belongs.

"W-what are you doing here?" she asks, anxiously picking at her nails.

"I've come to find my wife," I state simply.

She shakes her head, but I ignore it and take a step forward, the magnetic pull I feel toward her stronger than ever.

The second I'm standing before her, the warmth of her body seeps into mine, and I sigh in relief.

Reaching out, I cup her jaw, tilting her head back so she has little choice but to hold our eye contact.

"B-but you signed—"

I don't let her finish that sentence or even the thought. Instead, I press the length of my body against her and slam my lips down on hers, taking what I've been craving for the past two weeks.

She doesn't move to start with, she's frozen against me, and for several painful seconds, I fear that she's going to push me away.

Her hands lift and press against my chest, and I prepare myself to be forced back, but then...

But then her lips move against mine and her body sags.

I catch her, banding my free arm around her back, pinning her against me as her lips part, allowing me entry.

A deep groan rumbles in my throat as I swipe my tongue into her mouth, desperate to taste her.

Her hands side over my shoulders before her fingers sink into my hair, twisting tight as if she never wants to let go again.

We make out like teenagers, all tongues and teeth and very little finesse as we remind ourselves just how good we are together.

With my cock growing hard between us, I'm powerless but to reach down, grab her ass and lift her from the ground.

Her legs wrap around my waist a beat before I press her against the side of the cottage, ensuring she can feel what she's doing to me.

"Kingston," she gasps as I grind against her pussy, my lips dropping to her throat.

"It's been too long. I missed you, baby."

"Oh my god," she gasps as I grind myself against her, letting her feel just how true my words are.

I lave at her neck, sucking, biting, kissing; all the things I've been dreaming about.

Palming her breast, I lose myself in her taste, in the feel of her curves against my body, her scent, her kiss.

"We need to go inside before I fuck you right here," I mutter against her lips as my body spirals out of control.

"King," she moans, her hips rolling in time with mine, letting me know that she's fully on board.

Thank fuck for that.

I've no idea what I'd have done if she'd refused to have me here and sent me away.

"I need you, Tate. Fuck. I need you so bad."

Pulling her from the wall, I easily take her weight as I carry her inside through the door she emerged from not so long ago.

I don't take in any of my surroundings. My focus is solely on her.

"Straight through that door," she instructs, and when I follow orders, I find a small living room, or more importantly, a couch.

Lowering her to her feet, I make quick work of dragging her cardigan from her shoulders before reaching for the buttons running down the front of her dress.

My hands continue to tremble, but it's no longer with nerves, just pent-up need.

"Need you naked right fucking now," I confess as I make my way down the buttons.

The moment I'm confident that the fabric will fall from her hips, I push it from her shoulders, leaving her standing there in a navy-blue set of lingerie.

A set of lingerie I bought for her.

Fuck. Knowing that she's been wearing it despite putting this space between us brings me to my motherfucking knees.

Literally.

"Take your bra off," I demand as I reach for the lace of her panties and drag them down her thighs.

The second she's bare, I lift her foot from the floor and place it on the coffee table beside us.

"Fucking perfect," I murmur before diving for her.

"Kingston," she cries, her fingers sinking into my hair, holding me in place. "Yes. Fuck."

Her hips buck as I suck on her clit, plunging two fingers deep inside her and curling them the way she likes.

"Oh god. Yes. Yes."

"Fuck. You missed me too, didn't you, baby?"

"King, please. Please," she begs as I bring her to a fast and intense release. "Oh my god," she screams as she practically pulls clumps of my hair from my scalp.

I fucking love it.

No sooner has she finished sucking my fingers deeper into her body do I push to my feet, taking her with me and throwing her onto the couch.

She gazes up at me with lust-filled, wide eyes. Her lips are parted, her chest is heaving, her nipples are hard, and her pussy is slick and desperate for more.

I strip faster than I ever have before in my life and then crawl between her legs, ready to lose myself in my wife for the foreseeable future.

77

TATUM

Kingston looms over me like a vision.

I'm dreaming. I have to be.

Things like this don't happen to me.

I don't have men chasing me across the world, no matter how much I might have wished it would happen. I never believed it actually would.

He signed the divorce papers. The cottage has already been sold.

Why is he looking at me like I'm still his?

Like he's still mine?

My heart pounds wildly in my chest, but I find it almost impossible to focus on everything I should be thinking about right now.

All I want is him.

More of him.

Every single thing he can give me. All the reminders of just how electric we were together.

Nothing else matters.

Only sating this deep-rooted loneliness that's pulled me into its grip over the past two weeks.

He's here.

He came for you.

"Kingston," I whisper. It's so quiet that if I didn't know I said it, I wouldn't have heard it. But despite that, his reaction to hearing his name is visceral.

His eyes widen, the already dark orbs darkening further, his full lips part, and a warm puff of air rushes over my face.

"Tatum, I—"

"Please, King. I need you," I whisper like a desperate whore who hasn't seen any action in over two weeks.

"Shit, baby. I can't resist you."

Settling between my thighs, he wraps one giant hand around my hip, the other grips his cock, and in only moments, he rubs the head through my folds.

"Oh god," I moan, my muscles clamping down in the hope of sucking him in.

"Never letting you go again," he admits before thrusting his hips forward.

"Kingston," I cry as he stretches me wide.

"It wasn't meant to be like this," he mutters absently as he stares at where we're connected.

"W-what?" I stutter, my brain barely functioning as I watch him watch us with nothing but awe in his expression.

"I wasn't meant to turn up here and just fuck you into oblivion. I had a plan," he says, finally looking up at me.

I love the expression on his face. It's so open, so honest. I want to bottle it and keep it forever, because I'm the one who caused it.

He's here.

He came.

"Seems like the perfect plan to me," I say, sliding my hands up his arms and gripping the back of his neck. "Did you say you missed me?" I ask teasingly. I can't help it. He brings out the sass in me more than anyone else I've ever met.

"Yeah," he agrees, a smirk spreading across his lips. "I missed you, baby."

"Good. Then show me. Whatever else you had planned can come later."

His hips punch forward with such force it knocks the wind clean from my lungs.

But it's so good. So, so good.

Our bodies immediately fall into a rhythm. With every thrust, my hips lift to meet his.

My hands slide down his body, making his skin erupt with goosebumps and a violent shiver rip down his spine.

His visceral reaction to my touch alone makes me melt for him.

Gripping his ass, I pull, desperately trying to get more of him than I already have, although I fear that no matter how much I get, it'll never be enough.

He fucks me deeper, hitting that magical spot inside me with every thrust.

His eyes bounce between mine, emotion and desire warring in them.

I could drown in that look alone.

But all too soon, he ducks down, severing our connection in favor of another.

His lips brush mine in a sweet kiss. It's at total odds to what the bottom half of his body is doing.

It's a head fuck of the best possible kind.

"More," I whimper into his kiss.

"Everything, Tate. You can have everything."

Then he seals his lips over mine, plunges his tongue into my mouth, and his hips pick up pace. He doesn't relent until I've come twice on his magical dick. And only when I'm coming down from my second, does he allow himself to find his own release.

A low groan builds deep in his throat before his body stills for a beat before he lets go. His dick jerks violently inside me, filling me with ropes of hot cum, reminding me that even though it's pointless now, I didn't hesitate for a second to get him to sheath up.

Maybe all of this was just meant to be...

His movements slow, but he never pulls out of me. Instead, he drops to the side, pulling me with him and keeping my leg wrapped around his waist.

I attempt to swallow the messy ball of emotion that clogs my throat, but it's impossible. I'm feeling too many emotions all at once to even attempt to battle them.

"King—"

"Shush, baby," he soothes, clearly able to see the riot happening behind my eyes. And it only gets worse when he reaches out and gently brushes his knuckles down my cheek. "I missed you so fucking much," he confesses quietly, making my heart seize in my chest. "I'm sorry," he blurts suddenly. "Whatever it was I did, I'm so fucking sorry. I never wanted you to leave."

A weird laugh full of fear, hope, relief, and desperation bubbles from my throat.

His brow wrinkles in confusion, but he patiently waits for me to speak.

"You didn't do anything wrong, King. None of this was you. It was me."

He stills. "You're not pulling that 'it's not you, it's me' bullshit on me, Tatum. Don't even fucking think about it."

"N-no, I'm not," I assure him. "Things just...everything got on top of me. The past few weeks, they've..." I trail off, unsure of the right words. And even if I find them, I'm not sure he'd even understand.

"It's been a lot. I know that. But all you had to do was say something. You didn't need to run. To leave."

Ripping my gaze from his, I stare down at his chest. I want to say that I regret running away like I did. But the truth is, I don't.

I regret hurting those who care about me and disappearing without warning. But I don't regret my decisions.

I needed this time away. While I never achieved what I hoped I would, I have managed to find some clarity, some answers.

And finding Kingston standing in the middle of the little courtyard outside not so long ago, cemented them.

It doesn't matter how far I run or for how long, one thing is never going to change.

"King, I—"

"I'm falling—"

We both laugh when we attempt to start talking at the same time. His body moves and I gasp as his growing cock moves inside me.

"Sorry," I say. "You go," I whisper as my nerves return.

"Tatum," he says softly, his eyes searching mine. "Finding you gone was one of the worst moments of my life." My breath catches at the honesty in his tone. "Thinking you ran because of something I did...fuck, Tate, it fucking killed me.

"The apartment wasn't a home without you. Walking into the Warner Group offices knowing that you weren't there was just wrong.

"I missed you so fucking much. I had no idea what to do with myself. Where to put myself. I couldn't focus on work, and I hated being at home. Fuck, I even missed Griz, baby. That's how fucking bad it got."

A loud, ugly sob erupts from my throat.

He called her Griz.

"I need you, baby," he whispers, his fingers slipping into my hair at the nape of my neck and pulling me closer. "I...I love you."

All the air rushes from my lungs as his confession lingers in the air between us.

"I know I wasn't meant to. I know this is a business deal. I know all of that shit, Tate. But I couldn't stop it. Fuck. I love you. I fucking love you," he says looking borderline manic as he confesses it over and over as if he can't believe he's even saying the words.

"You want me to come back?" I ask, my mouth running away with itself.

He sobers, his expression turning serious.

"More than anything. I need you in my life, baby. It doesn't make sense without it."

"That's crazy. It's only been a few weeks," I say as if I don't understand what he's saying.

The truth is, I do. I more than understand, because I feel the exact same way.

The second I saw those flowers sitting outside waiting for me, everything that had been wrong with me since leaving Chicago fell back into place. My world felt right again. And all because of him.

His hand moves, the warmth of his palm burning my cheek before his thumb slides over my bottom lip.

"Yeah," he muses. "Crazy. That's exactly how I fucking feel."

Before I get a chance to come up with a response, his thumb is gone and it's been replaced with his lips.

His kiss is slow, gentle, and full of passion and emotion.

Full of...love.

My heart swells as I think about the fact that this incredibly beautiful, powerful man has just confessed all those things to me.

I didn't think he cared, and yet...

"Why did you wait so long?" I whisper into our kiss, unable to hold back the question.

He swallows, thinking for a moment as his warm breath rushes over my skin.

"Before you left, I had a conversation with Miles. He was frustrated because he wanted you to have an office on the top floor with us."

"King, no. You know—"

He silences me by pressing two fingers against my lips.

"I told him that you weren't ready." His eyes urge me to stay silent, not to argue with that statement. Instead, I settle for simply shaking my head. "I told him you needed time, that he needed to let you go to give you a chance to realize what you wanted."

"T-that's what you were doing? Giving me time to figure out what I wanted?"

"Yeah, and in turn, I've figured out that I don't want to live another day of my life without you in it." He pauses, rolling his lips between his teeth. "What...what have you figured out?" Nerves come off him in waves. "Is this where you really want to be, or..."

My heart fractures in my chest as he fully opens up to me. I can see all his fears in those electric green eyes.

"I love it here," I whisper. "I always have, and I always will. A part of my heart will always belong here in this village."

"But..." he hedges when I pause.

"But," I continue, "it's only a very small part. The rest of it, I left behind with you in Chicago."

His breath catches and his eyes widen with hope.

"What are you saying, Tate?"

I stare at him. My chest heaves, my entire body trembles, and blood whooshes past my ears as I play the words I need to say to him over and over in my head.

It's crazy. Only a few weeks ago, I hated him.

I literally thought he was the most irritating man on the planet. And now...

"I love you too, Kingston Callahan."

78

TATUM

I wake with a start, my heart pounding as if someone just jumped out at me and scared the living crap out of me.

I blink, my vision of the small living room of my rental clearing.

Weird. I don't remember lying down.

I was out in the sun and—

There's a noise in the kitchen and I sit up, realizing that I'm naked a beat before the reason for the noise appears in the doorway.

"Kingston." His name spills from my lips like a plea, making my cheeks heat and my thighs clench.

He's standing in a stream of sunlight wearing only his boxer briefs and looking like a fucking god.

Jesus, did he get hotter?

"Uh..." he starts, dragging my eyes back up to his face, a deep frown marring his brow.

He came for you...

"I can't find any coffee," he says, glancing back to the kitchen. "Where have you hidden it?"

Guilt twists up my insides.

Just tell him...

"Oh...um...I've actually been drinking tea."

"Tea?" he asks in astonishment.

"Yeah. It reminds me of Aunt Lena, so..."

"Okay," he says, accepting my reasoning without question.

I'm not lying. It's true. She was a tea addict through and through. Drinking it here does remind me of her, but also... suddenly, I can't stand the scent of coffee.

It's a real fucking problem.

"Would you like one?"

I snap my attention back to him.

"O-one?" I stutter like an idiot.

"A cup of tea, Tate. Would you like a cup of tea?"

His eyes drop to my chest as he waits for my answer, his tongue sneaking out and swiping across his bottom lip.

Everything that happened from the moment I found him watching me in the garden to the point where I fell asleep in his arms comes back to me in a rush of color, pleasure, and confessions of love.

Holy shit.

He told me he loved me.

"Y-yes, please. I'm just going to clean up."

The second I get to my feet, I discover just how necessary that is when his cum begins running down my thighs. Gross.

I move toward the stairs, expecting him to duck back into the kitchen, but he doesn't. Instead, he just stands there, shamelessly watching me.

"What?" I ask, pausing at the bottom step to look back at him.

He scrubs at his rough jaw, his eyes working their way down to my feet and then all the way back up again.

By the time they meet mine, they're blazing with desire, and it makes my temperature soar.

"I meant every single word I said earlier, Tatum."

A small smile plays on my lips as I remember everything he confessed.

"So did I." A laugh bubbles from my throat. "I can't believe you're here," I explain when he frowns at me like I've lost my mind.

"I can't believe you thought I wouldn't be. I need you, baby."

I shake my head, unable to believe he's telling me these things.

"But you signed the papers," I whisper.

He quirks a brow. The move makes him look so fucking cocksure. It does things to my insides that it really shouldn't. "Did I?"

"The cottage sold," I explain.

He nods, rubbing the back of his neck.

"Are you going to clean up or what?"

"Y-yeah. I'll be back. And we need to talk."

"Sure. I've got a few more things I need to say. Can you stay naked for it, though?"

My eyes drop from his to the fabric hiding what is arguably the best part of his body from me.

"You're not, so why should I be?" I sass before taking off up the stairs, hoping that he might lose that scrap of fabric before I get back downstairs.

I pause when I get into the bathroom and look in the mirror. For the first time in what feels like forever, there's a smile on my lips and a sparkle in my eyes.

"Damn you, Kingston Callahan," I mutter, shaking my head.

I pee before walking over to turn the shower on.

Pulling my hair back up into a messy bun, I step under the stream of water. I stand there for a few seconds, letting the powerful jets massage my shoulders as memories of what Kingston said downstairs play out in my head.

The old romantic inside me is doing a little happy dance.

He told me he loved me, that he missed me, that his life wasn't complete without me.

It's the thing dreams are made of. The kind of thing that only happens in movies and books. Men don't just drop everything and chase a woman across the world. It just doesn't happen.

Well, apparently it does.

And for little ol' me, too.

My heart flutters in my chest. It's so at odds with how it's felt for the past few weeks, I think there's something wrong for a few seconds. But then I realize that it's actually something very, very right.

I wash up before grabbing my razor to do some of the maintenance I've neglected for the past few days, because something tells me that that little session on the couch is just the beginning for us.

My insides tingle at the thought alone.

Once I'm happy that everything that needs to be hair-free is, I turn the shower off and reach for a towel.

Every one of my movements comes easier than they have since I first arrived here, and there is hope in my heart I haven't felt for... nope, I don't think I've ever felt it before.

He loves me.

Kingston Callahan loves me.

Just thinking it makes me smile and want to do a little victory dance.

I feel like a love-sick teenager again, only unlike a love-sick teenager, this is real. It's my husband telling me that he loves me, not some lanky, acne-covered man-child.

He didn't sign the divorce papers. His eyebrow quirk said that alone. Sure, that knowledge drags up a whole heap of other questions, but I don't have the brain power to even think about them right now. All I want to do is get back down to him.

I want to step into his body, feel the strength of his arms as they wrap around me, and breathe in the scent of his skin under my nose.

Slathering on some moisturizer, I pull on a long tank that's going to hide absolutely nothing with the short hem and wide arm holes before shaking my wild hair out and bouncing down the stairs like it's the best day of my life.

Hell, it very well could be.

His scent fills the air down here, and one look at the couch where it all happened makes my thighs clench with desire.

Oh, how I missed that man and his magical dick.

I pause, listening, trying to figure out what he's doing. But it's silent.

"King?" I call as I walk toward the kitchen.

My flowers are now sitting on the side, and I can't help but smile as I study them.

Turning away from them, I head outside, assuming that he's making the most of the warm afternoon sun. But my heart drops when I step out into the small courtyard because it's empty.

"King?" I call again, my voice sounding panicked.

My heart begins to race and my head spins.

He meant what he said to me, I know he did. I could see it in his eyes.

So where the hell is he...

I spin around, ready to race back inside, when something on the small table where I first found my flowers catches my eyes.

Stepping closer, I find a white envelope with my name written in his neat handwriting.

My hand trembles as I reach for it. I swear to god, if this is a goodbye letter after everything he told me since he suddenly appeared here and swept me off my feet—literally—then it might just be the end of me. I'm not sure I'll be able to take it.

The past couple of hours—even those I slept through—have been everything.

His touch, his words.

"Fuck," I breathe, holding the envelope at arm's length as if it's going to bite me.

I stand there for longer than I should, debating whether or not to open it.

Blowing out a slow breath, I force myself to calm down and see what he's left for me.

It's nothing bad.

It can't be. Not after...

But despite trying to convince myself that everything is okay, it doesn't stop my stomach from knotting up.

But not knowing is worse...

Tucking my finger beneath the flap, I pull it open and then pull the card from inside.

The back is blank, making my brows furrow in confusion, but not as much as when I flip it over.

Meet me at your favorite place in this village.

"My favorite place?" I whisper.

I love every part of this village and the memories it holds. But there is only one place that truly holds my heart.

I glance down at myself before running into the house to drag on some leggings and throw a zip-up hoodie over my shoulders to hide my exposed side boob.

In seconds, I have a pair of sneakers on my feet and I'm practically running from the front gate and down the street.

My heart pounds harder with every step as I try to figure out what he's done, what all this means.

Surely, it isn't what I think.

It can't be. It—

I round the final corner and my eyes lock on the cottage. However, I quickly discovered that it isn't the quaint building and pretty yard that holds my attention. It's the delicious man standing in front of it.

He nervously scans the street before him, searching for me.

My heart tumbles in my chest as I study him.

I'm sure there have only been a handful of times in his life that he's been nervous, and right now is one of them.

I stay hidden in the shadows for another few seconds before my need to put him out of his misery gets too strong.

I take three steps forward, and the second I move into the light, he sees me.

His expression morphs from one of fear to one of pure happiness.

His eyes widen, the green sparkling in the sun as his lips pull up into the widest smile I think I've ever seen.

'Tatum,' he mouths as if he's shocked to see me.

As I walk closer, he does the same. It's as if we're magnets, pulled together by something too strong to ignore.

After checking for cars, I pick up speed as I cross the road.

My need to know what he's up to has me running straight into his arms. He instantly pulls me into his body and drops his lips to mine, kissing me as if he didn't see me less than an hour ago.

"What are you doing?" I ask when he finally releases me.

Silently, he takes my hand and tugs me inside the cottage's yard, closing the small gate behind us.

"Kingston?" I ask as we move toward the front door.

He brings us to a stop and turns to face me.

I fight to drag in the breaths I desperately need as his eyes bounce between mine, studying me closely.

"This place has been sold, we shouldn't—"

My words are cut off as Kingston thrusts a box at me.

It's black velvet, much like the one that housed my engagement ring.

On instinct, I lift my left hand and glance down at my rings.

Kingston reaches for my hand and gently grasps my fingers.

"You never took them off," he muses.

Shaking my head, I say two words that are so painfully true, that they cut straight through my chest, only in the best kind of way. "I couldn't."

"Fuck, Tatum." He releases me before scrubbing his face. "This is for you," he says, pushing the box closer. "You need to open it before I do something I really shouldn't in Aunt Lena's flower beds."

I raise a brow at his confession.

"Baby, you're not even wearing a bra," he points out, his eyes dropping to my more than obvious nipples.

Wrapping my hoodie around myself, I find his eyes again.

"Please," he says, pushing the box closer again.

I take it, muttering, "What have you done, Kingston Callahan?"

He shrugs but doesn't say anything as I flip the lid and peel back some tissue to find—

"A key?"

"A key to your cottage, baby," he confirms as the world begins to spin around me.

I mean, I hoped when I found his note and then him standing here.

But—

"How? It's my father's. You can't just—"

"You served me, baby."

"You signed them, didn't you?" Emotion bubbles up my throat at the thought of no longer being married to him now.

"Baby," he murmurs, stepping closer and wrapping his hand around the back of my neck.

His eyes hold mine and refuse to let them go.

"Nothing in this fucking world could make me sign those papers. Not a single fucking thing."

79

KINGSTON

With my hands holding her face, I brush my lips against hers.

Keeping this a secret from her has fucking killed me. But I knew that she'd never accept it if I didn't deliver it right.

It had to be in person, and it had to be after I confessed everything else I've been bottling up inside.

The second her lips part, I lick deep into her mouth, trying to tell her with actions exactly how I feel about her.

Having her with me, her body pressed up against mine, suddenly everything is right again.

It just confirms everything I realized the moment I discovered she'd gone.

Tatum Callahan isn't just my wife. She's my everything.

Our kiss quickly turns heated, too heated for being out in public in this quaint little village.

It pains me to do so, but I manage to pull my lips from hers, breaking our kiss.

Resting my forehead against hers, I hold her eyes as her increased breaths rush over my face.

"Fancy showing me around your new place, baby?"

Her eyes bounce between mine and I smirk, able to read her thoughts.

She wants to refuse, to tell me where to go. But she won't, because she wants this place too much.

"I can't believe you've done this," she whispers.

"This place was always meant to be yours, Tate. Now it is. Your name is on the deed. It's yours to do whatever you want with."

"And if I want to live here?" she asks.

"Then we'd need to discuss how that works in reality."

She frowns, her brow rippling against mine.

"You'd consider it?" she asks as if the concept is impossible to believe.

"I want to be with you, Tatum. And if this is where you need to be, then..." I take in a deep breath. "Then we'd figure something out. I'm not losing you to another country. It's not going to happen."

Reaching for her hand, I place her hand against my chest, letting her feel just how fast my heart is racing.

"You're in here, Tatum. And I need you—" Wrapping my other arm around her back, I pin her against my body. "Right fucking here."

"King," she gasps.

"I don't care if you want to move to Antarctica. We'll find a way to make it work. Now," I say. "I'm dying to look around this place that makes you so happy."

She bounces on her toes in excitement.

"Come on then," she says twisting our fingers together and tugging me toward the front door.

She's like a little kid who's just been given the keys to a candy shop. I can't help but smile, my heart melting as I watch her open the door and skip inside.

I've barely crossed the threshold when she pauses and just breathes in.

"You okay?" I ask, noticing that her eyes are closed.

"Yeah," she whispers, her lips pulling up to a smile. "Just...

taking it all in. It still smells faintly as I remember."

I nod, letting her have her moment, and look around.

My eyes widen at the sight of the old fashion decoration. The walls are covered in red and gold swirls that make my head spin even while sober. The furniture and woodwork are mahogany and straight out of the seventies, and all the fittings are tarnished gold. It's...a time warp.

"Wow, this is—"

"Exactly as I remember it," Tatum says fondly as she takes off again, dragging me with her.

Every room she takes me into is the same. It's like nothing I've ever seen before.

It's not until we get to the drawing room that something other than the decoration captures my attention.

Releasing Tatum's hand, I walk toward the fireplace with my eyes locked on a photograph of two kids.

Picking it up, I stare at my girl. She's probably ten. She's got her dark hair pulled back into a ponytail, her eyes are alight with happiness, and she's wearing a pair of denim dungarees. Both her and Miles look out of breath, like they've done a million laps of the pretty yard behind them.

"I remember that summer," the girl in question says, stepping up beside me and turning the frame so she can see the image. "I never wanted it to end."

"You really love it here, huh?"

I expect her to agree instantly, but she hesitates, making me turn toward her.

"Tatum?" I ask when I find her chewing on her bottom lip. "What's wrong?"

"I do. I do love it here."

"But?" I ask, sensing that there is so much more that she wants to say.

"But...and I never thought I'd say this...but I miss Chicago. I miss Miles, and Lori, and Griz." I wince at the mention of the cat. Can't say that I've had the same feelings about the little furball.

"And me?" I hedge.

She laughs. "Yeah, King. I missed you too."

I smirk. It's cocky as hell; I can't help it.

"So, what are you saying?"

"I will always love this place. And I'm so incredibly grateful for whatever you've done to secure this for me but...I don't think I'm ready for this life yet."

Thank fuck.

"So..." I prompt, refusing to voice my relief that I don't have to figure out a way to live a life that's split over two continents just so we can be together.

"I think I need to come back to Chicago. For now, it's my home. It's...*our* home," she says hesitantly.

"Tatum," I say, stepping closer to her and wrapping my arms around her body. "I realized something in the past two weeks." She stares up at me with her big blue eyes that always suck me right in. "My home is wherever you are."

Her eyes fill with tears and her bottom lip trembles.

"Please don't cry. It's meant to be a good thing."

"It is a good thing," she agrees, her voice cracked with emotion. "I just never thought—"

"You didn't think I'd come for you? You thought I'd sign those divorce papers and forget about you? You thought you didn't change every single thing in my life?" I offer up. "Baby, you're it for me. Our marriage might have started out as a commitment to secure us other assets, but fuck all that. The only thing I want now is you."

Her tears finally spill over and I catch them with my thumbs.

"I think...I think I need to show you the bedrooms now," she says through her tears.

"Oh yeah?" I ask.

She takes a step back, grabs my hand and leads the way once more.

Every single stair creaks on the way up, as well as the floorboards once we hit the top floor.

"Master," she says, throwing a door open to reveal the ugliest bedroom I've ever seen in my life. The comforter alone gives me a headache. Thankfully, we move on fast, and I can only hope there's a less trippy room that we can make the most of. I'm all for enjoying a high, but fuck me, that was a bit much.

Thankfully, the next one is a little tamer, the third is Miles's room, and the fourth—

"This is your room," I say, releasing her hand and stepping farther into the pink room. It's the girliest thing I've ever seen with pink fairy lights strung up everywhere, pillows covering the bed, and a heart-shaped rug on the floor.

It's very different from the room I remember her living in at her parents' house. This is a little girl's room. That was...an adult's room designed by adults.

"What gave it away?" she teases.

"Well, Miles was never really a pink kind of guy." She moves closer and I rip my attention away from the room in favor of her. "Have you ever had a boy in your room, Tatum?"

She bites down on her bottom lip and shakes her head.

"Nope. I'm not that kind of girl, Mr. Callahan."

I smirk. "Oh really? That isn't what I've heard," I mutter as I crowd her small body with mine.

"You shouldn't believe rumors, Mr. Callahan," she teases.

"Oh, these aren't rumors, Mrs. Callahan. I think you'll find I have first-hand experience."

Sliding my hands up her body, I trace her sinful curves before pushing the hoodie from her shoulders and letting it drop to the floor at her feet.

A moan rips from her throat as I cup her braless breasts and squeeze.

"Kingston."

"I think we need to christen your new house, baby. Let it know it's got a new owner."

Before she gets a chance to say a word, I drag her tank from her body, exposing her chest.

Ducking low, I suck one of her peaked nipples into my mouth as I work her leggings and panties from her legs.

"Naked," she demands, tugging at my t-shirt and attempting to rid me of it.

Reaching behind my head, I pull it free as she goes for my jeans, popping the button and shoving them and my boxers down my thighs.

My hard dick springs free and she licks her lips before sinking to her knees and sucking me into her mouth.

"Fucking hell, Tatum," I groan, my fingers sinking into her hair. "You are exactly that kind of girl."

She stares up at me, her eyes wide with hunger.

The temptation to let her suck me dry is high, but just before I get to the point of no return, I pull her off me and throw her onto the bed.

Her chest is heaving and her lips are swollen as I crawl over her.

"You're perfect," I say before ducking to kiss her.

She wraps her legs around my waist, trying to encourage me to up the ante, but despite her desperate whimpers and the way her nails claw at my skin, I hold off, driving her crazy.

Eventually, I flip us and settle her on my waist.

"Your house, baby. That means you're the boss."

She sucks in a sharp breath before the most incredible smile spreads across her lips.

"Is that right?"

"Yep," I say, tucking my hands behind my head, giving her full access to my body. "Do your worst, Mrs. Callahan."

The way she smiles at me makes my heart skip a beat.

"Fuck. I love you."

Her smile grows, but instead of responding with words, she reaches for my dick and then sinks down on me incredibly slowly.

Her eyes hold mine the whole time she rides my cock, taking what she needs, letting me see and feel every ounce of her emotions.

Moving my hands, I hold them out for her to grab and she immediately laces her fingers through mine and uses me for leverage.

Her pussy ripples around me, her body sucking mine impossibly deep.

"You're incredible, you know that, right?"

Her body trembles as I say the words, her release approaching right alongside mine.

"King, fuck." I thrust my hips up, unable to hand over every bit of control and send her flying off the edge. "Fuck. I love you, I love you, I love you," she chants as she falls.

"Love you too," I groan as my cock jerks, spilling myself inside her.

Her body goes limp and she flops onto my chest, her chest heaving as she fights to catch her breath.

"I'll never get enough of that," I whisper, pressing a kiss to the top of my head.

"Same," she confesses breathlessly.

I laugh to myself, and she lifts her head to look up at me.

"What?"

"I thought you were going to fight me about this place."

She studies me for a beat before laying her head back on my chest.

"I don't want to fight anymore," she says quietly.

"But it's so fun," I tease, tracing my fingers up and down her back, making goosebumps break out.

"Yeah, sometimes. But I can't argue when you've given me everything I've ever wanted."

My breath catches at the honesty in her words.

"Well, I do try my best," I say cockily.

She falls quiet, and I wrap my arms around her, holding her tightly and embracing the moment with her.

It's a turning point, a massive one in both of our lives.

Although, I don't realize quite how big until she speaks again a few minutes later.

"King?" she whispers.

"Yeah, baby?"

"I'm pregnant."

80

TATUM

Those two words linger in the air between us. And for a couple of seconds, I wonder if I actually said them out loud, because he doesn't react.

But then, it's like the words register in his head and his entire body tenses.

"Y-you're...pregnant?" he asks as if he heard me wrong.

Squeezing my eyes closed, I pray that I haven't just fucked everything up.

Maybe I should have kept it secret a little longer, until we've figured all this out at least.

But he deserves to know. I've already kept it a secret long enough.

"I freaked out. I didn't—"

"That's why you ran," he says on a breath, finally figuring it all out.

"King, I didn't know—"

"Look at me," he demands.

I hesitate, unsure if I'm going to be able to look into his eyes without breaking down again.

"Tatum," he warns when I don't follow orders like a good girl.

"Kingston," I start, but he's not having any of it.

His fingers thread into my hair and he gently lifts my head, giving me little choice but to do as he asks.

My eyes are already full of tears by the time they find his, but what I see staring back at me forces them to spill over.

I don't see any anger, frustration, or disbelief.

Just love and concern.

"You were worried about what I'd say?" he asks, studying me closely.

I shrug one shoulder. "Yeah."

"Baby," he warns.

"I had no idea how you felt, King," I say, sitting up to put a little space between us so I can think properly.

He slips from my body as I move to sit beside him, and I instantly mourn the loss of him.

"Hell, I had no idea how I felt. Everything was spinning out of control. My feelings for you were big and scary and..." I draw in a deep breath, trying not to fall apart all over again. "Everything was such a mess. I just needed...I needed to breathe. I needed space. I needed—"

My words are cut off as he suddenly sits up and kisses me.

His hand wraps around the back of my neck and the second his tongue licks mine, my tears fall faster.

All my fears are instantly washed away, replaced by relief.

He's okay with this. Everything is going to be okay.

Time ceases to exist as he kisses me, but the second the warmth of his palm comes to a stop on my stomach, the sob that rips from my throat brings it to a swift end.

"Hey, it's okay."

"King, I'm pregnant," I repeat. "We're going to have a baby."

He studies me for a beat before the most incredible smile pulls at his lips.

"There isn't anyone else in the world I'd want to do that with, baby."

"B-but it's so fast. We're not even really married, we—"

"We are really married," he argues, holding up his hand to show me his ring.

"No, I know it's real. I just mean, we didn't do it because we wanted to. We—"

"Didn't we?" he asks. "There was no point in any of this when I didn't want to marry you, Tatum."

"But you hated me."

He chuckles. "Maybe. But I also knew that there was something very right about this. You felt it too; that's why you didn't fight harder."

I smirk. "I just wanted this place."

"Nice try, baby. But we both know you wanted my dick."

I swat his shoulder. "Be serious, King. This is—"

"How it's meant to be?"

"But a baby. That's—"

"Fucking incredible."

I sigh, shaking my head. "You're insufferable."

"That's why you love me," he quips.

"It's going to change everything. Your apartment—"

"Our apartment," he corrects.

"It's going to be full of baby stuff, and we'll be up all night. There will be diapers, and bottles, and poo. Lots of poo."

He cups my cheek and wipes away a tear I didn't realize had dropped.

"We'll figure it out. It's not like you have a job to distract you."

My heart sinks as I think about returning to Chicago unemployed.

I loved my job. I loved my team.

"That was reckless of me, wasn't it?"

"I'm pretty sure that you could sweet talk your boss into giving you your job back."

"Sweet talk? You mean a blow job won't do it?" I tease.

"Well, considering I was talking about taking it up with your brother, no, probably not."

"Oh ew, King," I say, swatting his shoulder again. "That's gross."

"You don't need to worry about your job, Tate. There will

always be a place for you at Warner Group or Callahan Enterprises."

I fall silent, unable to process everything that's spinning through my mind.

Of all the scenarios I imagined when I told Kingston the truth, him being happy about it wasn't one that I lingered on.

I expected him to be angry. Full of disbelief and frustration.

Pissed that I'd lied to him. That I hadn't been more careful—not that it's solely my responsibility, of course.

But this...this is something else.

"What are you thinking, baby?" he asks, holding my face firmly and looking deep into my eyes.

"I...I don't know. You've..." I shake my head, a soft smile playing on my lips. "Who are you?" I ask, laughing.

"The man who's in love with you," he says simply, his voice raspy with emotion. "The man whose baby you're carrying."

A sob breaks free as more emotion than I can deal with erupts inside me. Without missing a beat, he pulls me into his arms and silently holds me, supports me, and gives me everything I knew I needed but was too stubborn to accept.

My tears coat his chest, but he doesn't complain or try and stop me. Instead, he just allows me to expel everything that I've kept bottled up over the past two weeks.

I've no idea how much time has passed when I open my sore eyes, but I'm pretty sure I fell asleep again.

It seems that all I needed to help me fully relax was to have Kingston wrapped around me like a snake.

I don't think I've ever had two naps in a day.

Is this what I have to look forward to in the next eight months?

"Hey, sleepy head," he whispers as I begin to stir.

I remember him lying back and taking me with him, but I don't remember us ending up on our sides, him spooning me.

"S-sorry," I rasp, my voice rough with sleep.

"Nothing to apologize for."

"I haven't slept well since I've been here," I confess.

"Well, I'm glad I could help."

I groan, stretching my legs out and rubbing my ass back against him.

"Again?" I ask when I feel him hard against me.

"You're naked," he points out. "And sexy as hell," he muses, sliding his hand from my ribs all the way to my thigh. "And all fucking mine."

"I don't think I can go again. Not yet at least."

He chuckles, and I don't need to look back to know that he's smirking.

"I'm sure I can be talked into giving you a rest," he teases.

"King," I half-warn, half-moan.

I might be feeling a little sore, but that doesn't mean my muscles aren't tightening down with my need to feel him inside me again. And it certainly doesn't mean that I'm not slick and ready for him.

"Does this place have a bathtub?"

"Uh-huh," I mumble. "It has the best tub."

"Oh god," he groans. "What color is it?"

I laugh, knowing exactly what he's thinking.

This place is literally the opposite of his taste. Everything is patterned, colorful, cluttered, and a little gaudy. It's a lot to take. Aunt Lena loved it, though. And while it might not be my taste, I appreciate all the reasons why she did.

"Come on," I say, rolling out of bed. My muscles pull and twist, reminding me that I haven't had the full Kingston Callahan experience for way too long.

I'm at the door when I hear him moving behind me.

"Turn around," he demands, his deep voice bouncing off the walls and making my skin erupt in goosebumps.

Doing as I'm told, I twist to face him, finding him sitting on the edge of the bed with his elbows resting on his knees.

His hair is a mess, his eyes are hooded and dark, his lips are swollen from my kisses, and there are unmistakable scratches across his shoulder.

I did that.

My heart swells as I take in my man in his most open and vulnerable state. I get this. Only me. Possibly only ever me.

"What?" I ask, my brow furrowing as he stares at me.

Or more specifically, my stomach.

"I'm just trying to imagine how you're going to look in a few months with our baby growing inside you."

Without thought, my hand lifts, resting just above my belly button as a similar image fills my head.

"You mean, other than like a whale who's about to pop?" I tease, although honestly, I'm kinda scared. I'm rather fond of my stomach as it is right now.

"Never. You'll be hot as fuck," he says, pushing to his feet and stalking over.

Heat surges through my body as he closes in on me.

He's still hard, and the sight of him bared for me makes my mouth water and my thighs clench.

"Dirty girl," he muses, able to read my filthy thoughts. But before I get to act on any of them, he grabs my hand and tows me out of the room and toward the only door up here that we haven't looked inside.

I hold my breath as he reaches for the handle and then throws it open.

He takes a step forward and then gasps. "Oh, holy fuck, this is—"

"It's got the best bathtub in the world."

"It has carpet. In a bathroom. And..." He squints and moves closer to the wall. "Is that furry wallpaper?"

I chuckle as he strokes it, confirming that it is, in fact, furry wallpaper.

"Jesus. You're going to get this place remodeled, right?"

Fighting to keep a straight face, I look him dead in the eyes. "No, why would I want to do that?"

He studies me, desperate to see my lie, but thankfully, every now and then, my poker face is just good enough to pull things off.

"You're not serious, are you? I feel drunk just standing here."

I glance at the wild pattern of both the wallpaper and the carpet. It's...trippy.

"Oh, I don't know. I quite like it. And Aunt Lena loved it, and I promised her that I'd never redecorate."

"Right," he muses, finally looking away from me and turning the faucet on. It's a huge gold thing that fills the massive tub in only minutes.

"You said it's mine, right? My name is on the deed?"

"Yeah," he mutters as if he's already regretting that decision. "Your cottage, you can do—or not do—whatever it is you like."

"Perfect," I say, finding some bubble bath in the cupboard and pouring it into the running water. The tub instantly fills with inviting white foam. "What are you waiting for?"

I climb in, leaving plenty of space behind me for him to join.

The second he does, I let out a contented sigh as I lean back into his chest and his arms wrap around me.

Home.

"I missed you, King," I whisper. "Thank you for coming for me."

His hands spread over my stomach protectively. The move makes my eyes burn. But no tears come. I've shed them all. Everything from here on out is going to be happy.

"That was never in question. Have you seen a doctor yet?"

I still in his arms, silently answering his question.

"Tatum," he warns.

"I know. And I will."

"You're damn right you will. I will have nothing but the best for my girl and my baby."

Tingles race through me.

I want to tease him and defy him, try to convince him that a normal doctor will do us just fine, but I don't. Instead, I just snuggle deeper into his body and indulge in being in his arms again.

81

TATUM

It took quite a battle of wills, but eventually, Kingston conceded, and we spent a week together at the cottage.

To my shock, by the time we emerged from the bathroom and ventured downstairs, three suitcases were sitting in the hallway, and I discovered that he'd paid someone to pack up all my things at the rental and move them here.

The arrogant jerk really can get anything he wants.

His obvious show of power and wealth didn't irritate me to the level it once did, but I didn't let him know that. Instead, I told him what the old me would have said and teased him relentlessly about it.

Not that he cared. He just shrugged it off like he usually does before pulling me into his arms and distracting me the best way he knows.

I made the most of the week he granted me here and took him to every place I remember. We strolled through numerous Cotswold villages hand in hand, soaking up the spring sun and the quaint Britishness. We ate pie and mash in pubs and had takeout fish and chips. I even made him a Sunday roast like Aunt Lena used to. It was...well, it was nowhere near as good as hers. The parsnips resembled pieces of coal, the potatoes weren't crunchy on the outside and fluffy on the inside, and the gravy was lumpy as hell, but despite all its issues, Kingston ate it and did his best to convince me that I did a good job.

I didn't. It fucking sucked. But I appreciated the gesture all the same.

We left the cottage and the village that holds so much of my heart two days before we were due to fly out so that we could spend some time in London. I hadn't done it for years, and he's only ever been for business. We did all the tourist things and walked until the soles of my feet were tender, but it was worth it.

By the time we were sitting at our departure gate at Heathrow Airport, I was exhausted, so incredibly happy, but ready to go home.

I love England; I love Aunt Lena's house and the beautiful village it's located in. But right now, Chicago is my home. It's where my heart is. Well, when he's not chasing me across the Atlantic to confess his undying love, that is.

"Did you tell Miles what time we land?" I ask once we've finally retrieved our luggage from the belt and are heading toward arrivals to hopefully find a car waiting for us.

I slept on the flight, but it was restless and uncomfortable. I'm longing to crawl into Kingston's massive bed and sleep for a week.

Sadly, though, that's going to have to wait a little longer, because he's already secured us a doctor's appointment for later today.

No matter how much I try and convince him that everything is fine, that a doctor isn't really necessary at this point, he refuses to accept it.

As annoying as it might be, it's also sweet as hell, so I'm happy to go along with it.

When we haven't been out exploring together or rolling around in bed this past week, he's been reading up on the first stages of pregnancy.

The first time I found him researching was in the middle of our first night in the cottage. His jet lag was kicking his ass, and he was wide awake. He was so invested in what he was reading that he didn't notice me approach, and when I dropped down beside him and saw what he was reading, his cheeks heated with embarrassment.

"I just want to know what to expect and to understand what you're going through," he said to me. I swear to God, it was the sweetest thing I've ever heard him say.

Every day since, he's been happily telling me all the facts he's learned about the first trimester, and then also what to expect as we move into the second and third.

Every time he says something new, I fall a little harder in love with him. His excitement is contagious too. And while I was unsure about what I truly wanted my future to look like when I ran from Chicago, now I know without a doubt.

I want Kingston. I want our little family. I want to be standing by King's side as he and Miles take Warner Group by storm and turn it back around. I want to be a part of it all.

"I don't think I mentioned it, no," he says as we march through the doors to a small crowd of people waiting to collect loved ones. "Why?"

"Because he's right—" I don't get a chance to finish my sentence, because Miles takes off running in our direction and engulfs me in a hug.

"Or maybe I did," I hear Kingston mumble before Miles exclaims, "You're back," and holds me even tighter.

"Whoa, gentle," Kingston chastises, having moved closer. "You don't want to squash your niece or nephew."

Miles tenses while I silently fume at Kingston.

"We weren't meant to be telling anyone," I point out.

"Miles isn't anyone, he's—"

"You're pregnant," a very familiar female voice screeches before Lori emerges from behind Miles, quickly followed by Kian.

"Bro, you knocked her up?"

Turning, I glare at Kingston who just shrugs, uncaring that everyone in our inner circle is now aware of our little secret.

"Yes," I confirm, "but we're not telling anyone yet because it's early and—"

"You've got it. Your secret stays with us," Kian agrees, making Lori roll her eyes before she surges forward and pulls me in for a hug.

"I'm so glad you're back," she whispers in my ear. "Chicago isn't as awesome without you in it."

"Me too."

"You're not staying in England?" she asks hopefully. While we've chatted since Kingston gate-crashed my English pity party for one, we haven't really talked. We've both been too busy, and the time difference hasn't exactly helped.

"Nope. I belong here, for now at least."

She squeals in excitement before hugging me again.

"As grateful as we are for the welcome home party, is there any chance we can leave the airport anytime soon?" Kingston grumbles.

"Good to see that you're still a miserable asshole," Kian teases, slapping his brother on the back as he reaches for the light suitcase Kingston allowed me to pull as if I'm some kind of invalid.

"Pfft, as if that's ever going to change."

"I thought you said you loved me?" Kingston balks.

"Oh, Jesus. You're not going to turn into *that* couple, are you?" Miles asks. "Someone pass me a bucket."

"Suck it up, man. This is it now. Your sister is mine."

Miles cringes, his top lip curling in disgust. "Well, at least she isn't my responsibility. She's a fucking liability."

"Love you too, Bro."

Wrapping his arm around my shoulder, he drops a kiss on the top of my head.

"Missed you, little sister," he confesses quietly. "So, when are you coming back to work?" His voice is a little louder with that question, and Kingston's hand tightens in mine.

"You mean I still have a job?"

"Well," he starts as we emerge into the bright afternoon sun.

A black town car awaits with Lewis standing beside the driver's door waiting for us.

He smiles the moment he sees me, his head nodding in greeting.

"Well, what?" I ask as we come to a stop, allowing Lewis to deal with our luggage.

"Your marketing manager position has been filled."

My stomach drops, disappointment flooding through my veins.

"W-what?"

"In fact, the whole marketing department has had a massive reshuffle," Miles confesses.

Ripping my eyes from him, I glare at my husband. He hasn't said a single word about this.

"What does that mean?" I ask, my heart beginning to race.

"It means that Charles decided to opt for early retirement," Miles explains, mentioning our CMO.

My hands tremble.

No, surely he isn't going to—

"Congratulations, Tate. You're our new Chief Marketing Officer."

The world spins around me as I stare at my big brother.

Kingston steps behind me, his arm wrapping around my waist as if he's worried I'm about to drop to the floor.

"B-but I'm pregnant."

Miles shrugs. "It won't stop you from doing your job, will it?"

"Uh...n-not right now, but—"

"Tatum," he sighs. "Even senior management are entitled to maternity leave. And anyway, there isn't anyone else I'd allow to have the job. It's meant to be yours. It always has been."

Kingston leans closer, his warm breath rushing down my neck, making me shiver. "We're going to take over the world together, baby."

"So," Miles starts. "What do you say?"

It's everything I've never wanted, but right now, standing here with my husband behind me and nothing but hope filling my big brother's eyes, there is only one thing I want.

This.

All of this.

Lifting my hand, I hold it out.

"Thank you, Mr. Warner." His brows pinch as he hesitantly lifts his hand to mine. His palm slides against mine and I keep my mouth closed, torturing him a little longer. "I happily accept your offer."

"Yes," he hisses before stealing me from King and engulfing me in a bone-crushing hug. "We're gonna fucking kill it, Tate. It's going to be epic."

As much as I want to go home and freshen up before our doctor's appointment, my new and very sudden promotion meant that we all ended up going for celebratory drinks.

Lori was buzzing with excitement, and so were Miles and King. Kian was...well...Kian.

I guess this huge change in my life doesn't affect him like it does Miles and King as CEOs of Warner Group. I'm pretty sure I could see a little pride in those green eyes of his, though.

As predicted, there was nothing more that the doctor could tell us about my pregnancy, that we hadn't already learned. She took my blood pressure, which was normal. A freaking miracle if you ask me after the past few weeks. My pulse was good, too. She took blood, but we won't know the results for a few days, and she hooked us up with a midwife. But, just like I knew, and much to Kingston's irritation, there isn't much to do but look after myself until we have our first scan and learn a little more about our peanut.

"Can we swing by Lori's and pick up Griz?" I ask tiredly as we head across the city.

Kingston turns to look at me. "Baby, you can hardly keep your eyes open," he points out.

It's true. I'm fighting damn hard here. "I need my girl," I whisper pathetically.

"We can get her first thing in the morning. You heard what the doctor just said, you need to rest, take care of yourself."

"One stop for Griz isn't going to stop me from doing that," I argue.

"Tomorrow, Tatum," he says, pulling out the fierce CEO voice that makes my lower stomach knot with desire.

I silently chastise my body. I'm definitely too tired to go there.

I let out a heavy sigh that I hope lets Kingston know just how irritated I am about following orders right now.

"You two are my top priorities, Tatum," he says, resting his hand against my flat stomach. "You always will be. Let me do my job."

"Fine," I huff, sounding like a petulant toddler.

He smirks before wrapping his arm around my waist and giving me little choice but to rest my head on his shoulder and relax.

"I promise, I'll always give you everything you want and need. Including the cat."

"Aw, you love her, don't you?" I tease.

He harrumphs, letting me know that he really doesn't.

It's fine. I think the little love/hate relationship they've got going on is cute.

Thankfully, the roads are clear and only minutes later, Lewis is pulling the car into the underground lot and we're climbing out.

"We won't need you for the rest of the day or tomorrow," Kingston explains. "But we'll both be heading to Warner Group first thing the following morning."

"No problem. If you need me though—"

"Go and spend some extra time with your family, Lewis," Kingston says before taking our luggage from him and leading me toward the elevator.

"Aw, see, you can be nice," I taunt.

"I'm always fucking nice."

I chuckle. "Pretty sure you have plenty of staff who would say otherwise," I deadpan.

He scoffs as the elevator dings to announce our arrival, but he doesn't respond.

He can't. He knows how true it is as well as I do. It's what makes him so good at his job.

"Welcome home, baby," he says after opening the door and letting me step inside before him.

The second I'm inside, I breathe in deeply, letting the scent of home fill my senses.

Contentment washes through me, letting me know that I was right to return.

I love England, I love the village, and the thought of having a life there. But not yet. Right now, my life and my family are all here. It's where I need to be. Where I belong. With my husband, my brother, my best friend, and—

"What's that?" I ask, taking in the ridiculous addition to Kingston's living room.

"What?" he asks innocently, letting me know that he knows exactly what I'm talking about.

"That...that...cat castle." I stare wide-eyed at the most elaborate scratching post I've ever seen in my life.

The thing is pink.

Pink.

"Oh, it's not a castle. It's a palace," Kingston explains matter-of-factly.

"A palace," I muse. "I guess that explains the crown on the top." I'm about to say something else, although God knows what, when a familiar purr hits my ears.

"Griz," I call, searching the monstrosity before me for my girl.

At the sound of my voice, her little face pops out of a hidey-hole.

"Grizzy," I say, holding my arms out for her.

She immediately jumps into them and begins nuzzling my neck.

Emotion burns up my throat, not just because I have my girl back, but because Kingston knew I'd want her here. And he hasn't just got her here, he's bought her the most ridiculous peace offering.

The man in question steps up beside me and reaches out. I freeze as his hand moves toward Griz, waiting for the moment she notices and strikes out.

But she never does. Instead, she lets him tickle her behind the ear.

"What the hell?' I whisper, not wanting to ruin the moment.

"Oh, didn't I tell you?" Kingston says lightly. "Griz and I have come to an agreement. We're going to be able to live together in peaceful harmony from now on."

"Is that right?" I ask, looking between the two of them, trying to figure out what the hell kind of agreement a man and a cat can strike up.

"Yep. We're tight now, isn't that right, fluffpuff?"

I gawp as he reaches for her and lifts her into his arms.

He snuggles her into the crook of his elbow and roughs up her head, something she usually hates, but she...she purrs.

"You're a cat whisperer."

"Well, like I said before, I do have a way with pussy." He wiggles his eyebrows in amusement.

"Oh my god," I mutter. "I married that."

"Till death do us part, baby. There is no way you're getting out of those vows now. You're mine until the end of time."

I step closer to him, pinning Griz between us.

"Sounds awful," I tease.

"Uh-huh. Go and get that sexy ass in bed, Tatum Callahan, and let me show you just how awful having to put up with me for the rest of your days really is."

He swats my ass as I take off with a burst of laughter.

"You can have me if you can catch me," I call back, suddenly feeling a little less exhausted and a lot more turned on.

"Oh, baby, there is no doubt I will always do that."

And he does, over and over again.

EPILOGUE

Kingston

Seven months later...

We sit around the conference table in Miles's office and listen to Liam explain the growth of the company since we took over.

It's pretty fucking epic listening, if I'm being honest, but sadly that doesn't mean I'm fully focused.

I should be; I fucking love this shit.

But there is something else in this room I love more than knowing I've succeeded.

Tatum Callahan.

My beautiful wife and soon-to-be mother of our baby.

My eyes stray from Liam as they already have done a million times since she entered and sat down.

Honestly, us making her Warner Group's Chief Marketing Officer when Charles announced his early retirement was the best thing that could have happened to this company.

Sure, Charles was great. He and his marketing department

had run some unbelievably successful campaigns over the years. But times were changing, and faster than he could keep up with.

Tatum, however...she's had her finger on the pulse of what people want and need from Warner Group, and it fucking shows on the graph I should be looking at.

Sure, Miles and I have had a lot to do with the success, Liam too. But Tatum and her department...fuck, they have smashed it out of the goddamn park. And we're yet to hit the most successful time in the financial year.

Liam continues, and noticing my wavering attention, Miles kicks me under the desk. But it doesn't achieve anything other than giving me a bruise. My eyes are locked on my wife.

She's been struggling the last few weeks. I might keep trying to tell her that she's beautiful and glowing in a way I've never seen her before, but she's exhausted, her back and hips are aching and keeping her awake at night, and she's doing her best not to eat every piece of food that passes under her nose. I have no doubt that it's going to be a boy despite us not finding out at the scans. Callahan men breed men—it's just how it's always been. I don't feel like breaking tradition with that yet, no matter how much she tries to convince me that her gut is telling her that we should be buying everything pink.

She's aware of my attention, she always is, but that doesn't mean she looks back at me.

My little brat.

She knows I want her eyes on me, but she won't give them to me.

"Will you stop trying to eye-fuck Tate over the table?" Miles whisper-hisses, clearly not paying Liam any attention either.

"I'm allowed, she's mine."

"Don't I fucking know it," he scoffs, probably remembering the time he walked in on us going at it over Tatum's desk.

We were celebrating her promotion.

It's not our fault that Miles didn't knock. The windows were darkened for a reason.

"Jealous, bro?" I tease.

"Of you fucking my sister? Absolutely not."

"Not what I meant and you know it."

"Not the life for me," he mutters, earning himself a scowl from Liam.

I'm about to force myself back into this meeting when Tatum winces, her hand shooting to her belly.

My heart jumps into my throat, just like it does every time she makes a noise or does something that might signify that something is wrong.

I don't say anything. I've learned my lesson over the past few months.

Our boy is probably just doing football practice on her ribs. We were told at our last midwife appointment that our little fella is in position and ready—not that we needed telling. Tatum could tell from those little feet and the pressure of his head on her bladder.

She relaxes for a minute or two, but then winces again.

"Tatum?" I whisper, unable to keep my concern to myself. There is something in her expression, something that fucking terrifies me.

I know we're leading to a life-changing moment, and I'm so excited to meet our little guy, but also...knowing what Tatum is going to have to go through...fuck...I hate it.

I can't stand it when she has a headache or her back is aching with her pregnancy. Her giving birth is going to kill me.

'I'm okay,' she mouths.

She's also lying. I can see it in her eyes.

She blows out a slow breath, attempting to relax, but it doesn't work, and the next time her face twists with discomfort, she lets out a little whimper.

"Tatum?" I ask, interrupting Liam and turning all eyes on her.

"I-I'm sorry. E-excuse me."

She pushes her chair back and gets to her feet with the help of the table before shuffling toward the door, only she pauses before she gets there and grips her belly.

"Tatum," I call, jumping to my feet and rushing to her. "Baby, what's wrong?" I ask, covering her hand with mine, aware that every set of eyes in the room is focused on us.

She thinks for a moment, her lips rolling between her teeth. "I think...I think the baby is coming."

"Oh shit. How do you know?" I ask in a panic.

"Well...it's either that or I just pissed myself."

"Oh, Jesus. Fuck. Meeting canceled," I call before ushering Tatum out of the room.

"What do I do? What do you need?"

"Dry pants?" she deadpans.

"Umm...I don't—"

"What's happening?" Miles asks in a rush, spilling out of his office with wide eyes.

"I'm having a baby, Miles," Tatum says calmly.

"Shit."

"Yeah, shit."

"Okay, while you two stand there freaking out, I'm going to the bathroom to clean up."

"We need to be going to the hospital," I say in a rush, my voice a tone I'm not sure I've ever heard before.

"And we will, but not while I've got liquid running down my legs, and when my contractions are—" Her face twists in pain and her hands go to her stomach again. "Fuck, that really fucking hurts," she cries.

"Okay, we're going to the hospital right fucking now."

Wrapping my arm around her waist, I try to guide her toward the elevators.

"No, I need the bathroom," she demands, standing firm. "Miles, there is a packed bag in my office cupboard. Can you please get it and bring it to—"

"Got it," Miles says before darting off, following orders without question.

"Bathroom, Kingston. I promise I'm not going to deliver her on the toilet. There is time."

"Him," I correct as I spin us around and head toward the ladies' bathroom.

She goes straight into a cubicle and strips the bottom half of her clothes off before sitting on the toilet. The whole time, I stand there completely useless and totally clueless about how to help her.

"Oh fuck," she cries when another contraction hits.

"Fuck, baby. I hate this. I wish I could take the pain away."

"This is only the beginning, King. You're gonna need to man up. You—"

"I got it," Miles shouts, sounding a little too proud of himself for finding a bag before he rushes to my side. "Oh shit," he gasps when he finds his sister half-naked on the toilet.

"Miles, don't be a pussy," she snaps. "King, there are pants, panties and most importantly, sanitary towels in that bag. Find them all for me. Then we can—motherfucker," she barks.

"On it," I say, finally feeling useful.

I find the packet of sanitary towels first and thrust them at Miles so I can keep searching for what she needs.

"I am not qualified for this," Miles mutters, and when I glance up, I find him staring at the packet like it's about to bite him.

"For fuck's sake, Miles. It's no wonder you can't keep a woman for more than a night. Open the fucking packet and pass me one," Tatum demands. "I feel sorry for your future—fuck. FUCK," she bellows. "Will you two hurry up?"

"What? Why?"

"Are you timing them?"

"No. Are you?"

"Oh yeah, I'm sitting here focusing on a fucking stopwatch. They're getting closer. Fast."

"Okay, okay." I find what she needs and pass them over.

Miles turns his back, giving her some privacy as she redresses.

"Call the hospital, let them know we're on our way, and then start fucking timing. They're going to want to know."

"Yes. Yes."

"Oh Christ," he mutters, pulling his cell out and finding the right app while I dial the number for the maternity ward I've got saved in my contacts.

In less than five minutes, we've discovered that Tatum's contractions are now less than two minutes apart. We've got her dressed and we're heading for the elevator.

"Oh my goodness, is everything okay?" Judith asks as we approach, turning everyone's eyes out here our way.

"Baby's coming," Tatum says simply.

"Oh my gosh." She hops to her feet. "What do you need? I've done this three times; I'm practically an expert."

Tatum cries out again as another contraction hits.

"Where were you ten minutes ago while I was battling with these two clueless morons?" she asks.

"Hey," Miles complains. "We're doing our best. This is out of our wheelhouse right now."

"Dude, you looked offended by a fucking sanitary towel," I point out as Judith presses the button for the lift.

"Yeah, well. I don't have a use for them in my life."

Judith laughs. She's more than aware of Miles's shenanigans. She's had to send desperate girls away more than once over the years.

"Well, maybe you should open yourself up to learning a little about them. Might help you understand women a little better."

"I understand them just fine," he scoffs, not happy with her advice.

Thankfully, the doors open and we move inside.

"Tatum, would you like me to—"

"Motherfucker, I hate you, Kingston Callahan," Tatum cries, I swear crushing every single bone in my hand in the process.

"No, no, we've got this," I say. "Right, baby?"

"Easy for you to say. You're not about to shit out a bowling ball."

"Okay, now I know that isn't anatomically correct," Miles points out proudly.

"Shut the fuck up, Miles," Tatum barks.

"Good luck," Judith calls. "Send us pictures," we hear before the doors close, and we begin to descend through the building.

"Is Lewis ready?" Tatum asks.

"Yes," I agree.

"And the hospital bag is—"

"In the trunk like it has been for weeks now. We've got this, baby."

"Go—FUCK."

"They're getting closer," Miles points out.

"You fucking think?" Tatum hisses as we hit the ground floor.

He fumes behind us, not liking being chastised by his little sister. I get it. But honestly, he needs to learn when to shut up.

"Lewis, have you ever delivered a baby?" Tatum asks the second we have her inside. Lewis wasn't waiting by the door; instead, he's already behind the wheel with the engine running ready to go.

Even in the rearview mirror, I see him pale at the question.

"Um...no, Ms. Tate. I haven't. Could today be the day I do?"

"If you don't put your foot on the gas, it may just be."

"You really think he's coming that fast?" I ask, horrified.

"I do."

The second Miles closes the door, Lewis does exactly as she suggests and floors it.

By the time we pull up outside the hospital, Tatum's contractions are scarily close.

What happened to all the stuff I read about a woman's first baby usually taking a while? Trust Tatum to be the exception to that rule.

Thankfully, a midwife is waiting for us with a wheelchair. The second we open the car door, she takes over making all the demands, leaving Tatum to focus on her breathing and not giving birth in the parking lot.

We race through the hospital and into the maternity ward.

"I need to push," Tatum cries through her wails of pain.

"Okay, sweetie. We're almost there. You see that door at the end of this hallway? That's your room. That's where your baby is going to be born."

"Hurry, please," Tatum whimpers.

"Dad, you need to come with us," the nurse demands as we approach the door.

"Here, take the bag," Miles says, thrusting it at me. "I'll be right out here."

I glance back at him before following Tatum into the room.

He's pale and looks as terrified as I feel.

"You've got this, man. Look after my sister and nephew, yeah?"

"Always, bro. Fucking always."

Rushing into the room, the door falls closed behind me and I swear someone hits fast forward on my life.

I help the midwife get Tatum onto the bed before she quickly examines her and tells us what Tatum already did.

The baby is coming right fucking now.

It all happens so fast; I almost don't have time to panic.

Almost.

Tatum grips my hand in a tight hold, crushing as hard as she can, I can only assume so I can feel just a hint of the pain she is in right now. The other holds the gas and air mouthpiece to her mouth, and she sucks on it like she'll die without it.

"I can't do this," she cries after the strongest contraction she's had so far rolls through her.

"You can, Tate. You're doing so well," the midwife praises.

"I need painkillers. Give me everything," Tatum cries.

"I can't. It's too late."

"Oh fuck," she screams, her entire body locking up and her face turning beet red, and she pushes.

"You're doing so good, baby. He's going to be here soon."

"ARGH," she screams again before falling limp. But her relief is short-lived because another contraction hits her almost immediately.

"Push as hard as you can. The head is right there."

The midwife looks between Tatum's spread legs, and I find myself doing the same.

"Oh my god," I whisper when I find that she's right. "He's got loads of hair," I tell Tatum.

"I don't care, just get him out of me."

I smirk. It's the first time she's said he.

"Next contraction and you'll deliver the head," the midwife says. I haven't even registered her name. It's all too much of a blur.

"Okay, okay. It's—ARGH," Tatum screams, her grip getting even tighter, which I didn't think was possible.

"That's it. That's it," the midwife encourages before Tatum falls back with an exhausted cry.

"One more contraction and you'll have your baby."

I look down again and instantly feel a little lightheaded when I literally see a head poking out of my wife.

Oh god. This is really happening.

Someone is going to hand us a helpless child as if we're qualified to keep it alive.

Wrapping my free hand around the bar of the bed, I try to keep it together.

Tatum needs me not to lose my shit right now.

"It's coming," she cries before she gives it one final push.

"That's it," the midwife says as Tatum crashes back, exhausted, her eyes falling closed.

But the second a small cry fills the room, she's fully alert again as if she hasn't just been through all of that.

There is so much emotion in her eyes, so much love for our new little person, I fall for her all over again.

"Congratulations, you have a beautiful baby boy," the midwife says before placing him on Tatum's chest.

"Oh my god," she sobs, tears immediately falling as she stares down at him.

Moving closer, I rest my hand over hers on his chest.

"He's perfect, baby. You're perfect."

"I love him so much," she hiccups.

"Me too, Tate. Me too. Both of you are my everything," I say before leaning over her and pressing a kiss on her brow.

Long before Tatum is ready to lose him, the midwife lifts him from her chest, and another appears as if from out of nowhere so they can weigh him and check Tatum over.

After a couple of stitches, they cover her in the dressing gown from her hospital bag and return our boy—now wrapped in a soft yellow blanket—onto her chest. He's been weighed and checked over, but despite deciding to come out a little early, he's in perfect health and ready to take on the world.

"Ready to have a go at feeding him?" the midwife asks.

Tatum nods eagerly, although her eyes never leave our boy.

The midwife talks her through how to do it, and like any good Callahan man, he picks it up super fast.

"I'll leave you three alone for a little bit. Call if you need anything," the midwife says before slipping from the room.

"Well," I say, "that was—"

"Unexpected," Tate finishes for me. "Do you think Liam is still talking about that graph?"

I can't help but bark out laughing.

"Who cares? The most important thing right now is that I was right," I preen. "And you know what that means?"

Tatum groans.

"I get to choose our little man's name."

We agreed early on that if we had a girl, Tatum would name her, and if I was right and we had a boy then I would. I've been teasing her with terrible name suggestions ever since.

But the truth is, I've known from the very beginning what I wanted to call our son. I just have to hope she agrees.

Taking in a deep breath, I prepare to tell her.

I could have before now, but I didn't want her to veto it before she'd met him and understood why it was the right one.

"Okay, well...welcome to the world, Princeton Warner Callahan."

Tatum sobs before dropping her lips to the top of his head.

"You like it?" I ask nervously.

"I love it. It's perfect. I love you, King."

"I love you too, baby. And you, little man. You've no idea what's in store for you."

Lorelei
Tatum and Kingston's wedding night

"You look lonely." The deep, familiar voice rumbles through me as his shadow swallows me whole.

Sucking in a deep, hopefully calming breath through my nose, I close my eyes and pray for strength.

I love my best friend dearly. She has been hands down the best person who has ever entered my life. But the world she inhabits, the people she is connected with... yeah... not exactly my type.

I come from nothing, and despite working my ass off to try and better my life, I already know that I'll leave this Earth with exactly the same as I entered with. Unlike those currently surrounding me.

Watching Tatum get married was... a headfuck.

She looked beautiful—beyond beautiful. She was a vision wrapped up in the most incredible dress. She was so perfect that no one else in the room would believe that she was suffering from the effects of our drinking session last night.

She wanted to be good, but I'm pretty sure she was lying to herself from the second she thought about those intentions, let alone said them out loud.

She was marrying her brother's best friend. A jerk she's spent her entire life hating. A man her father handed her over to in his will. And if she wants to secure her inheritance, then she has to see it through for a year.

Crazy? Yeah, totally fucking crazy.

But also...

Some might say it's romantic in a way—secretly, I might just be one of them.

They've been enemies their whole lives, both doing anything they can to rile the other up. Now they've been brought together in a way they never expected, and well... who knows what the future will hold?

The sparks are already flying—and not just the angry ones.

They're hot together. Anyone with eyes can see that.

Disappointment niggles inside me, but I don't have time to focus on the fact I'm here as Tatum's only bridesmaid, alone.

Instead, I straighten my spine and attempt to prepare myself for turning toward Kingston's best man, his younger brother Kian.

"Not lonely, just... taking a moment," I say coolly.

Refusing to look at him, I track the closest barman's movements in the hope he can feel my burning stare and supply me with something that will help me get through the next few minutes.

But it never happens—he's too busy with a group of pretentious older men who are drinking top-shelf whiskey as if it's water.

The overt show of wealth makes my skin crawl.

"Well, you look too good to be having a moment alone. Care if I join you?"

But it's too late, he's already sitting on the stool beside me as if there isn't a chance in the world of me saying no.

I guess that's the kind of ego you grow when ninety-nine percent of the female population wants to screw your brains out.

Well, Kian Callahan, welcome to the one percent who would rather scratch their eyes out with a corkscrew than worship at your stupidly expensive shoes.

Schooling my features, I finally spin on my stool to face him.

"Seems like a pointless question, don't you think?" I ask, dropping my eyes down to where he's sitting.

If I didn't know that his navy suit had been tailored to fit him to perfection, then it wouldn't be hard to figure it out. The way he wears it... well, it's probably the only positive thing I can come up with about him if I'm being honest.

That and just how fucking good-looking he is.

I bite down on the inside of my cheek.

It's not fair. In fact, it's really fucking unfair that, not only was he born into one of the wealthiest families in the country, enabling him to walk straight into a high-profile, very well-paying, and powerful job, but he was also gifted with model-like looks.

How are the rest of us mere mortals meant to compete with the likes of him?

A rush of copper fills my mouth as bitterness floods my veins.

"I'm amazed I'm the first," he says smoothly before looking in the direction of the barman and immediately getting his attention. Of course.

It physically pains me not to roll my eyes.

"Macallan, please," Kian orders. "And another—" He glances over at me for confirmation of what I'm drinking.

I refuse to comply or allow him to buy me a drink. Buy—what a joke. Of course this wedding includes an open bar. Other than watching my best friend say her vows, it's the best part of the whole day. Hopefully, if I drink enough, I'll be able to ignore the stench of pretense that permeates the room.

You could leave, a little voice says.

Tate has gone. Kingston literally dragged her away to celebrate their nuptials alone.

Lucky her...

"I'm fine, thank you."

Kian's eyes narrow in irritation before his hand darts out, stealing my glass from the bar before me.

"What are you—"

"Pornstar martini," he says to the barman after sniffing my glass. My chin drops. "She'll take another."

"H-how did you..." I stutter like a fool once the barman has retreated.

He smirks, making perfectly symmetrical dimples pop in his cheeks before he winks cockily.

Jesus.

"I'm not just a pretty face, Lorelei," he rasps, his smirk growing.

His voice flows through me, and damn him if my thighs don't involuntarily clench.

It's a natural reaction to a virile man, I try telling myself. It has to be that, because there is no way on Earth I'm in any way attracted to this arrogant jerk.

"Debatable," I mutter under my breath as I turn my attention back to the bottles lining the bar. They're almost as pretty, and they certainly contain less bullshit.

"I'm sorry, I didn't quite catch that," he says, shifting his stool close so that the heat of his arm warms mine.

"Yes, you did," I say confidently. "Was there something you wanted other than to interrupt my peace, Kian?"

I don't look over to see his reaction. I don't need to. The reflection of the gold trim that covers the bar does the job perfectly well.

His nostrils flare and he sucks in a sharp breath as his lips part in surprise.

I mentally give myself a high five. I'm not sure it's often anyone gets the upper hand when it comes to any of the Callahan brothers.

"I don't feel like we got off on the right foot," he says, attempting to turn this back around again.

"Is that right?"

We've actually met a few times over the years thanks to our mutual friends, but I don't know him. I've never cared to.

He exudes more than enough of everything I hate to put me off for a lifetime.

I guess it should be expected that he's forgotten we're already acquainted. He was with some fake blonde bimbo the first time we met, and he was as big an asshole that night as he has been every other time I've met him.

"I was merely pointing out that it's tradition that the best man and bridesmaid hook up at a wedding if they're single."

"Then I guess it's a good job that I'm not single, isn't it?" I retort as our drinks are placed before us and my feet hit the floor.

"If that's true, then he isn't worthy of you."

Walk away.

Just walk away.

"And why is that?" I ask, unable to follow my own advice.

Spinning on the balls of my feet, I find myself at eye level with him. Many would cower the second his eyes locked on theirs. But while I may not be as powerful or important as him or anyone else in this room, I refuse to bow down to them.

Money doesn't make you more important. Your job title doesn't make you more or less worthy of anyone's time or attention.

The only thing that matters is the kind of person you are. And the one staring back at me with a mixture of mirth and expectation lighting up his green eyes is a selfish jerk who only cares about his reputation.

"Because a beautiful woman like you should never be attending an event like this alone if you're not single."

I raise a brow but keep my expression neutral.

"It's a huge risk when instead of missing him," he explains before throwing his whiskey back and pushing to his feet, moving closer. He towers over me even in my heels, forcing me to raise my chin to keep eye contact. "You could be spending your time getting to know me better."

His alcohol-laced breath rushes over me and his eyes bounce between mine as if I'm meant to be... what? *Impressed* at that pathetic attempt to pick me up?

"Fortunately for him, it's a risk he doesn't need to worry about. Goodnight, Kian. Good luck with your next victim." And with those words hanging in the air between us, I walk away, making sure I put as much sway into my hips as possible.

Want more?
PRE-ORDER NOW!

Missing Tatum and Kingston already? Download their extended epilogue HERE!

Want to be the first to know about my books in progress? You can join my Patreon for sneak peeks, special edition paperbacks, and more!
SUBSCRIBE NOW!

Have you met Zach?
Turn the page for a sneak peek of Hate You, book #1 in my spicy contemporary romance series, Rebel Ink.

HATE YOU
SNEAK PEEK

Prologue
Tabitha

I stare down at my gran's pale skin. Her cheeks are sunken and her eyes tired. She's been fighting this for too long now, and as much as I hate to even think it, it's time she found some peace.

I take her cool hand in mine and lift her knuckles to my lips.

"It's Tabitha," I whisper. I've no idea if she's awake, but I don't want to startle her.

Her eyes flicker open. After a second they must adjust to the light and she looks right at me. My chest tightens as if someone's wrapping an elastic band around it. I hate seeing my once so full of life gran like this. She was always so happy and full of cheer. She didn't deserve this end. But cancer doesn't care what kind of person you are, it hits whoever it fancies and ruins lives.

Pulling a chair closer, I drop onto it, not taking my eyes from her.

"How are you doing today?" I hate asking the question, because there really is only one answer. She's waiting, waiting for her time to come to put her out of her misery.

"I'm good. Christopher upped my morphine. I'm on top of the world."

She might be living her last days, but it doesn't stop her eyes sparkling a little as she mentions her male nurse. If I've heard the words 'if I were forty years younger' once while she's been here, then I've heard them a million times. She's joking, of course. My gran spent her life with my incredible grandpa until he had a stroke a few years ago. Thankfully, I guess, his end was much quicker and less painful than Gran's. It was awful at the time to have him healthy one moment and then gone in a matter of hours, but this right now is pure torture, and I'm not the one lying on the hospital bed with meds constantly being pumped into my body.

"Turn the frown upside down, Tabby Cat. I'm fine. I want to remember you smiling, not like your world's about to come crashing down."

"I know, I'm sorry. I just—" a sob breaks from my throat. "I don't know how I'm going to live without you." Dramatic? Yeah. But Gran has been my go-to person my whole life. When my parents get on my last nerve, which is often, she's the one who talks me down, makes me see things differently. She's also the only one who's encouraged me to live the life I want, not the one I'm constantly being pushed into.

That's the reason I'm the only one visiting her right now.

When my parents discovered that she was the one encouraging my 'reckless behaviour', as they called it, they cut contact. I can see the pain in her eyes about that every time she looks at me, but she's too stubborn to do anything about it, even now.

"You're going to be fine. You're stronger than you give yourself credit for. How many times have I told you, you just need to follow your heart. Follow your heart and just breathe. Spread your wings and fly, Tabby Cat."

Those were the last words she said to me.

Chapter One
Tabitha

The heavy bass rattles my bones. The incredible music does help to lift my spirits, but I find it increasingly hard to see the positives in my life while I'm hanging out with my friends these days. They've all got something exciting going on—incredible job prospects, marriage, exotic holidays on the horizon—and here I am, drowning in my one-person pity party. It's been two months since Gran left me, and I'm still wondering what the hell I'm meant to be doing with my life.

"Oh my god, they are so fucking awesome," Danni squeals in my ear as one song comes to an end. I didn't really have her down as a rock fan, but she was almost as excited as James when he announced that this was what we were doing for his birthday this year. Although I do wonder if it's the music or the frontman who's really captured her attention. She'd never admit it, but she's got a thing for bad boys.

I glance over at him with his arm wrapped around Shannon's shoulders and a smile twitches my lips. They're so cute. They've got the kind of relationship everyone craves. It seems so easy yet full of love and affection. Ripping my eyes from the couple, I focus back on the stage and try to block out that I'm about as far away from having that kind of connection with anyone as physically possible.

I sing along with the songs I've heard on the radio a million times and jump around with my friends, but I just can't quite totally get on board with tonight. Maybe I just need more alcohol.

"Where to next?" Shannon asks once we've left the arena and the ringing in our ears has begun to fade.

"Your choice," James says, looking down at her with utter devotion shining in his eyes. It wasn't a great surprise when Shannon sent a photo of her giant engagement ring to our group chat a couple of months ago. We all knew it was coming—Danni especially, seeing as it turned out that she helped choose the ring.

Shannon directs us all to a cocktail bar a few streets over and I make quick work of manoeuvring my way through the crowd to get to the bar, my need for a drink beginning to get the better of me. The others disappear off somewhere in the hope of finding a table

"Can we have two jugs of..." I quickly glance at the menu. "Margaritas please."

"Coming right up, sweetheart." The barman winks at me before his eyes drop to my chest. Hooking up on a night out isn't really my thing, but hell if it doesn't make me feel a little better about myself. He's cute too, and just the kind of guy who would give both my parents a heart attack if I were to bring him home. Both his forearms are covered in tattoos, he's got gauges in both his ears, and a lip ring. A smile tugs at the corner of my mouth as I imagine the looks on their faces.

My gran's words suddenly hit me.

Just breathe.

My hand lifts and my fingers run over the healing skin just below my bra. My smile widens.

I watch the barman prepare our cocktails, my eyes focused on the ink on his arms. I've always been obsessed by art, any kind of art, and that most definitely includes on skin.

I'm lost in my own head, so when he places the jugs in front of me, I startle, feeling ridiculous.

"T-Thank you," I mutter, but when I lift my eyes, I find him staring intently at me.

"You're welcome. I'm Christian, by the way."

"Oh, hi." A sly smile creeps onto my lips. "I'm Biff."

"Biff?" His brows draw together in a way I'm all too used to when I say my name.

"It's short for Tabitha."

"That's pretty. So... uh... how do you feel about—"

"Christian, a little help?" one of the other barmen shouts, pulling Christian's attention from me.

"Sorry, I'll hopefully see you again later?"

I nod at him, not wanting to give him any false hope. Like I said, he's cute, but after my last string of bad dates and even worse short-term boyfriends, I'm happy flying solo right now. I've got a top of the range vibrating friend in my bedside table; I don't need a man.

Picking up the tray in front of me, I turn and go in search of my friends. It takes forever, but eventually I find them tucked around a tiny table in the back corner of the bar.

"What the hell took so long? We thought you'd pulled and abandoned us."

"Yes and no," I say, ensuring every head turns my way.

"Tell us more," Danni, my best friend, demands.

"It was nothing. The barman was about to ask me out, but it got busy."

"Why the hell did you come back? Get over there. We all know you could do with a little... loosening up," James says with a wink.

"I'm good. He wasn't my type."

"Oh, of course. You only date posh boys."

"That is not true."

"Is it not?" Danni asks, chipping in once she's filled all the glasses.

"No..." I think back over the previous few guys they met. "Wayne wasn't posh," I argue when I realise they're kind of right.

"No, he was just a wanker."

Blowing out a long breath, I try to come up with an argument, but quite honestly, it's true. My shoulders slump as I realise that I've been subconsciously dating guys my parents would approve of. It's like my need to follow their orders is so well ingrained by now that I don't even realise I'm doing it. Shame that their ideas about my life, what I should do, and whom I should date don't exactly line up with mine.

Glancing over my shoulder at the bar, I catch a glimpse of Christian's head. Maybe I should take him up on his almost offer. What's the worst that could happen?

Deciding some liquid courage is in order, I grab my margarita and swallow half down in one go.

I'm so fed up of attempting to live my parents' idea of a perfect life. I promised Gran I'd do things my way. I need to start living up to my promise.

———

By the time I'm tipsy enough to walk back to the bar and chat up Christian, he's nowhere to be seen. I'm kind of disappointed seeing as the others had convinced me to throw caution to the wind (something that I'm really bad at doing), but I think I'm mostly relieved to be able go home and lock myself inside my flat alone and not have to worry about anyone else.

With my arm linked through Danni's, we make our way out to the street, ready to make our journeys home, and Shannon jumps into an idling Uber while Danni waits for another to go in the opposite direction.

"You sure you don't want to be dropped off? I don't mind."

"No, I'm sure. I could do with the fresh air." It's not a lie—the alcohol from one too many cocktails is making my head a little fuzzy. I hate going to sleep with the room spinning. I'd much rather that feeling fade before lying down.

"Okay. Promise me you'll text me when you're home."

"I promise." I wrap my arms around my best friend and then wave her off in her own Uber.

Turning on my heels, I start the short walk home.

I've been a London girl all my life, and while some might be afraid to walk home after dark, I love it. I love seeing a different side to this city, the quiet side when most people are hiding in their flats, not flooding the streets on their daily commutes.

My mind is flicking back and forth between my promise to Gran and my missed opportunity tonight when a shop front that I walk past on almost a daily basis makes me stop.

It's a tattoo studio I've been inside of once in my life. I never really pay it much attention, but the new sign in the window catches my eye and I stop to look.

Admin help wanted. Enquire within.

Something stirs in my belly, and it's not just my need to do something to piss my parents off—although getting a job in a place like this is sure to do that. I'm pretty sure it's excitement.

Tattoos fascinate me, or more so, the artists.

I'm surprised to see the open sign still illuminated, so before I can change my mind, I push the door open. A little bell rings above it, and after a few seconds of standing in reception alone, a head pops out from around the door.

"Evening. What can I do you for?" The guy's smile is soft and kind despite his otherwise slightly harsh features and ink.

"Oh um…" I hesitate under his intense dark stare. I glance over my shoulder, the back of the piece of paper catching my eye and reminding me why I walked in here. "I just saw the job ad in the window. Is the position still open?"

His eyes drop from mine and take in what I'm wearing. Seeing as tonight's outing involved a rock concert, I'm dressed much like him in all black and looking a little edgy with my skinny black jeans, ripped AC/DC t-shirt and heavy black makeup. I must admit it's not a look I usually go for, but it was fitting for tonight.

He nods, apparently happy with what he sees.

"Experience?" he asks, making my stomach drop.

"Not really, but I'm studying for a Masters so I'm not an idiot. I know my way around a computer, Excel, and I'm super organised."

"Right…" he trails off, like he's thinking about the best way to get rid of me.

"I'm a really quick learner. I'm punctual, methodical and really easy to get along with."

"It's okay, you had me sold at organised. I'm Dawson, although everyone around here calls me D."

"Nice to meet you." I stick my hand out for him to shake, and an amused smile plays at his lips. Stretching out an inked arm, he takes my hand and gives it a very firm shake that my dad would be impressed by—if he could look past the tattoos, that is. "I'm Tabitha, but everyone calls me Biff."

"Biff, I like it. When can you start?"

"Don't you want to interview me?"

"You sound like you could be perfect. When can you start?"

"Err... tomorrow?" I ask, totally taken aback. He doesn't know me from Adam.

"Yes!" He practically snaps my hand off. "Can you be here for two o'clock? I can show you around before clients start turning up. I'll apologise now for dropping you in the deep end, we've not had anyone for a few weeks and things are starting to get a little crazy."

"I can cope with crazy."

"Good to know. This place can be nuts." I smile at him, more grateful than he could know to have a distraction and a focus.

My Masters should be enough to keep my mind busy, but since Gran went, I can't seem to lose myself in it like I could previously. Hopefully, sorting this place's admin out might be exactly what I need.

"Two o'clock tomorrow then," I say, turning to leave. "I'll bring ID. Do you need a reference? I've done some voluntary work recently, I'm sure they'll write something for me."

"Just turn up on time and do your job and you're golden."

I walk out with more of a spring in my step than I have in a long time. I'm determined to find something that's going to make me happy, not just my parents. I've lived in their shadow for long enough.

———

I look myself over before leaving my flat for my first shift at the tattoo studio. I'm dressed a little more like myself today in a pair of dark skinny jeans, a white blouse and a black blazer. It's simple and smart. I'm not sure if there's a dress code—D never specified what I should wear. With my hair straightened and hanging down my back and my makeup light, I feel like I can take on whatever crazy he throws at me.

With a final spritz of perfume, I grab my bag from the unit in the hall and pull open my door. My home is a top floor flat in an old London warehouse. They were converted a few years ago by my father's company, and I managed to get myself first dibs. They might drive me insane on the best of days, but at least I get this place rent-free. It almost makes up for their controlling and stuck-up ways... almost.

Ignoring the lift like I always do, I head for the stairs. My heels click against the polished concrete until I'm at the bottom and out to the busy city. I love London. I love that no matter what the time, there's always something going on or someone who's awake.

The spring afternoon is still a little fresh, making me regret not grabbing my coat, or even a scarf, before I left. I pull my blazer tighter around myself and make the short journey to the shop.

The door's locked when I get there, and the bright neon sign that clearly showed it was open last night is currently saying closed.

Unsure of what to do, I lift my hand to knock. Only a second later, the shop front is illuminated, and the sound of movement inside filters down to me, but when the door opens it's not the guy from last night.

"Oh... uh... hi. Is... uh... D here?"

The guy folds his arms over his chest and looks me up and down. He chuckles, although I've no idea what he finds so amusing.

"D," he shouts over his shoulder, "there's some posh bird here to see you."

My teeth grind that he's stereotyped me quite so quickly, but I refuse to allow him to see that his assumptions about me affect me in any way.

"Ah, good. I was worried you might change your mind."

"Not at all," I say, stepping past the judgemental arsehole and into the studio reception-cum-waiting room.

"That's Spike. Feel free to ignore him. He's not got laid in about a million years, it makes him a little cranky." I fight to contain a laugh, especially when I turn toward Spike to find his lips pursed and his eyes narrowed in frustration. All it does is confirm that D's words are correct.

"Is that fucking necessary? Posh doesn't need to know how inactive my cock is, especially not when she's only just walked through the fucking door. Unless..." He stalks towards me and I automatically back up. I can't deny that he's a good looking guy, but there's no way I'm going there.

"I don't think so."

"You sure? You look like you could do with a bit of rough." He winks, and I want the ground to swallow me up.

"Down, Spike. This is Tabitha, or Biff. She's our new admin, so I suggest you be nice to her if you want to stop organising your own appointments and shit. I don't need a sexual harassment case on my hands before she's even fucking started."

I can't help but laugh at the look on Spike's face. "Don't worry. I'm sure you'll find some desperate old spinster soon."

He looks me up and down again, something in his eyes changed. "Appearances aside, I think you're going to get on well here."

I smile at him. "Mine's a coffee. Milk, no sugar. I'm already sweet enough." His chin drops.

"I thought you were our new assistant. Why am I still making the coffee?"

"Know your place, Spike. Now do as the lady says. You know my order."

"Yeah, it comes with a side of fuck off!" He flips D off before disappearing through a door that I can only assume goes to a kitchen.

"I probably should have warned you that you've agreed to work around a bunch of arseholes."

"I know how to handle myself around horny men, don't worry."

After finishing my A levels, before I grew any kind of backbone where my parents were concerned, I agreed to work for my dad. I was his little office bitch and spent an horrendous year of my life being bossed around by men who thought that just because they had a cock hanging between their legs it made them better than me. I might have fucking hated that year, but it taught me a few things, not just about business but also how to deal with men who think they're something fucking special just because they're a tiny bit successful and make more money than me. I've no doubt that my time at Anderson Development Group gave me all the skills I'm going to need to handle these artists.

"So I see. So, this is your desk. When you're on shift you'll be the first person people see when they're inside, so it's important that you look good. But from what I've seen, I don't think we'll have an issue. I've sorted you out logins for the computer and the software we use. Most of it is pretty self-explanatory. I'm pretty IT illiterate and I've figured most of it out, put it that way."

D's showing me how they book clients in when someone else joins us. This time it's someone I recognise from my previous visit, although it's immediately obvious that he doesn't remember me like I do him. But then I guess he was the one delivering the pain, not receiving it.

"Biff, this is Titch. Titch, this is Biff, our new admin. Be nice."

"Nice? I'm always nice. Nice to meet you, Biff. You have any issues with this one, you come and see me. He might look tough, but I know all his secrets." Titch winks, a smile curling at his lips that shows he's a little more interested than he's making out, and quickly disappears towards his room.

It's not long until the first clients of the afternoon arrive, and I'm left alone to try to get to grips with everything.

Between clients, D pops his head out of his room to check I'm okay, and every hour I make a round of coffee for everyone. That sure seems to get me in their good books.

"I think I could get used to having you around," Spike says when I deliver probably his fourth coffee of the day. "Only thing that would make it better is if it were whisky."

"Not sure the person at the end of your needle would agree."

He chuckles and turns back to the design he was working on when I interrupted.

My first day flies by. D tells me to head home not long after nine o'clock. They've all got hours of tattooing to go yet, seeing as Saturday night is their busiest night of the week, but he insists I get a decent night's sleep.

DOWNLOAD NOW to keep reading.

ABOUT THE AUTHOR

Tracy Lorraine is a *USA Today* and *Wall Street Journal* bestselling new adult and contemporary romance author. Tracy has recently turned thirty and lives in a cute Cotswold village in England with her husband, baby girl and lovable but slightly crazy dog. Having always been a bookaholic with her head stuck in her Kindle, Tracy decided to try her hand at a story idea she dreamt up and hasn't looked back since.

Be the first to find out about new releases and offers. Sign up to my newsletter here.

If you want to know what I'm up to and see teasers and snippets of what I'm working on, then you need to be in my Facebook group. Join Tracy's Angels here.

Keep up to date with Tracy's books at
www.tracylorraine.com

ALSO BY TRACY LORRAINE

Inked (A Rebel Ink/Driven Crossover)

Rosewood High Series

Thorn #1

Paine #2

Savage #3

Fierce #4

Hunter #5

Faze (#6 Prequel)

Fury #6

Legend #7

Maddison Kings University Series

TMYM: Prequel

TRYS #1

TDYW #2

TBYS #3

TVYC #4

TDYD #5

TDYR #6

TRYD #7

Knight's Ridge Empire Series

Wicked Summer Knight: Prequel (Stella & Seb)

Wicked Knight #1 (Stella & Seb)

Wicked Princess #2 (Stella & Seb)

Wicked Empire #3 (Stella & Seb)

Deviant Knight #4 (Emmie & Theo)

Deviant Princess #5 (Emmie & Theo

Deviant Reign #6 (Emmie & Theo)

One Reckless Knight (Jodie & Toby)
Reckless Knight #7 (Jodie & Toby)
Reckless Princess #8 (Jodie & Toby)
Reckless Dynasty #9 (Jodie & Toby)

Dark Halloween Knight (Calli & Batman)
Dark Knight #10 (Calli & Batman)
Dark Princess #11 (Calli & Batman)
Dark Legacy #12 (Calli & Batman)

Corrupt Valentine Knight (Nico & Siren)
Corrupt Knight #13 (Nico & Siren)
Corrupt Princess #14 (Nico & Siren)
Corrupt Union #15 (Nico & Siren)

Sinful Wild Knight (Alex & Vixen)
Sinful Stolen Knight: Prequel (Alex & Vixen)
Sinful Knight #16 (Alex & Vixen)
Sinful Princess #17 (Alex & Vixen)
Sinful Kingdom #18 (Alex & Vixen)

Knight's Ridge Destiny: Epilogue

Harrow Creek Hawks Series

Merciless #1

Relentless #2

Lawless #3

Fearless #4

Callahan Billionaires

By His Vow #1

Ruined Series

Ruined Plans #1

Ruined by Lies #2

Ruined Promises #3

Never Forget Series

Never Forget Him #1

Never Forget Us #2

Everywhere & Nowhere #3

Chasing Series

Chasing Logan

The Cocktail Girls

His Manhattan

Her Kensington

9 781917 034616